KILLING THE MESSENGER

Also by Christopher Wallace

The Pied Piper's Poison

The Resurrection Club

The Pirate

KILLING THE MESSENGER

Christopher Wallace

FREIGHT BOOKS

First published in the UK September 2011
This edition published May 2013

by Freight Books
49-53 Virginia Street
Glasgow, G1 1TS
www.freightbooks.co.uk

A CIP catalogue reference for this book is available from the British Library

ISBN 978-1-908754-19-6

Typeset by Freight in Plantin
Printed and bound by Bell and Bain, Glasgow

the publisher acknowledges investment from
Creative Scotland toward the publication of this book

à Cécile

Christopher Wallace is communications director of a major public sector organisation and former managing director of a leading advertising agency employed on successive government advertising campaigns. His first novel, *The Pied Piper's Poison*, won wide acclaim and the Saltire First Book of the Year 1998. He lives in Edinburgh.

Sometime in the near future.

C DAY MINUS 2 DAYS

Media Suite 1, Central Office of Information Exchange, London

'Do you think he'll be alright?'

The Prime Minister stood over the poor man's inert body, addressing the room but seeking out my reply. I knew the style. I knew he supposed I'd seen this before. I have. He also presumed I gave a shit. I didn't. And that I'd play along with his is-there-a-doctor-in-the-house faux-fretting. I was still deciding. My only interest was in getting my answer. He was only worried about his campaign. The crumpled, unconscious suit at his feet was right in the way for both of us. I made no effort to be convincing.

'Should be fine, I think. A bit stuffy in here.'

Meaning; he won't be fine, not for a long time. This was just the start of it for him. Probably deserved it.

The Prime Minister cradled his head and offered water to his lips. A touching scene. Can't take your eyes off it. Anyone? Silence. Time stood still. Where was my fucking answer?

You know that we are about to hypnotise the entire nation? You're looking at one of the side effects, how many more like him will there be? All kinds of shit about to happen and I can't find anyone who even cares. Do you care, Prime Minister?

So this is how it plays. My final audience with the man in charge.

Kept me waiting, solitary confinement. Half an hour at least. Then voices at the door – the coffee I'd demanded? No, good God, it's Him, the man himself. I straighten out, almost stand to attention. He's almost at me already, a tall man, making long strides, confident strides.

'Cal? You okay?'

Offering his hand. A smile that scans across my face. I'm not meant to notice but I do. I'm meant only to feel its effect as he locks both his eyes to my left then fleets across to my right, a move he's practised to perfection, a move that someone somewhere in his distant past taught him, showing him how to appear interested; looking into me, his audience, looking into my soul. I answer as trained to.

'I'm great, you?'

I say this as I shake the hands of his band of helpers, clocking in particular his private secretary, her and an old friend I've met before: the soon-to-be prone greasy man mumbling out the side of his mouth towards his earpiece, already fixing the Prime Minister's next appointment, nodding to me and pointing to his ear to signal he's otherwise engaged. His name badge says Jason Watson, Special Advisor. He pirouettes and heads toward the back of the room. I hear him saying no, repeatedly and forcefully. Someone at the end of the line is getting a doing. I'm tuning in, intrigued, but the Prime Minister wants my attention.

He looks around, there's no obvious place to sit, he finds this vaguely amusing, and wants us all to relax into the same state of mind. We drift to the front row and I pull down a theatre seat. He sits right next to me, bunched up tight though it clearly doesn't bother him. He takes a breath and fixes his eyes on the podium, begins to speak to it as if I'm still standing there.

'Cal, I wanted to spend a little bit of time catching up, seeing where we've got to with the campaigns. Do you have everything you need from us to get to where you need to?'

His opener. His scene setter. Telling me why we're here. He's stolen my meeting. Just like they are trying to steal my campaign. Not even launched yet but here I am, an impostor, pretending to be in control when really I have been marginalised into infinity. Paranoid? Not paranoid enough, that's my problem.

'You have an update for me?' He leans encouragingly closer then laughs. 'And of course, something new to pitch?'

Very astute, Prime Minister…Yes, the default reason for my presence is normally to sell: push my agency, broaden the campaign, upscale every last ad and execution. One of the best. Or worst. Look at what I've done to your colleagues after all. But I've met my match in you, haven't I? No, today I want to buy, I'm in the market for reassurance. I've got a screamer of a campaign to show you, it'll change the world, and maybe not all for the better. I'll turn you into a god that most will be happy to worship.

That's what our tests prove. But the downside is so steep, Prime Minister. There are those ill-equipped to handle so much abrupt joy in their lives and they're going to be our casualties. Damaged beyond repair.

'Prime Minister, to recap: we are C Day minus two – Prime Minister. Two days until the campaign goes live... We started out, what seems a long time ago now, on one campaign, the *Cohesive Communities* brief. It obviously developed into the *Together As One* concepts we presented originally pre-election, and that then evolved into the *Feeling Together* campaign once we incorporated the *Well-Being* brief. Somewhere along the line my agency also began working with The Sea of Tranquillity people, on what was another campaign, positioning them and their relaxation techniques. Since then somehow these tracks have grown closer and closer until they are approaching one and the same thing and it's difficult to separate the original from the *Tranquillity Now* stuff we've worked up in parallel. I need to know you are aware of and happy with that and the direction this is now going in.'

I hear myself droning on in a language that even I struggle to understand. The Prime Minister is still looking to the podium. I have no way of knowing if he's actually heard or engaged with any of this. Earpiece Jason has heard me though, and he was at the other end of the auditorium. His radar has already picked up that I'm off script and off agenda here. Out of bounds. His call is terminated and he's in hyper-rebuttal mode. Short strides, hurried strides, bring him over, fast.

'Why does it matter if the Prime Minister is aware of what your other clients are up to? You've got your brief; you know what's required, don't you?'

Ouch. I'm absolutely aware I'm being scanned by another set of eyes, this time not peering into my soul to find common ground and an unspoken bond that means I'll give him my vote. Not at all. This time I'm being sized up fast in terms of size and scale of threat. My time is almost up.

'Prime Minister,' I keep my voice as low and calm as I can. 'We're on schedule... everything is still holding up in the focus groups. In fact... effectiveness is going ever higher.'

And so I go on, trying to capture his eye, but he's performing now, smiling for a dash of milk and frowning to turn down a fucking biscuit from the enraptured refreshment team. Deflection. How can any of that be more important than what I'm trying to tell him? Prime Minister, we've primed the weapons and it all works like we, like I, told you it would. Now you're throwing this crazy Sea of Tranquillity gang on top of this and all the evidence suggests that it will send it exponential. That's enough to scare me. Prime Minister, can't you see I am scared? Why aren't you stopping this?

'Two campaigns, we are now finalising both. Sometimes they appear part of one and the same complementary thing; sometimes we argue about whether they should be two separate things. The brief, or briefs, aren't clear in that respect.'

The Prime Minister smiles a photocall smile whilst his whole entourage including his Earpiece Man and me, the drowning ad man, waits for his direction, something he's reluctant to give, choosing to play for time instead.

'Well Cal, you do have something to show me?' This time something like a real smile returns to him – or one he wants us all to take as such, not just me, the one being blanked. He turns to the acolytes. 'Normally Cal puts on a great entertainment, he knows I'm a sucker for the words and pictures thing, he could sell me anything. Frequently does.'

They give him the laugh he's looking for. Poor Prime Minister, too innocent to deal with a manipulative, snake-oil-pushing cynic like me. Laughing on cue, seals and hyenas. I join the game, flashing a token grimace to indicate appreciation of his flattery. I hadn't intended to show anything, this was meant as my showdown, where I'd find my answers. I pull the memory stick from my pocket and walk to the podium.

'Anyone know how to fly this thing?'

I find the docking point, the console and the plasma screen behind it spring to life as they upload the extraordinary data. An assistant's assistant leans across to enter the system password; I move only slightly to let her, standing my ground, enjoying the fleeting moment when she invades my space. She ducks under my chin to key in the codes. Clean auburn hair, scentless, a tiny silver chain at the back of her neck, resting on her freckles. A real human being, working for the Prime Minister.

The memory stick has everything on it to tell a story, but not the full story of course – how once upon a time there was an ad agency. One like most of its kind. One hundred and fifty staff on five floors of central London real estate, buzzing like a wasps' nest of ideas commissioned to help sell both the palatable and unpalatable. Visualisers, designers, programmers, progress-chasers, administrators, account men

– all arranged in a labyrinthine hierarchy of power that mutated daily according to the currency of ideas they possessed in that moment. And in that moment hating each other because of it. Wasting their energy on the deadly cross-departmental skirmishes that are the essential fuel of the collaborative creative process. So far so normal, what made this agency so different?

This: it stumbled upon an extraordinary formula, one that could truly change attitudes, behaviours and buying habits, all that and more. Oh yes, things changed in adland when governments realised they could sell policy like any product, change social behaviours by creating the craving for change. In any country in the world, who's the biggest advertiser, who's got the most to sell?

And then us, and something extraordinary. The formula. Focus group guinea pigs tested to destruction. Accidental alchemy, magicking up the stuff of dreams. Ads that have the audience salivating with an unbearable yearning, yet serve up the meal to be devoured then and there, all in the same communication. Create the need and satisfy it, problem and solution for the price of one: *Together Now!* as briefed by government is an anti-racism, anti-dishonesty, anti-everything-that-threatens stability campaign. A pro-community, pro-inclusion, pro-your-leader-as-living-deity as answer to that brief. Headache and tranquiliser served up on the screen. Alas, as with the best drugs, it comes with its side-effects, many as yet unknown.

The console display before me offers a choice of files it has accessed from the memory chip. As I line up the file icon, the plasma screen behind me automatically glides out from the wall mountings and angles itself above the front rows of the auditorium. It suddenly lights and extends to its enormous, twenty-four square metres of ultra high definition. Fuck me. Seriously slick gear.

The 'play' icon appears and the lights in the room dim of their own accord. I am about to offer some kind of commentary but I stop myself; these effects, this room and what they are about to see will do the job for me. Full fucking blast, they deserve nothing else. The man on screen speaks and we go into a dream.

Sometime later, the lights are back on. Show over. The Prime Minister is first to twitch back to life, gently nodding in silent agreement with himself. Of his squad of young helpers, one still has her head in her hands, unconsciously mimicking her Prime Minister's star turn. Her friend next to her is weeping, although she might not be aware of this. My bet is that if they could sign up right now to feel his pain, share his mission, conceive and then give difficult birth to his love-spawn then they would; sign up to do the whole lot in one great splat of a combined experience oh-yes-of-course-you-fucking-would.

'Quite something, isn't it?' The Prime Minister shakes his head slowly, a twitching grimace hinting that he has found a seam of guilty pleasure in here, somewhere. 'Powerful, almost unsettling... What do you think, Jason?'

We turn to the man who had been busy on the earpiece phone. Now set, presumably, to be a whole lot busier. Explain that. Explain what it did to you. He looks at me with a mixture of unrestrained contempt and bewildered admiration.

'This works, yeah? You're sure about this?'

I look at the evidence surrounding me.

'We've tested in over a hundred focus groups and eleven hall tests. It works.'

The Prime Minister nods. 'What does it do to the approval scores?'

'Sends them skywards, into orbit.'

He nods again, this time to Jason. 'Get me a briefing on those scores. I want to understand what we'll get.'

For once though, the sidekick isn't quite by the Prime Minister's side. He's begun to droop slightly, hand drawn over his eyes. Whatever it is that's taken him, he's not in the full receptive-poised-for-fucking-action mode we've come to know and love.

'Jason, are you okay...? You're looking a little green there, need to take a break?'

The Prime Minister sounds concerned, convincingly concerned. For all I know he might actually be concerned. Macho Jase waves away any doubts as to his stamina.

'I'm fine... Fine. Too much coffee today, catching up on me I guess.' He looks back to the screen, blinking furiously as if bedding in new contact lenses, ones that gave a dangerous new perspective. 'Quite something, like you said,' he mutters. 'Unsettling... yes, but really quite something.'

The others in the room are becoming accustomed to the light, re-orientating themselves to their day, taking comfort from the Prime Minister's interest in one of their number. The door opens and there's the head of another team, waiting to take the Prime Minister onwards.

Their relief to get moving, back to the real world, whatever that might be, palpable.

'I can make a briefing any time after the final groups are complete.'

I'm saying this to a departing audience, all packing up and keen to take their opportunity to exit. I'm saying it without realising I've slipped back into Account Man mode, as if I'm still part of Harlequin, checking for client buy-in. Not what I came here for. I raise my voice because I'm not sure if anyone wants to listen, but they have to. He has to.

'Prime Minister?'

I shout. Don't mean to but it comes out loud and sharp. Unfortunately loud. Unfortunate timing – as I'm screaming at him not to go, another commotion, a body slumps to the floor. Iron enforcer Jason has keeled over en route to the exit. Falling without warning like my words are a sniper's shot to the back of his vanishing head. He goes down from the feet up, the way a carefully demolished tower block peels into itself when detonated. Horizontal on the carpet before anyone has a chance to catch him. No matter, he now has the cooing PM crouching by his side. 'Jason? Jason... are you alright? What's going on...? Better get a doctor... an ambulance...'

Yes. Better get a whole load of ambulances Prime Minister, better get used to this because my guess is that we're in for a lot more, unless of course, you want me to pull it back. Unless you do want me to turn down the power and I've somehow missed your signal. Have I?

'Prime Minister?' I repeat, as groggy Jase-blubber pulls himself up; checks pockets, hair, earpiece, and realises he's drooling on the Prime Minister's sleeve. This distraction is all too convenient. I'm not going to stop.

'Prime Minister, one last thing...'

He turns, halting his progress to the door, still supporting his colleague. His eyes fix mine, my invitation to continue though he wants me to feel his impatience. I lower my voice.

'I want to know... I asked you if you knew these campaigns were now running in this sequence. The brief to do it like this comes from you guys... I'm asking you again... Why are we doing it this way, what do you want from it?'

Not articulated well, not smooth at all. Shit. I used to be good at this for fuck's sake. Listen to me. Why are we doing this? Why? I've reached out to my beacon and he doesn't like it, stiffening up the shoulders under his suit jacket, demon eyes like lasers staring into me. Who the fuck are you to ask me that?

Then a softening. The Prime Minister sighs, like he's indulging me, me the incorrigible one, going all uptight on him, freaking everyone out for no reason. Jason Watson is standing unaided now, even walking, where's the problem?

'Cal...' he says, in a tone that says listen up. 'You know what I want from this, and all of this?' His arm sweeps the room as if to indicate both the machinery of government and all the people in it. 'All I want is a happy country. I just want to make everyone happy.'

CAMPAIGN LAUNCH MINUS 370 DAYS

National Exhibition Centre – Alliance for Positive Mental Health,

Inaugural Convention

Greig Hynd took a moment to lift his glasses and rub his eyes, blinking furiously to kick them back into gear. He noticed the cup of coffee Catherine had given him was still in his hand. Taking a sip, he realised how long it must have been in his possession. More of an accessory than refreshment, stone cold, he looked through the throng for somewhere to offload it. Instantly, he was drawn into another encounter.

'Dr Hynd?… Elaine Bain, *Action Against Depression*. You must be thrilled with your day. I wanted to thank you.'

Greig smiled warmly at the woman addressing him, a professional smile, practiced; one he knew worked well and enjoyed deploying, even on occasions like this when he was tired and trying to gather strength for the big moment. It had been a good day. A great day.

'Elaine, thank you, how kind of you to say that…' Greig glanced around again for a surface to jettison his plastic cup. This done, he offered his hand, which was enthusiastically taken.

'… And so nice to meet you.'

He now sandwiched her hand between his, giving her his full unadulterated beam. She reflected it willingly back, unable to stop herself completing the set of hands with hers on top of his, so that to anyone watching there would seem to be some kind of tug of war going on in the midst of the networking free-for-all. Yet there was no sense of embarrassment. For him, this was natural territory.

'But Dr Hynd, we've met before…'

'Have we?' Greig tried to take her in; middle-aged woman, classic healthcare professional look, grey skirt suit, beige shawl, grey hair cropped tight, ethnic jade earrings and some kind of mischief in her eyes that spoke of her coming from the psychology rather than medical side.

'Dr Hynd, you came to see our groups just after we began. You made a presentation after our charity status was confirmed, you spoke about fundraising at the expense of taboo-reinforcing, and asked us to have the courage not to chase easy cash. You thought you were being rude but you were fantastic, it was just what we needed to hear.'

The flow of detail had Greig rewinding through his mental log of meetings. *Hope Against Depression? Anger At Depression?... Action Against Depression.* So many meetings, so many nights on the road, so many people taking his hand.

'Elaine... I'm so sorry, of *course* we met. It wasn't a meeting, it was a workshop you guys organised... A year ago?'

'Year and a half... you were the star of the show, we still talk about it, that's why there's so many of us here today.'

He listened to the words, at a loss as to how to respond. Yes, he'd have made some kind of pitch, something off the cuff that he'd improvised then and there.

She tugged at his hands one more time, pulling him towards her.

'And I hear you're a father again!'

Familiar ground. Now almost rehearsed.

'Yes, that's right. Little boy. Week and a half ago.'

'You must be so happy, what's he called?'

Greig shook his head. 'I know it sounds terribly negligent but we haven't had a chance to think about it. We had all the girl's variations worked out but could never settle on what we'd call a son. Keep meaning to fix it but...' He shrugged in a vaguely apologetic kind of way. His inquisitor looked at him in admonition.

'You should get back to your wife. Leave this for a while, sort your priorities.'

'I know.' He nodded, eyes rolling with faux guilt. 'This event today was meant to run months ago but got delayed twice, switched venue to something three times bigger, you wouldn't believe the time it's all taken. Overwhelming... but something's happening and the moment is now.'

An unhurried smile came back at him but instinct was now telling Greig to move on. The woman loved him. To hold his place in her esteem, and more importantly, to keep a hold of the boost she had just given him, he had to exit, fast. Always leave them asking for more. First rule of showbiz.

Another woman materialised to his left, agitated and businesslike, a strange combination at the best of times, doubly incongruous here.

'You ready to roll? We're almost an hour behind schedule.'

Greig took the arrival's trademark brusqueness with trademark equanimity. 'Catherine… meet Elaine Bain, *Action Against Depression.*'

'I'm Catherine Laing. I work with Greig.' The newcomer's words had an unspoken yet unmistakable territorial claim to them as she turned instantly to her colleague. 'We should clear everyone out of here and get them back into the auditorium if we're going to have any kind of proper wind-up.'

She turned back to the other woman. 'Sorry to drag him away… it's just…'

The woman signalled a departing nod in reply. Catherine Laing's cold eyes watched her disappear back into the crowd.

'Another convert to the fan club?'

'Wouldn't say convert, turns out she was fully signed up already.'

'*Anxiety About Depression*, where do they all come from?'

'Same place as us Catherine. A place for everyone, remember?'

A great day, great success. Problems for sure, thought Greig, but problems to do with success, being oversubscribed, over committed, over enthusiastic, an accusation that could never be levelled at Catherine.

'Okay then…' he sighed, '…you think we're set?'

'You better go and get plugged into the public address desk. I'll get these rooms cleared.'

She paused and Greig wondered if there was a possibility of an apology on the way, maybe for the hostility shown to Elaine Bain, maybe for being so downbeat on a day that already deserved celebration. Greig waited, but the tone remained the same.

'You take it easy out there. Some of these people are getting overwrought. I think we've got to be careful we don't overcook this.'

Overcook it. Greig rubbed his eyes again. *Overcook?*

'I know what I'm doing Catherine. I'll put my underpants on outside my trousers and save the world whilst I'm at it.'

'*Underpants?*' Another grimace, this time lingering.

'…Like Superman…'

'Whatever… you've just forced me to think about your underwear so

11

thanks for that. Anyway, you know what I'm saying. Feet on ground. Let's go.'

Greig didn't need another invitation to exit the conversational cul-de-sac. Catherine's problem seemed to be the very success they were having, maybe to do with the scale of events they were heading toward. A long way from the cosy lobbying that they had kicked off with only two years before. They had long left that comfort zone and were still gathering speed, yet only Greig seemed exhilarated rather than terrified by this. Could it really be the visualisation of him in his y-fronts that traumatised her? Right now, in this very hall, there seemed to be hundreds, if not thousands, of other women happy to fawn all over him.

He made his way out of the room, one of the few free rooms in the exhibition complex. Out of the six, five had been commandeered for themed break-out groups, each with their own main sponsor. Two thousand delegates passing through today, each paying only a token admittance charge. Quite a scheme, an impossible scheme open to abuse, but it had worked. *His* scheme, and he felt a glow of pride as he passed through the auditorium arena, pride that he had been right to trust his gut feeling, proud that he could trust these people. All of them. *His* people.

Greig became aware of a face on the horizon looking out for him. Bernie, arriving just in time to give Greig his cue. 'Hey chief,' he shouted. 'Catherine says we're ready to go.'

Bernie clipped the remote mic under his chin, muttering as he did so. 'Could you stand still for Christ's sake; I'll never get this on you otherwise… Pandemonium in here. Every session overbooked. Thought we were going to have a riot at the meditation seminar… that would have been ironic, wouldn't it?'

He paused to see if Greig was buying the joke, the lack of response not halting the flow.

'Come on… What's the matter with you?… It's a sensation! Happy punters… profit. They all want to know when the next one is…'

Greig tugged at the microphone to check it was securely attached.

'Remind me never to mention my underpants to Catherine again.'

Bernie nodded vigorously. 'Sounds like a good idea… Push this in and the red light comes on and you're live… see?'

'Red is on, red to go… Cool. How are we going to get everyone together?'

'We won't, there's not enough room, besides, there's going to be a lot of clearing up at the break-outs.'

Greig moved off again, pushing ahead, weaving a path through the crowd that Bernie struggled to follow.

'What do you mean, *clearing up*?' He called back.

'You know... Arguments... Getting carried away. A lot of people airing too many personal issues and then not getting them back in the box... half the place thinks we can change everything overnight, they're going bananas because there's no consensus.'

Greig had halted, progress blocked by a discussion. Hitting reverse, face set, he was pushing Bernie back in the opposite direction.

'There never is a consensus, that's why we work in this area, to celebrate our differences...'

Bernie winked at him, glancing downwards to draw Greig's attention to the hand pushing aggressively into his chest, Greig's hand.

'Just you tell them mate. There is no consensus, we are gathered to celebrate that there ain't no fucking consensus because you have to be mad to want to work with madness.' Bernie paused and offered an apologetic wince to acknowledge he'd gone too far.

Greig shook his head in a practiced headmasterly fashion. 'A twenty-seven-year-old bright kid going on fifteen...'

His pushing hand now pulled the offender toward him, close enough to whisper in his ear.

'Just be grateful I don't have this microphone switched on, otherwise we'd have just heard your own self-declaration of stupidity being the keynote address. Now go and gather the teams, tell them we want one last drive to get everyone back into the hall. Is the presentation stuff loaded?'

Bernie nodded, stone-faced.

'...And the Tranquillity stuff, it's working?'

Bernie nodded again.

'Alright then, go. Impress me. *Allez vite*!' Greig clapped his hands, as much for himself as the crowd he sought to address.

'Ladies and gentlemen, please!... Closing session now, main auditorium... please make your way to hear the mystery speaker, let's hope he's worth it!'

The remark drew a response, albeit slowly, and seemed to ripple lazily through the crowd.

Greig waved his arms, ushering bodies along the corridor, then made to move through the same crush he'd created. Once he negotiated his way into the central auditorium he felt a rush of adrenaline. The numbers. Two thousand? More, and all still here, hanging on to the very end of the day, and all gathered together, every seat taken, standing space filling fast. A tangible sense of expectancy. Applause starting as soon as he mounted the steps to the stage. Greig smiled, automatically, recognisably contrite. There was no podium and he was absolutely on his own.

He turned to the giant display screen behind him to see if there was any sign of life on it, hoping to see his holding slide. Instead he caught a view of his own face and his surprise at seeing it writ large on display, captured live. Laughter from the audience and another rueful smile from himself. He looked to the switch on his remote unit. Red to go.

C DAY MINUS 370 DAYS

Harlequin Advertising, Warren Street Central London

Ignition. The lift off. Harlequin Advertising, as it was then, reaches for the sky, reaches out and preposterously finds it within its grasp. The days of our pitch, when we thought we'd won over a dominant part of the CIO, the Central Information Office, as it was then.

And the very start of this, our pitch, our show, is recorded for posterity. The video taken of the rehearsal, shot on shaky digital with tinny, eerily echoing voices. A record locked deep in the vaults, and what choice viewing it must make. The pitch that was, the team that was, the times that were.

It's only our side filmed of course, no client present. Instead, we had agency people posing as the government buyers, the civil servants who commission this stuff, Roman Emperors in the Coliseum box, a thumbs up to tell you if you live or die. For as I recall, in those days, the dark days of the Vesey Empire, Harlequin was looking terminal. One account loss away from the great roster in the sky rather than the cornerstone of the multinational, multi-company labyrinth 'Sneaky' Pete Vesey would dream of. Triumph from disaster, the ascent to the stars all stems from the events of this day.

On the tape, we have our then MD, the aforementioned Mr Vesey doing the intro, selling a vision of his agency to his own staff, blindingly oblivious to the grim reality of their daily experience. They stare back impassively, not buying any of it.

Yes, when Peter plays his greatest hits it's only him who is humming along at the chorus, only him seeing the inner beauty at the ugly parade. To be fair to him, he believes it and maybe that's the point; if tenacity is what you're looking for, then he's your man. It's right there written in

15

his face and caught in the footage. If you choose to try and explain that the world is just not turning the way he's called it, then you've got a bit of a fight on your hands with conquering his delusion, ego, need to be loved and corporate overdraft just the start of it. A fight to the death. For later, though. For now let's savour the performance on tape. Peter reeling off the client list, bullet by bullet, explaining our presence on the CIO roster. And then, overdoing it, spilling into the planner's bit, the creative bit, and my bit. Peter in an unambitious brown suit, wool and cashmere, for this is before the days of international travel that would transform both Harlequin and his wardrobe.

It can't be that long ago when he was plain Pete, even Sneaky Pete, media seller, but now he's here as *Peter* Vesey, dignified supremo, relaxed yet aggressive, full of talk about *relishing the challenge* and an agency culture of the most difficult of briefs bringing out the best in us.

The script he should have been following is mine. Fortunately, the camera focuses exclusively on the warm-up man so that my inner turmoil as he mangles my carefully crafted copy goes unrecorded, as do the twitches and tics of Harry Rhodes, Director of Planning, as he awaits, like a condemned man, the dreaded passing of the presenter baton. Even in rehearsal, Harry's nervous and after countless rehearsals, and with a script telling him how and when and why we will arrive at his slot, Harry still manages to convey utter shock, dismay and sheer caught-with-pants-down horror when the moment finally arrives.

And to be fair again to Peter, it's hardly like he throws some kind of venomous curve-ball when he does. Sure he's taken our audience on some spontaneous tangented flight of fancy that will make them wonder if they've arrived in the wrong building, but the rhetorical hand-over – '*So what does the research tell us?… Here's Harry, our Planning Director, to brief us…*' – that he does manage to stick to. Throw in the slides with this bullet point summation and pie-charted idiot's guide to the issues and even a passing stranger could step into the planner shoes and run.

But Harry to take it on, lift the performance? No, poor Harry's as manifestly uncomfortable with his part in this pitch as he is in his role at the agency and probably as he is with his wife, kids and crippling mortgage at home. Harry, wake up man, it's your turn, we're meant to *relish* this challenge, weren't you listening? It's started bad, now's your chance to really fuck it up, so come on, get it all over with.

I'm being cruel of course. Harry's a decent man, never pretended to be what I needed him to be, no malice in him. Be near him in the pub and he'll stand his round. Get him on any topic other than the Harlequin Agency and you'll find him informed, intelligent, ticking any number of boxes as a good guy to have on your side. It's only the weight of expectation that brings Harry down. Down and out. Within a year he'd be gone, in the first purge of the new regime. My regime.

So, forgive me for asking, what the fuck *does* the research tell us then Harry? And here Harry's problems really seem to begin. His section has been crafted so that he presents a slam-dunk case of flawless, evidence-based, undeniable logic. *Your brief was X. We asked our focus groups Y. They responded with Z, so the creative proposition is Z. QED. Now what does that look like in pictures and words, Nick?* Except with poor Harry, no matter how hard we come down on him, no matter how much we coach, cajole and downright bully him, the doubts creep in – so that where the script will say 'The focus groups conclusively point to Z', what comes out of Harry's mouth is something like, 'The focus groups *seem* to point to Z', or, 'The groups, which were in themselves as challenging as the brief, *sort of* indicate Z, in as much as we could tell…'

The scary thing is that these are his *best* performances, done in rehearsal, when it doesn't count. *This might be what the research is telling us. Perhaps. Or it maybe not. It's not at all conclusive and I wouldn't want to be held to it. Over to you anyway, Nick, and best of luck.*

At last, we're arrived in the fertile 'Red' zone of the performance, where the storyboards, animations and crazy concepts of Nick Craig's Creative Department, as presented by our Creative Director, the aforementioned Mr Craig, here in loud shirt – loud enough to prove he's the real thing, a *creative* – will touchdown the ball our quarterback planner has thrown from deep. Only the concepts are not so crazy, more predictable and safe. The former has been thrown out in favour of the latter and it's safety we're selling here. That's the theory anyway, conveniently making a virtue out of necessity. *We don't want fancy ads*, said the focus groups, sort of. *That's all right*, said the Harlequin Advertising Agency; *we've not got any anyway*.

Nick's caught here on tape in full flow, with the charm button pushed fully down. Nick's 'tell' is all about his hair, his long blond and impossibly straight hair. The same hair he will sweep a majestic hand through to tackle a marauding fringe and send it back clean off his forehead to his crown, from which it will cascade relentlessly downwards to crowd in on his cheekbones so that he does the same again. Particularly when he thinks he's landed the killer blow. Nick and his hair; a key relationship in the workings of the agency. You can forget any decent creative output when they're not getting on. Hair kept occasionally under control by the restraint of a hair band when he's in full-on concentrated, brief-busting mode. Today though, it's show time, and it's all unleashed for the camera in full bouffant glory, the 'tell' on display with every third concept board. He's holding up one with '*Together As One*' written on it, then an image of a multi-cultural group of kids hanging out, the way they seem only to do in adland. Then the boards with the celebrity images, celebrities solo and serious, addressing the camera. 'This is my TAO' signs off hip rap star Tarzan, because of course, '*We're All Together As One*'. More boards, more personalities, this time unlikely ones – an elderly traffic warden is shown to have the words tattooed on his arm, a nurse in a hospital spots what she thinks is a name tag on a patient only to find it's a campaign ribbon kept close to a beating heart, everybody gets it, the fireman, the waitress, the full fucking line-up of the Village People and entire crew of the Starship *Enterprise*. Nick hits a play button and we have a jingly morsel of music – *together, together, as one one one* – he sways on his feet; infectious, isn't it? There's no stopping him now; the shirt is peeled off to reveal the T-shirt lurking beneath, you've guessed it, our TAO T-shirt with all the colours of the fucking rainbow. Infectious, unstoppable. The kids will dig it. We swear.

It's a star turn from Nick, best so far, even if he's had negligible competition. Touchdown. Better that he did on the day itself as it happens, as so often happens with over-prepared, overly cautious shows like this. Bit by bit we are robbing him of the spontaneity that gives his performance what appeal it might have. He's peaked too early. On the day his hair will be strangely subdued, lank and forlorn, reluctant to be teased into action. He'll endlessly shuffle the order of the boards, betraying the fact that he realises he lacks a killer opener. Just mediocre variations on a mediocre theme.

So we limp toward the Grand Finale. Almost. Before I begin, an introduction. Caroline Black, whose main job so far has been to sit looking attentively intrigued and convinced by the case presented, gets at last her own solo spot. *I'm Caroline*, she says, approximately, *and I'll be your Account Director, your main day-to-day contact should we win the account*. She then goes on to say she's been involved in the strategy development – bit of a long shot this but hey, if arriving late but looking gorgeously lost during the aforementioned strategy development meetings counts, then she's earned her spot, though her silent, mysterious and clueless allure. I'm being needlessly cruel about Caroline of course. There's history here. Bad history, obviously.

Anyway, she's smart enough to know the gig, which is to look friendly, non-threateningly intelligent and above all, willing. *I'm Caroline, and I'm the sort of air stewardess for the account, I'll cater for your every whim during this flight. When the real pitch begins, I'll look even more beautiful than I do on this tape; I'll have had my highlights done so I look a natural blonde, be better dressed, short black skirt suit and white blouse open maybe one button too many so that I'm businesslike and serious but still giving off some kind of charge so that you the client will find yourselves returning to me during the show, even though I'm contributing nothing other than my attractive presence in the company of grey middle-aged men like yourselves. And you'll think we don't notice, and will never guess that it's been designed like that for exactly that reason. Thank you and enjoy, you shallow fucks.*

The beautiful Caroline doesn't so much hand over to me, the final act, in rhetorical fashion – *So, Cal, where has this presentation led us, you shallow fuck?* – as smile knowingly, throwing a challenge to say something interesting. There's no landing pad for me then, no. I start from scratch, standing up to deliver the closing speech, to tell the jury that there's only one verdict they can deliver, despite the parade of hopeless and unreliable witnesses. At least that's what it feels like. I watch myself pull myself to my feet, no obvious enthusiasm for the project apparent in the all-important body language.

The mitigating circumstances for me are that I've worked on this thing for six weeks solid. And when I say solid I mean it, twenty-four seven. Thinking about it in my sleep, on the tube, in the bath, during sex. Hard to think about when I wasn't thinking about it, building a theory, knocking it down, then another one; selling a theory on the corridors of Harlequin, during lunch with Peter Vesey, the bar with Nick. Weeks of herding them together, bringing them to where they need to be in order for it to work, to convince, to look like a team rather than a desperate bunch of chancers throwing random shapes on the wall.

And they just don't get it like I do. Which puts me in a lonely place, as I see now watching that rehearsal reel. I've got more hair than now, a fuller face. The eyes though, are dark, intensely dark and glowing with a burning resentment that in another life could have made me a screen star in the smouldering hero/psycho mould that cycles in and out of fashion.

A youngish man, barely turned thirty, burning up even then, the Calum Begg as captured in that moment. Burning up with lots of things, but mostly just the sheer loneliness of it all.

Calum Begg stands/slouches and launches into the best rhetoric of the day.

'So, why, you're asking yourselves, should any of this convince me that Harlequin is the agency to make this work and deliver our objectives?' Followed by a recap, or what was meant as a recap, and sweep up of all the bits my colleagues have missed during the excitement of their spell in the spotlight. Except it is very much like starting again, building the case with a conviction hitherto missing. A compelling case, evidencing the success of our other CIO campaigns. We end on a non-rhetorical, a statement of certainty; after all, clients can only buy certainty. No matter what hopes Harry might cling to, you'll never hear of one falling for the indecisive lot – *get me the ones wracked with self-doubt, I liked their might-do attitude*. No sir. Harlequin offer a proven strategy, from a proven agency with the track record to match. Only one verdict possible.

All cringe-inducing. An unreal exercise.

Peter Vesey viewed the incriminating footage over and over for days, showing an appetite that verged on the clinically obsessive. Then he summoned me to hear his views.

'You're missing a bit here,' he says, pausing the play on his laptop screen, '...and here, you need a bit that links.' He insists on running me through the whole slo-mo car crash. The presentation needs work, the performers need to improve and I dutifully take notes. The entire future of Harlequin in my hands. Time running out, I get to a spare room and make a call. I get him straight away.

'Do you want us to win this thing?'

This is an odd thing to ask your client shortly before a pitch, but Nigel Richards can probably tell by my tone it's a serious question.

'I want the best agency to win it.'

'Nigel, drop the civil service shit. Do you want us to win it or are you happy to let fate decide?'

'Why do you ask?'

'If you want us on the account you'll have to help.'

'Things bad?'

'We're exhausted. Some of the guys don't get it and it's beginning to fall apart.'

'Do *you* get it?'

'*I* get it. I wrote the fucking book but no one wants to listen, and that's just *our* lot, before you guys pass your own particular scrutiny on it.'

'What do you want me to do?'

'Call Peter, check we're ready to roll, find some way of getting it into his head that the less he says the better. Otherwise… you'll get the Peter Vesey show.'

'Anything else?'

'Do some pre-sell on your guys.'

Nigel sighs, like it's a very long list. 'Anything else?'

'That should do it.'

'Okay. Done.'

'What about the presentations you've seen so far.'

'What about them?'

'Any good?'

'Interesting.'

'Interesting good, or interesting awful?'

'Interesting mix… Cal, do your stuff and see what happens, meanwhile, I'll make the calls. You can owe me.'

The line goes dead, Deep Throat signing off without ceremony.

CAMPAIGN LAUNCH MINUS 370 DAYS

National Exhibition Centre – Alliance for Positive Mental Health,

Inaugural Convention

'Hello!… Can you hear me ladies and gentlemen?'

Greig didn't need the recognition offered up from the floor, again the screen behind him showed the expression of mild shock as his voice boomed across the auditorium, drawing smiles in turn from the audience.

'Delegates, thank you…' He began again, speaking softly, sacrificing speed for clarity in his voice. He was experienced enough at addressing halls like this, but never on this scale, or with the atmosphere of semi-hysteria tangibly hanging in the air. He noticed, to his satisfaction, that these ingredients seemed to make him relax; it was going to be hard to go back to the rounds of health service meeting rooms with fluorescent lights, Stone Age heating and community centre lock-ups, if he had to.

'Thank you all for coming and giving your time, ideas, and energy in the spirit of exchange and enlightenment that was the concept behind today's event. I have final thoughts I want to share with you before we close the event, I hope you can indulge me, I promise I'll make it as quick and painless as humanly possible…'

Greig paused and turned round to look at the enormous plasma screen again, seeing himself on it doing the same. He waved half-heartedly to himself as if offering encouragement to his giant twin. A murmur of appreciation from the floor.

'…I had some slides?' said Greig, as if addressing a celestial control room watching over him and the screen suddenly changed; a PowerPoint slide replacing his image with a presentation title: *'Alliance For Positive Mental Health, Dr Greig Hynd.'*

'Okay, it works... Three thoughts then as promised, quick and painless... First thought, first slide please.'

The giant display changed, now the screen showed a photograph of a man, aged and weather-beaten, face contorted with rage and frustration, transmitting outright hostility to the lens capturing his image. Underneath it, a caption read: *'Serenity Now!'*

Greig nodded his head slowly in recognition at the screen.

'Delegates, colleagues... Those of us who work with the vulnerable, with communities under stress, with those whose mental health is damaged or compromised, those of us who deal with the wreckage around such individuals, those of us, by which I guess I mean all of us here today, who have chosen to work in this field so that we can offer something, will have no problem recognising this man, this scenario, this yearning desire in ourselves, our society, for some kind of peace... And yet...'

Greig pursed his lips, returning eye contact across the rows in front of him.

'...And yet ours is a society that seems to thrive on only the most negative of human impulses. For entertainment, for relaxation away from the stresses of modern life, we gobble up as much conflict and violence as the film studios, internet and video game makers can throw at us. We watch serial killers at work or maybe chill out watching any number of rational normal people rush to make first class fools of themselves in the pursuit of celebrity... and yet, and *yet*, the *same* audience for all this is the *same* audience we face in our working lives, looking for answers, dreaming of a get-away holiday, retirement, a second home in the sun where these rules maybe don't apply.'

Greig sighed for effect, again scanning his audience to check they were engaged, their silence telling him they were his, signalling his first revelation.

'I believe we have reached a tipping point in the gap between these two states. I believe this is unsustainable and that the consequences for continuing on this path will be...' He paused again, lowering his voice. '... *Catastrophic.* We cannot go on as a society where our coping mechanism for stress is the very thing that stressed us to the point where human values vanish. *Something* must give.'

Greig could hear murmurs of assent swelling through the rows ahead of him.

'Okay, second thought from me, another slide?'

The screen changed to show something completely different, a graph showing a humped curve spread out along a horizontal axis.

'This is what the statisticians call a distribution curve,' continued Greig. 'This is what they would call a 'normal' distribution. I want you to think of the area under the curve here as the population, in pure numbers, of our society. We can divide that total population as belonging to one of four states as shown here; thriving, doing okay, under stress and under treatment. Basic stuff, yes?'

He changed to a more sombre tone. '...I want to concentrate on this lot,' he pointed to a section, '...a whole bunch of people under threat, beginning to slide, vulnerable, hanging in there, under pressure and maybe scared of where it goes next if they can't keep it together. There may even be some of *them* in this room...'

Loud laughter, swift quiet.

'...Because the next stage is this lot...' He pointed to the last quartile. 'The people we deal with, colleagues. Those under treatment, needing help, engaged in therapy. And we all know that every day there are *more* and not *less* of them. Now, we've all grown up, grown up professionally with the assumption that there would *always* be more of them. Today I ask, *why?*'

Greig pointed to the midpoint and then to the end quartile.

'The difference between the points on this graph is represented in numbers of population, that's how this has been designed. Lots of people here in the middle where we hit our highest point, fewer people here where we hit our lowest. But you could also see this as time, or a progression. We, ladies and gentleman, delegates, colleagues, seem to have drifted into the business of jumping in to help drowning men here,' he pointed to the final quartile, '...instead of just stopping them fall into the river *here,*' he pointed back towards the midpoint. 'Imagine we could move this midpoint, this whole distribution curve five percent leftwards, so that more people thrived and more people got by. Imagine what that would do to the numbers entering this phase here, the final quartile... Imagine our working lives... Fewer patients, better care, better concentration of resources to those who really need it... Imagine our society, more thrivers, more contentment, productivity, happiness if we could move that midpoint, make our society feel better about itself... Imagine the violence, drug and alcohol abuse... you name it... imagine all of that on the decrease simply because as a society we *feel better.*'

Total silence in the hall. A silence to savour. He let it linger then snapped back into the performance.

'Final thought... No more slides... Instead...'

He turned round to the screen to see the graph still there. 'Can we have that camera back?' he asked. 'This time showing the audience here?'

The screen flickered and then changed to reveal an image of the hall taken from high up. Greig beamed at the assembly now starring in the same show.

'Okay not perfect, but good enough. Recognise that lot? It's *you*... Final thought. *You,* delegates, colleagues... *we*... are it... All of us in this room, however you feel right now, tired, stressed, uncertain... for all our individual weaknesses... we are it. I've spent the last two years travelling amongst you, listening to you, gathering the thoughts and theories I've just tried to articulate... And what I have learned comes down to a simple point. *Yes*, things have to change if we as a society want to avoid a catastrophe, *yes* there are economic, societal, health, law and order... any number of imperatives why governments will now have to listen to this... and *yes*, we, in this hall, are the best hope that society has. I hope you are ready to be heroes because that's what we all need to be to make this change... But I tell you, as one who knows you, having seen the energy and love... and love is a word I'm not ashamed to use here... *love* in this room... You can do it... you have to do it... and you will. Delegates, I've spent years trying to reason, to lobby... trying to persuade other people to let our issues onto *their* agenda. Well, let me confess before all of you. I've been wrong... We shouldn't beg to be on anyone else's agenda, we *are* the agenda!'

Applause. Not like in the movies with an instant crescendo. Not like that at all thought Greig, no. This applause took time to build and indeed enjoyed several moments when it might have petered out through lack of momentum. Whilst never quite reaching a point of euphoria, it was convincing enough by the time the screen flicked back to show Greig applauding it back. And in those moments, he would later reflect, there was no panic inside him, no crisis of confidence, far from it. He had never felt more free, less inhibited about what he was trying to express. Speaking without notes, so as to force himself into the spontaneity now rewarded, he had surprised even himself by the strength of his call to arms.

Then the sight of Bernie frantically waving to him stage left.

'...Greig? Greig... You still want to show that stuff?'

'*Stuff?*'

'...Your *good morning starshine* stuff...You were mad for it yesterday.'

Slowly it came back to him as he forced his mind to revisit the last day's build-up. He nodded to Bernie and raised his arms one last time.

'Delegates... Can I have your attention just once more, one very final indulgence?'

It took a few seconds for the crowd to hush.

'I wanted to share one more thing with you before you travel home... A few days ago, we received a visit from a couple of interesting people... working in the same field as ourselves but coming at it from a completely different place...'

Greig tried desperately to remember the names of the two academics whose last minute call had made such an impression. Stupidly, he'd taken no note with him. His mind was now absolutely blank as to any detail; their names, institution or academic base. He had no choice but to stagger on, the fluidity of his words from just minutes before now a thing of memory.

'...Working in the field of visual semiotics, no less. Anyway, we have a short piece for you now which I hope will send you home with a bit of a glow. They call this piece a sensory collage... and it comes from their studies of cerebral triggers and responses as a means of relaxation and surrogate meditation. Highbrow stuff but I invite you to view it, and imagine if a piece like this has a part to play in shifting that equilibrium in our graph, balancing our society. I invite you to enjoy it for yourselves, enjoy its warmth... they call it and themselves Tranquillity... Sea of Tranquillity. I hope you'll see why.'

A nod to Bernie, still crouched at the front of the stage. The hall began to darken as the screen washed away the image of the speaker and turned blue, deep azure blue, glowing like a jewel as the light in the hall darkened to pitch.

A sound, a beat, repetitive and steady, like a heartbeat, louder and louder as the tone of blue on the screen seemed to fluctuate somehow, sometimes in sync, sometimes slightly ahead of it, curiously creating some kind of tension in the disparity.

Greig watched, happy to be a spectator, surprised by the darkness around him but enjoying the temporary anonymity it blessed him with. The noise too was a surprise, way more powerful than he had experienced in any rehearsal.

The blue screen changed pitch and tone and slowly mutated through ranges of shade to show waves pitching gently; waves as seen from below the waterline, rippling accompanied now by the sound of a mantra-like chant growing in volume and intensity, slowing and speeding in random precision so that occasionally heartbeat, wave and chant hit perfect harmony, sometimes hitting an unsettling dissonance, and just as the former displaced the latter, the volume of the combined sound reached forward another level; impossibly, uncomfortably loud. As the visual vantage point moved up, ready to break through the waterline with daylight, warm tones of orange and yellow glistened through, growing in vibrancy. Then the breakthrough moment arrived, moving out of the water, colours and sound exploding together and the screen was washed with nothing but yellow, sunshine; intense radiant sunshine inside the hall, reverberations subsiding.

He began to turn away, when a flicker on the screen caught his renewed attention. A face was emerging from behind the yellow glow. This wasn't what he'd seen before. The face was of course recognisable; *his* face, captured on camera just before the address, when he'd smiled to himself, a joke at his own expense but now looking different – unselfconscious, open, warm, somehow perfectly at one with the scenario the filmed treatment had just run through.

His own dreamy meditation was suddenly cut short. Alarms suddenly ringing in his mind. Was this deliberate, who did this, at whose instruction? Sabotage or accidental? Why did the images seem to follow in logical order, what was the message these occurrences fluked together?

The lights were up in the hall, abruptly, instantly, before he had time to refocus. The screen was now back to his opening slide. *Dr Greig Hynd, Alliance for Positive Mental Health.*

He staggered toward Bernie, the latter holding out a rueful smile.

'Jesus, you're good at this stuff.'

Greig offered no response, still replaying the scene sequence in his head.

'I mean, seriously fucking good Greig. You should do this for a living…'

Bernie looked at him imploringly, wanting the boss to get the joke. The silence between them however, was soon interrupted forcefully.

'Greig… Greig… I love you!' An arm reached over Bernie seeking Greig.

It was Elaine Bain, swaying earrings and all, tears in her eyes.

'You were wonderful… we *can* do it…'

She reached forward again, intent on touching him, holding part of him, crushing Bernie against the edge of the stage in the process. Greig returned her gaze, aware he could not hope to reciprocate the same level of adoration, embarrassed at his own lack of willingness to do so, instead observing all around with professional detachment. This transformation was something of wonder, he thought, the power of the piece, he had been right to include it.

More hands stretching for him. 'Okay everyone, could we just calm down, there's a crush here... please move back...'

No one seemed to hear him. His microphone had been switched off by the remote crew. He reached through the crowd to lift Bernie clear, the pressure enough to make this a meaningful test of strength. He noticed Bernie had lost a shoe somewhere in the process. He noticed he had no hope of getting it back. A hundred or more reached out to him, only the force of those behind them preventing them from mounting the stage. And it was his own presence that was luring them forward. Hysteria. Unmistakable, as frightening as it was fascinating.

Greig turned sharply and ran to the back of the stage, eyes fixed on the door leading to the technical area. On reaching it he found it was open and he moved inside, heart racing, every sense telling him he was being pursued. A corridor, then another door, then the calm of the room they had used as temporary HQ, notes from the order run-through still pinned to the wall. The team had only just begun to reassemble, three of them in there, including Catherine.

'Greig!' went up the cry, disconcerting as he approached. 'What a show!... What a speech!'

Greig read the conference identity badge of the speaker, Natasha Skacel, one of the new enthusiasts that had come on board in the last few months. Attractive, young. Bernie had been pursuing her with no sign yet of any success.

'You liked it?' Greig asked cautiously, allowing himself a seat, wondering if he'd over-reacted somehow to what he'd just seen.

'You bet, loved it! Let's march on Parliament!'

For an instant, his heart sank. Was she serious? The laughter from her and her friend told him otherwise. He tried to hide his relief at hearing it.

'And what did you think, Catherine?' He pulled his chair closer to her.

'Think of what?'

Greig realised how tired he was as he summoned the energy to join her game, teasing out a supposedly reluctant response he knew she must be eager to give. He sighed and slumped into his chair. The door opened and Bernie limped in, casting a shamed look to Greig as he slumped to the floor, knees up, hands behind his head.

Greig turned back to Catherine. 'What did you think of it all, Catherine; the day, the syndicates, the presentations, and how it went down in the end?'

She drew herself near to him; face uncomfortably close to his, close enough to plant a kiss. Her face softened and Greig wondered momentarily if this indeed was her strategy.

'I think... I think I'm going to be sick...'

She stood up, hand to mouth, not visibly retching but enough alarm in her eyes for Greig to know that this was not play-acting. She swayed on her feet and Greig found himself standing and steadying her.

'Are you alright? A doctor?... Is there anything I can get you?'

She shook her head. 'I'll be fine, it will pass.'

They stood motionless, the attention of the room upon them. A glass of water was offered and Greig guided her back down to her seat.

'There's been comments about heating and air quality in that room all day... pretty poor, wouldn't be surprised if that's upset you somehow.'

Catherine snorted angrily at his caring, understanding tones.

'Nothing to do with that Greig... nothing at all... It was that... *thing* you insisted on playing... that bloody swirling loud thing. Makes me dizzy just to think about it... Plunging us all in darkness too... Disgraceful.'

'I'm sorry...' Greig began to apologise immediately although not entirely sure of her exact complaint. She cut him off anyway, raising her voice as if addressing the whole room.

'And *you* should be ashamed of hyping up our audience like that, promising things you have no idea if we'll even deliver. *Ashamed* Greig... This hysteria is not what I've worked for. I don't know where it's going or meant to go or where it is in your mind that you want to go and that worries me.'

'What do you mean, Catherine?'

'I mean you're out of control, Greig, and I'm out. I'm out of this... circus.'

Greig watched as Catherine drew her things together, anorak coat, handbag, today's themed conference satchel. *Circus*? Catherine paused once she had everything assembled, now staring over him expectantly, but expectant of what; repentance, apology? The silence that hung over the two of them now extended across the room. Greig noticed how Catherine seemed to think the silence was working for her, stance becoming visibly more proud, more aggressive. More pointed somehow, as the room's attention focused on the awkwardness.

Yet as the time passed, Greig felt any urge within him to reply drift further and further away. *Hyping up*? Yes. Absolutely. *Guilty*, he thought. The only way to be heard was to shout, why couldn't she understand this?

He studied her face. Her eyes were filling, glassy. Tears heading this way soon, tears of rage. She had played herself out and wasn't being let back in, and that for sure wouldn't have been how she'd imagined this would run. The days of the committee rule had probably just ended; maybe that was what she was testing.

'Catherine. Honestly… If that's how you see it I won't stand in your way. I can only thank you for your support and friendship.' Greig stood and offered his hand, an offer that was ignored as Catherine froze. *Not being let back in.* Greig let the silence hang again, silence that seemed to fall solely on her. 'Goodbye Catherine.'

Eventually she retreated to the door. He waited until it closed behind her.

'Okay everyone…' He clapped his hands, blowing in relief. 'Things calming down out there or should we go for that march on Parliament right now?'

Laughter. Laughter in the room and no answer other than the laughter to show they were on his wavelength.

'I propose…' he said, raising his palm to silence the team, 'I propose a stiff drink… anyone want to organise that… volunteers?'

Greig walked across to his coat, hanging on a rack by the door. He handed over cash from his wallet to two of the girls. 'Five bottles of… anything.'

He eased himself next to Bernie, still wilting on the floor.

'Bernie…?' Greig's arm reached round to hug his shoulder and pull him tight, voice hushing to a seductive whisper. 'Bernie, you were great today… Man of the match. I mean it. I'm so proud of you, and everything you did to keep things going. And I'm sorry about your shoe, really sorry. One day, I'll get you a new one, promise. It might even match.' A gentle rocking from Greig shook Bernie into acceptance of the joke, weak as it was.

'Bernie?' Greig continued. 'One last favour of the day. Could you go and find whoever mixed the Sea of Tranquillity stuff? I want to know exactly what happened out there and who made it happen, okay?'

Bernie wearily took Greig's hand to pull him up.

'You unhappy with it?'

'*Unhappy?*' Greig's eyes fixed in on some infinite part of the horizon as he let himself drift back to his moment of glory on the stage. 'I'm ecstatic. *Tranquillity Now,*' he said, smiling in relief. 'Way to go.'

C DAY MINUS 350 DAYS

Harlequin Advertising, Warren Street, Central London

We're back in the boardroom doing it for real. Today, ladies and gentlemen, we have not one but two surprise guest stars; besides Nigel, the unit's Senior Manager, we have not his boss, but his boss's boss, Duncan Sage, a god amongst the gods in the hierarchy of the civil service, his humourless elder statesman presence turning all of us a whiter shade of pale. Even worse, next to him sits an altogether more sinister proposition. Derek Rove, special advisor, beamed in straight from The Party, in amongst the sober suits here's a guy in black polo neck and jeans, a fucking jazz maverick looking for quirky improvisation amongst the onslaught of trad bullet points.

His presence makes me feel yet more clammy. I see him looking at Peter, sizing up, judging instantly, we are not the sexy agency he's looking to jive with. Fuck, holy fuck. Why is Peter so fucking square when he should be groovy? Why is Nick's grooviness so obviously of the faux variety and why is Harry still here shaking in his boots at the prospect of hypothesising the bloody obvious? At least Caroline is on form, giving it off as per brief, just enough to cover some of the cracks.

I remember Pompous Pete kicking off, clearing his throat, thanking them for coming, client lists, *our approach*, the usual shit. They had lined themselves up three in a row on the other side of the table in flagrant disregard of the sequenced chairs strategically offered to avoid this confrontational seating plan. No, they were meant to be integrated amongst us, part of the team from the off. All of it ignored when they planted themselves Cold War style opposite the screen, defensive arms folded tightly across chests.

Peter hadn't even made it to the second of the client list slides before

Derek Rove's interruption made the rehearsals a sideshow to history, the presentation that never was. Slide two of forty-three, one of which only had the fucking date on it and the special advisor man derails us.

'*One Future*?'

Peter can only offer up a counterfeit smile. 'I'm sorry?'

'I thought you were going to talk about *One Future*?'

By which I can surmise that he's less than wildly interested in our credentials in carpet retailing that Peter was warming into and wants to talk about the government semi-biggie we're already engaged in.

'Sure, what do you want to know?' responds our leader, sustained-through-all-too-obvious-effort-smile on show.

'How does a brief that says stop a few selfish people from killing the planet become the happy-clappy celebration of all that's good in life?'

This is serious heart attack stuff. Not delivered particularly aggressively but enough in tone and demeanour to trigger mass palpitations on our side of the table. One, because it's a slanted, devious swipe at one of our/ their star campaigns; two, because a happy-clappy celebration of all that's good in life is precisely what they are about to be presented with.

'Because that's what the focus groups said,' grins Peter, still employing the wide and preposterously unremitting grin/teeth clench to show that *he* personally, at least, is satisfied with this explanation.

Truth is, this is a less than brilliant answer to a challenging enquiry. A bit like a historian saying one side won the war because the other side lost. Only less illuminating. Someone speak for fuck's sake. Somebody has to.

'*One Future...* is probably your best performing campaign on any score – awareness, empathy, endorsement – changing attitudes. If you're referring to behavioural shifts then it's probably premature to see this yet, all our evidence says we've got to establish some kind of common aspiration to work towards before people will think about how they can contribute... a bit like showing the destination before starting the journey, because no one's going to start travelling before they know, even roughly, where the fuck they're heading... what else?... The *selfish few...* well you show me them Derek, do you think the selfish few recognise themselves as the *selfish few*, read the S*elfish Few Times*, watch *The Selfish Cable TV Channel*? You see, no one recognises themselves as the problem, and they get defensive when they think they're being labelled as such... so there's no choice but to work with the *whole* population, and strangely enough there's more chance of moulding *a society* through communications than targeting *individuals*… Not what the textbooks say but the facts themselves tend to back it up.'

I pause momentarily and pour myself a fresh coffee, even make a token gesture of offering the contents of the pot around the table. Not showboating but giving him the space to attack, if he wants to. He doesn't, daring me to plough on.

'Derek,' I said, consciously working both him and his silent colleagues in stereo, 'you're out there working at community level for The Party, what feedback do *you* get on the streets? I'll bet anything that you guys target everyone because no one sees themselves as the floating voter, the undecided. Me? I've decided. I've decided I can't make my mind up, I'm not who you're after…'

I wait to give him the chance to smile, and he's man enough to nod in acknowledgement. The stage is still mine. 'Basically our whole audience is made up of isolated lonely people who would like to feel part of *something*. Only they don't know what that is. Sounds corny but they *do* want to feel *together*, don't *you*?…'

I let it hang and sip my coffee. Stone cold, of course, disgusting; but I can mask this and pretend to enjoy it because I'm warming to a hot theme. My own. Again there's no challenge to stop me. I'm either winning this or wading into ever deeper waters.

'It comes up in research, time and time again. There's power in all this that gets routinely under-estimated… *Togetherise* everything and you are winning, believe me. People will notice it, will warm to it, will *vote* for it.'

At last he comes back, sharply. 'So why don't we?'

'Don't we what?'

'*Togetherise* everything?'

'You tell me Derek. You're the guys in charge. Maybe there's a failure in nerve if the budgets are anything to go by. These are under-resourced campaigns. *One Future* should have three hundred percent more weight behind it. You're running some kind of drug misuse scheme targeting junkies… with all due respect, they don't really consume advertising, engagement tends to be an issue because they're generally too stoned to notice the commercials. Talk to the community – *together we will beat it* – whatever, that's where the success is… As for racism, social harmony and integration… I'll ask my learned colleague here to strut his stuff, show you how we'd propose to crack it.'

Strut his stuff. Nick would never let me live this down but hey, I was on a roll, bypassing slides two through to forty-two so that Nick could unveil the T-shirt and thrust his fingers through his fringe like it's a martial arts assault on his scalp. Lift off. Almost. A pause to take in the mood of the moment. Everybody quiet, even our Managing Director.

Derek Rove purses his lips, this could be appetising or he's preparing to bite. Nigel Richards sits steadfast, giving no sign of being up or down. And then the silent man from the Ministry, the mute Duncan Sage, hitherto happy to let it all roll by, now showing ominous signs of intervention.

'I'm lost on the content. Where's the policy, the new government policy which is the point of having a campaign to start with? What is it we are telling the public with these materials?'

Telling us one big lie Duncan baby, if you listen to my boss, telling us nothing new, just like your brief and policy. You could guess that someone like Duncan Sage wouldn't like someone like me, in fact you could guess that me, sitting there, cup in casual hand, about to hit him with a persuasive yet strangely vacuous line about rational versus emotional, literal versus allegorical in communication execution would be the antithesis of everything he held dear. Smooth, shiny people like me are everything he spends his life avoiding in his quest for substance and order. That we get away with it and even earn a living from it probably irritates and intrigues a quizzical mind like his by equal measure. He sees no value in anything I do. And he despises the politicians in charge of him for falling for it too. I need to build a bridge. And everyone is waiting.

'Let me show you those test results.'

I flick through the computerised slides, move the screen cursor to highlight some of the attitude statements we'd asked respondents to agree or disagree with after viewing these same materials. *A Government that's close to me. A Minister who cares.* Perfect.

'You will remember we said that we don't ask panel members for their own direct response. We ask them how those close to them would react; a friend, a neighbour. Doing that we are accessing their innermost gut response to it all by making them false intermediaries. Authentic, valid, *emotional* feedback. Unfiltered. Look, over sixty percent agreement – *The Minister; a man I'd be proud to stand together with… The Ministry – People sharing my load.* Do you really understand how powerful, how different, innovative this could be for CIO? But if it's not what you want then yes, let's spell out the policy and see who's interested.'

I don't know how it's going down with them but I'm impressed, wishing the camera was rolling again to capture my lifetime's best. Duncan Sage is silent once more. It's Derek Rove who offers the first response.

'What happens if we treble the budget on *One Future?*'

Triple the budget? Jesus Christ. I try to feign nonchalance.

'More penetration, frequency, ubiquity. All of which gives a sign that the government cares about this, takes it seriously… It's almost like the campaign weight itself gives legitimacy to the message.'

And then, since it's going so well, an unplanned intervention from our side, from someone desperate to put his own fingerprints on everything going down, regardless of consequence. 'It's a bit like…' butts in our man with a revived smile, 'I suppose it's a bit like the big liars of history, the bigger the lie the more likely it is to be believed.'

Peter will later take some convincing that this wasn't the most helpful of metaphors to offer at this stage in the proceedings.

Caroline offers to refresh cups. Somehow we move on. Platitudes are exchanged. Nick juggles a few more concept boards until we are as bored with them as he is. Then they show the tell-tale twitches of wanting to go.

All out before midday. We are next to be seen waving them off the premises, the Harlequin Royal Family on the steps of our own little palace. Pete's whispering in my ear as they go. *Pushed the envelope there, Cal… Not so sure it was all helpful.* Nice fucking vote of confidence. Then he wants to go to lunch, replay it all again, presumably expecting me to reassure him over three courses that it *was* all helpful and that *he* was just great. He looks genuinely surprised when I claim to have a prior client engagement. I don't care. *Not all helpful,* like his lunatic input? Once everyone is clear I move in on Caroline and, for half an hour or so, she is to be my alternative appointment.

Instead however, another call comes through from our inside man on the panel. Deep Throat issues an immediate summons; this is either very good news or very bad news. There's no in-between.

CAMPAIGN LAUNCH MINUS 350 DAYS

Campaign for Positive Mental Health Central Office, Islington, London

She had been lucky to catch him in the office, he would later think, and he had been unlucky to be in when she called, spectacularly unlucky.

The day of the summit, the key meeting, Party Headquarters, where it would be so important that he project himself, the organisation, the whole agenda with nothing but pure assurance, the only thing they understood. And to prepare for this, to enter the zone, he could rest at home and watch his wife's tender care of his son, or stop by the office, cocoon himself there, pick up some power from the team. Of course it would be the latter that had the more appeal.

'Greig, there's a woman here, insists on seeing you. I've tried telling her you are tied up but she's getting more and more agitated. I'm really sorry.'

Natasha frowned as she spoke, one leg twisted round the other, a body-language that radiated her discomfort. Everything she does is charged with the strangest chemistry, he thought, watching her. Quite beguiling. Greig looked over her shoulder to the door where Bernie was now engaged with the unexpected visitor, voices raised.

'Sorry Natasha, wasn't listening. Who is she?'

'Says she saw you at the convention. That you'll know what it's about. Other than that she's refusing to say. Only to *Dr Greig*.'

Greig looked to his watch, half an hour until he had to leave. Cab already booked. He stood up, smacking his palms.

'Okay. Let's deal with it.'

The woman and Bernie's noisy debate abated once both realised Greig himself was heading over. The office floor had no reception area as such, just a set of sliding doors onto the sixth floor corridor. It was something

37

they had talked about addressing, to screen the teams working from the constant interruptions of deliveries, callers and impostors who would sporadically grind all workings to a halt.

'Excuse me, can I help you?'

He offered his hand to her but she showed no sign of taking it, instead taking a half step back as he looked to her. She seemed to flinch, falling back as if scared by him, eyes flashing with some kind of forced courage. Greig's every inclination, personal and professional, told him of the need to calm her down. A glance to Bernie, *what's going on?*

'Just the two of us I said. Just us alone.'

Her words were spoken through clenched teeth. Agitated, as Natasha had put it. She must be around forty thought Greig, well-dressed, nothing odd in her appearance other than the startled expression around her eyes. Maybe this was her big appointment of the day, *her* interview.

'Okay...' said Greig slowly, still trying to weigh it all up. 'I'm Dr Greig Hynd...' he stopped himself, forcing his best attempt at a natural smile. 'Listen, I'm sorry, obviously you know who I am, otherwise you wouldn't have asked for me... Look, I have an appointment that I'm about to leave for in ten minutes or so. I'm happy to have a quick chat if that would help...' Greig pointed to the conference table at the corner of the room. 'Otherwise one of the team could fix an appointment for later or even help you themselves if you want.'

Another glance to Bernie, the latter rolling his eyes momentarily in exasperation at the thought of wasting further effort. They waited for the woman to make her choice, she stalled as if overwhelmed by the range of possibilities on offer.

'What's it to be?' Greig slowed his voice, trying to sound soothing and relaxed whilst hurrying her at the same time, hoping to take whatever charge there was out of the atmosphere.

'Over there. Now. Just us.'

'Okay,' smiled Greig, taking a step towards the table. 'Can we get you anything, take your coat...?'

The woman shook her head, following on almost reluctantly, as if wary of walking into a trap. She clutched her handbag tight, holding it high with both hands, tight enough for her knuckles to shine white against its black leather.

Greig sat down and waited for her to do the same, willing the team to settle, to act normally, to hide their tension better.

'So, what did you want to talk to me about? I'm sorry,' he halted. 'We haven't been introduced, I didn't catch your name?'

She looked back at him, as if still fighting some urge to shy away. She spoke quietly, blinking slowly, reciting words as if to remind herself of her purpose.

'I know who you are. I know *exactly* who you are, Dr Hynd. I was there, remember?'

'You were where?... I'm sorry I...'

'At the convention. Thought it was wonderful, the start of something none of us had ever seen before, then the spectacle at the end... I know who you are...'

She stopped talking and closed her eyes, reliving that moment. Greig looked at his watch. This was a bad one, textbook personality disorder, straight from his early days of medical practice. Something that would take time, time he didn't have. He glanced furtively to Bernie, now back seated at his desk, twenty yards away. *How do I get out of this?* He suppressed a smile, then the urge to giggle. The woman's quiet meditation lingered on.

'The presentation. *Your* presentation.'

Her eyes were open again, alarmingly wide. Voice louder, alarmingly loud.

'What about it?'

'It was wonderful. A transformation. I thought you were like Christ himself, Dr Hynd. Thought you were Christ. Only afterwards, I had these rages, this anger in me that I couldn't understand. Couldn't sleep, uncontrollable anger. *Why?* You know why, Dr Hynd, don't you?'

Greig felt his pulse quicken and wondered if any of the team were tuned in. The question disturbed him. *Why?*

'These rages, have you talked to anyone about them?' said Greig, distancing himself as subject, speaking now as Dr Hynd, addressing his new patient.

'You *do* know, Dr Hynd. Because I've seen through you. You're everything you say you're not. That's why I'm angry, that's why I'm scared, because I can see the future, can see what you are going to do. You say you offer help but you offer damnation... You are...'

She stood suddenly, voice now shouting, shouting to the room, to the whole world around her. 'You, Dr Hynd... the Antichrist!'

Her hand dug into her handbag and emerged instantly with the flash of the blade being lunged toward him. The furniture seemed to dance before his eyes, waving in front of his face until Greig noticed there were two hands on it, each fighting for control; hers and Bernie's. Greig rose to his feet, slowly backing away, stunned. There were distant screams in the room, hysteria. *The Antichrist* mouthed Greig silently in disbelief. More screams, then a shout from Bernie as the knife became his, a clattering of the office doors as the woman made her escape.

Bernie winced, the knife slammed on the table in front of Greig, blood on Bernie's hand.

'Wow... Holy shit! Crazy bitch... Nearly cut my finger off... You okay?'

'Me?... I'm fine... How bad are you?'

Bernie examined the damage. 'I'll survive... Knew she was trouble.'

'Disturbed... Highly disturbed... She'll damage herself. Needs help.' Greig halted the diagnosis as he realised no one was listening, concern focused instead around Bernie's injury.

'Someone called the police? Are we taking you to hospital?'

Bernie held his hand high above head height, trying to slow the rate of bleeding. The blood continued to drip onto the table.

'Anyone got a cloth?' demanded Greig, showing no inclination to begin any search. 'Is he okay? Should he go to hospital?'

The office swarmed around Bernie.

Greig tried to engage Natasha's wavering attention. 'It's just that I really should get going.'

'*Going?* Going where?'

'Party Headquarters. I'll be late if I don't head off now.'

'My god, you're still thinking... After *this*?'

Greig lowered his tone, aware that Natasha's was creating an audience. 'I've got to go... We could wait months for another slot... Besides, what would they think of us if I cancelled now, with *this* as an excuse? Bernie, you're okay?'

'Yeah,' mumbled Bernie, now clutching a bandaged hand. 'No damage done. Not to you anyway... You're right. What's staying here going to achieve?'

Bernie understands, he told himself. The police, the procedures, statements; the whole day would be gone before it had begun.

'And keep an eye out for any more mad women. You seem to attract them.'

Greig was grateful for the cue, however half-hearted, grateful for the exit Bernie was offering.

'I'll do my best… Listen, regarding the police. Think it's really… appropriate? I'm thinking of all the publicity, and the help that poor woman really needs. The police? I'm just not sure…'

A roomful of silence again. Broken by the weary announcement from the injured man. 'Cancel all calls to the police.'

Greig pulled his overcoat on and headed for the door.

'Thanks Bernie… Probably best we keep these locked from now on.'

He realised he was talking to himself. The office was still clustered around Bernie, first aid being administered en masse.

'Bernie?' he called, hesitantly, reluctant to raise his voice in any way that might cause more alarm.

'Yes, Boss?'

'Thank you.'

It sounded hopelessly crass, even to himself, but what other words to say it, to say *you saved my life*.

Bernie shrugged, grimacing at the pain or the awkwardness of the exchange. 'Just make sure you nail the Party. Make sure they get the message.'

Greig turned up his coat collar and headed out. 'I'll… try. As I said, I'll do my best.'

C DAY MINUS 350 DAYS

Portcullis House, Westminster, London

Portcullis House is a government building, but a sexy one if there is such a thing, a political building where members of Parliament hang out. It should be off-limits for Nigel but he's relaxed about entertaining me there. After his session with the Special Advisors they want me over and fast.

He watches me passing through the security check at the rendezvous, waiting for me on the other side of the glass partition, handing me a visitor pass to wear with pride.

'Mr Begg... And are you one of the great liars of our age or do you just aspire to that?' I'm impressed by Sir Nigel's use of fluent deadpan as he guides me to the canteen area, nodding in recognition to a host of anonymous, non-introducable colleagues as we progress to our own plastic corner of the room.

'Me?... Listen, I'm just an entertainer... Comedy act... Parties, weddings, anniversaries...'

Nigel sits down. 'Make yourself comfortable. Derek Rove will join us. You take whatever he says; it's non-negotiable, right?'

'What do you mean, how do we stand?'

'Just be patient... Don't argue with him. He's hot for you right now so don't give him any reason to cool. These guys have got the ear of the Prime Minister and they're chasing something new. Don't piss him off or he'll find someone else...'

'I'm not looking to piss anyone off... tell me for fuck's sake, what's the score?'

Nigel hunches forward. 'When he says it, you will take it all as news, okay?'

I nod, moving forward to join the conspiracy.

'The *One Future* thing... You'll get double budget but you must show a plan and write something that commits you to deliver what you talked about. Okay?'

Double money. Fuck me.

'The drugs misuse thing. They want to go big on that... They'll throw in knife crime and gun crime budgets to make it some kind of *Together Crime* thing you talked about. But again you'll have to write a plan telling them how it will work.'

'Another pitch?'

'No. Yours.'

Implication upon implication explode in my head. There must be millions in all this.

'Timescale?'

'Urgent. All required yesterday. Hope is a precious currency, in short supply. The hope is your agency can make some. The PM's in trouble, wants to be seen to be doing something on crime. And Climate Change. And *Cohesive Communities*, of course.'

'What the fuck's that?'

'New name for racism, or anti-racism to be precise.'

'I thought we'd just pitched for that today?'

'You did, successfully.'

'But that's a different title from this morning.'

'Things change fast in communications.'

'You're telling me... So where do we stand with *Together as One*?'

'Run it. Still fits. Same budget as multi crime.'

'Ours as well?'

Nigel blinks. Harlequin is about to sink under the weight of the work. And money.

'When?'

'Same.'

Supernova. Where's the catch?

'Nigel... Don't you see that if all these campaigns are happening urgent urgent, they'll land on top of each other. They'll all just merge.'

'*Togetherise everything*. A plan, Cal. We need a *togetherised* plan.'

'Why so hot for plans all of a sudden?'

'Because then we can see if it works with the other plans.'

Nigel Richards isn't stupid. He knows as he offers the bait, I'll go chasing it, playing brainless mutt chasing the fat cat he dangles tantalisingly close. He'll get his knighthood for this.

'Other plans?… And how do you want me to play that in with *my* plan, given that I know nothing about them?'

'You're in the same boat as me Cal, and don't go squeezing Derek Rove for detail. He'll get suspicious if you push him.'

'Need-to-know basis?'

'Exactly. You'll get told what you need to know. No more, no less. And remember,' he says, pausing to tap his cup with a teaspoon to signal the importance of the announcement he's about to drawl, 'make sure you remember who your client is here. *I* am your client, no matter whatever else you are told. It is *government* money we are spending here, not *Party* money, so that makes *me* the client and means *you* keep me in the loop. Understood?'

Nigel Richards' words swish and sway around, drifting in and out of the general hubbub washing around us.

'*Understood*? Cal?' he repeats.

I lift my spoon and tap my cup, looking around at all the activity in the canteen. Dozens of meetings just like this. Researchers, lobbyists, parliamentarians and their flotsam hangers on; all hunched over plastic tables, drinking from plastic cups, sitting on plastic chairs. Quietly frenetic, something going down. There's a connection to all of this, there must be.

'Let me get this right. The Party's in trouble. The new PM has never really replaced the old PM, in hindsight always an impossible task. But our new guy still wants to show he's got balls. And he's looking to set up a whole host of initiatives in order to drastically reshape the whole personal image thing. And then throw an election.'

I pause and take in another sweep of the hall before fixing Sir Nige in the eye.

'Close? *Togetherised* enough?'

A thin, thin smile from the CIO Unit Manager.

'Might be. Might be wrong. Might be all about setting up a platform for the old PM to come back to. Anyway, I'm not the man to ask. Derek Rove is. Only…'

This time Nigel pauses and plays out his own version of the sweep of the room.

'…Only, if you ask him, you'll blow any chance of everything we've talked about. Your choice Cal. Why would you *need* to know?'

A warmer smile from him to conclude. One I match with my own. We sit in theatrical, satisfied silence slowly invaded by the sound of footsteps drawing close as the newcomers draw up chairs alongside. Derek Rove and assistant. We get introduced. I then wait for the very fucking special advisor's word on things.

'You'll be wondering about today…' he says, swirling coffee in his cup.
'Guilty.'

'We were impressed, it confirmed a number of things we've been thinking, so well done.'

A nod from the advisors.

'So here's how we're going to play it.'

Another pause in delivery, as if to check I'm compliant. He gets a sombre nod back.

'We want a plan. Nothing overly long or complicated. Just a couple of sides of paper. We want a schematic of how all the things we talked about today can run as one big campaign of three separate phases. We want you to work it so that each separate component has enough weight to cut through substantially on its own, but also to complement the other components so that the sum of the parts is greater… yadda yadda…'

A hand gesture to articulate the rest of the premise. Am I following? I am. He continues.

'Once we've got that, we'll let you know how your agency stands.'

I feel a sudden, huge deflation. This guy is determined to keep us all dangling.

'Okay, timescales?' he says, à propos nothing. 'We want everything… we need a plan that has everything wrapped within six months, that is to say produced, run, the lot, all elements, one after the other. Starting whenever's feasible. Nigel here will talk you through the budgets.'

I'm confused now, is he talking about getting my plan in six months or, Jesus Christ, the whole thing being over within this time? Nigel can sense my confusion.

'You better get that plan to us as soon as you can Cal if we're going to meet these kinds of deadlines.'

Nigel then turns to his colleagues. 'Never normally a problem for any agency to achieve the impossible, just a matter of budget being high enough.'

Nice joke at my expense, perfect dig from Civil Servant to Political Advisors about an outside agency, everyone given their appropriate place. Not that I give a fuck, my heart's racing. This not-so-special special advisor has given me to understand that he'll decide who he's going with once he gets my plan. Then he goes and blows this tough guy stance by telling me he's desperate to have everything done and dusted in a fucking nanosecond, meaning it's impossible for him to have any other players at the table. Not only is it all mine, it's all mine at any price I care to call.

I hear the drag of his chair as he and his assistant make to leave. *Things to do, kamikaze diaries.* I understand and shake his hand warmly. *A pleasure*, I mean it, oh yes. Sir Nigel is man enough to let me have the moment; a hand on my shoulder and then he too, exits.

A hundred meetings continue all around my island table, none of them with a hope of coming anywhere near what has just passed at mine.

CAMPAIGN LAUNCH MINUS 350 DAYS

Party Headquarters, Grosvenor Road, London

A taxi ride across the city, passing in a blur. He'd wanted to sink low into the seat of the cab, to hide from the faces outside. Arriving at Party Headquarters he had given himself up to be processed like some kind of suspect himself at reception. A temporary ID badge showing him as he was when taken by the camera, ashen, haunted, not there at all.

He took another deep breath. *Antichrist.* Thought of his daughter, his favourite memories of her as a baby. Of teaching her to swim, the two of them in the pool. Concentrating on the detail, searching for calm, anything to help him focus. Around him, above him, in all the corridors, rooms and open-planned space between, the Party machine buzzed with its own importance. Accountable to no one, far removed from the victims its policies created. Perhaps he could make it all change.

'Mr Hynd?'

Greig drew his coat and briefcase together and extricated himself from the deep jaws of the leather sofa. A wait of only twenty minutes, nothing as compared to what he'd endured at the other parties. So far.

He followed the swinging hips of the Party intern sent to fetch him from one room to another. The only difference being he'd made it from ground floor to third, progress of sorts, again standard territory for all parties. This time with offer of a coffee, taken; a drink which arrived with the players, both sporting their own Party mugs.

'Dr Hynd? Derek Rove. Thank you for coming. These are my colleagues, Jason Watson, Ann Riordan. Apologies for keeping you waiting, busy time for us as I'm sure you can imagine.'

Handshakes all round. Jason Watson bristled with nonchalance as he was introduced, an adolescent air to him. Here, in this company, Grieg felt strangely old and sober and wondered where the determined air of irreverence came from. Was it a natural reaction to the deadly dull and serious world of deal-making and back-stabbing that was politics, or was it more calculating? Greig took in each in turn, reading them, a lifetime habit turned professional necessity. Derek Rove; suited in a grey pinstripe, white shirt, open collar. All of it straight from a high street window, probably of the moment but oddly creased and uncomfortable on its bearer. What age would he be? Mid thirties but lined by his life of endless meetings. *Yes, right there in your face Derek.* Jason Watson: similar vintage, more rotund and with a radically different take on Party wardrobe, jeans and sweatshirt, his bearing the legend 'Kent State University' in studied retro fashion just to tilt things further towards a campus ambiance. Training shoes that looked suspiciously shiny. Then the woman, Ann Riordan. Small woman, fine features, fine boned. Older than the other two. A considered ignorer thought Greig, silent withdrawal as a *political* statement. The others had to make some kind of effort to shut him out, eyes only for each other, for her it was a probably a pillar of her being, the stack of notes, diary and all manner of tabulated order sat before her on the table top. A defence, realised Greig. A barrier to hide behind. The process person in the room. The one with the power.

'... Anyway... anyway... Dr Greig... sorry, Dr Hynd...'

Derek Rove broke off from his whispered exchange with Jason Watson to finally turn to Greig, swivelling in his leather chair like some chat show host with the words of his producer ringing urgently in his ear. *Bring him in now, he's looking bored! Now!*

'Dr Hynd, you've travelled far to be with us today?' Derek Rove flicked through his notes as he spoke.

'Not especially. We're based in Islington.'

'*We?*' interrupted Jason Watson.

'Alliance for Positive Mental Health.'

'Well, thanks for coming anyway, Greig. We are interested of course in hearing what you have to say about your... *alliance.*'

Derek Rove seemed to have given up on his search for illuminating detail and spoke with a resigned let's get-it-over-with air. He turned to his two colleagues.

'Guys, how do we want to play this?'

Although he spoke to both of them it was obvious that the response he sought could only come from the woman in possession of the most notes.

'Dr Hynd, welcome to Party Headquarters. I hope we didn't keep you too long. Conference next month. I should perhaps explain who we are. I'm Ann Riordan, and I'm Convenor to the Policy Secretariat, Jason is a Policy Co-ordinating Special Advisor with the Party and government, and Derek has a role in Strategic Liaison. Is there anything you would like to ask regarding ourselves and our roles before we begin?'

Only the one, thought Greig, *just what the hell does it all mean?* He shook his head. 'No, thank you Ann, you've made it perfectly clear.'

'Anyway, as ever with the Party there's a lot going on. Perhaps you could just refresh us on who and what you represent?'

She spoke with an icy formality as if determined to establish a divide she would then make it her business to maintain.

'*The Alliance for Positive Mental Health.* An organisation of health professionals, primarily, although open to anyone who has an interest in, or can contribute to, an agenda of well-being. We started as an organisation of those involved in the effects of mental health issues – dealing with patients and the whole coping mechanism the health service and society uses to deal with the effects… and gradually got more and more interested in the *causes* of poor mental health on a societal level. We are a response to the *vacuum* that exists in terms of policy with regard to well-being.'

Even as Greig spoke, he could sense the complete lack of engagement his words were being met with, from the lack of eye contact any of them were willing to give, to the immersion in previously scribbled notes, to the satisfied smile Jason Watson shone to his partner in crime. His eye sought him out.

'You have a point to make?'

'I was just thinking of that song… you know the really old song… When all the broken-hearted people, something, something and unite… there will be…'

'… the answer, la da da,' chorused Derek Rove.

Greig watched the two men share an exclusive appreciation of the quality of their harmony or humour, or both.

'So Greig,' said the singer, '…you're here for all the broken-hearted people, finally united as per the musical prophecy. Yeah?'

The final *yeah?* was thrown over to Greig, somewhere between a challenge and a no-hard-feelings reassurance. Underlying all of this though, thought Greig, was a clumsy, brutal pitch. This is all a game. Impress us or we don't play.

Greig sat still, concentrating on maintaining his own calm and patience. *Someone tried to kill me today. I rushed here from that. This was meant to be important.*

'I'm not broken-hearted, Jason. Anything but. I am worried though, if that proves anything.'

Greig stared back, weighing up his options as he did so. Leave now, storm out? None of the people he was with gave him any impression that they had real influence in the Party. Conduits to influence at best. *Strategic Liaison?* Gatekeepers, determined to show their Party muscle. And what they don't understand they reject. The business of politics.

'But *who* are you Greig? What are you representing here, why should we take notice of you?'

This was all on the record, pre-supplied for these idiots in a hundred different formats long before today's session. Another deep breath.

'I am Greig Hynd. Practicing Clinical Psychologist. Background psychiatry, which makes me even more of an oddball. I still work, have to because the Alliance is a voluntary, part-time organisation with no staff overhead. We have ten full or part-time organisers themselves self-funded through other work or via sponsorship. Three of our people are paid for in full by drugs companies. A contradiction, you might think, since our whole ethos is to get away from a chemically dependent society, but we are pragmatic enough to take their money right now for the greater good. *Who* do we have? Membership? We've got half a million associates rising by fifty thousand a month. Our conference events are inevitably over-subscribed in terms of number of issues and participant numbers. So,' paused Greig, turning to Ann Riordan, '… I do sympathise with your challenges in organising your own party conference. We have begun regionalising ours, and now have a sort of never-ending tour. Because of who we are and what we are interested in, it has to be face to face, has to be personal. Yes?'

He clapped his hands in conclusion, wondering if he had succeeded in startling them. Then starting again, speaking more softly.

'So, who am I, what have I got? I've got me, then ten helpers, then half a million, where we're going I don't know, but I know it's somewhere and that's why I'm here.'

'Can you tell me more about yourself… any affiliations?'

Affiliations? wondered Greig. Strange word. Awkward word delivered with unease. Meaning political affiliations. What baggage was he carrying?

'We have heard, for instance, that you have been visiting other parties.'

'Guilty. We've received many invitations from many parties to discuss what we're about. I took the view that it would be negligent not to take these up. But am I *affiliated*? No. And the Alliance? We're still waiting on offers.'

'Sea of Tranquillity?'

'Sorry?'

'A strange bunch. No?'

A strange tangent, thought Greig, temporarily thrown.

'I wouldn't know... I've never met them. They've dealt with some of the admin staff. Why do you mention them?'

'Same thing. They're touring, looking for backing, resource. Had them in here last month. Spoke very highly of you. Almost in terms of partnership, something we *had* to back... Have you got any idea of the number of approaches we get, every one wanting something, backing for the cause, whatever it is?'

Greig looked to the door, enticingly near. He looked to his coffee cup, long since empty, with no sign of replenishment on offer. *My rages,* she had said, *an anger I cannot control.* He shook his head and rose to his feet. Something that seemed to cause surprise on the other side of the table.

'Have I offended you?'

Greig ignored Derek Rove's words and continued to draw together his things.

'I'm sorry Greig, but that's the way it is. You'd have to be very naïve to think you can come in here and expect us to just roll over to join your...'

'... *You, You, You,*' cut in Greig, standing at the door. 'What about *us*?' He stopped, satisfied with the riddle he'd just set. 'Incidentally guys, it was *you* that invited me here, something that seems to have been lost in translation. Or maybe I'm being naïve again. Of course... *You* invite *me* in to tell me how uninterested *you* are. There is no *us*, not here, in the great inclusive Party.'

He gestured towards Ann Riordan's notes. She looked back, bemused.

'No matter,' he sighed. 'I've taken up enough of your valuable time, and vice versa. I'll leave you to get on with... strategic liaison...'

'Greig. Please sit down. What do you mean *us*?'

Greig looked back at Jason Watson. 'Are you interested? I mean *really* interested? Not going to break into song, not going to start redrafting conference speeches whilst I go through it?'

There was no sign of an answer from any of them, in itself an answer, he realised. He stayed standing, not angry but aware of the need to appear close to it; the only way he could maintain their attention. *Someone had tried to kill him, that's how important it was.*

'I don't know about Sea of Tranquillity or whoever coming round here. I couldn't give a damn. I know why *I* came here and why you should be interested. I came here to say that you guys, and since *you* are the party in power, *us*, …have no policy whatsoever about mental well-being. I know you think you do, like all the other parties think you do. I know you think that committing to spend billions clearing up the mess caused by inadequate provision of mental health *is* a policy… So we have a policy vacuum. No goals, no objectives, no explanations of how society should *feel* about itself and how we are going to help it toward that. How government and all its offices should be trying to make their public feel. Imagine the benefits to us, us as a society if everyone just *felt better* and thought that the government cared about how they felt, wanted them to love *themselves*? And if you can't get your heads around that, just imagine the damn votes, because people like people who care, although right now there might not be so many of them in your Party.'

He realised he was lecturing, with nothing coming back at him. Time to stop.

'Dr Hynd,' said the woman panellist, hesitantly, 'I think that perhaps you should come and address our Health Policy Development Sub-Committee on this. They would be the most appropriate policy development unit for you to engage with at this stage, I would think.'

She turned to her colleagues, seeking endorsement for the resolution she had offered. Greig cut short the process; he was still standing, folding his overcoat over his arm.

'Not interested.' He strode to the door and placed a hand on the handle. 'I've told you what I want, wasted enough time. If you want to make policy, not talk about developing a committee to discuss one, let me know. If you want me to work with decision makers, let me know.'

He opened his arms, offer made. And then a final thought.

'Incidentally guys, you might be interested to know, we did have one of the broken-hearted people with us today, at our office, a lonely disturbed soul let down by your policy. She was waving a knife around, looking to damage anyone, or herself… mainly looking for help that she's never going to get from here, is she?'

Greig turned and headed out. He noticed his hand that went to close the door behind him was shaking.

'Dr Hynd!' called a voice from the room. Ann Riordan, standing. 'Dr Hynd, please don't leave like this. If we've offended you then I'm sorry. But we cannot respond to threats and bluster.'

Threats and bluster? Damn. Why couldn't they see it?

'Okay, now you listen to me. I've been round the other parties, this is true. I've briefed them. Like you, they are not good at handling new ideas. Of all the parties though, I thought I'd find the most common ground here. But...' hunched shoulders, palms up, '... I was wrong. I've been a health professional all my working life, training, teaching, and practising. I grew up with a younger sister and older brother, an absent father and an alcoholic mother. Somewhere along the line I took responsibility for all of them. Somewhere along the line I learned that the best hope for my mother was when I helped her cope with her condition, to understand and empathise and then help her get over it rather than punish, rather than hide the damn bottles. And I did that, not because I'm a wonderful human being, but because I'm a *rational* being and I wanted a *normal* life. I had to create normality around me. I've done that ever since. Help people because I want a normal life. *You?* You're meant to be interested in helping people. I thought that was the whole point of the Party. I haven't heard one thing yet from you about it. I honestly don't know what you're in politics for, it's a damn mystery to me. Anyway, as I say, I got it wrong, so my apologies for that. Did I threaten you? I know what it is to be threatened, I don't think I did. I tried to give you a wake up call.'

Greig closed the door again. His hand had stopped shaking. He walked to the staircase through the open-plan throng of the Party. *I don't know what that was about,* he thought, smiling politely to a gaggle of Partyworkers clustered round the vending machine, *but it did me a lot of good.*

He paused momentarily as he handed in his ID badge at reception. Go home or head back to the office? It was five o'clock, he had promised his wife an early return for once but knew there would still be activity at his own HQ. Automatically, his steps took him to the subway station, down the escalators to the bowels of the underground. Once on the platform it was as if the crush of the crowd pushed him into the train carriage rather than any conscious choice on his behalf. The high of his final flourish was deserting him as tiredness set in. The crush of those around him in the carriage contrasted achingly, angrily with his need to be alone. These were the same people he had just sworn it was his life's work to help, he realised. This same ignorant mob invading his personal space from every angle. Saint Greig, perhaps human. Perhaps a hypocrite like those at the Party Headquarters. *I know exactly what you are,* she had said. Where now Dr Hynd? You're supposed to be the man with all the answers.

C DAY MINUS 350 DAYS

Soho, London

I walked back to Harlequin through a car wash of heavy drizzle and swooshing traffic, soggy and slow, taking in the events of the day. A day that was not yet over. I had to think of the sell to Vesey, how much to share, how to position it all; there was also the entire agency, ready to commit mass hara-kiri or throw itself into an orgy of celebration given the word on the pitch, the result it still waited to hear. In theory, everything depended on developing an acceptable plan, so the champagne should be kept on ice. However, there was no doubt that Harlequin were in for something substantial, and that was surely enough to trigger righteous drunkenness. My phone rang, again. I had been ignoring it. Caroline; five missed calls. Then I remembered lunch. Shit.

'Caroline? A thousand apologies, I got called over to meet Mr Richards and that nice Mr Rove… I completely forgot. Listen, can I take you to dinner instead? Right now, if you want…'

So it was that lunch became dinner and my own private celebration. So it was that Caroline agreed because she had something to tell me rather than the other way round. I arranged to meet her an hour down the line in an Italian joint off Firth Street where I spent the aforementioned next hour placing calls and drinking vintage Barolo because, strangely, I could not face going back into Harlequin. Lonely in triumph, a new one for me.

Placed call number one, first of three. Nick Craig. One glass down.

'Nick?… Yeah. Cal. You can release the hounds Nick. All done bar the formalities. They loved the work… T-shirt, you name it. Blew them away. Abandon ship, that's an order. Vesey? I'll call him next. You've two minutes to clear the building. Well done, couldn't have done it without you.'

Placed call number two. 'Harry?… Cal. Congratulations, you did it.

They need some work done on an implementation plan but it's ours. Listen, let's go somewhere with this one yeah? We've proved we're a match for anyone, nothing to be shy and bashful about. You going to step up to the fucking plate or what? Build a career on this one. Enjoy. *Your* achievement. Now get out before Pete Vesey comes calling, which he will. Nick's taking the team out right now, grab that bandwagon. One minute to get out.'

Placed call number three. Last call. Two glasses of rich red making me relax into the role, holding court from the new red-checked table-clothed desk that is by now my workstation, complimentary focaccia in a basket to my left.

'Peter? Hi. Cal. I'm still at Portcullis House. Been here forever. Routine meeting with Nigel Richards hijacked. Yeah? That's why I'm calling. Where to begin?… Derek Rove seems to be the man in charge. They are lining up a raft of policy announcements, initiatives, god-knows-whats of which our pitch was part. The good news is that we've passed through our flaming hoops today so the race thing is ours as we've called it. *Budget*? Big, for sure but we have to finalise the plan first… Listen, it looks to me like a pre-election plan. We have to consolidate all the elements… crime, drugs, environment into one huge Party pitch. That's the real brief, always was, get it? *Together*?… Yeah, good idea. I was thinking the same. A drink? I'd love one but I'll be here for another while. I'll give you a shout once I'm clear. Maybe you want to take Nick and his team out meantime if they are still there, yeah, Nigel Richards gave them a call, he needed some new visuals sent over for reference, let it slip out. Yeah, I'll call you later.'

A waiter hovers over me, waiting for me to close down the call; it must have had the air of wind-down from the moment I got through to Peter. He offers more bread and I wonder if he's listened in to what I was saying. But then I'm well into my fourth large glass and care less and less. Besides which, a beautiful woman is about to join me.

She actually arrives a full half hour later, and as she smiles and makes her way across to my corner I can smell that somewhere in the delay she's been to freshen up and change aura. Impossibly fragrant and happy. Is this the woman I was on parade with first thing this morning? No wonder we won the account. This woman's gorgeous and might be the answer to everything.

'Wine?'

'Yeah but not red, could I get something lighter, white?'

The waiter offers his selection.

'Whatever, the best. A bottle.' Caroline smiles.

'So what did you have to tell me then? Show me yours and I'll show you mine.'

'I think I can guess what yours is Cal,' she says, taking in the near-empty bottle that has been my table companion.

'Whatever. What's your news?'

'I'm leaving the agency. I'm resigning. I'm going to RSGG.'

Caroline has the decency to look a bit shamefaced about this. Thinking, as she would, that she's somehow letting me down. And, in that instant, I do feel a momentary wobble. The wine has slowed me down but the wiring in my brain soon went through permutations. This was great news. I could smile, be magnanimous. I could love her.

'RSGG? What have you got there… Promotion, better offer?'

'Account Director. Digital Team.'

'Congratulations. Honestly. It's what you deserve. I know some guys from RSGG. They're a good outfit. I'm sure it will work out for you. Cheers.'

She raises her glass to mine. Somewhere between let down and radiance.

'I thought you'd be annoyed.'

'Cheers.' I insist.

'Cheers… To the future… Harlequin and CIO, *Together as One*? Can we toast that too or is it too soon.'

'Oh, we can toast it, for those of us who are staying with the agency it's our future…'

'They've confirmed it?'

'That and a whole bunch of other things. For the next wee while we're going to be an extension of Government, CIO, the Party, MI5, FBI… and all points in between.'

She raises her glass again. Laughter in her eyes; clear, warm, affectionate eyes looking to me.

'I don't know how you did it. I hope they give you a knighthood.'

'Who?'

'Peter Vesey, Nigel Richards, all the sleazebags. To be honest, I don't know how you can stand it… It's one of the reasons I'm leaving.'

'You don't like government work?'

'I don't mind it at all Cal. It's what goes with it… I mean look at this morning for god's sake. Peter going on about the world's greatest liars.

Harry not understanding the brief or where it's going, Nick so arrogant about his little pile of nonsense. And we all just watch it play.'

I can feel myself relaxing, almost a new sensation. This combination of Caroline, red wine and pizza bread is a potent one. She's beautiful and I'm stinking drunk, stinking of garlic. Is this really happening, could she be mine? I ask for some water.

'It's all about egos... Our business. Egos. Mine included. It'll be the same wherever you go. RSGG, wherever. Why do they have their names in the title if it doesn't matter to them?'

'Then why not you, the Cal Begg Agency?'

Music to my ears. I can hardly speak for the stretch of my smile.

'That would be fantastic. Any thoughts on clients?'

'I think Nigel Richards for one.'

I groan. 'CIO's roster is a closed shop precisely to stop that kind of thing. Influential client choosing his best mate. Got to go through the circus of government procurement...'

'But someone does it, everyone starts somewhere.'

'Sure, absolutely. We resign and start up and hey, four years later, we can pitch to be on the new roster. Assuming we're still in business.'

'So start *now* Cal.'

A mournful shake of my head.

'It's all happening *now*, Caroline. All the new ground; happening now. I can't go anywhere until I've proved that it all works. Until then I'm just another Account Director. After that it's open sesame. That's why I'm stuck at Harlequin and Peter knows it.'

A waiter materialises just as I begin to share my melancholy in this moment of triumph, robbing the moment of its poignancy as he flirts with the woman opposite me. I feel I've already let her down, broken an illusion she might have had of me. An important illusion... She feigns interest in the choice of dishes.

'Hungry?' she asks.

'Fucking ravenous.'

'Rrr... ravenous,' she repeats, rolling my Scottish Rs in her teasing mouth. The menu goes down.

'I'll choose...' she says.

The gnarled garçon reappears and the two of them discuss what would be good for me, the spectator at my own banquet. At last he's gone and she fixes me in the eye, coming on stern and serious, still lovely.

'And what about us, Cal?'

'*What about us*?' I parrot.

She laughs as if these games are what she enjoys, although it soon transpires they are not.

'Why are you so determined to make it difficult?… Us, Cal, are we going to be an item… or not?'

First she ordered my food. Now this, the seizing of the initiative. Was I making it difficult? How can she make it so easy?

'I would, really, very much hope so, Caroline, I've thought about nothing else since I first met you.'

There's no doubt that the wine has helped with this. I think I lean over and take her hand at this point too, embarrassed about the watching waiter but warning him off, proud to do so.

'I've thought about it too. Never thought it would happen, not whilst I was at Harlequin.'

She gives my hand a squeeze to authenticate the sentiment, and I feel a flashing guilt over my declaration. *Thought of nothing else.*

She's still holding my hand, moving close to speak softly, as if passing on some great secret. A fun secret.

'You know, I know absolutely nothing about you. I know you work hard, that you're from Scotland, and can guess what you're going to wear on a daily basis. Apart from that, nothing. So tell me, open up.'

'Where do you want me to start?'

'I don't know… Your family Cal, all the time I've known you, I've never heard you mention them. Are they in Scotland?'

Welcome to my world, Caroline, welcome to my universe. A small one, of which you are now the major part, like it or not.

'I've got no family in Scotland. Aunts and uncles maybe; no one I'm in touch with. My father died three years ago, just before I joined Harlequin. My mother went when we were very young. My brother is somewhere in the Far East, Thailand. Maybe Vietnam. He used to be in London too though we never exactly hung out together. Always working, worse than me, if you can imagine that. Better looking too. He took a holiday two years ago and never came back. I get texts and emails telling me where to send the money.'

'You send him money?'

'Why not? He's got better use of it than me. I like to think of it as a kind of partnership thing. I do the work, he has the fun.'

'What about your fun?'

'Right now, this is it. There's not been much room for anything else for a while.'

'And you really don't know where he is? Are you not interested?'

'He used to tell me. Used to send me updates of where and who and what he was up to and why he needed cash to keep doing it. Then, gradually, these got shorter, and shorter. So that now, I'll get barely a sentence. Maybe I could work it out if I followed the trail and read backwards. You see, he was always a really, really intense guy. My mother dying so young... he had barely started school. Anyway, when he went on this trip he really loosened up and I thought my thing would be to support him. I liked seeing him enjoy himself. Now I get my single sentence stuff which either means he's too busy enjoying himself or turned back the other way. To be honest, I'm not inclined to look too closely. *Really* intense.'

Caroline doesn't seem satisfied with this answer, or her starter, or her Pinot Grigio. I watch her working up a theory between the three.

'What if it's not him? Someone else? Identity fraud. Shouldn't you check it out?'

It is a theory. I can't stop myself from smiling.

'Could be. Fair point. A bit elaborate for the four hundred a month I send but could be. To be honest, I've got enough paranoia as it is, I'm not really in the market for anything new.'

Still, she won't let it go. Something else is on its way, stretching a basic riff into a song, then a suite. I can feel the whole West End musical taking shape. She's now holding both of my hands, pitching from the heart.

'Have you got any time, Cal? I mean holidays. You must have loads. I'm taking a month off between finishing at Harlequin and starting over at RSGG. Why don't we head out there ourselves, track him down. You *must* be worried about him. Shit, *I'm* worried about him and I never knew he existed before I sat down here. Come on, I've got friends who've done the Thailand bit, the beaches, islands, it's fabulous, Why don't we? Tell me yes, Cal.'

And here, at this point, at this table in a restaurant in Soho, we reach a big fork in the road. She's going to sort me out and reach deep for the inner Calum Begg and I can suddenly see the beginning, middle and end of our relationship playing out in my mind before the main courses have arrived. Before we've gone anywhere near consummating our thing beyond holding hands over a table. Decision time, choice of paths. One marked '*Happiness, normality, fulfilment, love*'. The other signposted, '*Disaster, lunacy, solitude*'.

'Caroline, we've just won the biggest piece of work any agency in London... any agency in Christendom is going to get its hands on. I've no time right now. The next three months are going to be kamikaze...'

And so I steer off in the chosen direction. When I replay this in my mind I can still see the hurt in her eyes for those moments. We still have our hands together but suddenly I am aware of them, conscious of the gesture rather than any need. She doesn't argue against the analysis. Doesn't utter a word.

'Are you hungry? Do you need this?' I ask, sensing her suddenly restless, drifting out of my range. Needing to get away.

'I can come or go.' She shrugs. 'Why?'

'Listen, I do want to get away with you Caroline, get away right now. Your place, my place. Any place we can go and just be the two of us for the very first time. And just make love.'

Eyes widen, eyebrows rise, not necessarily in delight. Not necessarily in shock either. Wrong-footed, working out the options. She's already said she is in, so to back out now would be killing it before it has any chance. A mouthful of white wine.

'Your place, darling. If you want.'

I do, so we leave. Staggering out into London's mid evening, holding hands in a cab. Making awkward exchanges about the fucking traffic and favourite bars. Then arriving at mine, a token inspection of the premises and then getting to it. The kissing and the rest. Doing it without music or lights, our different phones and their multi ringtones' sporadical ringing as the only soundtrack. A woman in my bed. What a day it has been, not over yet. I can't say it was great, our first time, in fact it was just like that, a first time. I can't paint a picture of soft focus pink glow to it all. But we are more together at the end of it than we were before. Were more of the item we'd agreed to be, and afterwards there is a movement to somewhere new; Caroline teasing about the stark and sterile décor, me defending the sleek minimalism. Caroline giggling at the white, hospital ward roller blinds that grace every small window, lingering over the only discordant note of personality that clashes with the show-home blandfest – the framed Beatles print, an original shop promo piece for *Rubber Soul*.

'You like this? Bit before your time surely?'

'My father's. Before his time too. People ask what it was like growing up in a house with no mother, no females, and all I can say is that we were a Beatles house rather than the Rolling Stones. My father was firm on that. Made sure we never forgot it. And this Caroline, where you are now, is a Beatles home.'

'I've no idea what you're talking about, Cal, I'm interested though. Honestly.'

Caroline laughing in her eyes, wrapped in a towel, mug of tea in hand, reaching out. My happiest memory of the whole relationship. And then me, toiling with the impossibility of it all, explaining the disaster zone that was my family.

'I believe, that somewhere in the past, when the Beatles and the Stones were it, that you tended to declare for one or the other, if you were into music.'

'That's years ago.'

'For sure, but my dad was obsessional about them, the only band that mattered. He was nostalgic for it. Better times maybe.'

'Was he serious about it?'

'Deadly. Wouldn't hear a word against John, Paul, George or even Ringo. We went along with it. And that poster is there to remind me. My one concession. You still don't know what I'm talking about, do you?' I move closer to her, begin to whisper. 'I'm talking about value systems, false gods and the like. Growing up with no religion, no ideology and having a gap that needs to be filled. Growing up without a mother's love. The need to believe in something, and my father either believed in the Beatles and made us love and worship what he loved, or he gave us that to fill the gap. And there are worse things to believe in than the Beatles. Besides, it's the one thing I have to connect with him. One way I can talk to him. Even now.'

'Do you miss him?'

'I didn't know him at all. Only as a parent and that's different isn't it? I look at that picture and try to imagine what was going on in his head. But all I can see is the fab-fucking-four.'

Caroline puts down her cup. Pulls me close.

'I wonder what goes on in your head. I...'

Another call on my phone cuts her off. The flashing screen telling me about a text arrival, marked urgent.

'From Nick. He's in a karaoke bar off St Cuthbert's street. Half of Harlequin there. Fancy it?'

'Do you?'

I look to the bedside clock. Eleven. I sit up.

'*Our* moment, *everyone's* moment. Let's do it. We can be there in half an hour.'

'*We?*'

'You don't want to come?'

'I'm okay about coming along. It's just arriving with you at close to midnight... kind of obvious what's been going on if we turn up together.'

'You embarrassed about that?'

'Not exactly. I'd just... maybe have a little time before we announce anything. You know?'

'We can share a taxi. Once we get there I'll give you a five-minute start. Let you make an entrance. I'll come in later, won't drop a hint of anything. Promise.'

So the final, most forgettable part of the day is set. Another taxi, another part of London. Nick had done his job of getting everyone out, racking up an epic bar bill on his agency credit card, a bill that would be transferred to the first job-bag for the new *TAO* campaign which itself meant the first job of the campaign account director – in this case, me – would be to find some feasible way of hiding these very same expenses. But I am okay. These moments in adland are rare. Rarer still in Harlequin-land and something has to give. Me? I am in adman heaven. Account win. Advertising Valhalla. I am the Prince of the city, with my Princess, so I think, in tow. I watch her walk in to the bar and immediately follow, any agreement on the decorum of our joint but discreetly separated arrival out of the window. I match her step for step, a half yard in her glorious shadow as she makes her way to the Harlequin set. Caroline locked in immediate celebratory embrace with the traffic team, waltzing around in rotation only to be confronted by the unexpected presence of myself, there way ahead of our agreed schedule. Her look of surprise, utterly genuine, probably enough to throw most off the scent of recent goings on. Me? I want to freeze time here, hit pause forever, live in that place where everyone is happy. Instead, I'm dragged violently to the other side of the bar.

'Cal, you fucker, you lucky, lucky fucker...' drools my creative director. 'We fucking pulled it off... We pulled it off for you. *You* thought we were shit didn't you, but we fucking pulled it off.'

Nick graciously offers his glass to me in salute.

'Well done anyway, you lucky fucker.'

Well done to you Nick. Congratulations. *Together as one.* Whose line was that anyway and does it really matter?

Over his shoulder I watch Caroline work the tables and instantly want to be alone again with just her. Away from the madding crowd. Why have I brought us here?

Nick conjures up another tray of drinks and offers me my pick, which I am grateful to receive. Another arm around my neck, another bruising hug dragging me sideways. Here's Harry Rhodes, a glassy eyed, happy – relatively happy – drunk Harry Rhodes.

'Cal… You must be thrilled. A fucking triumph, *your* triumph. Cheers!'

Harry and I clink glasses in silent salute. He gulps his alcohol like there's a gun being held to his head. Sighs at the debauchery around him.

'What's up, Harry?' I ask this more out of irritation than concern, though my words probably sound shot through with good-guy empathy rather than how-fucking-dare-you-be-miserable-and-drink-on-my-tab annoyance. Yin and yang, me and Harry. His is the curse that condemns him to permanent melancholy; mine is to notice this.

A shrug from Harry that seems meant to convey something along the lines of it's *nothing, don't worry, not your problem.* For me, this is just further encouragement.

'Harry, level with me, what's wrong?'

Normally, I'd expect some kind of playback on a new chapter of marital strife, a household pet gone AWOL, domestic shit. Not this time, and as I press, I can sense this, so that when at last he does reply, I'm almost as spooked by my own intuition as by what he actually says.

'*Togetherised…*' is what he says.

My turn to shrug. *What do you mean, esteemed colleague?*

'Togetherised together,' he mumbles, 'gives you the creeps, doesn't it, or am I the only one?… I don't think we appreciate just how high risk this is all going to be.'

Fucking defeatism before we've even started. Before we've even celebrated winning it all. 'There's no risk Harry, we'll get it all done, we have to.'

'Not that,' he grimaces, like his insides are shredding just thinking about it, 'I mean we're going to get everyone to love the Party. Whether they deserve that love or not. Surely that has to fall down somewhere, surely that will crash at some point in the road…'

I stare at him, giving no encouragement either way.

'...And what you said today, Cal, so impressive, so right. I think we *do* all want to belong to something, but couldn't it be something more than just those clichés we parade in these bloody ads?... These horrible, cheesy, soulless ads. Yes, they tap into something quite profound, don't they? Leave me feeling quite scared in a strange kind of way, like we don't really know what we are playing with here, do we, Cal?... Or maybe you do... I find myself wondering what it is we've started. No going back now though, I guess...'

I shake loose from Harry's limp embrace, realising for once he is absolutely right. There is no going back, none at all.

CAMPAIGN LAUNCH MINUS 350 DAYS

Campaign For Positive Mental Health, Islington, London

The lights were visible from the street as Greig approached. So late, nearly seven o'clock, and the office still in gear. Regional conference schedules pinned to the walls, maps, piles of correspondence, unopened mail. Bernie hunched over a multi-coloured spreadsheet, two fingers on his left hand bandaged.

'Hiya, Captain. What's the news?'

If Greig had hoped for quiet he'd chosen the wrong place to find it. Yet somehow he knew he'd also been looking for the reassurance that the machine was still functioning here, that someone, somewhere was doing something. Natasha approached as he sat down and leaned his head back in the chair.

'Let me hear yours first. How's the injury, did you call the police in the end?'

'No. We thought homicide central might have a bit of a rush on at the moment. Assaults on fingers are a low priority, even if they need sewn back on to the hand that nearly lost them.' Bernie studied his injuries anew, as if musing on the possibilities.

'Good, so that's it?'

'Well, we should probably write our own record of what happened. Health and safety, statement for the file.'

Greig groaned. More wasted time.

'You look as if you could do with something,' said Natasha, brightly. 'What's it going to be?'

Natasha and Bernie had assumed responsibility for the daily management of the office since Catherine's sudden departure. A seamless transition, with the long hours and never-ending organisational wrangles their reward for taking it on. Natasha though seemed to thrive on the new duties. More and more Greig realised he had no idea of how the office now functioned in a practical sense. Every day there were letters to sign, messages to record for the phone-in service and pieces to record for the web logs. Apart from that everything was magicked away. Greig was grateful for that.

'What have you got... whisky, gin?'

Natasha smiled and raised an eyebrow.

'If you're serious I'm sure we could sort out something.'

'No, not serious. Green tea will do. That's strong enough.'

'How are you after all of this... And how's your boy, wasn't something happening there as well today?'

'He's okay, I hope. He's been in for tests. I'll catch up with my wife on how it went when I get home.'

'Is he... is it serious?'

Greig sat up, much as Natasha's voice soothed him, this was not information he would choose to share with the half-dozen staff within earshot. His son.

'Not particularly good,' he said, voice close to a whisper. 'Not particularly bad but not good either. Something not right. Autism? Deafness? Trouble with breathing. They're checking it out.'

Just talking about it seemed to draw whatever energy he had left in him out in one swift spiral. His voice drew to a halt.

He found Natasha's face suddenly close to his.

'Let me know if there's anything I can do. You should be home.' She placed a hand on his shoulder. He had to stop himself from placing his own on top of it. More guilt.

'So,' interrupted a voice. 'What *is* the word from Party HQ, Greig?'

There was more than a hint of trepidation in Bernie's question. Trepidation and impatience combined somehow. Was his defeat so obvious, wondered Greig.

'Yes Bernie... Let's get everyone around. I've a few things to say... I don't want anyone to waste their time on a cause... It's only fair that I tell it straight...'

The tone of his reply wasn't meant to be ominous but immediately Greig knew he had his team worried.

'It's been a tough few months. I know things have got a whole lot bigger, I don't know if we've actually got a whole lot happier, which would be ironic, to use Bernie's favourite phrase, since well-being is what we are all about. Personally, I have a few challenges at the moment, combining my other work and family commitments…'

He looked for some kind of reaction, getting nothing but blank exhaustion.

'Anyway, we had this meeting today. Some of the operators within the Party. I felt sure, *still* feel sure, that they will have to recognise a common agenda, and that's what I went to discuss this afternoon.'

The sound of the office telephone ringing out interrupted Greig's flow. Bernie glanced at his watch as he peeled backwards to answer, and Greig glanced up to the clock on search of the same information, ten past seven. Late. Who would call now? Greig waited whilst Bernie closed out the call.

'Anyway… An opportunity may exist. But I have let you down and let…' Greig scanned the faces again whilst he searched for the right words to assuage the guilt. He caught Natasha's look of sympathy and stayed there, locked eye to eye. '… My own stupid self-importance get in the way. It's probably right that I…'

Another phone-ringing interruption and a flash of temper from Greig.

'Damn, who the hell is so intent…' He reached for his own mobile, the source of the call, an unrecognised number. He silenced it and threw the device back to his desk.

'I'm trying to say… that maybe it's time for someone else…'

Another call. This time it was Bernie's phone ringing out to halt the address. To Greig's dismay Bernie stood and took the call. He waited to see if it too would be closed out quickly, something that Bernie showed no signs of doing. He gave it some more time, grimacing apologetically to the rest of them before deciding to continue, but Bernie himself interjected.

'A guy called Nigel Richards on the line, insists on talking to you. Central Information Office.'

The department name was only vaguely familiar to Greig. The name even less so.

'Tell him to call later.'

'He said you would say that and that you should talk to him if you know what's good for you.' Bernie held out the phone.

Greig sighed as he raised himself from his chair and made his way across.

'Was that him on the other lines before?'

Bernie nodded. Greig turned his back to the room and placed the receiver to his ear.

'Greig Hynd. What do you want?'

'Dr Hynd...' said a voice on the line, a voice that was friendly, even chirpy; a voice whose owner clearly thought he had every right to call at this hour and demand instant attention. 'Can I suggest that you stop whatever you are doing right now and come and meet me? Whatever you are doing is unlikely to be as important as what we have to discuss.'

'Meet you where?'

'Anywhere you like Dr Hynd. Anywhere that we can both get to, quickly.'

'And meet about what?'

'About what you were talking about today. About policy. Helping people.'

The words had Greig intrigued. This was a call from Government, yet it was the Party he had been with earlier. Crossed lines, CIO asking for an urgent meeting, it had to be significant, surely?

'Can you come to our office, should I come to yours?'

The first pause in the conversation from the other end of the line.

'...Perhaps it would be best if we met somewhere neutral. Name the nearest bar or hotel to you and I'll be there within half an hour.'

'Okay, let's fix that. See you soon.' Greig passed the phone back to Bernie.

'He wants to meet somewhere near... bar or hotel. My mind's a blank... Tell him one, I better wrap the group here.'

He strode back to the gathering he had called, clapping his hands.

'Okay! Apologies but we'll have to finish there. Interesting meeting today and it seems there might be a part two so please let me get back to you all once that is concluded. Hopefully I can explain all later.'

Greig lifted his coat and phone and made his way across to the door.

'Bernie!' he shouted, looking back. 'Where is it I'm going then?'

CAMPAIGN LAUNCH MINUS 350 DAYS

Paddington, Central London

Arriving at the bar Greig realised he had no idea who he was looking for. For this rendezvous, he was entirely in the hands of the man who'd arranged it. He surveyed the layout of the place, torn between a need to find somewhere hidden and discreet, and the logical need to make himself visible enough to be spotted, the blind date backdrop already making him squirm.

'Dr Hynd, I presume?'

Greig turned to find the voice belonged to a middle-aged man with a kindly undertaker countenance.

'Nigel Richards… CIO… Pleased to meet you. Would you like a drink? Yes… *Orange juice*?… Splendid.' Nigel Richards took a slow step towards the counter.

'Orange juice times two please.'

Greig took a mental note to hide his gnawing sense of resentment for being here, a feeling he had directed at his host; unfair, since it was he who had accepted the meeting and Bernie who had presumably chosen the venue. A shit-hole. They were meant to have things to discuss. Big things, though this seemed unlikely according to his own instincts, watching Nigel count carefully from his wallet, the wallet taken from a crumpled raincoat. Another middle-man, another time-waster, another false lead.

'Now then, where to have this?' Nigel Richards asked aloud, scanning the unpromising landscape, glasses in hand.

'Here's as good as anywhere,' sighed Greig, pointing to the bench nearest the bar and parking himself down. He had promised to be home hours ago. A demanding day, for sure, one of the worst. Tests on his boy. Tests that would doubtless point to the need for more tests. A son he could not reach. A screaming woman with a knife in her hand. The Party HQ debacle. This damn bar.

Nigel Richards placed the two drinks down into neutral space between them, then paused to contemplate, almost as if he was about to give grace for them. Eventually he began to speak, fixing Greig sternly.

'Okay. Listening?… This is an off the record chat, between two civil servants, in a bar, in an after work, informal, shoot the breeze way as happens. Are we clear?'

'*Civil servants?*'

'You work for the Health Service, don't you Dr Hynd?'

'I suppose so, but I'm hardly a civil servant.'

'*Public* servants…' cut in the other. 'With no authority or agenda other than their own curiosity. Again, are we clear on this?'

Greig waited for the space around him to empty as two men lingered close to watch the television screen momentarily before moving off. He was about to be sounded out and it had to remain secret. Maybe this would be worthwhile after all.

'Okay, this fifth amendment stuff… fine. Why did you want to meet me, why so urgently?'

The smile re-emerged across Nigel Richards' features.

'Well Greig… We have been talking a bit, fighting talk at that, enjoy ruffling the feathers at Party HQ do we?'

'Why would you be interested?'

'There's the thing, yes. CIO's part of the government, and in government everything is communications and communications is everything. So we are told to get interested Greig, and that's what I'm doing. Okay. Simple question. What do you want, Dr Greig Hynd?'

Greig studied his glass. Going through the parade all over again. What would he give, the long impassioned pitch; the short pugnacious pitch? The abrupt pitch. He clapped his hands, loud enough to startle those gathered around the television screen, loud enough to jump him back into character.

'The Alliance for Positive Mental Health exists to promote the concept of positive well-being. It's about creating an environment where a society of individuals cherish and nurture the notion of a 'fit' mental state.'

'Dr Hynd,' came the cut in from the other side of the bench. '*Dr Hynd…* With all due respect, spare me, I've read the speeches, the website, the interviews. I get that. What do you want?'

'*What do I want*?… I was trying to explain.'

'Explain in terms of money, funding… power? Help me here. What's the game plan for you, your organisation?'

'To influence government, decision makers…'

'*Influence decision makers*? You've got one right here, Dr Hynd. You had three this afternoon, people of huge influence. Yet you merely harangued them to no obvious purpose. Although,' he paused, suppressing a dry smile, '…the Party does like to have its chain pulled from time to time, never underestimate that.'

Nigel Richards searched across the table for a response to his accusation. Seeing none in Greig, he continued, though in a softer tone.

'The benefits you propose your agenda will bring… productivity, less crime… a more harmonious society… these are of huge interest to government… surely the next stage is some kind of trial of your approach, some kind of project to test it out.'

'This is no *project*. I'm talking about a shift across a whole society; it only works across a whole society, everyone in or everyone out. No middle way. That will take leadership, policies, intent. It's not a damn project.'

'So what *is* it exactly you want?'

Greig paused. This was not a normal conversation, not what he was used to. Somewhere back he and Catherine had worked up a list of objectives and milestones that might contain the specific detail that Nigel Richards seemed so interested in. But the list had been obsolete ever since it was written, existing only to spur Greig's ambition higher. Bigger events, bigger aspirations, that was the journey he had embarked on. Lesser detail. Bureaucratic detail.

'Look, if you don't see it, let's call it quits for tonight. I'm tired of explaining…'

Another interruption, an aggressive interruption, the other man's impatience finally matching his own.

'Dr Hynd, with due respect, you haven't explained anything at all. Suppose I'm convinced by your concepts… where do we go from there, how do we make it happen?'

'By shifting societal attitudes…'

His partner thumped the table. 'But *how*?'

The two men waited for the attention that was upon them to dissipate.

'You haven't worked it out, have you?' said Nigel Richards.

Greig stayed quiet.

'Do you want to be in government, Greig?'

None of the detail, nothing in fact *worked out*.

'I'm not a politician.'

A gentler smile. 'Oh I think you're a very skilful politician, Greig. A natural.'

Greig tapped his hands, gently, silently.

'I want to be in a position where I can make these things happen. I'm not in any party; I'll go wherever the ideas take me.'

'And you have ideas. A precious commodity. Something new, especially now. You understand?'

He didn't. He kept quiet, the silence becoming easier to give.

'We have a vacuum of ideas, as you say Dr Hynd. It's been that way for a long time. A Prime Minister desperate to demonstrate he's not like the last one. Maybe even willing to call an election out of bravado, to prove that he's the people's choice after all. And he'll need to fill the shop window with new people, new concepts in order to mark a break with the past. Precious commodity, ideas, you see?'

This was the same stuff Bernie would eagerly read aloud from the news and opinion sites he surfed endlessly.

'It's for you to demand Greig. *Minister for Positive Mental Health?* Could that be yours?'

Greig listened intently, replaying the words in his head. *Minister for Positive Mental Health.*

'Are *you* serious? And are you authorised in any way…?'

'I'm not authorised, Greig. Informal chat, remember? But I am meant to find ways to make things happen.'

Again Greig followed the words, and the meaning behind them, hearing them as if on an echo delay, repeated over and over.

'Mr Richards. I'm flattered. But let's have a bit of reality. Ministerial posts, elections? There's a few steps missing. I'm not a Member of Parliament; I'm not even a Party member. This is fantasy talk about being a Minister on the other side of an election. And so, with that, I'll wish you a good night and thank you for your time.'

A hand reached across the table and held his arm.

'Greig, your time is now. Join the Party, call Jason Watson. Arrange to pick up where you left today. Name your price. You might be surprised.'

A glance at his watch; ten o'clock. The events of the day. He'd be arriving home next, very late, apologising to his wife and then announcing he'd been offered a place in the next cabinet, in a dingy North London pub. Then to her news.

'It's delusional isn't it?'

'Why don't you tell me if that's the case or not Dr Hynd, after all, you're the psychologist.'

'Can I bring my people?'

'*People*?'

'The team that work for me.'

'Not my decision. There may be jobs available. Depends on what you negotiate when you join, if you join. Also at constituency level.'

'*Constituency*?'

'Well, you would need a constituency wouldn't you? That would need to be addressed. Quickly.'

Quickly, yes. Join the Party, trade his ideas, his credibility. *Name your price.*

'You are serious, aren't you?'

Nigel Richards stood and straightened his coat.

'Politics. Always serious.'

Greig stood to face him.

'And the other thing I should have mentioned. Delicate matter...'

'What?'

'None of this counts for anything if there is anything embarrassing, anything swept under the carpet about your personal or professional life that would make anything we've talked about... difficult in any way.'

'You mean hidden scandal?'

'Quite.'

'Nothing. Absolutely nothing.'

'Thought as much, you have that air about you. Still, you might want to think about that, sleep on it. None of us have led entirely faultless lives.'

He offered his hand. Greig took it, a firm handshake.

The two walked to the door.

'You're heading my way, tube station?'

Greig shook his head. Where was he heading? At that moment he didn't know. Anywhere to be alone, to reflect.

'This way.' He pointed in the opposite direction.

'Well, goodnight then, sorry, one final thing... Sea of Tranquillity? Mean anything? Are you involved with them?'

'Vaguely, we used a kind of montage they made at a conference we had. What about them?'

'You might want to see if you can get them under control. A bit over-enthusiastic. Not shy about using your name in conversation either. Just a thought.'

Not shy about using your name. Greig followed Richards.

'What do you mean? Is there a problem?'

Richards patted Greig's arm.

'You've had a lot to take in tonight, haven't you? No, not a problem. You should just be aware they've latched onto you and your organisation, and you had better make sure you're comfortable with that or do something about it, whilst there's still time.'

Another pat on the arm.

'It was just a thought, nothing more. Goodnight Greig. I look forward to hearing how you get on.'

A lot to take in. Yes. He realised he was walking without any idea of where it was he was heading, waltzing through the light rain to nowhere in particular. Was he being taken for a fool, was any of it real? Nigel Richards was real; authentic to his sensible shoes and battered briefcase, but who was controlling him? A taxi pulled up and Greig saw that it was his own hand that hailed it, one move ahead of his mind. *Take me to my office, there's nowhere else to go.*

The lights were still on as his cab pulled up outside. Team still at it – what *would* happen to the team? I will *negotiate*, he told himself, even mouthing the word negotiate as he sought his office pass key. A glance to his still silenced mobile phone; four missed calls from his wife. No message. She would have to wait, and for once it would be worth waiting; Mrs Hynd, wife of a government minister. He wouldn't call now, she would only ask what was going on and demand to know then and there in the same call, robbing them both of the moment, a moment worth waiting just a half hour or so more for.

'Hello?' shouted Greig to the empty office, scanning towards Bernie's workstation.

'Greig?... At last, where have you been... we gave up, thought you'd been kidnapped or something... How did it go?'

The voice came from the opposite end of the room, a female voice, one that Greig was almost too tired to recognise.

'Natasha. Still here, alone?'

Greig walked over to Natasha's desk. Dropping his briefcase dramatically to the floor, he wheeled a chair to the side of her desk and threw himself into it, feet up on the desk top, head in hands. A quiet sigh.

He felt her eyes upon him. Sympathetic eyes, busy empathising.

'No good? Forget it Greig. We'll get the bastards yet. They'll have to listen someday.'

Her voice was soothing, almost like a pair of hands on his shoulders, massaging away his anxieties, yet at the same time it triggered a new wave of guilt. *No good?* Very good, actually. As good as it could be. Greig closed his eyes and placed a finger to his lips, silence fashion.

He sat still. Too tired to notice how long the moment was lasting, concentrating on his breathing, breathing heavier to the point of almost snoring, running the events through in his mind; the first national conference, the regional conferences, the campaign contributions racking up, the special advisors to Nigel Richards. Here. Telescoping time, exponential speed. If it were true.

He opened his eyes to see Natasha had moved, now sitting on top of her desk, next to his, looking down on him with soft concern.

'It's okay, Natasha.'

'What are they offering?'

'A place in government. At *ministerial* level.'

Her eyes seemed to widen and charge with wonder. 'Which Ministry?… more to the point, which Minister?'

'A new one.'

'Oh my god… *You?* You did it! You grumpy bastard, you've really done it, what are you acting all sore for?'

'Natasha… It's never this simple. There will be a catch…'

Greig stopped, his feet had been thrown to one side and he now found Natasha in front of him, shaking him gently.

'We did it. We're there, don't you see?'

What he wanted to hear over and over. Closing his eyes, her voice calmed him, but her words seemed to halt just as Greig was drifting headlong into them, letting himself go. He opened his eyes again and this time she was closer. He launched a gentle kiss, meant somehow as a kiss of thanks, yet he found his arms drawing her in, pulling her to him. His hands once more holding her shoulders, squeezing them, holding her rigid as the kiss grew, hands that then wandered down, undressing her with an urgency that he was incapable of holding back; blouse buttons, the waistband of her skirt, her clothes peeling away and falling. A hand cupped a breast for him to kiss, the other pushing her close to him in the small of her back, almost toppling her to the ground before she could hold him back. *Greig, Greig…* She was whispering to him, saying it in a way that he understood was an appeal for calm. She gently prised him away from her back and he realised with shock that he had been digging his nails deep into her. He stroked the same skin by way of apology. *Greig*, she said, stopping him again. She stood free of the chair and took off her shoes, bra following. *Greig*. She lay down on the floor, beckoning him to join her. One hand ran over his eyes, rubbing them, tired eyes. His other hand already taking off his shirt, throwing it down for her to lie on. The hand still wearing a watch. The hand that had hailed the taxi on the street, a lifetime ago.

Moments later, brief, tender yet mechanical moments later, he was already beginning to deal with the afterward. Greig took a deep breath and surveyed the scene all around him. His eye lingered on the clothes scattered around them, lit by the harsh fluorescent strips above; intimate clothes incongruous against the office backdrop. He rushed his clothes quickly back on, fully dressed in seconds.

'Sea of Tranquillity?' he asked aloud.

'I'm sorry?' laughed Natasha, head to one side. 'Didn't see that one coming.'

She was still naked, almost provocatively so.

'Is there a file on them somewhere? It's what I actually came back for. The guy, the government guy… he gave me a warning shot. Something about them using our name… I need to know right away.'

'If you really need to know, right now…' drawled Natasha, now speaking with the air of the soothing counsellor, someone talking another down from the window ledge. '*Sea of Tranquillity…* Catherine's contacts, should be a file over here…'

She padded in bare feet across to Greig's side of the office, browsing through the storage behind Catherine's old desk.

'I can look up whatever emails are stored on the shared drives, or do you want to do that whilst I search for hard copies?'

Natasha was still showing no inclination to dress. Greig tried hard not to notice, the effort overwhelmed him. What had he done?

He closed his eyes, burying them under guilty hands. Another deep breath.

'Natasha, I've got to go. But I need a complete record of everything we've ever had or sent to these damn people by start of play tomorrow.'

He was talking to the space around her rather than to her, issuing instructions as if addressing a committee of workers, all placed on emergency footing, addressing staff rather than a woman he'd made love to only moments before. A ludicrous formality; bizarre, he thought, inexcusable. He walked to the door, leaving sharply, without saying goodbye.

C DAY MINUS 345 DAYS

Central London, Raffaelli Restaurant

For all his faults, and fuck knows there are many, Peter Vesey's choice of restaurants easily trump mine; perhaps reflecting the modus operandi of a man who lunches for a living. Here, on this occasion, our first serious tête-à-tête since the pitch win, we are to be found in a corner table of some kind of underground vault. Our space lit by flaming torches and the warm glow of the reservation system console, wine racks latched to the bare stone walls above us. The smell of fresh bruschetta and thyme seems to suggest conspiracy, especially when mixed with the damp of the cold cold stone. Yes, this was the London of Medici princes, busy plotting in their medieval Florentine catacombs, although actually somewhere between Soho and Pimlico, in a side street off a side street that has been styled after the subterranean lair of a decadent baroque castle. And here, somewhere around the second bottle of Amarone, I realised I was dangerously pissed, agreeing disconnectedly with everything my man says. Anyway, the word from my man is he wants to seize the opportunity.

'I want to seize the opportunity Cal, understand?'

It seems churlish to disagree. I do understand, vaguely... *Seize* the opportunity. Of course. What he means is that he wants *me* to seize the opportunity. For him.

Peter raises his glass. 'Are you with me, then?'

I raise mine by reflex, without really understanding what it is I'm toasting other than another swig of Amarone.

'These moments come rarely. We've done exceptionally well. But we'll never be what we can be unless we shape up pretty fast. We're in the big league now. Big boy's rules. That means change. The Board see it that way too. They want to see your plan.'

This last bit is a twist on an old theme. Of course I've heard the stepping up to the plate mantra ever since I joined Harlequin, Peter being a serial abuser of every sporting metaphor going. *Personal Bests, Team Relay, Olympic Trials* – oh shit I've heard them all. But here's a new slant. *The Board* are interested. The question duly arises in my befuddled drunken mind; just who the fuck are the Board he's so reverentially referring to?

The initial guess would have to be that Peter is referring to the shareholders in our parent holding company NBN Holdings, since Harlequin has no board itself. The mystery men of NBN are just that; mystery men, the elusive, anonymous men in grey suits. *Interested in my plans.* Fucking wonderful. I already have been performing two parallel tasks, both at breakneck speed, each more urgent than the other. The first, to plan the actual campaign, cascading that into production, research, development and client contact schedules, media planning and purchasing liaison on top of that. However, all of this was a mere sideshow to the exercise the man himself demanded I concentrate on in syncopation; the forecast of revenue and fee return on the very same work against the costs for actually doing it. So that now I am living in spreadsheet city, or more precisely, living in the Bermuda Triangle of Project Management software, interconnected accountancy spreadsheets and Agency Traffic Action Forms. A no man wilderness where no work actually gets done, but profit projections can be tweaked endlessly until Peter and his 'Board' can be satisfied. For the first time in my career at Harlequin, Peter needs more than a simple projection of what we'd make. He needs a minutely detailed account of how the vast fortune we stand to make would land and where. And now the same 'Board' want another plan on top of this. Holy fuck, is this what all the wine is about?

'Peter, you've had me running in circles over this. I've amended the forecasts to a point where they're losing any sense of reality... Pounds pesetas potatoes yen Zen... We'll make millions, you know that. How much beyond that I don't know. Who the fuck *are* these people, can't you explain that there's a point where we've actually got to produce this stuff rather than fill in balance sheets about what it'll bring us... If you won't, I'll fucking tell them...'

My voice must have been raised towards the end of my little spiel because people on the other tables begin to look round. Peter waves away the concern of the waiter, patting me on my arm.

'Cool your jets Cal. It's not like that at all.'

He nods, in a magisterial kind of way to shut me up whilst he orders up some coffee. Double espresso. I need to sober up.

'The Board is changing. There are new investors coming in. Obviously I'm not in charge of that process but once the new line up is confirmed, I'll brief you. Meantime some of the existing and prospective members simply want to look at the shape of it in terms of size and structure. That's normal, Cal, especially given the amount of work we've just been awarded.'

I wait a moment to check that it is permitted for me to respond.

'Then why are they asking me? It's your agency.'

A deep breath from Pete. A leisurely sip of espresso.

'Because you're in charge now, Cal. It's yours…' Portentous pause. '… If you want it.'

My hand reaches out to my glass. A sip of luminous red silk.

'Mine, as in what, what's mine? Managing Director mine?'

'Yours to run. You'll get a title.'

The glass is still in my hand. Another sip, then I raise it. 'Cheers. Thanks very much.'

My thanks are solemnly accepted. The king is dead. Long live the king. Ruler of all in Harlequinland.

'Congratulations,' offers Peter, magnanimously clinking his coffee cup.

Shared smiles. Even the waiters seem to join in our moment, the passing of the torch. The highest office Harlequin has to offer has been placed in the care of the next generation. A new era has begun. Perhaps.

'What about you, Peter?'

A quizzical tilt of his head. Eyes of surprise.

'That's what I have still to brief you on. With the new investment will come changes to the structure of Harlequin Group.'

A firm stare. *Do I follow?*

Yes, almost. *Group.* Interesting word. Another new word, unless the alcohol is fooling my hearing. Harlequin Group, says Peter. New to me.

'What structure?'

'Harlequin will become a holding entity, under which we will have Harlequin Advertising, Digital, Public Relations, Public Affairs and Communication Optimisations. These will largely exist as virtual autonomous sub-divisions of Harlequin, staffed up according to pitch needs or client projects, or offered as a tailored integrated solution.'

Another fixed stare from which, through our caffeine-and alcohol-and years-of-working-together-fuelled telepathy, I am to understand that this is a serious, non-negotiable, and above all, *done* deal. *Get it?* Not that I have anything to worry about. I'm a newly appointed Man Without a Title Yet In Charge of a Virtual Autonomous Sub-Division. And I'll report to guess who.

'I take it you will be the MD of the Harlequin Group itself?'

The question merits no direct answer, Peter choosing to reflect openly on the immense challenge his own new role will bring.

'I'll be looking at acquisitions, expansions, strategic alliances… building the Harlequin brand… our client offering has to be as broad as the best in class, better than that in fact…'

It is a vision, of that there's no doubt. Obviously a bit of a blurred vision for me at that point, selfishly obsessing about my own place in the firmament, whatever, wherever that was.

'These other… wings… *Harlequin Digital, Harlequin PR*… will they have their own Managing Director?'

'Why do you ask that?'

'Just trying to understand how this all fits together, the practicalities. Are we taking on new people, or are you going to wear all these hats?'

Two glasses of grappa arrive by the command of Signor Vesey's hand. I'm prompted by him to take mine.

'We may or may not recruit, over the long term; it depends on the level of client demand for specialist services… These are virtual divisions. We already have the skills portfolio; it's just how we field our team to best fit the opportunities as they arise. Cheers.'

I'm forced to sip before continuing. 'But Harlequin Advertising will be a real entity with a real MD in the form of me?'

Peter's eyebrows lift north of skywards. It seems to go without saying.

'There is clearly client demand for that service so we will tailor something to fit it, yes.'

There's a hint of frustration creeping into his responses, like I'm being deliberately slow in the uptake here.

'Peter, virtual divisions with virtual staff tend to have pretty virtual clients paying absolutely virtual fees. That's my issue if you're interested.'

Peter's face falls as if the grappa's gone sour. I'm throwing his gracious gift back in his face. Cue more frustration in his voice, coupled with hurt. A wounded man. Correction; an honourable man, wounded unfairly, hit below the belt.

'Cal, this is about stepping up to face challenges, seizing the opportunity and you are either with that agenda or not. This is the Grand Prix; don't join in the race if you want an easy ride on cruise control.'

Words of wisdom, of sorts. Words that make more sense then and there than in the cruel light of sober reflection later. For all the bluster and usual clanking metaphors there is a cunning strategy in there; are you in or out? Commit or quit. Now my grappa tasted sour.

'What plans and what timescale?'

A bemused look from my man. Genuine, sincere bemusement. What do I mean?

'You said the Board wants to see ideas on shape and structure of my bit.'

I see his face reanimate like the power supply has just been restored. He thinks I've finally got it. He talks faster, excitedly.

'End of the month. Basic ideas. How are you going to take what you've got and use it as a platform? How are you going to build on the campaigns we have planned and get more? What's the structure that will maximise the potential of the opportunity?… And so on…'

I'm trying to get a practical understandable instruction from him. The riddles grow tiresome.

'You mean how are we going to staff up to meet the growing demand?'

A narrowing of the eyes. 'We will not staff up for the sake of it. That's precisely what we will *not* do. No. I want a plan that addresses the business priorities.'

'What *are* the business priorities?'

He pulls his chair closer to the table, leans forward. 'Don't you think you are carrying too many passengers?'

Peter's eyes still have a lingering air of menace. I am being given to understand that we two are an island, everyone else is rubbish, and that moreover, I risk his wrath if I do not begin to move against them. Time for more grappa.

'Peter, we have a mountain of work to get through over the next few months. You cannot be serious, clearing out who we've got before we've got over that…'

'Now's *precisely* the time,' interrupts Peter. 'Before they've wormed their way into the new campaigns. If you're talking about peaks in workload, isn't that what freelancers are for?'

I glance around, checking to reassure myself we are not being eavesdropped upon.

'Who are we talking about here?'

'You tell me Cal. Who do you absolutely need? Who genuinely adds value to the brief?' He pauses, a reptilian glint as he sips from his glass.

'Nick, Harry… Hugh?… It's your call, Cal… We want to see your plan. We want to see your ratio of costs to income right down. I would suggest that this has to be one of your highest priorities.'

If it all sounds self-evidently, fatuously, fabulously hokum in retrospect then I can only apologise. In my defence, I can only state I was in the presence of a master of this kind of bullshit, someone who had made a career out of it. That I did not stand up, walk out and resign without ever turning back I can only put down to that, my exhaustion, the alcohol, the food, and of course to vanity and ego. And yet, oh yes and yet, even accounting for all of this and another gallon of grappa it still should never have been beyond me to smell the great fucking rat on the loose in that restaurant, for I have just been handed responsibility with no power, no power whatsoever. I have been in charge of Harlequin Advertising since we turned down the dessert menu and I seem to have run it to the point of bankruptcy by the time we've finished our first coffees. I have, to be fair, been given the chance to turn it around and by my silence and taking of the wine I have accepted this challenge.

Truth be told, there's a little game going on here; I'm taking Peter for a fool who can be worked round and he's taking me for a fool who can be manipulated. One of us has it wrong of course, but that I will only discover later.

CAMPAIGN LAUNCH MINUS 344 DAYS

Finchley, North London

Dishes jettisoned rather than stacked in the sink. Debris crunching underfoot as he laboured to make any impression on the accumulated mess. It was, Greig thought, as if there had been a party here. One that he had missed.

The door creaking open behind him, his wife.

'Made a fresh pot of coffee, want a cup?'

She scratched her head, yawning. Ignoring him.

'Sorry for being so late again last night. Quite a day. Should have called but it was meetings meetings meetings…'

'We've got a meeting ourselves today, half past nine. Harlands Medical Centre, on the other side of the city. You'll have to help me get Ben and Sophie ready.' Neutral eyes, neutral voice. Greig was as troubled as he was impatient at his inability to read her.

His mind a blank. 'Harlands?'

'Respiratory clinic, recommended by Hilary… You don't remember… Dr Hilary Bruce, your son's paediatrician.'

A sign of emotion in her response, although not the one he was hoping for. A missed episode. Another one.

'Did you hear me coming in last night?'

'What?'

'Just wondered if I woke you.'

'Wasn't sleeping.'

'Sorry anyway… Listen, can we talk, there's so much I need to…'

The sleepy form of his daughter materialised, staggering in a semi-comatose state towards him. He stopped to embrace her. *Morning sleepyhead, some cereal, juice?* He parked her on a stool and looked round for his wife.

'Anyway, I really, really need to catch…'

Halted again, the sound of the doorbell.

'Shit… The taxi.' She quizzed the kitchen clock. 'So early?'

'I'll go.' Greig paced the hall, opened the door and signed for the delivery, returning with the bouquet and an air of subdued triumph.

'Flowers!'

His daughter's delight seemed isolated. Greig pursued his wife to the sink and pushed them to her.

'For you… For us. We got it.'

'Got what?'

'Recognition. We're about to be offered a place in the Cabinet.'

At last a smile, if sceptical. 'How's that going to work then?'

'That's what I want to talk to you about. Got to think up a plan.'

'You and Catherine worked up endless plans.'

Missing episodes, had she forgotten? 'Catherine's been gone a while.'

She put the bouquet in the sink. 'Your new team then. Natasha, she's bright. What about Bernie, isn't this their chance?'

He moved to stand alongside as she cleared a breakfast setting. '… They are all about *getting* influence, not delivery once you've got it… This is important… I was getting a pretty hard time yesterday from the government guru for not having this worked out already.'

She put down the plate, turned slowly, rotating to face him. 'Well, it's a point, isn't it?'

He slumped to the table, head in hands.

'Okay Greig,' she softened. 'Try to get home early tonight and we can see. There has to be something about prioritising which parts of the machine you can get your hands on first. Which bits can be quickly realigned to the new agenda the quickest?…' She broke off the thought. 'Now, you will need to help me get Ben up, time to move.'

He straightened up as instructed. '*Machine*?'

'*Government* machine, sunshine. Wake up.'

A stolen kiss to the back of his daughter's head as he followed his wife's lead out of the room.

C DAY MINUS 300 DAYS

Harlequin Communications Group, Harlequin House,

Warren Street, London

How to describe it? A *Board* meeting? Peter Vesey doesn't like the word Board, because we aren't, strictly speaking, a board. The agenda is headed 'Management Board', but he doesn't much like that either. Why not call it what it is, he would reason, a *team* meeting, to discuss matters of interest to the team. And there's my problem, because under Peter's divide and rule modus operandi, here is a team that will never see itself as such. Agenda? Who cares? Yes, the Agenda. Prepared and circulated by the new Managing Director, or whatever my title was to be, with that very item topping the list. Item one, New Structure. Let the Coronation begin. Or not. Pete's in the chair and he has different ideas. How come? My fault. I have told my leader we are pulling in separate directions, that the campaign is in danger, slipping timelines and that anarchy reigns; the obvious solution being to clearly put me in charge. Mr Boss however has only heard the problem part of the equation, and it transpires that this pushes some particular buttons on him.

'I won't let you screw this up, understand? I will not let that happen. You are not acting like a team and you better start doing so because otherwise you will screw up the biggest opportunity this agency has ever had, understood?'

Peter is not shouting but he's not far off. Those kind of volume levels, nostrils flaring impressively, fist thumping the boardroom table. Seven of us in the room at that moment, his remarks aimed at the air above us, all of us assuming that his scorn is directed at someone else. Me? I've called the meeting, won the account, created the opportunity; Hugh McDoughnut?

87

Hasn't even signed an expense claim against the account. Not guilty. Andy? Busy as ever elsewhere. Harry? He feels guilty and inadequate at any time; it's his default setting, nothing new here. Nick? Maybe we're getting warmer. He's been beyond precious since the pitch win, pouting spectacularly under a succession of ruthless hair bands, revolutions in his mind telling him that it's his creative vision that our client has been seduced by.

'I want a plan, an execution plan that delivers the campaign within client timescales.'

Another thump of the table and blank looks around the same table.

'Everyone has a copy of the schedule, Peter. There's no shortage of detailed plans and schedules…' I offer truculently.

'Cal?' says Andy. 'Can I, may I?' Fuck, I think. Something's coming.

'With all due respect, there obviously is something wrong, because otherwise would we have been pulled in here for an emergency Saturday meeting?'

'Actually, if you look to the agenda, you'll see why the meeting was called.'

Cue hurried glances around the table as exhibit A, my fucking agenda, is re-read by the panel.

'No, no…' The precious document is thrown to one side. 'You're absolutely right Andy. Obviously there is a problem. And we are going to tackle it; we will not screw this up. Where are we at with the creative development?'

Attention turns to Nick, who does his best perplexed look.

'Ready to go. Just waiting on a new brief.'

Eyes back to me.

'Nick, you've had a brief. Had one two weeks ago.'

'That was just the old brief, rehashed. Not a new brief.'

'You mean the brief that won us the pitch, the one the client bought? When they said "*we'll have the one you presented as fast as you can please*". Why would we need a new brief after that?'

'Because…' says Nick, arms open, looking to draw the good men and women of the fucking jury to his side, 'because they *changed* the brief, added two entirely different campaigns to it, so that it's something new to what we presented. Why else would you give us that back but with a box full of numbers that we are meant to decipher as part of the new brief?'

Nick's voice has raised itself to dramatic level, as in amateur-dramatic level, as in a theatrical it's-so-obvious-why-do-I-have-to-point-it-out way.

'A matrix Nick, how many times do you want me to explain it?' I ask, although realising that the answer is obviously one-more-time. He doesn't want explanations though, he's playing to the gallery. Cal's box of numbers, exhibit A. Proof that this is out of control.

'We take all the audience segments by demograph along the top, seven in total, from affluent young ABC1s to elderly C2DEs, then we take each emotional scenario of belonging and isolation along the side, ten in total. What's in the core of the matrix is just a code for each audience-specific execution we have to develop. One piece of paper, simple. As I have said, if your department would prefer, I'll copy the same brief seventy times if you would find that easier.'

My turn to appeal to the jury, relying on their intelligence to follow at first explanation the pride and joy that is my innovation and gift to the world of creative brief development.

'*Simple?*' Nick jeers. 'Even our own planning director says it's an incomprehensible crock of shit. How are we meant to work it, what's wrong with a brief that just says what the ad should be about?'

All eyes naturally fall on Harry, mine included, throwing dangerously acute daggers at his implied treachery.

'I didn't say it was unusable,' he whimpers, face screwed up with the pain of having his ass wedged between two chairs, philosophically speaking, '… unorthodox, for sure. Definitely not traditional.'

His voice has actually grown more confident in the space of a sentence, concluding with a sense of certainty that he tries to convey to the room. I loathe his lack of spine so much it could melt the air.

'Enough! We will give this client *what* they have asked for *when* they have asked for it. And you…' An angry finger pointed at Nick. '…You better cooperate and start working and stop disappearing to celebrate or it will be done without you.'

'*Disappearing to celebrate?*' queries a wincing Nick, somewhat bravely. 'Who's been spreading that shit?'

Peter chooses not to respond. Instead, in an ever-not-so-fucking-subtle way, he chooses to seek me out, alone, for some meaningful eye-to-eye. Like he is planting a fucking great flag. *There. The two-faced bastard, right there. Calum Begg. He told me.* Nick's eyes burn into me.

Peter begins again. Another group address.

'I am told,' he says softly, patiently, waiting for us to dig the gravitas, '…that the government is planning something very new, totally innovative and wildly ambitious. They are staking everything on its success, and will put millions, literally, behind it.'

'Have they seen the opinion polls?' asks Andy. 'They will need it. Our man's a deadbeat. He will never win an election, and now they are saying that as Prime Minister he won't even last long enough to call an election. Approval ratings below ten per cent!…' Andy catches his breath, eager to follow through with his own punch line. '…And that's in his own Party!'

Peter waves down Andy's gleeful résumé of our client's imminent demise.

'They know they need something extraordinary to pull this around. That's why they will give it absolutely everything it takes.'

'But surely *that*…' says a timorous Harry Rhodes, taking anything but inspiration from our MD's situation report, 'that will cut right across the combined campaign they've commissioned from us?'

'That is the campaign they've commissioned from us, you fool, that's what I'm trying to tell you! *That's* how important this is to them!'

Commandant Vesey has snapped so furiously that I swear there are glassy tears ready primed in Harry's eyes.

Harry draws together what composure he can.

'Okay. Alright. But let me add just one thing to that. One thought: if they think the campaigns are so powerful that they will revive the Prime Minister's standing, then… well then it just won't happen. They'll never let him do it.'

'Who?'

Harry turns back to Peter, conviction growing.

'His own Party. They hate him. They want him *out*, not reinvigorated.'

And as the others digest that, I too have just had a thought, that of poor Harry, his wasted talent. Where did he conjure that from? History would prove that he is right of course, that his reasoning powers are well, well ahead of ours. And maybe we all know it even then. But there is no appetite to pursue his logic, or where it would take us. Nobody stands to gain anything from it if it were true. More convenient all round to pretend nothing has been said. Default setting.

Silence reigns. I push an agenda toward Peter, pointing to item one. I look to him, the telepathy talking. *I won't contradict your status as the man who knows if you address this, now.* He glances downwards, reading with barely concealed distaste, as if I have presented a car repair bill.

'The other issue to brief you on today is the restructure of Harlequin towards group status. The Board have decided to invest in a broad front of communication vehicles. We will look to acquire and grow towards critical mass, and I will lead that process. Harlequin Advertising will become a subsidiary of the group with immediate effect. Any questions?'

Another silence that indicates either communal, telepathic empathy or, more likely, total confusion. Questions, from me.

'You are stepping up to *Group* MD, right?'

He nods. Progress. Open admission. Good.

'So who is the new head of Harlequin Advertising?'

This should seal the case. Instead he chews over an answer, face growing ever more serious, before speaking as the magisterial Harlequin *Group* head.

'This morning's meeting shows you are a long way from being a unified team ready to be led. I think that until you are it would be wise to continue meeting like this on a weekly basis to ensure the campaigns are delivered. Understood?'

In all honesty, it is hard to understand. Yes, it has been a mess, yes, we are a rabble. But the chief architect of this disorder, the man with the gift of contagious, infectious confusion, is the man who says the price for our anarchy is his imposition of more of the same. It makes no sense at all, generating friction rather than harmony throughout the team. Maybe that was the strategy. In any case he is up on his feet. Meeting over, purpose served, whatever it was.

C DAY MINUS 299 DAYS

Party Headquarters, Grosvenor Road, London

A Saturday meeting followed by a Sunday meeting, a progress meeting with Derek Rove at Party Headquarters. Welcome to the seven-day week of your high-achieving highly secretive communications man. *Can I trust you?* Derek's opening question on the phone. Stupid question, who is really going to say no? And these are the guys running the country. So yes, Derek babe, what do you want to tell me?

He wanted to tell me to be prepared to explain everything from scratch to some influential people, tell them how it would work and when it was planned to work. One last thing. *Tell no one.*

I rock up solo as requested and loiter at the unnamed head office reception area. First face I see is Nigel Richards doing the same. He bows, curtly. Voice friendly. Words not.

'Thanks for the call, you bastard.'

'Nigel, that's not fair, Derek Rove specifically said tell no one. I had the full-on can-I-trust-you pitch. What do you want me to do?'

'Remember who your client is, my friend. I won't forget this next time you need a favour.'

'Come on...'

Nigel turns a deaf ear, acting like he's consumed by regret, let down from the highest height.

'Well, fuck you then,' I mutter, loud enough for him to pick up.

He's close enough for me to see his effort to hide his smile. A turn and a wink of the eye. *Fuck you too Cal, watch yourself.*

Derek Rove arrives, breathless, harassed. Like Nigel he has struggled with the Sunday Best/Weekend Dress-Down wardrobe dilemma and sports a bizarre mix of high-tech leisure attire meets power suit. He greets us with a grim smile that seems to both thank us for coming and apologise for calling us here.

'Anything you see or hear today stays between us. Okay? Otherwise you, and all your agencies, are history. I'm serious. Are we okay with that?'

Presumably, if I'd said no, the meeting would have ended there and then. Presumably, my silence is all he wants to hear, because he accepts it greedily.

'I want you to act normally, talk us through it as if you're briefing any normal client. And don't ask any questions about who's in the room or not in the room. You don't need to know, so don't go hunting for clues, alright?'

Derek Rove is grilling me eyeball to eyeball; I can see his are red and chronically starved of sleep, manic. Even worse than mine. Again I say nothing, relatively easy to do given I have no idea what the fuck he is on about. Holy mackerel, this guy is even worse than Peter Vesey for spinning riddles, between them they could create a vortex. I catch a raised eyebrow from Nigel, the pair of us finding common ground in the unspoken quiet; we are both beginning to hate this guy.

'Good,' says Derek Rove. 'Follow me.'

He takes off across the floor, launching himself upwards once we reach the bottom of the stairwell. I glance back at Nigel following sulkily behind. *What's going on?* Nigel delights in silently mouthing his reply without breaking languid stride. *Fuck you.* Charming. I can but hope it is a joke. We reach some kind of meeting room on a landing at the top of the stairs. A sexy room, glass walls. Rove opens the door and brings us in without knocking. No space for us at the table, so there's an immediate bit of chair dragging and re-arranging of furniture to break the ice before any kind of introductions. Six people in there, one Very fucking Important Person. I make to set up my laptop with the projector screen and notice my hand is shaking.

'Have you been offered a coffee or anything?' asks the VfIP.

I'm about to answer in the negative but an interjection from one of the Party faithfuls saves me bother.

'There is no coffee in this place. Not on a Sunday. Not even for an ex-Prime Minister.'

This seems to trigger great mirth in the room. I roll with it.

'*Especially* for an ex-Prime Minister,' counters the man himself, generating more hilarity, most of it enthusiastic rather than genuine. The screen offers up my presentation icon. I look round and notice Nigel

Richards has quietly taken a seat at the back of the room. As welcome as a bishop in a brothel.

'Ah well, water then. Shall I?'

I signal my thanks and the ex-Prime Minister pours me a glass, smiling a regal smile. He has aged since last seen doing his thing in public, and I try to think of when that last was; sometime in the previous year, a documentary about his Peace Envoy work, or the paparazzi shots of the holidays in the Tuscan villa. Older and more grizzled, but impressively relaxed and easy; looking as if he has years of youthful vigour left in him, light years more than his haunted, hapless successor. The man I had been expecting to see in this room.

'Okay. We have Cal Begg of Harlequin Advertising here,' shouts Derek from his lonely pew. 'I've asked him to brief us on the campaign we have planned to support Government's push toward societal unity and cohesion. Cal's going to tell us how it's all going to work.'

So there we were, that was as far as we were going to go with introductions, the stage was all mine.

'Thank you, Derek...' I looked to the ex-Prime Minister, aside from myself, the only man in the room comfortable in his jeans and white linen shirt.

'Let me show you some ads.'

C DAY MINUS 260 DAYS

Harlequin Communications Group, Harlequin House,

Warren Street, London

Then Nigel Richards, the man who tells me never to meet anyone on government business without his legitimising presence, calls me to fix up another meeting with some shadowy people who have government money. He says it is imperative that I meet them at Harlequin. And on my own. Yes, meet sans Nigel; he cannot be seen in this kind of company. Welcome to the world of communication with third party NGOs, semi-autonomous quasi-publics who may or may not be within a sniff of public money to do something that moves their agenda forward, without committing government to actually act on said agenda. Confused? Let me put it more simply. Governments don't like change; they tend to be more for the *impression* of change, an altogether easier-to-manage kind of thing. So how to buy off someone and let them make merry with something that's pretty harmless? Easy; you give money for them to have their own campaign. You send them to the Harlequin Advertisings of the world where they can lose themselves in endless discussions about their fabulous expensive-but-pointless-because-if-it-really-was-going-to-change-anything-we-wouldn't-be-allowed-to-do-it awareness raising campaign.

Welcome then to Harlequin Advertising, you esteemed guests and so-I'm-told new pseudo clients, welcome, Sea of Tranquillity. Both of you.

Unlikely revolutionaries. Unlikely brief. Unbelievable brief given that Nigel and CIO are meant to be paying for this out of taxpayer funds. There are two of them in our boardroom, talking me, and my colleague Nick Craig, through the story-so-far of their particular thing. Pat Brosman; bearded, glasses, hair that can best be described as between styles, the yellow teeth of a third-rate secondary school geography teacher with relentlessly rustling nylon over-jacket that he refuses to take off. His colleague, Angela Thompson, from here on known as Angela Tranquillity, is in similar need of an urgent makeover. Bubbly curls frothing out from her scalp to cascade chaotically on to her woolly-jumpered shoulders. But the thing about Mrs Tranquillity here is that underneath her soulless housewife thing, a trained eye like mine can spot a caged sex-minx trying to get out. This woman, minus the glasses and just about everything else, is beginning to get through to your author, especially with the way she looks so earnestly towards my side of the table to assure that I am getting it, the 'it' being whatever the fuck her partner is droning on about.

The programme as explained by the duo; we are to enter into the zone of hypro-meditative-stimulative-ecstacised-hay-fevered happiness. I'd like to. Instinctively I'm all for being led into a zombified trance. But I don't have the time.

'Angela, that sounds good. Although maybe it would be more appropriate if one of the creative teams go through that experience first. Nick?'

My Creative Director looks torn.

'Cal, as you know, we're pretty tied up with existing work. I don't know quite who you have in mind.'

Which of course is Nick's icy dig at his newly appointed puppet-leader about the lack of resource and creative department overload. Who do I have in mind? Freelancers, Nick. Hire up some cheap-but-willing guinea pigs to sample the product.

'Freelance. Call up some senior guys who we trust.'

Mrs Tranquillity offers support. The soft smile again, soft yet focused with laser intensity. Nick smiles an affirmative, a new smile from him, subconsciously mimicking what's being given to him. The soft smile of Angela Conspiracy. Some hours later another debrief, this time with a former colleague, this time in more intimate surroundings. Caroline has a way of laughing, giggling with a gasp, incredulity to the point-of-orgasm that I never tire of hearing. Lying down, one hand on my chest, the other propping up her head from her elbow, every inch of her trembles as she gives in to it. Tonight, a catch up; catch up on our news, the scandals, my agency and her new one, the latest on her coterie of friends, their careers and love-lives, a retinue of names and events that wash over me as I marvel at the glow of her skin. There had been a plan to get out, to meet some of these faceless names, many of whom were eager to put a face to mine, or so Caroline tried to sell it. But my more urgent need was to get close, to connect, kiss every last inch there was to caress, to rub her into me like some kind of magical lotion. Caroline, lying there in profile, oblivious to the adoration I felt for her. A laughing, joyful presence in my bed.

'Honestly, how can you stand it?' she asks, biting her lip in an attempt to stifle the mirth she feels at the mere prospect and all the comic lunacy it entails. '...Bloody Harlequin... don't you want to get a great big gun and shoot the whole lot of them?'

'Funnily enough,' I reply, running a hand through her hair, 'that's what Pete wants me to do, homicide apart.'

'Fire them?'

'Build a new team. Get the ratios of income and expenditure aligned to industry-leading margin. But essentially, yes. Fire them all.'

She sits up, a hand across her mouth.

'Oh Cal, it's comedy central, isn't it? Peter Vesey... How does he think it runs, what exactly is it he thinks he adds to this so that he shouldn't go too?'

'He handles the international aspects. Collects air miles at the behest of the Board, pursuing group-wide international assignments and alliances.'

She rolls off me onto her back. 'Meaning?'

'Fuck knows,' I murmur, burying myself in her warm skin. 'And that's without mentioning the new lunatics at large, Sea of Tranquillity.'

'The what?'

'Sea of Tranquillity. New client. Government backed, apparently.'

She smiles whilst computing the comic potential. 'Sounds like a spa treatment... Or a tribute band...'

'Or both. I've signed someone up to try it. You could join them, why should I be the only one wasting time on their vacuous new-age drivel.'

She laughs at my gold-plated grumpiness.

'Oh Cal, just surrender to it... There must be something that they've got if they've managed to get public backing... and you could be the man at the dawning of the age of tranquillity.'

Moments together crystallised in my mind. Times passed that now play back with only hurt and longing. The two of us barricaded in my flat, music playing, floating over us, waiting for the take-away food to arrive, delivered through the evening rain outside to my doorstep.

We had planned to go out. Meet and entertain the same named friends she had talked about, a few drinks, introductions, a meal, more drinks, maybe a club, dancing. All laid out ahead of us. But, when she arrived *chez moi*, and I caught up with her beauty, and faced the sheer desire to have her just to myself, we were in familiar burrow-down-and-hibernate territory. London on our doorstep, a city she wanted to embrace, something I wanted to hide from.

'I'm sorry, I know I promised but I really can't face it. I'm tired, talked out, all I want is to be somewhere where I don't have to fight to be understood. Can you understand that?'

I feel her going cold.

'We need to get out more, *you* need to get out more.'

My hands skim over her soft skin, looking for a response, tickling and caressing in all kinds of places. She doesn't stop me but has flicked a switch somewhere.

'Cal, listen to me. Your life is a disaster, or heading that way. You talk about these people… There's not one of them you actually like, yet you give your existence over to them, and there's nothing else going on in your life apart from that, is there?'

Sitting right up, cross-legged, naked and proud, like some seventies yoga poster. I address her breasts.

'There's you, both of you.'

Pushing me off. Serious conversation time. And now, even worse, T-shirt back on. Erotic buffet cancelled.

'Caroline, please. Just give me a break. It's been a tough few days. This is not what I need, although I know it comes from a good place. A lovely place.'

As I ramble on, proving my point about having expired in the part of my brain that can normally pull these kind of words together with relative ease, my default algorhythms kick in; I start to think about the countdown to the campaign launch, the jettisoning of staff as discussed and demanded, I start to think about tomorrow's workload and calls, about my reward for all this, whether I should hold Vesey to ransom for an immediate salary hike and bonus, and I start to think about Caroline, not what she'd said. The symptoms she'd described, no. I'm thinking about some kind of pendulum thing in our relationship, about how close I'd come to saying '*I need you*' or even worse. Thinking about how I did need her and her presence in my life. Good god, she was right. I hated them all.

'Caroline, listen to me. Of course there's truth in what you say and I hear it. I've just got to get this campaign out of the way and I'm out of it. They're all mad, inadequates. I won't miss them. Nuts. Every fucking one...'

I looked for agreement but her attention had drifted, moved on.

'I need to get away from all this, are you listening Cal?... Take a break, with or without you. Take a car, just head for the hills, a cottage somewhere, and talk about something else.'

'The driving would stress me out more than work.'

'I'll drive.'

'Your driving would stress me more than mine.'

Shakes her head, like she can't let herself roll with it. '...We'll take a train for god's sake, escape for a few days.'

'Yeah, timetables and shit, waiting on platforms, taxis to airports...'

'Cal!' she shrieks. 'Can you hear yourself, hear me? I'm asking you for something and you deflect it all, because you're so desperate to stay inside this prison you've made for yourself.'

'Prison?'

'Your cell, your food, your clothes...'

'Prison clothes, yeah?'

She sighed like I was pretending not to get it. 'You wear the same clothes all the time Cal. Eat the same food. Play the same music. And make the same excuses.'

I was stuck on the clothes thing: this she had wrong, surely?

'I wear a clean shirt every fucking day, what are you on about?'

Dressing in a hurry, exasperated. 'Shirt? Yes, maybe a white one. Button down collar, linen. How many of them have you got? And some jeans. Cal's uniform they call it. The people you work with. The ones you hate.'

The pendulum thing. What she might have seen once as charming eccentricities now bug her to the point of irrationality, where once being the Prince of Harlequin was something to be admired, something impossibly glamorous and powerful and intoxicating enough to have her aching to get close to it, now it's a nothing, a bankrupt currency. *The same clothes*. I never saw it that way. More about managing choice so my head can be somewhere else other than selecting the outfit for the day. The emperor's new clothes. *All the same*. I curl up on one side.

'Cal, Cal?' A hand to my face. A caring, though almost medicinal hand. 'I'm sorry, I didn't mean to hurt you.'

I put my hand on hers. Too spent to reply.

'Are you okay?'

I nod. *Yes. Great. You can go now.* Didn't you hear? It wasn't the Beatles on, it was John Lennon and the Plastic Ono Band. Never saw it that way.

'I've got to go now, take a break from this. I've got work tomorrow as well. You'll be okay, won't you?'

She knew I wouldn't reply and left without waiting.

CAMPAIGN LAUNCH MINUS 230 DAYS

The Fortnum Club Hotel, Kensington, London

Greig drained the very last drops from his cup and scanned the hotel lobby one more time. Above the reception desk the three clocks showing time around the world had moved fifteen minutes since he last looked. She was late, very late. Maybe she wasn't coming after all. The thought gave way to another, how had he been persuaded? This in turn gave way to a feeling of anger, resentment at Bernie for suggesting the rendezvous, resentment at himself for agreeing.

The waitress came over to him. Heightening his self-consciousness. 'Another coffee?' She spoke with an East European accent. Pretty girl. But she wouldn't recognise him, a minor relief. How life had changed. Being stood up by a former colleague was now a potential media scandal. Dr Greig Hynd, hanging around aimlessly in hotel lounge shock. He looked forlorn says our witness, the beautiful Katia from Riga, not like a man with all the answers, not like someone with the key to happiness. 'No thanks, I'm fine.'

'Hello Greig,' said a voice over his shoulder, a flat voice, empty.

'Catherine. Are you well?'

Greig stood up to offer a greeting kiss, an offer refused, leaving him to hang awkwardly as Catherine installed herself in a chair. She surveyed the art-deco rounded leather seat with some distaste, a look she then cast up and let spread to the rest of the surroundings and its décor.

'This is the kind of place you frequent now, I suppose.'

'We can go someplace else if you'd prefer,' he said, sitting down. 'But you can't fault the service…'

Even as the last words left his mouth the waitress rematerialised, as if primed somehow to prove his point, her professional smile contrasting with the difficult atmosphere that had descended on the table with Catherine's arrival.

'What can I tempt you with?' he asked, the conciliatory tone already an effort.

'Just water.' Catherine folded her arms as she spoke.

'So how are you?' he asked again, same voice.

'I'm not well Greig. You can probably tell that, can't you?'

Greig paused in reply. Now his choice, as he saw it, to answer yes to confirm her own judgement and score points for empathy but admit there is something wrong, and by extension accept a measure of blame for this state, or respond in a cheery negative and score less for observation but at least try to lift her.

The truth was, she looked only slightly different from when he had last seen her; anaemic, yes; thinner, yes. More pertinently, she seemed to carry a sense of defiant hurt. What had it been, the best part of a year since she had left?

'Are you telling me that you're not well? Do you want to talk about it?'

'I'm not your patient Greig. Anyway, you're the one who wanted to see me. I hear your team has had its problems of late.'

'Actually,' he said, slowly, emphasising his careful choice of words, '… we're doing pretty well. Extraordinarily well. It's why we need you, if you are in any way interested in joining us.'

'Do you mean the Campaign for Positive Health, or the Party?'

The neutral tone to her voice gave Greig the impression that the question was perhaps genuine, even if some of the words were somewhat loaded. As he made to speak, the drinks arrived, served with a painfully slow geisha-like ceremony. He waited impatiently for the waitress to exit the scene.

'Maybe you were right about this place. I'll make sure we choose somewhere more sympathetic next time. This time I thought it might be better to meet… in a neutral place, not the office, I didn't think that would be good for either of us.'

Catherine's face seemed to offer some encouragement.

'Catherine, what can I say?… There are a whole world of opportunities for us… to put into place everything we'd ever talked about. I wouldn't say we'd finally won or use crass language about something that's only beginning, but the fact is that the opportunity exists, right now, and we've got to take it. Being in government, at the heart of the agenda. What do *you* think? Have I got it so wrong?'

'I saw you. Of course I saw you, like the whole world saw you, performing at the Party conference. I was surprised and perhaps not so surprised, it was always where you would end up, wasn't it? And you were very good at that rousing stuff, I can see why they would want you. But for me it's all shallow, I'm afraid, all that punching the air and staged ovations. *All Happier. More Together*, more belonging and no explanation of how. All politics I suppose. No substance.'

Greig nodded as she spoke, as if agreeing with every word, tuning into the criticism in masochistic compassion. He glanced around to check nobody was in earshot.

'Catherine... If I was honest enough to admit that there are elements in what you have just said that trouble me too... would that be enough to make you want to be part of the solution? We have power now. I need you to help me use it.'

His voice had grown steadily more soothing, slower and yet somehow intense as he spoke. His professional voice, he realised. Designed to get her defences down, to dismantle first the hostility and then the distrust. Maybe she knew this. Maybe she was sensitive to it, and took on an extra layer of antagonism as an automatic reflex. Perhaps it was all simpler than that; perhaps she was as she said she was, simply ill, destabilised by something, and something that she was keen to blame him for. Complicated. Simple. Whatever, as he spoke it became obvious that the only one at the table convinced by his sincerity was Greig himself. Catherine? Unengaged, elsewhere, deliberate or otherwise.

'Catherine,' he continued, leaning forward, still looking to break the stalemate, 'I guess I'm reaching out to you, as someone whom has been on this journey from the very beginning... why not be with us when it bears fruit? What do you say?'

She returned his gaze but showed no sign of responding, no sign either that she was truly listening. He wondered just how ill she was and how appropriate it was for him to be pressurising her into some kind of executive role now, when it mattered. When it was going to be about power, rather than making arguments. And making arguments had been what she was so good at. Her fight had always come from within. Perhaps it had burned her. It burned them all in the end.

'Your family?' she said, breaking the lull.

'What about them?'

'How are they? Did you take them to the conference?'

'My family are fine. Seeing even less of me of course, but fine. These are important times. It seems every day takes us to a new threshold, new direction, whatever. It's tough. Everything we asked for, but tough.'

'How is your son?'

'He...' Greig broke off to scan the room. Why was she asking this? 'He's doing better.' Greig asked himself how much he had ever shared with Catherine as to his son's condition, or how much she might have been told. This wouldn't have been natural territory for her to explore when she was at her best and he felt an element of resentment that she would think it appropriate now. His son, his poor son. Born with such hopes. And every day, the expectations of what might be some kind of normal life for him were being gently lowered. *My poor son.*

'He's doing fine Catherine. We take care of him. Forgive me for asking, but are you under treatment yourself just now? Perhaps I should have asked sooner. So full of myself. So preoccupied with everything that's on.'

Something in his words seemed to sting.

'Yes, I am taking therapy. A number of treatments. Anything to help. I'm recovering from a breakdown. One caused by a combination of things but one of those factors you should be well aware of, if not responsible for.'

'*Me*? Are you saying I drove you to a breakdown?'

'Overwork. Unreasonable demands, lack of support... and then, to tip it all over the edge, the speech... or rather the presentation you made at the convention. I was right at the front. Deafened, frightened. The flashing lights, the images... How could you? How *dare* you?'

Suddenly, nearer the answers he had been seeking. The reason for the meeting. He pulled his chair to the table again. He thought about reaching out for her hand but withdrew it at the last, tapping the table-top by way of compensation.

'Catherine, I'm sorry, I don't follow, *my* responsibility? I've been trying to find out ever since that presentation how it happened, who put it together in that way, and even how we met Sea of Tranquillity to start with.'

'*Your* responsibility, Greig. You decided to play their segment. Your choice.'

'Not for it to run the way it did, to run the same thing I'd been shown. But it was you who brought them in to start with. Maybe you could tell me about them?'

This time his voice had been raised.

Catherine's empty stare looking back at him.

'I'll ask them myself,' he said softly, out loud, looking around to avoid Catherine's eyes, unintentionally attracting the attention of the eager waitress once more. Three steps and she was over at the table, eyebrows raised. A flat sweep of his hand. No, nothing thanks.

'Are we done?'

Catherine didn't move.

'What did they offer you?'

Greig shot her a look of confusion; the stop-start nature of the exchange beyond exasperation.

'I've never met them. You brought them in. What did they offer you?'

'I meant the Party. What did it take to get your performance at the conference, on a platform with the rest of them, selling out?'

Selling out. She had no idea what was offered, or what was asked, yet the assumption was of some tawdry deal.

'A sackful of gold, Catherine. Or should I say, silver? Yes, silver pieces. That sound right to you, confirm your judgement?'

A shake of the head from Catherine. *We are done.* He had no interest in her anymore. Done.

'I think,' she said, deliberately, as if determined to offer her view only now, when it no longer mattered, 'I really do think they are evil. A shallow kind of evil. I can see how that fits. And that you and them, the Party, you deserve each other.'

'And Sea of Tranquillity. The people who triggered your breakdown with their flashing lights and wall of noise, where do they fit in? Good guys?' he snapped.

Catherine's eyes opened wide, a light going on in her head. An awakening in progress. Even the trace of a smile forming as she stood, unburdened.

'Oh, *they* are evil. The worst of anyone. And they already have you, don't they? You deserve that too. You want to know more, to know how they got into the Alliance? Ask your questions closer to home instead of playing games with me. Ask Natasha Skacel. I hear you've been seeing a lot of her.'

Catherine scanned the lounge one last time, sour smile still playing on her lips. It was almost, he thought later, like she'd finally grown to like the place, comfortable in it. Sorry to leave it. He watched her move to the swing door exit. Deliberate in every movement, as if giving him the opportunity to call her back.

A presence materialised by his shoulder. The waitress, smiling hesitantly. A lightness about her, an absence of demands, lack of baggage. *Run away with me. I'll cherish you, and you'll ask nothing of me, that's why I'll love you.*

'Would you like the bill?'

He reached for his wallet, then halted. 'No, I have a room here. Can you add it to the bill for that?'

A glance to his watch. Five thirty. He had the best part of two hours still free. He gathered up his case and journals. A stair and a corridor, passing a table with a bowl of fruit and orchids and the scent of citrus furniture polish that marked the midpoint between him, his own breakdown, and the sanctuary of his room.

He negotiated the preposterously complex electronic key and the room was open to him. Another smell, some kind of rose blossom bath lotion, almost welcoming. He lay on the bed, head in hands. Two stolen hours, a luxury, of sorts. Restless, he moved for the television remote, again hopelessly complicated, beyond an average psychologist. He groaned, studying its multiple buttons and symbols.

'Something you need to catch?' said Natasha, emerging from the bathroom.

'Just trying to make the damn thing work. Just want to vegetate for a while... Why is it you have to have a degree in nuclear physics to turn on a damn television?'

She moved into his line of view to block his sight of the television. She was wearing a white bathrobe; the rose-scented fumes now overwhelmed the bedroom. She eased her shoulders free from the robe to stand naked before him.

'Natasha,' he said, leaning forward to kiss her breasts, '...we need to talk.'

'Of course,' she said, unbuckling his belt. 'It's always good to talk.'

C DAY MINUS 210 DAYS

Harlequin Communications Group, Harlequin House,

Warren Street, London

There was I feeling good about life, relatively good that is, in the scheme of things, and my scheme being pretty fucking big at that moment in time. I'd checked progress against the plan for delivery of all campaigns and then relayed the – relatively – good news to Nigel Richards that we were green to go, on schedule, and that he owed me, in the form of Harlequin, shit-loads of money. Didn't even mention Sea of Idiocy. That fell to Nick Craig, ambushing me at reception just as I was about to exit for an overpriced cup of coffee froth in designer cardboard, the anticipated taste of which was to haunt me for the rest of the afternoon, destined to be forever tantalisingly out of reach.

'Cal, I need to speak to you,' he said, cutting straight to the point. Unusual. Dangerous.

'Can't it wait? I've got a meeting on, cappuccino rendezvous. Join me if you want.'

'No. Now. Here,' he said, like something was seriously fucked up.

He pointed to the boardroom like he was going to fire me.

'Okay,' I said calmly, aware the receptionist would be tuned in, 'let's do it.'

I followed him in and we sat down. An awful room. A never-quite-there room. A room we would periodically try to make funky with a selection of choice ads on show, and then periodically try to make formal, replacing these with neutral, understated modern art. I sat and endeavoured to make myself comfortable. *Calm down Cal, he can't fire you, it would have to be the other way round wouldn't it, you moron?*

'So, what's up Nick?'

He swallowed hard. 'Zane Parry has attempted suicide. He's been locked up for his own safety. Sectioned. Al Norris is sick too, we don't know where he is. And Brian is refusing to have anything more to do with the brief, wants paid up and any therapy costs on top. They're scared shitless.'

I took in the news with all the gravity the situation demanded, nodding silently. Nick was wound tight, looking, unreasonably, for an immediate response. After all, he had had more time to absorb the news. He, presumably, knew who the fuck these people were.

'Zane Parry?'

'The freelancer we used on the Sea of Tranquillity stuff. A copywriter. Al Norris is his partner, art director. Strong team. Brian's another copywriter we drafted in. Cal, we're killing them.'

Freelancers. Creative freelancers. Of course.

'So, Nick, what are you actually telling me?'

Nick stared straight at me. Determined as ever, his face resolute, jaw square, saying fuck all.

'I'm telling you,' he started, 'I am *trying* to tell you,' he continued, as if it were my fault somehow that he couldn't string it together, 'that these guys need our help. That we *are* going to help them, and we need to get that organised. And quick.'

'Nick. I get that you think we need to help them. Whatever help means. But help me first will you? From the top. Who are these guys, why is it our call to help them and how?'

'Okay,' he says slowly. '*From the top.*' Deep breath for effect, deep breath which you might read frustration, or anger, or solemn gravitas, or asthma. 'Episode one,' he begins. 'You and I get to meet the Sea of Tranquillity outfit and try to figure out what it is they want us to sell. An hour's worth of harmless chat later we agree to send a creative team to sample their offering.' A pause, a look up to me, *Continue?* Of course.

'Episode two. We don't have any spare creative team because all creative staff are working flat out. So we hire a couple of freelancers to take this on, Zane Parry and Al Norris. They in turn ask to work with Brian Lee, and I agree. Episode three. Zane and Al begin sessions. They go to a semi-detached town house in Peckham and get all kinds of stuff... music, interviews, meditation, endless talking about what chills them, and what bugs them, what scares them. They get to look into computer screens that swirl and glow in response to what they say. They learn how to load some of this stuff into ads. Unfortunately, at the same time, Zane and Al get their minds blown.' A tilt of Nick's noble head, hand through outrageous fringe, the full hair tell. 'Literally.'

Hmmn, I mutter. *Minds blown.* Heavy.

'Chapter…' he pauses to correct, 'episode whatever, these guys are in a mess. Suicidal, heading towards a breakdown or already there. We *owe* them. We need to sort it out. That's what you and I have to agree on, Cal. Then we'll have the next episode to look forward to. Sorting out this so-called client.'

Nick had presented the story forcefully, focusing almost exclusively on the plight of the heroic Zane and Al. It was clear where Nick was leading his audience sympathies. There are still, unfortunately, a few loose ends to tie up in the epilogue. Like just how sane is anyone called Zane to start with?

'So, Nick. Forgive me for asking, but have we got any evidence for any of this?'

A weird thing to say for sure, yours truly falling swiftly into bad cop mode to counter Nick's hijacking of the saintly cop cameo.

'Evidence? Where are you coming from?' he demands. 'We *know* these guys, trust them, why else would we have used them for the assignment?'

'Nick, I only want to know if this is what the guys are saying to us, to you, or what we are surmising. I thought one of them is missing anyway, is he phoning in his claim from a secret location? What is it you think we can do?'

He slouches in his chair malevolently.

'Firstly. The guys will need medical help, probably specialist psychiatric help. We've exposed them to something very dangerous so we have to pay whatever it costs to put them right. Secondly, they can't work whilst they get treatment and since they are freelance they have no other source of income. So we have to put them on a retainer to keep them going, put them on staff. The last thing is legal advice. They will need lawyers to help them sue these Tranquillity people for damages once they've got some kind of strength back. We should set that up for them as well. It's the least we can do.'

Welcome to the parallel universe that is the particularly polar topsy-turvy realm of Nick Craig. An inverse world where black is white, up is down, and creativity rules. Where more loyalty is given to those outside the agency than in, where people are hired only at the point when we are sure they are unfit to work, where legal expenses are granted so staff can sue our own clients.

'Is this what the guys are asking for or what you feel inclined to give them?'

'It's what any decent agency would offer after what we put them through. It's the only way we'll get anyone to work with us again once word gets out.'

'I'm not sure we'll have any work to give out to anyone after word gets out that we're on hand for any basket case. There's nothing to be done, Nick.'

And with that, I'm up on my feet, making my way to the door as the petulant counter-eruption gets underway.

'*What*?'

Nick's hand grabs my shoulder, pulling me round to face him.

'We're going to leave these guys to hang after what they've done for us?'

It's a trite question, and one that begs a better one. We're standing toe to toe, he's the one shouting, I'm quietly goading, confident he won't hit me.

'What exactly *did* they do for us, Nick?'

My shadow boxer is wrong-footed. '...I told you, they went to these people. Sampled the product.'

'Did they write some ads? Have we got anything to show for it?'

'Who gives a fuck?' my man counters. 'They're ill, and *we've* made them ill.'

Nick doesn't seem to get that I for one could not give a shit. He doesn't get that his merry men have been handed a campaign win, campaign expansion and then an entirely new campaign on a proverbial plate. Somewhere in all of this Tranquillity stuff might be a way to make another, bigger campaign, or to make my campaign better. That's where the focus should be, not on charity relief.

'Listen Nick, there's nothing we can do right now. If you want a second opinion check out Vesey, next time he swings back in town. Maybe he'll see it differently.'

This time Nick does look as if he's ready to hit me, and fair enough, it's a smug answer I've served up here. Pete Vesey to see it differently? More than unlikely.

'I thought that *you* were meant to be in charge here?'

'I *am* in charge Nick. And I'm saying drop this.'

Nick slouches, sighing. There will be no fist fight, no physical combat. The energy evaporates from his body and he looks about ready to cry.

'That's a shit way for us to treat people. Is that your final word?'

I nod.

'Then I'll have to think about my own position and whether I'm happy to work for an agency that operates like that. Without decency. Without soul.'

If you ignore the fact that an agency *with* soul is a self-evident oxymoron, this is more encouraging. Will he really resign, or is this too much to hope for?

'Don't let me interfere with whatever spiritual journey you think is appropriate here, but you might want to check out where we are with the Tranquillity brief. We've committed to giving them a campaign, and I'll make sure we do with or without you Nick. Over to you.'

Nick glowers. 'This is unsustainable, Cal.'

I think he's making reference to his position. This time though, for once, he's ahead of me and says something that ruins the good mood he's pushed me into.

'You think it's smart, a clever way to impress Vesey by squeezing the agency tighter and tighter, pushing out campaigns like we're a fucking sausage machine. You think you can go on like that so one day you'll clean up. But you'll never get your prize from Vesey. And there will be a price to pay for the way you are treating people. For making everyone hate you.'

'I think that's all Nick, I'm going for my coffee, catch you later.'

I said my words as soon as he was finished with his fucking witches' prophecy, then waited for the door to close behind him and pulled over the boardroom telephone. Time for someone else to take some heat.

'It's Cal.'

'And a good afternoon to you sir, are you working well, hitting the heights for your best loved client?'

'I'm actually calling about our least loved client, although it's one our best loved client saddled us with.'

'I see. And the reason for a call to me about another client?'

'A heads-up Nigel. We're going to have to fire them. Tell them to take their account elsewhere. For an outfit that trade with the name "Tranquillity", they seem to piss off an awful lot of people, including our entire creative department.'

Silence at the other end of the call. I felt a loneliness creeping over me, I'd been stuck in the hated boardroom for over an hour. All I'd wanted was the luxury of a cappuccino in a cardboard cup, and fifteen minutes free from this.

'So you're feeling sore Cal, what do you want me to do about it?'

'Take these people away from here, we've enough to deal with right now. Why did you push them our way to start with?'

Nigel gives a near silent sigh. 'A favour. It was meant as a favour, Cal. These guys seem highly influential, flavour of the month in certain circles. If it's not working out then give them the push. Your call… Have *you* talked to them?'

'I met them once. Underwhelming. We sent two guys to get under the skin of their thing, who they managed to completely freak out.'

'*You* Cal, have you spoken to them about this?'

'To complain or get a grip on this thing?'

'Both. Look, don't let me tell you how to do your job but I'd have thought it worth at least a proper conversation before you bin the thing.'

'That's okay with you, even if it all ends badly?'

'Have the conversation. If it doesn't work out it doesn't work out.'

'Right then, I'll go for it.'

I stood up, enjoying a moment of relative empowerment, ready to close the call and make my escape. A moment of passing empowerment because, right on cue, in strides the form of my new captor. Presenting live in person, sneaking in fresh from his world tour, Mr Peter Vesey, back in town to kick ass. He gives me the sign to say I can close my call and pulls up a chair. The call changes in tone as I try to do just that as fast as I can, whilst giving nothing away lest Peter demand I pass the receiver so he can have his own heads up from Sir Nigel de Richards.

'I will do, thanks for that, I'll let you know how it goes.'

There's a suggestion of a question mark at the other end of the line as Nigel wonders why the tone has changed.

'How are my campaigns, anyway, everything coming along nicely?'

'*Everything*. I'll update you later. Okay?'

An intuitive Nigel Richards knows that someone has come into the room.

'Are you all right there Cal, sounding a little stressed?'

'That's great then. I'll give you a full update by Thursday. Cheers.'

I hang up on Nigel presumably silently quizzing an inert telephone in the same way my Chief Exec looks at me now.

'Everything under control Cal?'

'Just about. How did the latest bout of globe-trotting go?'

He didn't smile or flinch.

'You had a meeting at Party HQ?'

Heartbeat, increasing heartbeat, masked by my open smile. *Hey, let me share the experience with you, where have you been?* 'Last week. Wanted to go though work in progress all of a sudden.'

He spreads out the fingers of both hands across the table top, not drumming them, but examining them as if in some kind of awe. Executioner's hands.

'You didn't think to tell me?'

And now I begin to get it. He's pissed off, missed his invite to the ball.

'They sprung it on us. Sunday morning meeting, called in on the Saturday before. You were in Shanghai, Sydney, San Francisco, work in progress, detail meeting, what would you have wanted to do?'

Another look to the hands. He doesn't like this. This is not how a minion greets an international big cheese on his return. No sir.

'And who was there?'

'Nigel Richards. Derek Rove. Bunch of Party people with forgettable names and, yes indeed, our ex-Prime Minister.'

'What did he say?'

'He loved it. He said, I want a good effort for this campaign. Something like that. Give it a good shout.'

'How was he introduced, where was the current Prime Minister?'

'He wasn't introduced. No one was. No one mentioned the current Prime Minister.'

He takes a deep breath and sighs. It's hard to tell if there will be another line to this enquiry. Equally it's hard to tell who or where his source of information is. Peter smells a rat, and whilst you can question his intelligence and absurdly high self-regard, he doesn't tend to let go once given the whiff of a fellow rodent.

'What next then?'

'Deliver the campaigns.'

'Same timescale?'

'Shorter. A week and a half shorter, plus a trailer thing for the Party conference.'

'Conference? They had one four months ago.'

'Emergency conference this time. Party constitution stuff, Party unity, whatever the excuse was to have another conference with all the big players in tow.'

He nods sternly. I feel like I'm apologising for the shortcomings of the Party. For its dismal leader being outshone by his predecessor. For its disastrous show in the polls. For its plots and treason.

'So what's going on?'

Hmmn. Yes, that's the big question. What *is* going on, in the Party, in Harlequin, in the world at large, where to begin? Yes, the ex-Prime Minister had asked us to make a good campaign, and we had agreed, indeed I, like the pre-programmed automaton that I am, had fired back immediately that we would do the very best we possibly could, he had instantly corrected me. A *good* effort. That was what was required, good, as in save your best for later, when it counts. Get it? Don't prop up a losing side. We'll tell you when we want the best, understood? Sort of. It means re-writing some of our killer lines, blanding them down, but so be it, if it pleases. Can I ask why? No, they said, absolutely not. Just do exactly what you are told, Secret Squirrel, otherwise all bets are off.

'Anything you want to tell *me*?' Vesey has evolved, through design or sheer boredom, from bad cop to good. There's nothing I can tell him, or want to.

'In terms of what Peter? I can tell you I'm tired, working flat out, that I wish some of my colleagues would grow up, but you've heard it before.'

A smile. Sardonic, sour, but a smile all the same.

'Things are not going well here, Cal. I know that.'

He clears his throat. An awkward moment is coming.

'You've been acting a bit... erratic. It has been noticed, and I'm concerned. I think it might threaten the success of the campaigns, and I won't let that happen.'

This time I look to my hands, gripping the table top, what the fuck? 'Erratic?'

'I gather the campaigns have changed course a bit since your meeting at Party HQ and your colleagues are in the dark. At the same time you've driven them as hard as it's possible to go, being, as I understand it, pretty unreasonable. There's disquiet, Cal, and I have to ask, are the campaigns in danger?'

I make to speak, to demand a list of the malcontents, the conspirators stupid enough to think this man's their saviour. Make to speak, to bang the table in a fucking rage. And stop. *Erratic?*

'I'm sorry to hear that's the message you've been getting. The campaigns are in no danger. Some of these people are, but not the campaigns. We're on track.'

A slow, gentle nod, indulgent, pompous nod.

'I asked you for a plan. There's no sign of one. Income projections? You're always late. You bully the team who you clearly think aren't up to it but you have no strategy to clear them out.'

He hits pause so that I can answer if I choose. Did I bully the team? Of course I did, but only to get some kind of performance from them. My vision? Make a famous campaign and get the fuck out.

'Peter, you yourself described most of the team as passengers, and they are. We've got the biggest ever core research programme on our hands and Harry thinks this is a burden. Nick has the chance to be world famous, make a campaign every government on earth would want to copy, is he excited? No, he wants to be a charity for burnt-out freelancers. But if *I'm* the problem, I'm happy to go. Right now.'

At this I realise I've got to stand up so that this looks real, and yes the door looks good. Better even than it did an hour ago.

'Okay Cal, calm down. Sit down, let's talk.'

Talk is not high on my list, but Peter's talk is what I'm due.

'You do need a plan. And you need to share it with me.'

Peter leans toward me to check that I get the sincerity of the diagnosis.

'You need to work out what you want for the business, the rewards it will get and *who* will share it. Who do you want to keep Cal, who do you want to let go? Then a plan for how you're going to do that and how much it will cost. That's why income projections are important. Not for me, for you, otherwise you'll be floundering, yes?'

I have to accept it, if only to escape. *Guilty as charged. Have mercy.*

'Can I ask... What are *you* doing, Peter?'

For a moment it's him looking startled. '*Doing?*'

'...All this running rings around the world, what's the purpose behind that?'

A strong, flat smile.

'I'm doing it on behalf of, at the behest of, the group Board. They want me to look at the potential for strategic alliances.'

I am none the wiser.

'To what end?'

'To the ends of the earth, I'm afraid.' He laughs. 'Once you start on that path it takes you to the players. The players don't come to you!'

The humour in this is lost on me but has him cracking up under the weight of his own very-in-joke. He pulls himself up on his feet, still gagging ruefully. A hand is offered, like this is a farewell or start of something new.

'You have to keep me involved, Cal,' he says, eye contact over the handshake. 'I can only help you if I'm involved.'

I can agree with him on this one at least, there's more truth in it than he knows.

CAMPAIGN LAUNCH MINUS 180 DAYS

National Exhibition Centre, Emergency Party Conference

Together we win. So read the giant banner on the outside of the building. So read the conference programme, and the frame surrounding the picture of himself on his ID card. *Special Conference. Dr Greig Hynd. Accreditation Red. Heston Constituency.* He looked at the photograph of himself, a handsome, open and confident Greig Hynd, shot many many months before, in a session arranged by Natasha. With a friendly photographer they had successfully captured a warm Greig, a soft, compassionate Greig, a steely Greig and a concerned Greig. But always a handsome Greig. If they had shot him nearer in time to today, he thought, maybe they would have come closer to how he actually felt; edgy Greig, unconvincing Greig, the trapped man. Linger and mingle, that was the order. Don't get drawn, especially on the subject of Party leadership, the likelihood of an imminent snap election, your ambitions in any future cabinet. Smile and press the flesh, what you're good at.

What he was good at? Less than two years ago in this very venue he had worked the crowd to the point of frenzy. Done it unknowingly, effortlessly. Enjoyed it, even, they were his people then, every man, every woman, and he had loved them. But here, whose people were they, the Party people? A bickering bunch poised to jettison one leader, and bring back another, whom they had presumably loved, then hated, and then inexplicably loved again. Bickering and fickle.

'Got you another, disgusting though it is.'

Greig turned his mind from past to present to see that Bernie had materialised and was offering a plastic cup of coffee. Greig took it without acknowledgement.

'That guy. Over there. Bald with glasses talking to the red T-shirt. Any ideas?... He was waving at me a minute ago.'

'The bald guy?... Hmm. I see. Is he not one of your supremos from constituency land, some big cheese from Hestonshire?'

'Assistant Party Secretary, Heston. You're right. Thanks.'

'Met any famous people whilst I was away?'

Greig ignored the question, his mind telescoping down into a field of thought involving his new Party constituency, its gruesome Party meetings and the lousy hotel he and Natasha were obliged to stay in pending his purchase of a permanent base there. The picture on his ID, the smiling, shallow Dr Greig Hynd. Heston Constituency.

A glance to his watch; three o'clock, the afternoon session was already half an hour gone; he himself was due on in an hour and a half, following on from the Secretary of State for Justice, and the Minister for Transport before that. Both presumably offering up new prizes and initiatives hurriedly thought up since the less than enthusiastic reception of the previous batch. Another irritation took hold of him.

'Bernie, is this an Emergency Conference or Special Conference? Keep reading both. Hearing both. What am I meant to say?'

'*Welcome to the Conference*, I'd guess.' Bernie shrugged. 'I mean, it's a loaded question. The word on the street is, apparently, that if you declare yourself as attending the *Special* Conference, you are declaring for the Prime Minister, and his appeal for unity. *Emergency* Conference, on the other hand, is saying fuck that, we are here to sort this, which means getting rid of the Prime Minister and replacing him. If you want to sit on the fence, stick with *This Conference*, and offend nobody.'

'That's what I said last time,' snapped Greig.

Another shrug. 'Then why fuck with the formula? Say what you like... only mean what you say.'

Greig glowered at Bernie. *Mean what you say*, cheeky bastard. Glowering with envy, he realised, what he'd give to be an observer, on the outside. *Mingle*, he'd been commanded, yet what did they expect? Mingle through the minefield of Party politics. They'd also told him to steal the show. That he was today's wild card. That would get them top of the evening's news ratings. The full works, Derek Rove had said, without irony. The *let's be the agenda* stuff, seize the initiative, it's what the Party wants to hear. *We need the distraction*.

Another burst of activity as a roving pack worked over Greig and Bernie with a flurry of handshakes and backslapping; *looking forward to hearing your speech, Greig. We hear it will be one of the highlights.* A smile back, a hug back, a flinch to move the other way, time pressing, more people to meet, enough to send them on their way.

Greig's sweep of the arm to indicate the area of the hall he was moving to cast his attention over to the attractive blond girl chatting animatedly to a youngish man taking an interest in her. She could work any room, he thought, once more filled with envy and more besides. Beauty and naivety, a dangerous combination. Dangerous for all. And all day she had been doing it, the missionary work, engaging complete strangers with gushing tales of Greig's call to conference, of his quest to save the nation's mental health and happiness and Party fortunes in the process. Hitting on them relentlessly, passionately, with more belief than he had himself. Sometimes she would rush breathlessly back, replaying every line of whatever exchange she'd had, how she had overcome initial cynicism to reach understanding, or how they were already there and word was spreading. And sometimes she'd instinctively stand too close, right into his body space. Then he'd be caught between the need to have her there and then, and the need to remake the distance so that it wouldn't be so blindingly obvious to the watching world that they were more than just colleagues.

Innocent Natasha, sometimes even doing what she was doing now, grabbing her victim by the hand and leading him over so that Greig could meet that person and bless them, and she could give proof of the depth of her devotion.

'Greig! Greig, this is Cal Begg of Harlequin, the advertising people who have worked up the visuals to go with your speech.'

'Calum Begg, Harlequin. Pleased to meet you.'

Greig shook the hand being offered. The hand of a man in his late twenties or early thirties. A man out of place in this environment, almost more so than Greig. Grey linen jacket, white linen shirt and jeans in a zone where suits and ties abounded. A man with an unnerving coldness to his eyes in a zone where everyone was making an effort to look like everyone's friend.

'Cal. Thanks for coming. What have you got for us?'

'As I was explaining, or trying to explain, in my usual cack-handed backwards forwards kind of way to the very patient Natasha, we've re-cut the sequences from our campaign ads so that they are less identifiable as highlights from a government campaign on specific themes of race, justice and environment, and much more generic about community. People reaching out for each other. In line with your speeches and agenda, in as much as we can understand it.'

He paused, looking to Greig for approval, as Greig rehearsed the speech in his head. An hour to go. Unapproved visuals arriving by courier. A fiasco.

'Shit. That sounds terrible, and I'm meant to be good at communicating. I'm sorry.'

A grimace from the newcomer. 'What I meant to say,' he continued, fixing Greig with an expression of serious intent, 'was that of course we understand your agenda, it's a very compelling one, with or without our visuals to accompany it, which only try to show that we as a species are more fulfilled when we work together than alone.'

The uneasy smile of the stranger had subsided as he spoke, so that by the time he ended they were in a different place altogether, one where meaningful truths had come to be exchanged. Or so it felt. Greig found himself memorising the words.

'You communicate well enough, Calum. Cal?'

'It's Cal,' said the newcomer, literally standing taller as he spoke.

'Cal,' said Greig, softly, 'okay Cal. I'm taken with that. But now the difficult bit, and you have to understand I'm not getting at you here okay?... I've got less than an hour to go, and a conference hall full of the Party's great and good, on live broadcast. You arrive and tell me there are new visuals. What's going on, is this incompetent, unfortunate or what? I'm confused.'

Greig watched Cal quickly scan the immediate circle to see who was tuned in and what level of discretion he would have to employ. He drew closer so that only Greig, and possibly Natasha, could hear. Another invasion of body space.

'We supplied the stuff two weeks ago. You've probably rehearsed to it, yeah?'

Greig nodded, encouraging Cal to continue.

'Government campaign. *Together as One*. We were led to believe this would be a government conference. I don't know what got lost in translation but this is obviously a Party conference, so we cross some kind of line ethically speaking. So we took a flier and rejigged it. *Together everything. Happier nation*. Does that fit? We wanted something with more power to it for you. Believe me, I want you to blow them away today because for one I believe in what you want to do, and secondly, it's good business for my agency. Look at it, if you like it, use it. If not you've still got the originals.'

The three heads which had been locked together came up for air.

'And why so late?' he continued. 'It's right up-to-the-minute stuff. We've tried to make it topical, of the moment, it'll make sense once you've seen it. Look.'

Greig pondered his choice as Cal offered him the hand-held player to view.

'No,' he said, turning it away. He watched Cal's face fall momentarily, before regaining its normal tightness. 'I trust you. If you're saying this is better I'll use it.'

'Fantastic,' said Natasha, squeezing Greig's hand. 'I'll get to the control room and tell them to load the new version. Same length?'

'Yes. Everything the same, just a different edit, some new images.'

It seemed this was all it required from the newcomer for Natasha to wrap her arms around him too, planting an enthusiastic kiss on his cheek. A mixture of jealousy and relief ran through Greig's veins.

'If you're going to change it, better give a heads-up now. Still running it once you've spoken?'

Greig looked to Bernie, weighing up his choice.

'No. Run it first. I'll read to it. Improvise.'

Bernie stared back, almost in disbelief. '*Read*? You've never *seen* it before. What if it doesn't give you anything to say? You just going to stand still and watch it?'

A smile, the first genuine smile of the day from Greig, sharing his glance between Bernie, Natasha and Cal Begg. 'I trust him. You'll have to trust us. Natasha? Can you brief the conference sound and vision people? I'm going to disappear. Get myself in performance mode. Cal… it's been a pleasure. What is it you do at…'

'Harlequin Communications,' rescued Cal. 'Managing Director.'

'Really?' said Greig, without thinking, then moving to correct himself.

'… Sorry, that probably sounds pretty awful. Managing Director, really?… What I meant was… I don't know, these are high stakes we play for. I hope you're good.'

Cal Begg put forward his hand. 'A pleasure too, Dr Hynd. And yes, I'm good. The best.'

I damn hope so, thought Greig. Or it all ends here. A deep breath, and he felt himself relaxing for the first time in a long time. Another breath and he took off, hunting down some private space, somewhere in this vast cavern of a venue.

One quick call to make. There was no answer, to his surprise and slight relief, so that when the chance was offered by the automatic machine, the message he left was to both his wife and history.

'Darling, there are only a few minutes to go, I don't know whether you'll be watching with the children but I'll be thinking of you all as I speak. I'll do my best, for you, for all of us… and if it's not what they want, or not good enough then that's alright, maybe it's a sign we should step back from this for a while, let someone else fight the fight. Maybe I've done my bit already?… I know you will understand that. I miss you. Love you all. Have faith. However this plays.'

He switched off the phone, putting it back in his suit pocket. Alone in the hiding room. At the rehearsal two days ago, he'd been shown the four vantage points at which his speech would be scrolled on the two-way glass so that he could prowl and devour the stage like a feral beast and still find his cues without falling. Alternatively the offer of a lectern still stood, for those wanting to fly with more of a safety net. He was going to perform with neither. He was going to walk out, introduce himself, press play and improvise. There was a monitor in the room giving the relay from the stage, using the same cameras and feeds from the live TV coverage. He watched as the Justice Minister reiterated her shopping list of aspirations, an endless series of empty bullets; safer streets, a fair deal for victims, zero tolerance. Still, it was enough to bring the top table to its feet, and with that the hall, in half-hearted ovation. Follow that.

He was led through a maze of corridors to a small, dimly lit holding area just offstage where he was miked up.

He put an arm around his stage hand to draw him near. 'You've got the new visuals, yeah? Three minutes. When I say play go with it.'

The stage hand seemed hardly committed to the new brief and Greig found himself smiling at the haphazard nature of the event. A major speech, major platform, no higher profile imaginable yet no one, including himself, had any idea what he was going to say.

A signal from the stage hand: *you're on*. Greig walked into the lights, raising a hand almost automatically to acknowledge the polite but far from raucous applause. The stage space left for him to do his thing was far smaller than at rehearsal, the scene now crowded with the podium and panel seats for the conference chairman, Party chairman, other guests, and astonishingly, Party leader, the man whose crisis had necessitated this conference. Again automatically, Greig strode over to offer his hand, then working down the line to shake all hands, only realising halfway through that he was both eating into his own time and probably offending Party protocol. Time to be spontaneous. He looked up.

'Good afternoon. A pleasure to be here. I'm...' he paused to lift his ID badge, reading it aloud to well-received comic effect, '...Greig Hynd. Proud to represent Heston, all its people, all our people. Let me show you what we are about.' He gestured to the offstage area to play the video feed. There was no one there yet the performance demanded he keep up the pretence that there was someone snapping into action. After an agonising pause, the hall lights dimmed and the screen behind him dissolved its *Together We Win* legend into a montage of moving imagery and colourful pictures, coloured to the point of saturation in garish reds and yellows, of solitary people. Greig was intrigued, these were not the usual image library shots of studies of isolation and despair, but candidly real shots of ordinary people, albeit until the reverse colour-coded psychology; the brightness of the colouring making these people seem plastic, fake, lonely facsimiles of the real thing. The soundtrack played; heavy electronic drum and bass, again not sinister within itself but cold, emotionless, before giving way to more authentic sounds of guitar and hand-clap, itself a stepping stone en route to the sound of voices, and an a cappella choir version of 'We're all in this together'.

He realised that he could recognise the people being featured in solitary portraits on the screen, they were the very delegates he had been mixing with in the hours before this speech; identity card shots, people waiting at security, always captured alone, artificially alone. And then these shots segued into the same people captured in groups, happy gatherings, the hugs, handshakes and kisses of the conference now showing in mellow black and white. Reverse psychology because this was surely the message: together is natural, alone is false, an unnatural state. Greig smiled, waiting in the gloom for the visuals to finish. *Together We Win*, in simple pictures. And he himself would win. The gamble would pay. He had his cue. He would now react.

The music slowed as the screen fixed on the final image, a group shot, presumably taken at the previous conference, the auditorium crowd on their feet during one of the more sincere ovations. The party united, for once. *Together*, read the wording now superimposed upon them. The hall lights went up, to applause which had started before Greig could even begin to speak.

'What we are about?' he asked, almost shouting to be heard as the reaction to his own words amplified the reaction to the video.

'Yes,' he answered, '…what we are about.'

He walked forward, arms outstretched, an invitation to calm.

'I'm not going to keep you long. Not going to bore you with attacks on anyone else's policy or theory. I'm not even going to try to tempt you with an aspiration, because what I want to say to you is very simple… *Together, Now!* That's what I want to say. All that needs to be said.'

A fresh round of applause halted his flow, again giving him the opportunity to be seen to fight against the very reaction he had sought. A measured smile. A lowering of his voice. Relaxing into performance, feeling good about himself and the message he had chosen to deliver.

'For our society, being together, with common values, and in pursuit of simple decency is all we want. It's our natural state… but one we get distracted from, by others who want to buy us off with empty promises, or scare us apart with prejudice and division. I could talk for hours about my vision for a happier, healthier society. But in essence it's simple, because we are the party of togetherness. It's our natural state… where the strong help the weak, the young help the old, and everyone helps each other. *We* can make it happen, and *we* in this room, at *this* conference are our people's best hope. If we don't make it happen, nobody will. That's our challenge, but I know we can rise to it. Thank you. *Together now*, ladies and gentlemen.'

His ending was so abrupt he surprised even himself, and the silence that followed seemed to hang. Then came the earthquake, the roars, the cheering, the materialisation of the Prime Minister next to him, raising his arm in a boxer's triumph to the crowd. It would only be later that Greig would realise the significance of the Prime Minister's gesture, that it was a signal to the others, not to him, a claim of ownership, of his performance, his agenda, of Greig himself.

He left the stage to be greeted by more hands seeking his own, hands that patted, hugged and did everything they could to touch his success. In the crowd that engulfed him waited the previously elusive Derek Rove, pulling him free and into private audience in a quiet corner of the hall.

'You're staying over at the conference tonight?'

'Hadn't planned to.'

'You will. Breakfast meeting tomorrow, seven o'clock. Election briefing. Highest level. This is top secret. Understand?'

So secret, Greig would later realise, that he had been given no detail of the what, who or why he was to be involved.

'Natasha,' he said, extracting himself from her ecstatic embrace. 'Complications. I've got to stay tonight. Can you see about finding a room?'

'With pleasure.' She smiled, tugging at his ID badge. 'I'm sure *everyone* will be keen to fit you in.'

Greig felt himself blush and struggled for words with which to respond. No matter. Soon she was gone, on the case, replaced by another helper.

'I think she's seriously in love with you.'

Bernie's voice was deadpan. A comment or a joke, was it so obvious?

'What do you mean?' He tried to sound as natural as he possibly could, but still heard himself resonating as a hopeless phoney.

'Smitten. Idolises you. Do anything for you kind of thing. That's what I mean.'

'I see… Do you really think so?' Phoney tone, phoney question. An insult to Bernie's intelligence, the man who had saved his life. Sometimes, thought Greig, when all the guilts landed on top of each other, it was like they would collapse in on themselves, create a black hole that could suck the joy from the landscape. His question hung, unanswered, Bernie's lack of appetite to make a reply matched by his own lack of desire to hear it.

'Who do you see tomorrow?'

Greig struggled to focus.

'At the breakfast briefing?' Bernie quizzed. 'Jason Watson told me you're being hauled up before the movers and shakers.'

'I don't know. Thought it was meant to be a great secret. Should I have asked?'

'Probably more important to decide what the ask is.'

'Ask?'

A shake of the head from Bernie.

'As in what you are going to ask for. You're the darling of the conference. You can get anything you want, I thought you'd have realised that.'

Bernie finished with a look, one that Greig hadn't seen before, one that confirmed his worst instincts. Everything had changed. For all the conference goodwill he'd just created, the undying respect and loyalty he'd taken for granted from one of his closest aides was fading away, and there was nothing he could do about it.

'I'll work on it Bernie. Do my best, as always.'

'As always, Captain,' Bernie replied. The words echoed in his mind as Greig tried to compute if they were loaded in sarcasm, sincerity, emptiness or plain mischief. Wherever they belonged he suddenly felt tired and vulnerable, sorry beyond belief; wherever they belonged they made him want to cry.

C DAY MINUS 179 DAYS

Flat 37B New Mills Court, Highgate, London

Caroline had been restless when we went to bed and I was unaware of her having slept at all. Now she insisted on dragging us out to a red-eye breakfast at a sandwich shop, had us running out before dawn as if my flat was on fire. Something brewing. I knew it was time to be attentive but couldn't help trying to steal a glance at the headlines of the newspapers being delivered in their bundles at the door. *Greig Hynd: Kingmaker.* Crying out for my attention. Instead this, the inquisition.

'Enjoy yourself last night?'

Loaded question. What was the problem, too drunk, sober, sexy, unsexy?

'Yeah. Thought it went okay...'

'Liam, did you like him?'

Rewind in my mind. Liam somebody. Something dull in insurance. Boyfriend of Ella, Caroline's confidant. A cornerstone in last night's foursome.

'Of course... Didn't really get to talk to him but...'

'He thought you hated him. I can see why.'

The accusation unveiled. 'Ella said that?'

'He said that. To me. He's my friend too.'

Accusation substantiated. Shit. Damage limitation time.

'Want me to call him? Apologise, explain?'

She picks disconsolately at a rancid fruit salad. 'To say what, I'm sorry you're so boring that I ignored you all night but you're just not worthwhile enough for me to make any effort...?'

I shrug. 'Not exactly, but something like that maybe.'

She doesn't roll with it. I cup her chin, force her to look at me. 'Hey, what about look I'm sorry but my head was someplace between London and the Party conference where I took part in the political coup of the decade. But my wonderful girlfriend has pointed out my errors and I'd do anything to make it up to her.'

'It's not about me Cal, not even about Liam. Do it for yourself. Get a life.'

So the post-mortem on a night's soiree inevitably heads into the cul-de-sac of Cal.

'You don't want me to call him then?'

She lets this drift. Try again.

'Shall we go?'

Staring into space. I can feel the potential gains of such an early start drift to a meandering death.

'Caroline, what is it? I am truly sorry if I was hard work last night.'

'Always hard work Cal, never anything but.'

Time to plead guilty. 'Let me make it up tonight, just the two of…'

She cuts in. 'I'm going to make changes, Cal.' Doesn't look at me.

'Yeah?'

'I'm going to pack in my job.'

Relief. 'You've only just started. Thought you liked it.'

'Not right away… Maybe in a year. I've been thinking about teaching, getting out of the industry, I don't want to end up like you.'

Is this her idea of humour? Sadly not. She gives every sign of meaning this.

'Getting out of London too,' she continues.

My heartbeat quickens. 'But not right away?'

She frowns at the irrelevance of this. 'Don't you want to change, give yourself the chance to be happy? You're so good at putting things across, the only time you come alive… surely there's something more positive you can do with that.'

It's early and I'm tired and tired of hearing the same riff. But still in damage limitation mode. 'Maybe you're right. I should think about it.'

'Do you mean that, or are you just saying it?'

Of course I'm just saying it. Buying time. Time to convince myself. 'Let's talk tonight.'

She's too smart to be sold just like that. 'Why not, Cal, at least it'll make a change from your fucking agency.'

I get up and throw some money at the counter. Lousy breakfast, lousy value, but happy to pay anything to escape. Outside I stop to buy a newspaper.

CAMPAIGN LAUNCH MINUS 179 DAYS

Premier Express Hotel, National Conference Complex, Central England

Greig prised himself free of Natasha's softly stirring arms to re-camp in the bathroom, studying himself in the mirror, almost searching for recognition.

Half an hour later he was in another hotel, waiting in the lobby area, staring at a picture of his raised-arm triumph of yesterday. On all the front pages of the early editions, Conference special. As yet unwrapped bundles of newspapers in the lobby. It was very early, but he'd been grateful for his excuse to escape here.

'Dr Hynd?'

He followed the Party functionary to the lift; another security check, another screening of badge and ID before they arrived at the door of the suite. A knock on the door, another Party face to usher them in. *Take a seat, wait here.* Greig allowed himself to be processed and was pleasantly surprised to be left alone, sinking into a velvet sofa, listening to the hum of the air conditioning unit, smelling the acrid scent of the nylon net curtain drawn tight across the window. Drifting to a different place. Then voices through in the adjoining room coming closer. A door opened and a man entered. *Be resolute*, Derek Rove had advised. Greig realised what he'd really meant was be prepared for a shock. The ex-Prime Minister stood over him, offering too broad a smile for this early in the morning. Offering his hand. He did not introduce himself.

'Good morning! Can we get you anything?'

Greig shook his head. *No, thank you.* His price, he panicked. Why hadn't he worked out his price?

The other man drew closer. 'Greig. Thank you for coming to meet me at such an early hour, it's appreciated. I wanted to see you for a number of reasons. Firstly, just to tell you how much I enjoyed your speech yesterday, and to thank you for your contribution to the Party over the last while. You've provided a stimulus and energy that is greatly appreciated and you have my gratitude for that.'

Full eye contact all the way through, noticed Greig, someone so sincere or so good at faking it that it was immaterial if it was genuine or not. Impressive, the only option to give in to it, to go along.

'And your call for unity… for *togetherness*, well what can I say… I know you meant that at every level from society up but it would help if politicians led that wouldn't it?' Again the eyes hooked into him with the gentle laugh that had been signalled. Greig realised he was being coerced into the other man's reading of the presentation, his own speech being sold back to him.

'Of course it's what the Party needs. There's been too much division. And it has to end if we are going to do the job the country needs us to do. That's why I've been asked, Greig, to come back, as Party leader. Something I'm considering, but only if I can count on people like you. That's the other reason why I wanted to meet. Can I count on your support?'

Greig found himself nodding in emphatic unity as the pitch was laid before him, found himself almost committing to ready agreement with it. Almost. He was facing a master salesman, someone trying to get him to buy without mentioning the tariff, getting him to pledge loyalty without making any offer at all. He stayed quiet, searching for the appropriate words, it seemed almost impolite to mention. *What's in it for me?*

'Can I ask where is the Prime Minister in all of this?'

'He will resign at ten o'clock this morning, Greig.'

Another laser-lock of the eyes across the table. *Yes, you heard me, do you know what I'm saying?*

He did. He was talking to the new Prime Minister, his predecessor was gone. Forced out. And a new regime was already carving up the future.

'I'm sorry if it sounds parochial, but there is another agenda that I have been pursuing, that of the promotion of positive mental health for our society. Where does that stand in terms of priority now?'

Greig almost had to stop himself from saying something like 'in the new order' or 'next regime'. Words associated with a coup. But here he was discussing his terms for joining it. *A natural politician* Nigel Richards had said.

'Greig. I trust you, and I'm asking you to trust me. I will share with you some thoughts about the future that are highly sensitive. I'm not going to insult you by asking *if* I can trust you, I'm only telling you that I do, that I believe that I can do great things with you in partnership, and that by sharing what I'm about to I'm giving you proof of that. Okay?'

Significant moment coming. Not yet eight o'clock and here he was, face to face with a new, come back, Prime Minister. Already on the inside of one of the most sensational events in modern history, and under pressure to declare himself in or out, conscious that things were moving impossibly fast and that the wrong call now could close off endless avenues of opportunity in an instant.

'The Prime Minister will go, voluntarily, for the sake of Party unity. A courageous politician. We will match that courage by taking over government and then calling an election. A significant part of our manifesto to rebuild and reinvigorate the country will be the very things that mean so much to you. I'm telling you it's now our fight too; and that if we are elected we intend to make the nation's health and happiness our top priority. The only issue for you will be whether we are too ambitious, not whether we will do it or not. You can implement it, Greig, as a minister, if you join us and help us win the election.'

Greig felt the silence hang over him. He was obviously not going to get any more detail when the talk was at such a seismic level of significance; likewise he was not going to ask for any since to do so would somehow indicate a lack of the trust he had been asked to place in the future, and all its overlapping and intertwined scenarios: his future, the Party future, the Prime Minister's future and that of the country. His stomach rumbled noisily. Still not yet eight and yearning for early sustenance.

A hand reached out to him from across the table, offered to close the deal.

'Join me for breakfast?' laughed the new Prime Minister, flashing a practised smile. '... You sound as if you could do with it.'

C DAY MINUS 179 DAYS

Nirvana House, Underhill Mews, Croydon

The taxi dropped me at the precise address I'd been given, guided by supposedly error-free satnav, which is when it dawned on me that the rather grandiosely titled *Nirvana House* was in fact an office suite rented in a grey concrete box in an anonymous corner of London. It had taken somewhere in the region of an hour just to get there, during which I'd managed to rebuff my driver's cheery banter to the point where the swipe of the windscreen wipers against the dismal unrelenting rain passed as the journey's entertainment. A wasted hour of which I grew ever more resentful; we were due to launch in a matter of days, presuming the Prime Minister would survive his ongoing special/emergency conference. History would show of course that neither came to pass, not that I was to know in the back of that cab, perhaps if I had, my own history would have played out somewhat differently too.

As it was I was stressed about what Harlequin was supposed to deliver, angry at any grit in the ointment that threatened our smooth ascendancy to greatness. Step forward the enigmatic Sea of Tranquillity, newly moved up in priority, but not it seems, in terms of staff numbers. I move through the office block's vacant reception to the third floor and hit the plastic buzzer. Angela Solo arrives, flustered and charming in equal measure, and she's the only show in town.

'*Cal.* How good of you to come. Pat has had to go to a conference in Manchester and I'm all that's left. I've dragged you right across town when it would probably have been easier for me to drop in on you. I feel terrible, do you mind?'

We were standing at the door at this point. She had greeted me with a kiss, something that took me by surprise given we'd only met once before and that the only reason I had dragged my sorry ass across town was to resolve the dispute and atmosphere of hate erupting between us. She held on to my arm as she spoke.

She led me in, past a pyramid or two of unpacked cardboard boxes and wardrobe files, presumably representing the archives of Tranquillity. We settled in a clearing, two chairs at the corner of what must have been her desk; a clear, see-through single piece of plastic moulded into workstation art, computer terminal tucked underneath, monitor sitting proud, cable plugging it into the universe.

'Been here long, Angela?'

'I'm sorry. Chaotic, isn't it?'

The question was too rhetorical to merit an answer. I peeled off my jacket, damp from only a minute's exposure outside, now almost steaming in the aggressive heat of my client's HQ. Something else wafting in the air, I scanned around and saw the scented oil diffusers, three of them burning away to set the spiritual tone.

'Can I offer you a tea, coffee, water?'

Angela Ambiance has an especially winning smile that I'm inexplicably warming to. Still sporting the bubble perm that blights the top of her head and most that's underneath.

'Tea would be great.'

She takes an age to return with it, I'm left to chill out in the silence. No calls, no emails coming through to my Blackberry, nothing to do but wait. Then she's back and serves up slow, like she knows I've been running like a lunatic, like she knows this little bit of intimacy is a day lounging on a beach compared to how it is elsewhere.

'Have you been following the Party conference events, Cal?' she asks, offering me a cup, and I notice she's peeled off too, some kind of silk wrap going on here, a Chinese thing, red, drawn into a bow at the midriff.

'I was there yesterday. Travelled up to meet Greig Hynd, soon-to-be Minister for Niceness or whatever.'

She smiles indulgently. '*Greig*? Yes, we know Greig. How was he? Thrilled?'

'I didn't really engage with him. I was there to hand him the ammunition. He's on the up, for sure.'

'Ammunition?' A coy tilt of the head. An I-know-I'm-not-supposed-to-ask-but-will look.

'Just some visuals to give context to what he was saying. Turns out he simply played them and then played off them. Guessed he would. And it caused a sensation.'

'*You* did, it was your idea?'

'My idea to give him some new moving images, yes. Fought like fuck to get it out of our studio but it looks like it paid off.'

'And *you* suggested it. How clever, Cal.'

Put it like that, yes. *Clever*, there's no denying it. She lets me purr in pleasure, stroking away. This woman is giving me a hard-on for myself.

'You said you know him, Greig Hynd?'

'More Pat than me. We were involved in some of his conferences with the Alliance for Positive Mental Health. There's quite a bit of overlap in the agendas, although obviously theirs is medical whereas ours is spiritual. Same goal though.'

'Maybe you should amalgamate…' I deadpan, 'the Sea Alliance for Positive Tranquillity.'

'*Cal…*' she drawls, drawing closer in admonishment and I realise how much I like the sound of her voice, and how I'm throwing myself into this cynical, naughty boy thing so that she can play the schoolmarm in response.

'Is that your only recommendation for us?'

I shake my head, bemused. And entirely relaxed about being bemused.

'Angela, I have not one single idea about what to recommend, as I have not one single idea about what you want. We sent two guys here to find out and we're no further forward, except they are now missing in action. To be honest, I wonder if you might be better served going to another agency, we're absolutely overloaded with work right now and I can't pretend you would be top of our list.'

A knowing smile, with a trace of hurt that I instinctively want to correct. Gone too far, just as we were getting cosy. 'I'm sorry… I shouldn't have said…'

A hand goes up to halt any continuation.

'It's alright. I understand. Do you want me to respond or is it too late for that?'

'No, tell me what *you* think. Let's be honest with each other, that's why I came here.'

'Yes. And I do appreciate you coming here when you are so busy, and with much bigger clients… Let me tell you a few things though. Firstly, you are busy because you are the best, that's why we want to work with you, and I mean *you* Cal…'

Absurd as it sounds, and as awful as it reads in replay, I took this magnanimously, with stoicism. Yes, I *am* great Angela. Thank you for the endorsement.

'But there are things we can offer Harlequin... We know things you don't about the psychology of unity, the signalling we all, as individuals, are predisposed to respond to. All around you Cal, packed inside these boxes, all our research. Information you can access. And we will be a *paying* client.'

'You have budget? This is one of my concerns. We don't do charity...'

'We *will* have budget. Significant budget.'

'But what is it you actually want to promote, Angela... I mean I get the agenda in its broad sense... meditation, self-calm whatever, but what exactly is the brief, is it a technique you guys have or is it just the value of that you want to push?'

An emphatic shake of the head. Pulling closer.

'No, no. What we want to sell is *consciousness*.'

'Right.' My heart sinks. '*Consciousness*, then. Can you elaborate?'

'We want people to wake up to what goes on around them. Wake up to their own potential, potential for happiness, potential to live without guilt, without burden. Without leaders. Wake them up to how they are being manipulated.'

'Manipulated?'

'Overdosed with news, celebrity, all fodder... All a façade to keep them docile.'

'Right.'

'You seem unconvinced, Cal.' The can't-you-see-it anguish.

'I'm sorry. Just trying to figure it out... You are going to get government money to campaign about not needing leaders and you are going to use advertising?... The very thing that has been designed to manipulate to get an anti-manipulation message across?'

This seems to make her relax, like all-of-a-sudden, despite the odds, I am fucking getting it.

'So clever, Cal. So very cynical. Want to try something?'

'Sure,' I say. 'I'll try anything as long as it's mostly legal.'

'Good,' she says, face radiant. 'I want you to start by watching something. Watching and letting go, follow your mind wherever it leads you. Just five minutes, and then you can tell me what you think of it, will you do that?'

Angela Audience moves to set me up in front of her computer screen, leaning across me to call up the file to play, humming to herself.

'I'm going to leave you alone so that there are no distractions for you. Ready?'

Why not? I move to activate it and she places her hand on mine to guide it to play. She sings quietly as it begins, as if she's transfixed herself at the thought of whatever it's meant to show. Then she retreats. It has started.

And what comes up? A revolving montage of images, people shots, culled from yet another online catalogue. Standard stuff, all usual stereotypes on show; shopping housewives, football teams, old couples dancing in a class. So far so predictable, these roll one into another, in silence. The same type of pictures I make a living recycling to sell things, doesn't she realise? Then the mood seems to change without a noticeable breakpoint. More stereotypes, only now captured alone. Solitary people standing strong and proud. Achievers, the independent, a gallery of the resolute. And then it has changed again, I can hear whispers of children singing as the colour tone subtly fades, sepia browns and reds dominating. I'm aware I'm feeling unsettled, restless. The people I'm looking at now don't suggest the same attitude they did before, though it's hard to work out why. Not them but the backdrops behind them, all of it conveying isolation, dislocation rather than comfortable self-reliance. Fragmented people. Adrift. Something terribly haunting to it. I look away, where the fuck is she?

Avoiding the screen I focus on my watch; five minutes she had said, though it seems that a lot more time than that has passed. Stolen time. I'm more than just disconcerted. I take a deep breath, to togetherise myself.

'So what do you think? What did it bring out in you?'

Angela's reappearance startles me. Not that I'm not glad to see her.

'I think... Well, it's very good. I can't help thinking that it's not so unlike what we played at the Party Conference yesterday.'

She seems delighted by this scrambled reflection. 'Really? Then maybe we are on the right lines then!... Ready for something else?'

I'm wary of agreeing to phase two if it's anything like the first, though equally eager to leave it behind. *Sure, let's go for it.*

She ushers me to the floor, wanting me to kneel opposite her. Close my eyes, lean my forehead gently on hers. Follow her breathing.

This is a new way to take a brief, and one I'm not fully convinced by.

In fact, I feel I'm being set up for some kind of prank, my arms hanging uselessly by my sides. Angela Sensual-Touch is massaging my fevered brow. *Get this*. Fingers through to my scalp, kind of thing they do at the more expensive hairdressers, here as part of the search for the inner Cal.

'Cal,' she whispers, 'there's nothing you cannot do. Nothing for you to be afraid of, for you to put up this shield of cynicism to protect you. Lose that and give in to it, Cal. Nothing you can't have, nothing you cannot have if you want it with purity.'

My hands are resting on her at this point, somewhere just above her waist, ostensibly to stop myself falling over. Starting at just above the waist and then moving upwards as I'm encouraged by her mantra to reach out for anything I feel like having. I can feel her skin beneath the silk, nothing else beneath the silk so that I'm beginning to feel the sides of Angela Breast as my gentle fingers voyage on their own journey of discovery.

'Anything you want Cal, if you believe in it truly.' She's got something special going down in head-massage terms because it feels as if I'm about to be relieved of mine. And in the space of my time in her presence my needle has moved from 'curious to know' through 'would like to' to the section marked 'desperately needs to have sex with' where it is stuck, with the pressure rising dangerously. Every time I close my eyes as instructed, the last pictures in the sequence flash back to me. People bereft, adrift. My grip on her grows tighter.

'Understand?' she asks, breaking off. Once more, it's rhetorical.

She stands up abruptly, leaving me on the floor.

'A campaign about consciousness. You can do that, can't you?'

Why not? I think. After all, I can achieve anything. Almost.

'I'll speak to Pat about what budget we can give you to work with, and when we'd like to run. Does that sound good?'

It doesn't, to be honest, because I'm squatting on the floor, neither severing ties with a time-squandering pseudo-client nor reaching a glorious new physical/spiritual plateau of understanding with the supremely manipulative Angela Tease who has bought and sold my compliance without me even noticing.

'Sure. I'll see what I can do.'

And with that, I took my leave of Nirvana, never to glimpse it again. Back out to a sky that had somehow managed to grow even darker, and in ways I couldn't even begin to guess.

C DAY MINUS 178 DAYS

Harlequin Global Communications, Harlequin House,
Warren Street, London

It seemed like the rain would never end and that all the Togetherness I had
worked so hard to promote was going to be flushed out before anyone
had a chance to glimpse its greatness. Another morning, foul weather, foul
mood. I rock up at Harlequin before eight and guess what, the whinging,
hand-wringing, clinging form of Harry Rhodes is already lying in wait.

'Cal... Cal... Thank God you're back. I left loads of messages...'

Harlequin's Director of Planning is not lying; I survey the mess that
is the scattering of papers and post-its on my desk, a desk that has been
abandoned for all of what, ten hours? And here he is hinting at dereliction
of fucking duty.

Have you not seen the news? prompts Harry, probing more gently.

'What fucking news?'

'The Party Conference. Prime Minister resigned yesterday, emergency
leadership ballot today with guess who heading back...'

This *is* news. And somehow I'd missed it. Of all the days to sink into
a black-hole melt-down and lie with my head under a blanket waiting for
the headaches to subside I had chosen this one. I tried to think it through.

'It's okay, Harry. We're covered. I met him at Party HQ over a month
ago. He's already fully briefed on the campaign. Loved it. Gave me to
understand he was the real client all along.'

Harry grimaces. Not what he wanted to hear.

'Spit it out Harry, try to be a man for once... What is your problem?'

'Problem?' He winces.

'*Problem* Harry. There's always a fucking problem. Soon as I see
you hovering at my door I think here's fucking Harry, he has a problem
because there's never anything else, is there? Never here comes Harry

with a solution, because that's not how your interpretation of fucking planning goes is it? I've got some shit, I've fucked up, where's Cal to sort it out? That's the game, yeah Harry?'

This time even I am stung by what's being said, pausing only slightly to wonder how such an insipid vacuum of a man can draw out such anger in me. Harry grinds to even more of a halt, but I'm determined to get him moving. Preferably out.

'So, once more, and with all due respect, what *is* the fucking problem?'

Poor Harry's eyes have gone glassy, watery even. And then he rubs the same little eyes, in wonder, in hurt. Speaks softly, slowly, reducing the volume level and making me realise how I've been shouting.

'It was meant to be a heads-up, Cal. That's all. There will be a new Prime Minister. If it's a return for our old friend he'll call an election. As fast as he can.'

Harry has pulled himself together. I can be thankful for that. Still there's no sign of a point to this supposedly urgent briefing.

'So?'

'The minute an election is called our campaign is pulled.'

It's those buttons again. He can't keep his twitching fingers off them. Nuclear codes hit in merciless sequence. Rockets launched. All out war declared.

'Harry. Thanks for your analysis. I can't help but notice there are about sixteen 'ifs' in there. *If* the Prime Minister goes, *if* it's our man, *if* an election is called… This wouldn't be about you looking for another excuse to weasel out of the research plan would it? Finding it tough again Harry? Listen to me. I want every focus group, every output, every fucking frame of every commercial examined and optimised like we agreed. I want it scheduled and run as agreed. Otherwise I'll have your fucking head on a skewer, understood?'

This time Harry is less fazed, managing to stare back at me, blinking only occasionally as I let rip.

'Cal. Please listen to me. You're not seeing it straight. They are going to call an election and pull the campaign. We are going to incur cost that we have no need to. We are working ourselves to exhaustion… look at yourself Cal… There is no need for it. You need to call Nigel Richards. We need to hang fire, for everyone's sake.'

Harry is right in one respect, I am tired, beyond exhaustion, but because of help like Harry's not in spite of it. I stand up.

'Harry, if you don't get out of here and back to your job I will fire you. We have our brief and no instruction to drop it.'

He takes an age to get to his feet.

'I'm not sure Peter Vesey would see it that way, Cal.'

'Well good for him, but since he's busy setting up Harlequin Transcontinental, we'll just have to see it my fucking way for now, won't we?'

'He's downstairs, Cal. I saw him on my way in. Clocked in at six. Asked for all the info on Sea of Tranquillity and the Positive Mental Health stuff.'

He must have seen some kind of surprise writ large on my face at this, enough to make him stop and savour a small victory.

'Yes,' he said, eyes narrowing, finally finding the door. 'Another heads-up.'

Some time later, another presence materialises at the same door. Hugh McDoormouse loiters for who knows how long before I become aware of his anti-presence. Mr Finance, Harlequin's numbers guru, venturing skyward up three floors from his basement burrow, and with no sign of nose bleed.

'You okay, Cal?'

'Awful. What do you want?'

He shuffles on his feet, unsure whether to come in and make himself welcome or to stick with the relative safety of the doorway and throw in his master's commands from there. Two steps in and he sees my eyes, then it's a fast reverse. He's got the nerve to actually be walking backwards as he talks to me.

'Peter has been chasing me for the latest financial forecast out-turns. Wants to see them today. This morning, preferably. How are you fixed?'

Forecast revision. A plague of fools. The pounding in my head is about to bring the plaster down from the ceiling.

'He'll have to wait.' I mumble. 'Thought he was in orbit anyway.'

'*Orbit*, Cal?'

'Flying around, fucking around, you know the jet-set trail…'

Hugh is blind to the funny side of it all. Vesey has parachuted back into Harlequin unexpectedly and unhappy Hugh is all a-hover.

'So what can I tell him?'

'The words fuck and off spring to mind.'

'Cal, please…' he cuts in. I close my eyes and I've got those Tranquillity images playing in front of me again, studies on a theme. Drowning men volume one. Desperate drowning people planted in your mind, gratuitously, ruinously.

'Fuck... off!' Although it hurts me to shout it's what I seem to be doing, and to be doing well. Hands down, eyes open, Hugh is gone, successfully dispatched. Things look ever so slightly brighter. For the luxury of that moment. It doesn't last. Another visitor, again some indeterminate time later.

'Cal?'

'Mary.'

Mary from Traffic at least has the confidence to come in and park herself opposite.

'Hey Cal, you look fucked.'

'Thanks for that, is that what you came to say?'

Mary shakes her head. Loves me enough to smile as she does so.

'Mr Vesey wants to see you. Urgent. What you done this time Cal?'

Oh groan. '*Me*?... Fucked if I know. Why would he be upset with me?... Apart from refusing to fill in his income spreadsheets and keeping the whole thing going whilst he cruises the oceans in the agency yacht. Actually, maybe that's it, me actually giving a fuck, turning up for work when I feel like death. That'll be it, won't it?'

'Why is your phone switched off? Why is your office phone unplugged? I've texted and emailed but you're offline.'

'It's been a rough day, Mary. One day, that's all. It happens.'

'Want me to tell him you've gone home, sick?'

A pause whilst I consider the offer. A good offer. The problem is, Mary behaving like a decent human being has got me mellowing out, moving towards the light, it's like a magic wand, Mary's tough love. *Mary, would you hold me? Just for a second? I'll behave myself, I promise. It's not like that.* I wonder if she can see the sudden need in me. *You look fucked.* 'It's okay, Mary. I might as well face him now. I just hope he doesn't push it, because I'm honestly not in the mood.'

'Sure you know what you're doing?'

This is a question I've heard myself ask of others. This time though, I get the awful realisation that it's coming from a nice place. I really am in trouble.

'Doing my best.'

She offers a hand and hauls me out of my chair. A pat on my back then sends me down the stairs; down, down, down to face the summons that has been issued on me, a wanted man.

Knock and enter. No pause. One loud knock as a signal of intent. What the fuck does he want... Figures? Choose your own, Peter. Heads on a plate? Have mine.

Except he's sitting still, looking at me, not saying a word. He gives every sign of thinking, which means he's either a very good actor or that he genuinely is working it through. I take a seat opposite, uninvited. And we stare at each other. *His* meeting, his summons. We wait. He looks tired, creased, worn down by the strain of doing whatever the fuck it is he's been doing.

'Good morning,' he says, signalling nothing of the sort.

'Good morning,' I parrot. 'Your emissaries tell me you want to see me.'

'You never gave me your plan, Cal. I'm still waiting.'

Of course, *the plan*. It's all about the plan. Or rather the planned cull. On the to-do list Pete. Then do everything single-handedly and fire myself to reach an infinity profit margin.

'Any plan I could have given you would have been instantly obsolete. Things are changing every day. Fluid. You've seen the news, no one knows who's in charge or driving what. I've got to keep my options open in terms of resource.'

'Account handling,' he says, followed by a silence, in which it transpires that it's meant as some kind of question. I shrug. Help me here, you pompous oaf.

'How are you coping with account handling? Who do you field, who do you team up with for meetings and presentations?'

Odd question, this, given that he's dictated current policy of me and me and my shadow for company.

'Caroline left and you didn't let me replace her. What are you looking for?'

'A *plan*, Cal. I was looking for you to work this all out. How the agency could cover the bases without being exposed to unnecessary cost, without being exposed...' His voice tailed off, strangulated with something approaching anguish.

'What are you getting at, Peter, you okay?' I say, mixing real curiosity and faux concern to impressive effect, stepping right into the booby trap.

'I've had a complaint, Cal. A serious complaint. I'm trying to figure out what might have happened and if over-work or stress had anything to do with it.'

I sat down again, fighting the tension inside me that made me want to hit someone. A complaint? Which one of them, Nick, Harry, Hugh?

'Who's complaining about what? It's been tough for Christ's sake, how am I expected to get the work out on time on these deadlines by being Mister Nicey-Nicey? The assholes I have to work with wouldn't be able to make their own fucking sandwiches if I wasn't there handing them the bread...'

I heard myself meandering into a vaguely psychotic riff on agency catering, heard myself ranting like a lunatic and pulled up the plug.

'A *client* complaint, Cal.'

'*Client*? What do you mean? Nigel Richards, the departments, the Party, they are all sound, all...'

'Pat Brosnan, Angela Rix.' He trumps. 'Sea of Tranquillity. I believe you had a meeting recently? A meeting to set things straight after a difficult beginning. I believe you used the words *false start*. Complained about lack of brief.'

'I'd hardly say complained... Pointed it out, positioned it that we were struggling to understand what they wanted... Listen, what's there for them to complain about? These are *valid* points. *Serious complaint?*... Fuck off!'

Flailing again. Going down and not knowing it. He raised his voice.

'A meeting *you* asked for...' he droned, 'between yourself and Angela Rix, at which they say you behaved in an inappropriate and offensive way which left her highly distressed.'

Angela Anguish. Hard to imagine. Cue a fast, silent replay of the encounter in my mind, the montage, the massage, the intonations. Vesey staring at me; *explain yourself.* I couldn't. What had gone down? I was completely lost.

'Can you think of anything you did that would provoke that kind of response?'

I shook my head.

'Did you shout at her like you seem to shout at everyone these days?'

My head in my hands. Why would she do this to me?

He lowers his voice. 'Cal, were you hitting on her in some way...'

'Absolutely not... If anything it was her, she...' I stopped, words jamming, mouth dry. The impossibility of explaining it.

He heaved a heavy sigh. The judge who has to send you down but takes no pleasure from it.

'I'm going to see them. I'll hear what they have to say... I did warn you about situations like this, fronting them alone when there's no one to back up your version of events.'

'My *version*!' I exploded. 'My fucking *version*. I've worked with you for six fucking years. How many times have you had to apologise for my lewd and unsavoury behaviour? These are *nothing* people, a *nothing* client determined to get their nails into the agency. They've already sent two of our guys round the twist. They have a problem with *me*? Fuck them. I refuse to have anything more to do with them.'

'They feel the same way about you Cal, if it's any consolation.'

Something about the way he said this. A feinted smile. The twitch of the head as he spoke, the shuffling of the papers on his desk to tell me the meeting was over, somewhere in there was visible the pleasure he was taking in the whole procedure.

'Wait. I'm telling you there's nothing in the allegation, and nothing in them.'

This time Peter stands, like his authority is on the line. Starts slowly, gathers pace and volume as he loses it, almost as if he wants to show me how it's done.

'A *nothing* client, you say. You don't say they are close to Greig Hynd, our new Minister, the next owner of our campaign whom you've already met for yet more one-on-ones without keeping me informed. You don't say that they've got a pot of government money to spend on their thing, and you're not telling me a thing about the meeting you had at which something went down because I just don't believe allegations like this come out of thin air!'

He's standing over me, bawling. I'm sitting taking it. A role-reversal captured for posterity by a witless witness who walks in without knocking, so urgent is his news.

Hapless Harry Rhodes freezes in terror at the spectacle.

'What is it?' screams Pete Vesey, vexed by Harry's very presence, and the hesitant aura of indecision that goes with it.

'Just thought you'd want to know as soon as possible.' He turns to me. 'Sorry Cal, Nigel Richards couldn't get hold of you either, he called me. The PM's back in, he's just called a general election. Our campaigns have all been pulled.'

C DAY MINUS 160 DAYS

Cal's Cell, Highgate, London

I bought myself a new poster, had it fast-framed for instant pleasure, waited patiently for a good half hour before taking it home on the Tube. I then spent hours gazing at John Lennon and the boys in the capes and hats that made for semaphore ski gear as they joyfully cried *Help!* Did I feel so down? No, not really; I didn't yet realise it was all dissolving. Live on your own and there's nobody around to give you that perspective, work on a permanent war-footing with all those above or below and it's much the same trip except everyone is willing you to fall. Such is the perspective that only comes with distance, a very long distance, of which more later.

But I did appreciate her coming round, as the late great John would have said, and to prove it I had made extra special efforts in the cooking department, after months of wanton neglect. When I say *cooking*, I probably mean *cutting*; tomatoes and mozzarella, bread, cucumber, celery. The list is hardly endless. Yet there was something new here, if she had chosen to see it. The evening *chez moi* would be unusual in that I had made this effort rather than rely on the expertise of the carry-out brigade.

She rang the doorbell even though she had her own key. A sign, so obvious in retrospect, blind to the then fool, on his hill, still living in yesterday. She came in through the front door and before I'd even offered her a glass of wine, or taken her coat, massaged her feet or asked her how her day might have been, I hit her with the full force of a Calum Begg daily debrief. Everything coming out in one long torrential howl.

'Fuck *me*!... you wouldn't believe how it's been. So much to tell... you know they've called an election, obviously you know, well Vesey seems to think it's my fault, like it's my fucking doing, and then I get a call to swing by Derek Rove, officially to find out where they will park the

145

Christopher Wallace

Togetherness campaign, unofficially to tell the party how to fight a new kind of election... clueless, they were red fucking hot on all the fucking *detail* they can squabble over until polling day... And I hear myself saying *raise* the fucking game Derek, sell aspiration, sell emotion rather than logic, sell that you'll die for the people's right to be happy, to be secure, even better, you'll die for their right to demand happiness and security, fraternity... sell *everything* and promise *nothing*, and I hear myself sounding like that fucking Greig Hynd... did I tell you he couldn't say two fucking words to me, all shy and withdrawn, then put him on stage with the show and he's some kind of flamboyant *freak* waving his arms about, punching the air... Golden boy... *Tranquillity Now!*... Anyway, they're *buying* it, we meet them offsite in the next few days, another debrief, maybe Dr Happy will be there himself. You listening Caroline?'

Talking at her, her sitting quietly on the sofa, looking at me. To be fair, showing no sign of interrupting, perhaps recognising my need to offload.

'Caroline?'

'Cal, I want to talk.'

Don't we all, but some of us talk for a living, talk until it kills us.

'Well sure, let's talk. Been a hell of a day but I would love to listen, catch up with your news. Didn't mean to ambush you on the doorstep, but you wouldn't believe what's going down at Harlequin central.'

As I said this, the urge to do just that; talk, or even listen, began its magical process of evaporation, as I realised how lovely Caroline was, and that she was here in my flat, and that there were no other eyes upon us and that we were alone.

'God, how I've missed you. Can we go and lie down, just hold each other?'

She stiffened as I pulled her toward me. Rehearsed stiffness. 'Cal...'

'Okay... let's eat! I have a surprise for you... made something, actually found out how a knife works...'

'Cal...' she cut in, neither hungry nor curious to know where I was going with my faux-jaunty kitchen rap. 'Cal... I don't want this anymore. It doesn't make me happy, and I don't think it's good for you either to sit here waiting for me.'

'I don't mind waiting...'

'Cal,' she said. 'You don't understand what I mean...'

The tailing off filled in any particular points that had maybe failed to register. I realised my cherished notion of a night of conversation and

146

wine-drinking and thought-swapping and body-sharing was out. All gone.

And with that realisation went my urge to share, to speak, to do anything except burrow down in the relationship-free zone of my Beatles poster.

'Cal... Cal? Listen, I really think it's important, and I'm speaking as someone that really... cares... wants you to do everything you want to, wants you to be happy, do you believe me, Cal?'

I was looking at her, thinking of whatever brief times we had had. Instantly bitter that it was over, my bitterness being the last friend in the world I had left.

'Cal, you need to get away from here, this flat, the job, the crazy ambitions you have. You need to give yourself the chance to be a normal person, Cal. You're suffocating. There's nothing positive in your life Cal, you have to change it.'

So spoke the only positive thing in my life as she turned herself into a negative.

'Are you listening to me, Cal, will you try to do something about it, will you promise me you'll at least think about it?'

As she droned on, it gave me the time to pace the floor of my cell, so to speak, to play out the permutations in my head. In her intonation and exhortations she'd made a remarkably quick transformation. She sounded uncannily like just another fucking client. Another list of demands.

'Caroline, are you talking to me as a partner, someone who'll be with me on that journey, as my girlfriend... or are you just someone else dumping me with another fucking brief?'

A killer rhetorical. She dug into her satchel to retrieve the keys she left on the side-table next to her. Then up and out silently, lacking the grace to say goodbye, leaving me to stare again at the new poster she'd manifestly failed to notice. She closed the front door carefully, and I heard it click shut. No need to move for quite a while, time that once more evaporated. Trying to see faces, like my father's in John Lennon on the wall.

CAMPAIGN LAUNCH MINUS 50 DAYS

Downing Street, London

Greig shook the Prime Minister's hand and left the room on the second floor. Still smiling, he followed the assigned member of household staff down the stairs, along the corridor and out towards the front door. As he passed through, all around him were signs, portraits and items of historic importance to remind him where he was. He promised himself he would replay this moment later, savour it more than he was allowed to now, all passing by in a blur as he was escorted out.

Of course he had had a briefing on how to behave, the decorum on how to receive the appointment to Cabinet. Again this had registered somewhere in his mind, but too deep to be of practical use when facing the real thing.

He paused by the doorway, strictly taboo according to his brief, strictly the preserve of the Prime Minister himself, but in Greig that day simply a natural reaction to the cheers of the crowds held back by a gentle barrier, and the wave of photographer flashes that lit the street once he had shown his face. Still smiling.

He had thought they were three, perhaps four deep. Watching on the news later in the day he would see that number easily doubled. TV cameras, newsmen, radio mics, visual audio feeds of every persuasion set up in some kind of aggressive defence against those being ejected from the Prime Minister's office that day.

What is going on? they clamoured. He could have asked the same himself. Still smiling. A step forward, onto the pavement, speaking out over the roof of the ministerial car awaiting him. Breaking taboo, again, forgetting himself in the freedom of that moment, now part of the charmed elite. Untouchable.

'A wonderful moment, not just for me, not just for the Party, not even just those that voted for us. A wonderful moment for everyone in this country, a chance for us to make a change. The Prime Minister has shown courage and imagination in taking on this challenge, and I thank him for his faith in me, faith I hope to repay. But it's not about me, or even the Prime Minister. It's about all of us, the courage and imagination of us all to make our dreams a reality.'

Watching the same performance on the news channels later in the day where it threatened to surpass even the triumph of the newly re-elected Prime Minister, Greig was struck by the poise and ersatz gravitas on display. He was the only one watching who would not believe the delivery was not rehearsed, the only one who could possibly know the depth of improvisation utilised. Greig would take a mouthful of red wine and allow himself to savour the talent that had surprised him then, the same talent that had transformed a daunting election campaign trail into an effortless cruise to the finishing line. A victory cruise.

True, he had inherited an efficient local party machine in his adopted constituency. True, the rushed nature of the general election and the focus on a return of the former Prime Minister meant that Greig's lack of background to any relevant local issue was lost in the dramatic sweeps of the opera being played out on a national scale. Equally true, that he had played a key role in the gathering momentum behind a manifestly refreshed Party, with exciting new initiatives for which it sought an urgent mandate.

That the National Well-being Initiative was viewed by the opposition as a weakness through which they could attack the whole Party manifesto would be an amusing footnote of history for some, a critical part of a painful post-mortem for others. For Greig it was the decision that would give him his platform, or rather launching-pad to office. For the opposition, the lack of substance, lack of detailed objectives, lack of tangible outcomes was an opportunity to exploit, unaware that for a natural, spontaneous operator like himself, this was precisely the ground in which he'd thrive. Impossible to catch, impossible to outrun, his star had risen the more he had been targeted. Pushed into an ever higher profile by the very side out to beat him. A natural politician, as they had discovered to their cost. A national figure they helped build.

He endured a brief programme of last minute campaigning on what would become his home territory. On election night he was gone from there as soon as his result was announced, driven to Party Headquarters and a midnight rendezvous with his wife. It was the first occasion they had faced any kind of Party commitment together, not that it proved a trial, anything but. They held hands as the Prime Minister topped up their glasses of champagne, charm gun full on, the cheering making the team pull closer together. Genuinely intoxicating. He had felt his wife's eyes upon him as the plaudits were given, he had felt some kind of forgiveness, some kind of vindication for the sacrifices they had both made.

And then he had left his wife sleeping off the excesses of the evening to answer the Prime Minister's summons. A kiss on her dozing cheek. A new start. A chauffeur awaiting him. Another meeting with the man who held his destiny.

'Greig,' said the Prime Minister, rising to embrace him.

'Prime Minister,' said Greig, wrapping his arms around the other in genuine affection.

A satisfied nod, a shake of the head at the improbability of it all before the Prime Minister cut to the matter of business.

'You know how important your agenda is to us. You know how glad we are to have given it, and *you,* its rightful home within the Party. I want you to succeed. I *need* you to succeed, and therefore I don't want to place you in a position where there is any possibility of you losing focus. I am offering you a role working for the Health Secretary where you will have specific responsibilities for the development of our Positive Mental Health programme.'

The Prime Minister waited, indicating his offer merited some kind of immediate response. Greig paused to think through the scenario. He was one of the first in to see the Prime Minister yet had been offered a relatively junior role. His particular piece within the cabinet jigsaw was obviously one of the more strategic ones that had to be put in place before others would be placed around it, or above it. His piece. *Tranquillity Now.* The years of campaigning.

'I am sorry Prime Minister, but I will decline. I do not see the role as influential enough to make the kind of impact we discussed.'

A dry sniff from the Prime Minister. An offer of tea which he himself then poured. A shifting in his chair.

'What would you consider to have enough influence, Greig?'

'Minister for National Well-being. The most senior role within the Health Service, with cut-across to the education, justice and community portfolios.'

A rehearsed answer, for once.

'I'm not sure I am in a position to offer you that, Greig.' The Prime Minister was suitably solemn of both voice and expression.

'Then we are done.' Greig rose.

'Sit down,' came back the order. 'If I give you what you want, I want immediate results in return. I do not want the Party ever to be in the mess we were four months ago. I want a completely changed landscape within six months. I want results, proof that we are making a difference, understood?'

Understood. The first thing Greig began to understand was that he was being offered the post he had pitched for. The price and expectations that went with it were something he would have to work out in slower time. For the present, there was a victory to digest, the realisation of so much hope and ambition. A sleeping wife and young children. And there was a smile on his face he found impossible to control.

'I understand.'

'Then we *are* done, Greig. Congratulations. Get working.'

Greig followed the steps of the man waiting for him outside the room, steps that went down, down and then out, out to the audience waiting to adore him.

C DAY MINUS 50 DAYS

Harlequin Global Communications, Harlequin House,

Warren Street, London

Between the election being called, the campaign being shelved, truce declared at Harlequin, there was time to reflect, take stock, reassess priorities, mend broken relationships and get in shape for what was to follow. Yes, a better man would have taken this path. Me? A prolonged sulk. A sulk against the agency that refused to be led. The client that refused to be serviced. A boss who refused my best.

To be fair to me, which to be fair, no one in particular was at that point in time, nobody knew with any kind of certainty that this was an interruptus, rather than an end. The party we had given everything to serve was far from a re-electable certainty. As far as I was concerned, we stood on the verge of a colossal one-way bet on the wrong fucking horse. We had backed the party of the returning Prime Minister, before anyone decided they had always loved him, before they had forgotten or forgiven the wars, the spin, the piousness that had become intolerable first time round.

. And where we, I, Harlequin, our *thing* had upped the stakes dramatically was by not only backing the horse least likely at the starting post, but by backing the wayward left-field faction of that horse, if you will, in the form of Dr Greig Hynd and his groovy revolution. By accident or design we were seen to be aligned with his movement's excesses and would stand or fall with it. The faction most hated, reviled and targeted by opposition struggling to comprehend its luck in being offered such an inviting target. A target every bit as elusive as the objectives and purpose that had made it so. As Dr Hynd's road show begins to turn the tide this judgement begins to look more and more inspired, with more and more percentage behind it, in addition to your humble author who had wandered into it without a firm promise of anything from the slippery Dr Hynd. Yet as his particular star rose, so too did anything in even vague orbit. Step forward you client/ adversaries/insurgent faction now account-managed by Pete Vesey his very self, you are the power behind the new throne, Sea of Tranquillity. Step forward and welcome to the end game.

The morning after election night; a seven am call from Nigel Richards.

'We need to talk, Cal. It was made clear to us that the Party believed it would win and win decisively, and that when it won its foremost priority would be a campaign for community cohesion not unlike the *Togetherness* initiative you yourself developed. That brief is on its way Cal, how might we prepare for it? I need you to think big.'

'Nigel. I guessed this was coming. But what's new? Any clues?'

'Cal. Would you respect me if I were to break ministerial protocol? What can I tell you?... Our new brief might be the property of the new Minister for Well-being. That brief might not be so far removed from what your agency has already been engaged upon. Think about how *Togetherness* equals *Well-being* Cal. That's what I need you to be thinking about.'

A thousand different currency signs flash in my head as Nigel Richards maps one campaign into another.

'Nige baby, you'll have to pay us for what we've developed so far…'

A calming voice from my government contact speaks of public money. *Relax*.

'Budget will not be the issue, Cal. They will want this fast. They want it running whilst the election euphoria is still tangible, when they can get away with anything. That's where they're ahead of even you. Just get it up and running.'

'What about our unmentionable friends, Nigel?'

'Who?'

'Sea of Tranquillity?'

'They are history. Not part of the equation, not part of the future.'

'Okay Nigel, let's meet and talk. Bring whatever you've got to Harlequin, six o'clock. I'll have thoughts for you then.'

And in between times, thoughts for Mr Vesey, Mr Senior Vice President, Mr Chief Executive Officer of Harlequin Global Scheming and Manoeuvring.

Vesey the man appeared that very morning seeking me out in my new haunts of the fifth floor digital studio. Things must have been looking up, and he himself seemed keen to present an image of a man at peace with the world and at ease with his mission, back-slapping the guys and gals hard at it at the workstations, peering into their screens and feigning interest in the designs on display. *Dave... Nice work... This the latest version?... Keep it up. Christina... Settling in?... This is looking good... Kenny, how's that wife of yours, had the baby yet?*

'Yes boss,' says Kenny Chance, deadpan, comfortable enough with Peter's arm around his shoulder but far from melting into it. 'Two years old now, Peter.' A hundred smirks reflected into the Apple Mac screens as Mr Vesey seeks to retrieve the situation, firing off a range of retaliatory gambits in the hope that one of them might land. *Only kidding... knew it had been a while. Things move so fast in the digital world... You never keep me up to date.* The last one accompanied by a thrown look to yours truly, only I wasn't for catching it.

He let the laughter subside, magnanimously hugging Kenny one more rueful time, the swirl of his feel-good orbit carrying him over to me, where, bizarrely, I get the same treatment; hand on shoulder.

'Had a call from Nigel Richards yet?'

'First thing this morning. Before breakfast.'

'And?'

'Meeting tonight to compare notes on the new regime.'

He taps my shoulder, as if to indicate there's some deep thinking going down in the Vesey brain central processor. Then he speaks again, louder, opening up his comments to the floor.

'Amazing, isn't it? Go outside the agency and it's like a public holiday... election over, sea change in government... new leader... almost like we're all still in shock at what's happened. And then in here, we're already working on what they can deliver... No time to slack off and enjoy it, because this is where the real power lies, yes? I look at a room like this and I'm proud of the sheer professionalism on display.'

A weird address this, one to make me at least wonder what all the jet-lag had taken out of him. Around him there were absolutely no signs that anyone else was tuned in, let alone ready to respond. The morning after the election, and our senior statesman arrives out of nowhere to make his landmark acceptance speech on behalf of us all, to our toe-curling pleasure.

'Okay,' snaps Sneaky, indicating he's 'off' the wisdom thing and back 'on' the usual roving remit. 'Let's have a chat, now.'

We took the staircase descent to his office, giving time to swap pleasantries about the previous night's election results and key moments therein. He had watched them come in at home, turning down the chance of sharing the experience at any number of business clubs eager to share his commentary. He seemed surprised that I, without similar family commitments, would choose to do the same.

'Did you watch Greig Hynd?'

'What about it?'

'Bit disappointing after all the fireworks of the last few weeks. No?'

Greig Hynd's constituency result was one of the earliest of the night. He had given a perfunctory acceptance speech.

'I thought he did the job. Routine gig. What else could he do?'

Peter paused and shook his head, careful not to walk and talk into a never-ending free-fall. 'That's the thing, isn't it Cal? He's painted himself into a corner. Every time he opens his mouth from now on there will be this huge expectation that he's going to turn it on again… So he'll have the pressure to live up to that expectation, plus the risk of pissing everyone off by just banging on in the same way. He's got to deliver now, hasn't he… He called you yet?'

'Greig Hynd?' This time it was my turn to stop, why would Greig Hynd contact me directly?

He smiled, like I would never get it. 'One; he owes us, two; he'll be looking for a new spectacular very soon. Just wait.'

Wait we would have to. At least until six o'clock when the first indications of where my new best friend had landed and what he might want could be up for exchange with Nigel Richards. Until then there were other things to do.

'Since when have you been working out of the studio room?' he asked, easing into the executive chair behind his desk, inviting me to do the same opposite.

'So, since when Cal?'

'Three weeks or so, can't remember exactly.'

'Can I ask *why*?'

'I need people… *like* people around me. I was enjoying being on my own in that office less and less. Spending too much time banged up, walls closing in…'

Raised eyebrows, his tell of surprise, or rather his deliberate tell of surprise.

'So your office is lying abandoned then?'

'For the time being.'

'So we can give it over to someone else?' he asks, with a tone that somehow suggests this is a hypothetical, rather than practical question. Like he is probing to see how deep-rooted and serious this is. Like I'll fold somewhere along the line. *Okay Peter, you know me too damn well. I was never serious about this all along, I want my office back, my seat of power restored to me at once.*

'If there's someone that wants it, yes.'

'Isn't it a bit hard to have sensitive conversation in an open-plan studio?'

'Not yet. Nothing that these guys shouldn't hear. In many ways they should hear how tough it is with clients.'

'I meant with staff.'

Sensitive conversations. Quite. I get it, we're on the trail of Cal's plan.

'There's always the boardroom for that. The thing is... I have been spending time in the studio. Trying to get my head around the digital side, how we hyperlink all the websites, the digital content file servers, how the uploading and downloading all works. Blogs, automated replies. Something tells me it will be important.'

'Technical stuff?'

'The line between technical and creative becomes thinner and thinner. One dictates the other. For campaigns of the future we'll start with the possibilities on the technical side and work backwards long before we get to the brief.'

'I see,' he says, clearly bored. Detail he has no interest in.

Coffee has arrived. I test the water.

'Speaking of briefs, or working for no brief, what news of my friends at Sea of Tranquillity?'

A sip passes his lips.

'Do you mean in terms of their charge against you or their campaign?'

He knows of course I mean both. He knows how easy it would be just to tell me how he sees it, even display some of that professionalism he lauded earlier. But he has leverage and wants me back in his pocket. The cool detached Cal hanging out with the boys in the studio has set off an alarm within him. He wants the nervy, twitchy Norman Bates version back, and as soon as possible.

'Cal, you really should just level with me about what happened with

Angela. Something doesn't hang together on this, something not quite right.'

'*Nothing* happened. Have you spent any time with them, ever heard anything of substance from any of them on anything? These guys are bad news, Peter. World class at sucking you in, promising everything. Taking you to a great big dead end. Find out what floats your boat and then beat you with it. Bad news they should have a fucking health warning. They are a *cancer*.'

He loves this. A full, confident smile from my leader, getting me where he wants me.

'So.' He exhales. 'You don't like them then?'

Oh I like them Peter, as you can tell, especially that lying bitch who's probably jerking you off right now, as we speak, only you won't have realised it yet.

I return his empty grin, silently, reaching out in the dark for a reverse gear.

'Nice boots,' I declare. 'Fruits of your world travel?'

He can't help but glow with pride at the compliment and offer up the offending footwear for further view. Deep tan, pointed toe with silver side buckle, Latin stuff, a Gaucho business boot.

'Got them in Madrid,' he says admiringly. 'One of these things that once you see you just have to have.'

I shift in my seat, time to enjoy my coffee.

'What took you to Madrid? Part of the business travel or purely pleasure?' A slow and gentle nod. Check. *I get you Cal.*

'Business, Cal. Strictly business, duty free shoes aside.'

Time to push the envelope. 'Can I ask what kind of business, any connection to what we're doing here?'

'Every connection,' he replies, with that tone of faux surprise. *You don't get this, a clever boy like you?*

'The Board want us to be globally networked. Ready to act when and if there is any interest from abroad in the kind of thing we were doing for government here. Like-minded partners, that's what we want to set up. Simple. Only hellishly time-consuming and complicated in practice. Thankfully, now we have more time.'

Hard swallow. Lukewarm coffee. *Like-minded partners.* Other agencies run by cunts across the globe. All at the behest of the Board.

'I don't think there will be much time. I think the *Together As One* stuff is dead in the water. I think they want something new, and in a hurry. Smart enough to cash-in on the post-election euphoria whilst it lasts. It's all going to come together very quickly. It'll have to.'

A narrowing of the eyes from Peter. Maybe the coffee doesn't taste great after all. 'This is what Nigel Richards is saying?'

What I'm saying, Mr Boss. Me, here in front of you.

'I'll see him this evening. See what kind of update there is.'

'I want you on top of this, and I want to be in the loop. Understood? And no more fucking up.'

'Excuse me?'

'Where are you going to take this, Cal, just to an adequate campaign or are you going to seize this opportunity to clear out the dead wood and make a truly great campaign? It's up to you.'

The rising intonation suddenly stops.

'Let me get a brief first, Peter. Maybe we should chop and change once we know what we're meant to be doing.'

I heard myself talking with what struck me as restraint that went beyond the routinely admirable and well within the heroic. Why this feeling of being constantly on trial. Was I on another charge?

'Incidentally we seem to have passed it by, but can I ask where exactly we stand with the Tranquillity mob and their allegations? Kind of handy to know if I'm about to be fired for alleged misdemeanours given the rest of the gig you've given me.'

'I told you to leave it with me, Cal. I'm still talking. I will get to the bottom of it, I assure you. Meantime, I'm afraid, they still want nothing to do with you.'

'Which suits me fine, only I'll need to know if we have any commitments to them in terms of campaign.'

A deadly pause as Peter silently reconfigures his strategy one more time.

'I'll be straight with you, but you have to trust me, which I'm not always sure you do.' He lets that hang uncomfortably in the air. Clears his throat. 'Keep me in the loop Cal, otherwise things will get very, very difficult.'

Fear and loathing. What I want to say is no, I don't trust you but tell me what's happening anyway.

'I understand. I've always understood. So what's the deal?'

'Angela and Pat are in a position to give something very valuable to our campaign. Something that can increase its effectiveness exponentially. They have mountains of very specific research on the coding and subliminal triggers that make an audience more likely to engage with any piece of communication. Emotionally engage. It would complement our work fantastically.'

The Sea of Insanity duo, I realise, are uncaged again. Busy wanking Peter off. Their thing, their talent. How to shake them loose?

'You say *research*. Have they got anything of practical use?'

'Absolutely practical use… We've been making ads built around one emotional climax, Cal. Three separate ads for three scenarios. It's wasteful. They've got the techniques to make a minute-long sequence a constant pummelling of emotional peaks. Imagine the impact!'

Peter punched a clenched fist into a semi-closed palm. Smack, smack, smack. What could we not do to our audience, where could we not lead them?

'And they have shown you how this can work?'

'Yes,' he replies with deadpan affront.

'Could you share it with me?'

'They have an entire portfolio of colour code, sounds, scenarios most likely to impact against each demograph. We over-lay that against our existing scripts. Your matrix thing of audiences, scenarios and outcomes.'

My *matrix* thing. Fashionable again, of course. 'Right. As simple as that. Forgive me for asking, but why hasn't this been done before? Why don't they do it themselves if they are so smart?'

Peter leans forward, a co-conspirator now, excited yet secretive in tone. 'It's highly sensitive work, I think they've had to bend a few rules in order to have this information to start with. I don't think the Institute of Psychiatry or Mental Health Council would particularly approve how they got their results, so to speak.'

There was a lot of hand activity at this point, hands being thrown left and right, hands being vigorously washed. *Hey, we've all done it* hands, so to speak.

'You mean they abused their guinea pigs?'

My question went unanswered, save for more hands, traffic cop blocking hands. *Don't push me, we don't need to know.* I began to relax for some reason. Maybe because it made some kind of sense. They had to have something hidden.

'Anyway,' says he, anxious to get to what he sees as the real point. 'No one has ever had the opportunity to research it like we will, with a client willing to bankroll that to the tune we will…'

Back to the traditional fist pummelling. We were going to hammer our audience, in the name of Tranquillity. Still, again it all made sense. Even if their theory was bunkum, the research process could smooth it all out, help us find something that could get a faster heartbeat to it. My mind began to drift to the self-promised land of my post-Harlequin future and the one epic campaign that would give me the exit credential, the ticket-to-ride CV. Maybe back within touching distance.

'And I want your plan on how that's going to work in reality.'

Back to the *fucking plan*.

'I've got one more, maybe even two, rounds of business travel. After that, I'm all yours. Keep me involved. And think about what you will do to the passengers.'

'Can I ask a question? Sea of Tranquillity are sharing their spoils with us, what's in it for them? They don't strike me as the charitable type.'

'I've offered them a deal,' grins Peter, teeth glistening in pleasure. 'They help us with our campaigns, we'll help them *get* a campaign. Simple.'

My turn to raise hands, stop! *What the fuck*?

'They've had some kind of offer from way back, from our friend…'

'Greig Hynd?'

'The very same. He said he'd get them funding to promote their relaxation thing. All I've said is that Harlequin will use whatever influence we have to make that happen. And the more effective they make our campaign to start with, the better their chances all round.'

Peter's satisfied smirk has enough wattage to illuminate the room, fading only with the arrival of his temp PA, back to remind him of his latest international commitment. Our meeting is being adjourned before I've had the time to fully savour the fruits of his negotiation skills.

'In the meantime,' I rise to my feet, 'I'll have to wait to hear from their lawyers, or fucking Interpol on the progress of their indictment against me.'

My boss can hear this but pretends not to, pretends to be engrossed in the dialling tone he's getting from his phone. *Board*, he mouths, silently, ushering me out. *Keep me in the loop.* Oh yes Peter, easy. We're all in the fucking loop, whether we like it or not.

CAMPAIGN LAUNCH MINUS 33 DAYS

Party Headquarters, Grosvenor Road, London

So much to take in. The workings of the House, the make-up of his departmental team, the wider legislative programme of the government. The protocols of cabinet meetings and the mundane reality of the side-job as a newly elected Member of Parliament. Minders or assistants for every single aspect, steering him from one commitment to the next in relay, as if Greig was the baton to be passed day and night between teams intent on getting what they needed out of him and throwing him forward as quickly as possible. And here he was, on the move again, this time in the back of his ministerial car, chauffeur at the helm to take the cargo to Party Headquarters. The journey across London was taking over half an hour, precious minutes stolen from the schedule where every second seemed to count.

'Anything interesting?' Greig nodded toward the briefing paper that had Bernie's attention.

'This? Nothing boss. Unless I've failed to spot it.'

'How many more to go?'

Bernie switched his gaze between the thin pile of papers he'd managed to sift through already and those in the thicker folder still unopened. 'Couple of hours maybe… is it always going to be like this?'

A good question. These were the papers he himself was meant to read, a duty he'd temporarily delegated to his newly appointed Special Advisor now sharing his trip across London. Dutifully, as ever, he had accepted the mission, got to grips with it immediately, without pausing to ask questions of his own.

'I don't really get either, how you can go to a cabinet meeting with the Prime Minister and all the King's men, and then get summoned across town to face some Party committee people who don't have a real job between them.'

'They pulled you out of Cabinet?'

'Not exactly, the meeting was over. But I was heading back to the department and I get told I've got to come here, urgent. All I'm asking is…'

'Do I *have* to?' said Bernie, smiling.

Greig turned in exasperation. 'Exactly.'

'Depends what you've done boss.'

'But that's exactly it!' snapped Greig, hands colliding together. 'I haven't had the chance to *do anything* because of all these damn meetings.'

Bernie raised his arms in meek surrender, *not me*.

'Sorry,' he said quietly. 'Obviously, I'm not getting at you, but the absurdity of…' His voice tailed off as he looked outside. A homeless vagrant was searching through a waste bin for anything of value. A young man. The working world rushed by. 'I've got one of the biggest departments, staff of hundreds. Sexiest office I've ever seen, legions of staff and officials, already ambushing me with initiatives to cut, hospitals to close… It's like they are scared to let me think.'

Bernie nodded and placed a marker in the file of papers in his lap. The car had reached standstill once more, they had arrived at Party HQ.

'Jason Watson, wasn't it?' he said, getting out onto the pavement. 'I'll see if he's ready and we can get started straight away.'

Greig watched him enter the building, holding back to gather up the papers he had spread across the seat. Papers unread. He leaned forward to thank the driver and realised he'd forgotten his name.

'Thank you, that was great. Will you…?'

'I'll wait for you here, Minister,' the driver cut in. Greig mouthed a silent thanks, his own chauffeured car, still taking some getting used to.

Inside the building he saw Bernie waiting at reception, beside him was another man he recognised from what seemed like a distant past.

'Mr Richards.'

'Minister,' replied Nigel Richards, giving no hint of either the history the two men shared, nor pleasure in the other's progress since their last meeting.

'We're in Jason Watson's office.' Bernie began to stride toward the lift.

'All of us?' asked Greig. 'Are you part of this, Nigel? Thought it was a Party matter?'

Nigel Richards hadn't moved. 'I've been invited along as an observer. Perhaps it would be appropriate if it were just you and I that met with Jason.'

'Really?... Bernie's one of my most trusted.'

'I think it should just be the two of us. Sensitive issues, Minister.'

Greig shrugged apologetically. 'I've no idea...'

'I'll wait down here somewhere,' the junior offered. 'Give me a chance to get through some more papers.'

Greig moved reluctantly away. 'What *is* this about?' he demanded quietly of Nigel Richards. The two walked into the lift in silence, no reply forthcoming.

Jason Watson was waiting for them at the door to his room, the open-plan area thinly populated at this time of the evening. Nevertheless he seemed to usher his guests in with haste, almost in fear of them being spotted.

'Greig, good to see you, haven't seen you since...'

'Since the election night.'

'Yeah, quite.' He pointed to the seats opposite his desk. 'Guys, please.'

Greig sat and observed the exchanged glances between the other pair. Secret signals. It was all beginning to get wearing.

'Okay. What have I done?' He slapped his hands together, thinking of Bernie's remark.

Jason Watson pushed himself forward, seeking his eye, rising to the challenge.

'Okay, why not? Let's start there. What *have* you done? You are having an affair with one of your assistants. You're a married man with children. A minister in the new government. Public property, Greig.'

He would later come to think that his entire life could be divided up into two parts; the one before this moment, and the wholly unsatisfactory, despoiled and sullied one after it. Not the moment before he started the affair itself, not even his life before becoming an elected Party politician. He would divide his life into the time when he could face the world full on, with confidence and integrity. When he could ask a question like *what have I done*, and face any answer. Then the life after.

'*Sensitive issues*,' he said quietly, turning to Nigel Richards. 'What do you want from me, am I on some kind of charge?'

'Grow up, Greig.'

Jason Watson's snapped words stung. Greig was not being facetious; it was hard to know how these things played out. More new territory.

'You are the Minister for National Well-being, Greig. Having an affair is not likely to do much for your family's well-being. That's the issue, frankly, and how the media will run with this.'

Greig had formulated the obvious question in response but stopped himself from asking; if the men in this room knew about this then it would only be a matter of time before it leaked wider. How had he been found out, had Natasha been indiscreet? All immaterial. The only thing that mattered was how this would run.

'You want me to resign?'

'We want a way out of this mess, without embarrassment to the Party.'

'Then I'll resign.'

'That will embarrass the Party.'

It took an effort of will not to bury his head in his hands, to close his eyes and just wish it all away. An affair; that's how it must seem, he realised. Not how it was for him; a sporadic, on-off, spontaneous arrangement whereby the help and support given by one of his team occasionally veered off any normal path and crossed well over into dangerous territory. Why had he needed it? Why had he fallen into this. An *affair*. He had been due to see her tonight, a catch-up that would probably have strayed into a familiar illicit zone. Now off the agenda. Permanently.

'Are we done here? Guilty as charged. You don't need to know the detail, only that it's over. I'll deal with it.'

The two others stared back at him, unmoved. Greig remembered other meetings in this building where he had more successfully challenged the passive antipathy to his pitch. Not here, not today. He lacked the energy. They wanted him to stay for some reason. He was in the wrong; he would stay.

'Is there anything else likely to come out Greig, anything about... anything else?'

Nigel Richards' question, delivered in halting, cringing, reverse-apology civil servant style, sent a charge of adrenaline and anger through Greig, an injection of energy he was almost grateful for; how dare he, was this not hard enough?

'No other affairs. No homicide... genocide... So no, Nigel. I don't think so. What the hell are you doing here anyway, I thought this was the Party's little embarrassment?'

'I'm here...' Nigel Richards paused, icily, 'here because obviously it's the government's embarrassment too. And sadly,' another pause and exchange of glances with his Party colleague, '…because I've been over this ground before.'

His eyes sought out Greig's, as much to convey his professional detachment as the sincerity of his words. Greig gave his gaze back in silence, as his seething resentment, and all the energy that came with it, waned once more.

'Natasha Skacel is popular within some areas of the Party. Well liked. Made an impression in a very short while, much like yourself, Greig.'

Greig turned to Jason Watson. Yes, Natasha was popular. Of course she would be. What was the point?

'A little flaky perhaps, highly strung. *Naïve*.'

'She's young. Twenty-five years old. Is that a crime?'

Greig felt his words hang in the stale air. Words instinctively offered in defence of his dedicated assistant. Words to hang himself with. His lover. His *young* lover.

Jason Watson continued regardless, as if not hearing. 'Some in the Party were surprised to hear that you had a wife and family at all, Greig, given the kind of profile Natasha took at the conference… I have to say, when you brought your wife here on election night there was almost shock.'

'Jason!' Greig's hands were clenched, unable to tolerate the slow-motion replay of betrayal and misdemeanours. 'Like I said. Guilty as charged. It will be sorted. Why are you doing this to me?'

'It's not a matter of doing anything to you, in fact it's not about you at all, Greig,' reasoned Nigel Richards. 'I know it's sore. I know you'd rather get the hell out of here and get on with it and believe me I feel the same. But we have to think about how all of this might unfold. One thing I can assure you is that it will only be the start of it unless we can get a proper fix on it.'

He had reached out to place a hand on Greig's arm as he finished. Greig couldn't remember the other ever having touched him before. He nodded back. *Okay, I get it.* The hand withdrew.

'A young woman. Headstrong. Happy to pass herself off as your partner… How is she going to take it when you end the relationship?'

'I'll sort it.'

'Great. Good for you. Then what? Has she got anything that can damage us?'

'*Damage*? Why would she want to damage us… Don't you think this is all a bit extreme for god's sake?'

'She's known to tell some fanciful tales about launching your career, about Mental Well-being conferences that end in chaotic adulation, hysteria that she herself orchestrated, mass hypnosis, and all of it silenced and covered up. You're not even *aware* of it are you? But *you* can *sort* it? Frankly, I'm not reassured.'

An effort not to hide his face in his hands. The shock of what he had just heard had him blinking at the table in silence. Every time he opened his mouth they came back with something worse. Not a single response left in him, no sign of the courageous defiance he had hoped could close down this whole ghastly episode, no; only the beginning, as one of them had said.

'Greig,' said Nigel Richards, comforting hand once more on his arm. 'Is there any shred of truth in any of this... Any way it could be perceived to be true?'

'She says all this... She really says all this?'

Jason Watson shrugged. 'With a drink in her... When your wife is about.'

Greig rubbed his stinging eyes. The sadness was overwhelming. The campaign, the ambitions, the cabinet career over in an instant. Not even begun.

'It would have to be a bit of a stretch to call any of it the truth.' He felt himself struggle to give any impression of composure. 'Whether anyone has the inclination to make that stretch, is another matter. Perhaps they will. It's politics, isn't it? Whatever... Look, just tell me what you want and I'll play. I resign, abdicate, plead guilty, insanity... Anything. Just tell me.'

'We need a strategy, Greig, that's all. One that's thought through. I wouldn't have thought resignation is an option given the profile you have had and how early we are in government. This is about getting out of this mess, and *we* are here, believe it or not, to help you.'

'Just tell me what you want. Maybe it's best I go anyway.'

'Drop that. There's too much invested in you. Besides, if you insist on leaving things will get very, very messy, Greig. Open season, and no one to help you.'

Greig realised with a jolt that he was being threatened.

'Investigations, enquiries... you could forget about earning a living as a doctor whilst that was going on, not to mention what the attention of the media hordes would do to your family.' Nigel Richards winced at his own prognosis. He too seemed to sit ever closer, invading Greig's space and his ability to think.

'Yes,' Jason Watson, gripped with enthusiasm for this vision of Greig's grisly fate. 'Simply not an option. Okay?'

Greig found himself still reeling from the not-so-veiled threat.

'What do you have in mind?'

'It's your decision, Greig, you tell us.'

'*My* call. Really? I have the suspicion you want me to arrive somewhere and are going to keep up this bad cop good cop thing until I arrive there, yes? Why don't you save time and tell me what you want. Otherwise I will walk, and we'll just have to see if your dark predictions are accurate.'

The two men on either side of him eased back slightly, deflated momentarily.

'Short term,' said Jason Watson, remarks aimed at the room rather than directly at Greig, musing aloud, or trying to give the impression he was. 'Control the girl, keep her quiet, occupied. Don't give her a grievance or time on her hands. You'll know how to do that. Then you create a bigger story elsewhere... an initiative, do something, become famous for that rather than anything extracurricular... give the media something else to focus on, the Well-being agenda. Medium term? Consolidate. Tidy up, sell the results, in the Party, out of the Party. Redefine the persona you want to be recognised as... create that image, then be it.'

Jason Watson's voice trailed off, becoming ever more distant in Greig's mind. The mantra of launch or re-launch, manufacture and re-shaping of political identity as if they were talking about an exciting new brand of eau de cologne was at best a curiosity that failed to engage him, at worst a trivialisation of everything he'd been working towards.

'And you need to do it pretty fast too.' Nigel Richards was now hitting a confident, chiding tone.

The two men looked to him for acceptance of the urgent mission being sketched out in such a compelling lack of detail. Would he accept it, his challenge, mission, his punishment, whatever it was?

'Listen. Just let me... *please* let me just absorb this first. I'm not sure I really follow where it is you want me to go.'

The two facing him both began to speak, words colliding, frustration apparent. Nigel Richards waved deference to his colleague, the floor given to the stern-faced man of the Party. The marketing speak was gone, it was back to stark threats.

'You don't have time, Greig. This happens immediately.'

More masked intent. The two of them, sitting on top of him, squeezing out his air. The walls in the room, the darkness outside, a ministerial car with its engine running, his mistress in a hotel room probably ringing him on an unresponsive phone, his wife putting his children to bed, his son in a world of his own. The sadness as he thought of it all making it difficult to breathe let alone hear what they were saying. *Redefine your persona, keep the girl quiet, keep her occupied, give her no cause for grievance. Highly strung.*

'You're telling me to leave my wife for her, to keep her inside of all of this, to shut her up. That's it, isn't it?'

'It's one way of keeping control, short term.'

Greig found himself nodding, more in shock than agreement with the master plan. The impossibility of it all. Leave his family to save them from him.

'We are finished,' he said, quietly, pushing his way up out of his chair.

He left the room and followed the steps back down towards reception, now deserted except for the solitary shape of Bernie slouched over two piles of papers.

'We okay?' he asked, shuffling the files back into order.

Greig made to speak, but realised he was in trouble, the battle between desire for expression and nausea suddenly swinging violently towards victory for the latter. His steps gathered momentum as he launched into a sprint towards the toilet. The first act, he would later recall with bitterness, of his new persona, to be violently sick in the Party HQ.

C DAY MINUS 31 DAYS

Ministry of Well-being, New Kings Beam House, Blackfriars, London

One meeting. One room. One afternoon in London. An office at the Central Ministry for Health. Dr Greig Hynd's new hangout. Creepy building, never been before or since, looks like a hospital, smells like a hospital. Fluorescent lights, long corridors, white gloss finish on everything; the reception displays and desks, ceilings and floors. No white coats but medical clues abound, the floors of the block dedicated to areas of bodily concern, the names on the doors as you pass them, all Doctor this or that, the pro-fitness, pro-positive-diet, pro-counselling, pro-propaganda on pop-up stands that threaten to fall as you try to breeze past, following your porter. No trolleys or stretcher-bearers. Must have been their day off.

'I know we are pressed for time but it would be of help if you could give me your take on what it is you want to achieve here. How you would judge whatever campaign is run as a success. What attitudes and awareness do you want to see changed and how?'

I had started by reaching out to the man in charge, Dr Greig Hynd, Minister for National Well-being. I had met him before, when he wasn't a Minister, and he made it clear he remembered that. Thanked me, even. Because of that limited history, I found myself unsure of how to address him, was it the formal 'Minister' now that he was so elevated, or was he still dear old Greig-baby to old pals like me? He looked rough, in need of friendship, face truly miserable. He had been twitchy last time we met, although then he had the excuse that he was just about to go on and perform at the Party conference, to go on and be the star of the show in fact. Now, in power, he was somehow deflated. Nigel had hinted about something else which was a bigger preoccupation, and you could guess that this might have something to do with the urgent need to generate positive publicity and show that he could deliver as well as promise. Not that I expected to get him to fess up his misdemeanours and shortcomings right then and there. Not at all. I was serious, just what the hell did they want?

He was not to be drawn though, looking to his advisor to fill in the gaps as required, or at least to have the first go at it. The advisor was his right hand Bernie-something, still looking about twelve and in shock at being a Minister's Special Advisor, a college student at a poetry tutorial about to air his sixth form poetry ramblings of angst. I turned to him, trying to look encouraging, interested. It would be an effort to sustain this as he pointed to his graphs and equally indecipherable schematics and weaved his impenetrable tale of *Thrivers*, who were, well, thriving, the *Doing Okays* who were mostly sorted, those bottom-of-the-class who are already *Under Treatment,* and not forgetting the bunch trapped in the shaded zone of the graph who were *Vulnerable* and only just hanging in there. I knew how they felt. Still, according to Bernie's stumbling spiel, we could have less people undergoing mental health treatment and consequently soaking up Health Service resources and generally draining society if more of us were getting by, more doing okay and more thriving. That meant making everyone *feel* happier, making them *strive* to be happy. Simple.

Time to test the theory, or my understanding of it. 'So, a measure might be, for example, if I follow you correctly and please correct me if I don't…' I smile, still reaching out, building a rapport or something acceptably close, 'a measure like acceptance of an attitude statement like "*I am responsible for my own happiness*"?'

Bernie halts, like he lacks the authority to endorse this route, from his earnest gaze you can tell that only our Minister can give the word. Though he himself sits mute, arms folded, eyes elsewhere, head elsewhere. Four of us in the room about to change history, five if you count the silence. This is not a promising start, no sign of the fireworks to come. We four men – Nigel Richards, Greig Hynd, yours truly and the young Bernie – had enjoyed the fragrant fresh presence of Natasha at the start. She had been keen to stay too, I would have guessed, but Dr Greig gave her a prescription to go, a fool's errand that she didn't seem to take too well and hardly had him thriving either.

'Or "*I aspire to happiness*"?'

'Who doesn't?' chuckles Nigel.

'Is it more about being prepared to work for my own happiness then?'

'Wow, that's pretty good,' enthuses Bernie the kid, replaying it, chewing over it, taken aback by the accuracy of the fit. *Hey Bernie, I do this for a fucking living.*

'...Got to be careful about the word "work". Wouldn't want people to pick it up that it's all about having a good job and the rest following...'

Back to silence.

'Being prepared to treat my sense of happiness like my personal fitness... part of who I am that I should consider as something I can control and cherish?'

Nigel Richards reaches for the graph. He's looking puzzled.

'Can you say that again, in English?'

Fuck off Nige, I'm on a roll here, work with me, work with me Bernie, transcend your youthful limitations, work with me Dr Feelgood, Dr Greig.Wake up.

'Something like; "*happiness and fulfilment are things I should seek to exercise my own control of and manage in terms of my own response to challenges and success. I will seek support from others and support others on the same path*"... And that is pretty good because if we can make that a shared belief, and then a shared experience, it's a very powerful thing... Togetherised, magnified.'

'Absolutely!' The man claps his hands together so loudly they must be hearing it down the corridor and wondering what the fuck is going on. Greig Hynd is with us now, enraptured. 'Absolutely it Cal, you got it. Can you make it happen?'

'We'll see,' I say. 'There's still a lot to think through... How we can support that mindset change, how exactly we stimulate it... And what is the role for government in all this private, personal stuff?'

'Partners, leaders, friends.'

He says this with such conviction I still believe he meant it. Even after all that came to pass. My friends, *the government*, he really did buy it. *The government, your friends.* God bless him. Times when you could have sworn he meant it all...

'I'll put myself out there,' he offered, softly. 'I'm not afraid to take it on, if it comes to that. I've spent the last ten years going against the grain, facing down ridicule, indifference. I *know* this works, I know we can *transform* everything through it. We've come too far to be afraid of the final step, yeah?'

Four of us in the room, shaping this thing that would engulf us all. Four of us, each with our own unspoken take on just what our man meant.

It was to Bernie that he sought his initial and immediate endorsement, the years-of-struggle bit being only relevant to him. But what was the uptake he was looking for? Dr Greig Hynd's proposed Christ-like ascension to the role of universal saviour meant his disciples had to move up a few gears as well; potentially putting them in sainthood territory too. I could see Bernie squirming at the thought of it all, writhing inside his boy-to-man body. Let me sleep on it boss?

Nigel Richards wore a different face, altogether brighter, livelier, encouraging. Nigel was running through the angles, presumably, and finding most of the odds on offer favourable. Here was a minister offering to be the front, the fall guy, the owner of everything that would go down with the campaign, for good or bad. This was not how it normally worked. None of the caveats or escape clauses on show, far from it.

'Everything or nothing.' A slap of hands from our Minister to show that he meant it. Cranking it up. Nigel Richards thought he had a point.

'By which you mean if we win, we win big, and if we don't, we fail by some margin. I see. The question is, can we pull it off. Cal, what do you say?'

I've grown to hate this kind of talk. The we're-gonna-be-big routine. Even as recently as a year ago I might have gone for it, played out the role as Nigel seemed to want me to; why of course, the biggest, best and most successful ever! Except. Except now, with the wisdom and pain that passes as experience I'm more into managing expectations mode, not that this seems the easy option with everyone around me reaching for the sky. Not with only the vaguest notion of how sincere, or how insane my client is. *The government, our friends.*

'Well, we can certainly be famous. You can guarantee that. Spend enough across the right media. We can get noticed, get inside our audience's heads. Develop enough scenarios, select the ones that get under the skin and maximise them; yes we can guarantee that. Where it goes from there is over to you guys.'

A twitch from Nigel. *Don't upset the Minister.* Just give him what he wants.

'You *can* guarantee a winning campaign. Simple as that. Right, Cal?'

There's about eighteen different levels of hidden code in what he's just said, and how he's said it, ranging from *just go with it*, to *what the fuck are you playing at*, and up to *don't fuck up your big moment on my watch* and way beyond.

'Listen,' I start back, addressing Minister Hynd, already sizing up his cross. 'We can get the messages out. We can create a great need, a wave of want for… Tranquillity, Togetherness… whatever. I'm only saying, *just* saying…'

The words stutter to a halt, just as I have their undivided attention. What *am* I saying, I wonder, slow motion in an azure blue ocean of choice gently lapping in my brain. I've halted because the magnitude of that choice is overwhelming. Everything I wanted, right there in front of me. And as I found the words to say what it was that was troubling me, I realised I was the only one in the world who could fix it. And that another great fucking fork in the road had just opened up. Should I become one of them; or leave quietly, do an adequate job and keep my distance? Because this would be the campaign to end them all, and I knew it right then.

'What's wrong?' demands Nigel Richards, as if I'm short-changing him.

'It's a big ask to make anyone turn to the government for salvation once they feel the yearning for some kind of solidarity, spiritual solidarity at that. Probably the last, least likely partner you could think of. Communication will be much better at creating the need than making the marriage.'

'But *not* impossible?' he prompts, digging to see what I've left hidden.

'Impossible? We will have to see. If you are asking how it might be done I can think of one possible way. Maybe the *only* possible way. If it works, we will have created a monster. Are we sure we could live with where it would take us?'

The last question aimed obviously and exclusively at our minister. Is he on the wavelength. Does he even care? He meets my eye but shows negligible intention to engage. Four of us in the room, who is getting it?

'So, not impossible then?'

And I turn back to Nigel, veering toward agitation, like I'm the fucking problem here, lowering the whole tone. Government brainwash is not an issue.

'We have a matrix, of sorts, of all our audience by demographic segment, by which I mean age, social class, stage in life, you name it, down one side… and we have twenty-odd scenarios listed down the other – situations where someone might feel alone, vulnerable, isolated. These have been developed through research. Expensive way to bring it along, but hey, who's counting? So we have ranked in order, for each segment, exactly what our audience fears the most, like walking a lonely street at night, being taken ill in a public place, being really alone, whatever... Then we bring those scenarios to life in script form so that they are recognisable for those we want to be... haunted by them. So that we amplify every inadequacy we expect our audience to feel. Of course we'll have to cut fast and loose with the rules and regulations on what we broadcast, but there are ways...'

'Too much detail,' cuts in my minder. 'The Minister doesn't need to know.'

'Okay... Strike that from the record,' I drawl, though the room proves immune to my humour.

'The genius bit...' I start again, spreading my hands in mournful glee, '... is that once we know the scenarios, we can predict the responses to them. From there, it's straightforward to construct our offer, our way out for them. We can offer a dialogue about how our audience *feels*. We can offer understanding... *the government, my friends.*'

Nobody gets it. Not least Nigel. '...Dialogue?' He frowns, almost apologetically to the others. 'How could we manage that on this scale?'

'Automate it.'

'What?... Press one for all the answers, two for some of the answers and reassurance, three for total reassurance...?'

'Nigel!' I shout, hand hitting the table top. 'Listen to me. For every scenario there are a set number of responses, by each audience segment. From those there are only a limited number of enquiries we could expect to receive – *where can I get help, why do I feel this way, am I the only fucking one* – if we've done our job correctly we will know the range and content before we even begin. We will have answers prepared for each. A matrix of responses, of dialogue. It's multi-dimensional. We take on the requests in whatever format, text, web, blog, call, and we set up automatic recognition and automatic response. On a fucking huge scale.'

'The whole country,' says a voice hitherto silent, hitherto detached from all of this. 'Everyone in our society, in meaningful conversation with government about how they *feel*?'

I turn to the Minister. He gets it. Oh yes he gets it. 'Exactly.'

'And the endpoint?' asks Nigel Richards, either on the outside or keen for us to understand he's on the outside. 'I mean, where do we go once we are locked into all of this, these exchanges with however many millions?'

'Nigel,' I groan, as my Minister nods silently. 'That engagement is enough, don't you see? They come to us in need. Everything else is irrelevant. Since when was dialogue not an end in itself?'

Wise words, greeted in silence. Silent assent, we are on our way. Detonation.

'Tell me how much it will all cost.'

Yes Mr Richards, I will name my price, whatever I choose to make that. Because now you've heard this you are in almost the same position as me. Pay to make it happen and do your best to control it, or move aside and watch someone else do it. Give over your nuclear bomb to someone who might be as responsible as you, or may be not.

'I'll get you a figure as soon as I can. It's likely the most costly part is the research into the dialogue paths. But that information, as they say, is priceless.'

Nigel looks to the Ministerial team, or Minister and boy helper. 'You will probably need to get a slot with the Prime Minister's team, Derek Rove and Jason Watson, at the Party office too. This is big. We need them on side.'

Again, he seemed far from happy at the prospect of running the hyper-ambitious campaign that he himself had pushed for. *This is big*, he had noted through clenched teeth. Unconventional. There was no sign of gratitude to his account director either, architect of the said extravaganza. We were carving out a future, step by heavy step, with few signs that this was a future any of us wanted, yet still drawn towards it all the same. An architect of need. I would create the desire, and offer up salvation from an unlikely source. Tabulate another matrix. The call and response that would have us all looking to government. For everything.

'I want to be the face to all of this. I don't see any other way.'

Carving out a future. Greig Hynd, Minister, superstar. This is where it begins to slip out of control. I've been allowed the luxury of musing on the mechanics for all of five minutes before our man takes us to a very different place. Nigel Richards wants to know where.

'I don't follow. Cal has most of the scenarios already worked out. The scripts and executions are tailored to each audience segment. It's their experiences that will be the face of the campaign. That's what makes it real enough to get the audience engaged. Unless I'm mistaken, Cal?'

Playing this back I can almost hear the panic in his voice. Control slipping, slipping so early.

'You're absolutely correct. I'm not sure there's room for anything else. After that the communication gets a little crowded, obscured. The government role is all in the response mechanisms, and that has to be a consistent voice.'

'Personalise it, Cal,' cuts in the Minister. 'I've seen it done. It will make the ads, the executions even more compelling, add an urgency to these dialogues we need. And we need everything we can possibly throw at this. I can't afford to try and then fall short. I've seen, first-hand, the extraordinary work of some people who are experts in this that we need to talk to, that you need to work with…'

'I'm not sure.' I try to stop him, my hand gripping the table. 'Let me try to work it out.'

He shakes his head. 'It could be incredible. Putting your talents and this together.'

'This?' asks Nigel Richards.

'Sea of Tranquillity,' he says, stating the obvious, stating his need. 'They do this. It's their expertise.'

'No,' I hear myself saying. 'No. No. No.' Louder, stronger.

'What's the problem?' demands the Minister, like it's *my* problem.

'I don't trust them. Their methods or their intentions. I cannot see how our campaign, which I have been led to believe is important to you, could withstand the blow to its credibility that would come through association with these…' I pause as my mind seeks out the appropriate, though acceptable, moniker; fuckheads? Amateurs? Nigel Richards fixes me with a stern stare. Watch yourself. '…These *people*.'

'I see. But I have seen their results, it's what we need, I have no doubt of that. But are you saying there is a reputational issue?'

My campaign slipping away. Already becoming our Minister's campaign.

'Greig. You must be aware, surely. I mean the turmoil they have created in our organisation, the baggage that goes with their contribution to our conferences?'

We all turn to the taciturn Bernie, a welcome, though unexpected, source of support. Turmoil, baggage? Snap, my friend. I'll match and raise.

'I know, Bernie, of course. But the *power* of what they did. If we can contain that… just get them on a more responsible professional footing…' Dr Hynd looks earnestly toward me at this point, meaning this as a compliment, a normal campaign. Too fucking kind, Minister.

'Don't you see?' he implores.

The silence should tell him his advisor advises no. But I make a contribution just to make sure.

'Where they come from, their whole agenda, is suspect. We cannot, should not, go near it.'

I've laid it on the line. Told it like it is. Put the Minister in his place. Now he does the same to me.

'I want it. I'll have it. How do I make it happen?'

He turns to his civil servant flunky. The man paid to make things happen. The man who normally turns to me. Not this time.

'Get them to run their own campaign. Separate but complementary. Same themes but different outcomes. Let them do it themselves so that we can distance when we have to, if we have to. But make sure it all adds up to the same thing.'

The Minister is taken with this scheme.

'We can do this?'

'We have done this. Funded campaigns through third parties. In fact, we already have these particular people working with one of our roster agencies.'

'Really?'

'Harlequin,' he confirms, in neutral tone, taking no satisfaction as all eyes return to the only Harlequin representative present. Another fork in the road, leave them to it, let them work it out, or stick with it, find some way of winning back control. Cover yourself.

'I'll find a way to make it work. If you get clearance from your Mr Rove and all the President's men. If we get to brief the Prime Minister. I want to know everybody's in for this, and all that will go with it.'

A smile from the Minister and his servant, reptilian smiles. Too easy for them. The wrong agreement. The wrong campaign. Spiralling away from me. Four men in a room, scoping the campaign? One man in a room, shaping the campaign. Two others content to just pull his strings. The cruel laboratory of Dr Hynd.

'You give us a plan to set this up and deliver the campaign as fast as is humanly possible,' he says, 'and I'll take you to the Prime Minister.'

Knock it up and you'll have your day with the top man. See what the fucking Wizard of Oz has to say about it all, as if he'll fucking help you.

CAMPAIGN LAUNCH MINUS 27 DAYS

Queensgate Serviced Apartments, Kensington, London

Greig turned each lock in order; top, middle and bottom, the sequence carried out in quick, ritualistic fashion. He then took the ten paces or so through the hall to the lounge/dining room area and switched the top light on and off twice before moving through and switching on the lamps, his signal to the waiting driver outside that all was well, he was safely installed for another night. He did not wave down as he had once done, when the routine was fresh, when he had felt guilty at being nested whilst the chauffeur had at least one more journey to make before he could feel the same. No wave down. Instead he watched his hands shuffle the piles of reading matter stacked on this dining table into a fresh, more symmetrical arrangement. More logical. Creating space for the new arrivals swiftly to follow from the depths of his briefcase. Without sitting, without even taking his coat off he began the new ceremony of dispensing the colour-coded post-its that would give the pattern to tonight's reading. Red for urgent, material importance, orange for information, lesser importance, green for background, unknown importance. Soon the colours were dancing before his eyes. Lighting up the room whose own colour code was limited to shades of magnolia; cream carpet with matching sofa, white glass table, white chairs, stainless steel console housing the inert television and cable installation. Down the hall, the same single bedroom too. White suites in bathroom and kitchen to complement the white-washed walls. There had been flowers in the now empty vase the day he had moved in, a gift from the landlords, a welcome offering. They had stood out like neon jewels over the course of the settling in week, even in their decaying state, killed mercifully by the recycled air of the heat control system he had yet to master.

A collection of coloured stickers all around him, representing work that would carry him deep into the night, ministerial reading, constituency reading, cabinet reading. There had to be those who had a talent for it all, he realised, must be those for whom it was an easier task, those who could genuinely discern the difference between the important and not so important, with or without coloured clues, rather than exhaust themselves by reading all as the same despite every effort otherwise. Decisions to be made, in theory. Decisions already made, the reality. The only choice he was now being asked to exercise was how to position what had always been decided. How to sell the bad medicine.

But there was a comfort in such exhaustion. No idle space left to wonder about his abandoned family, unpredictable mistress, unfathomable ministerial colleagues. Or even how he was going to pay the cost of running these households whilst serving his self-imposed exile in exorbitant, anonymous chic. All pushed out of his mind by the demands of the job and the homework he set himself to go with it.

He drew a glass of water from the kitchen tap and returned to the dining room table. Coat thrown across the opposite chair. A hand unbuttoning his collar, feet kicking off their shoes. The disagreeable hum of the ventilation system, though agonisingly below the threshold of legitimate complaint, resonating in his ears, the smell of the vanilla furniture polish he was sure they simply released with the same air conditioning system to create the illusion of a cleaning service that could warrant a rental surcharge, lingering in his nose. All fading into soft background focus as his eye returned to the two green post-its to his left. Background, importance unknown. To be read later, not now, not priority. His hand reached out all the same. The files he had asked for. He opened the first. *Harlequin Advertising*. Background, status, achievements. He found himself looking at a picture of a man he did not recognise. Peter Vesey. Chief Executive. Owner. CIO Roster Performance. Interest waning, he left it open, pushing it to his left, and picked up the other file. *Sea of Tranquillity*. Background. Agents, known activities. No pictures, though names he did not recognise. Turning the page, he scanned the list of activities and associates. There in black and white, a name he did recognise. Natasha Skacel, Campaign for Positive Mental Health. He took a mouthful of water and slumped into the chair. Importance unknown. He reached for a red sticker.

C DAY MINUS 24 DAYS

Harlequin International Communications Holdings, Harlequin House,

Warren Street, London

I wrote myself a checklist. Page one of a new workbook, a clean start. Top of the list was to speak with Vesey, get his understanding up to date. I couldn't think of any other way of making progress, given the Tranquillity aspect of this. Maybe he had seen this one coming, maybe it was his way of guaranteeing himself a piece of the action.

My Managing Director was out of the country again so I was happy to leave a message. *New client demands, biggest ever, seize the opportunity, briefing the guys, need you involved.* Calculated language. I wasn't going to let any of this be played back to me at any point in the future as incriminatory evidence. No way – written in notes to myself, rehearsed language. Company man. Team player.

Instinct told me that the digital, blog, dialogue side of the campaign would be a key front. Now it was all set to play I needed my own handle on how that might work, meaning endless technical tutorials staring at computer screens alongside our studio head, Kenny Chance. The detail, as well as the communal feel to the open-plan workstations, was strangely comforting, as was the politely reverential attitude of my teacher, probably delighted that such interest was being taken in his work.

'This is as big as it could ever be, Kenny, a world first. I've made promises of all the wonderful stuff we are going to deliver. Now we've got to figure a way of just doing that. Whatever it takes, new kit, new software, hired hands, you tell me and the studio gets it. Then you tell me how it works and how I can access it all. The dialogues will change right to the wire. The ads and segments, *YouTube* slots, they will all feed off each other once the thing goes live and we can see how it should evolve. Are you okay with this, are the guys up for it?'

A scratch of the head, semi-shrug, smile somewhere between determined grimace and match-winning elation from Kenny. *We'll do our very best.*

'Think we should gather the guys round, bring them in on this?'

He does, we do.

'Stop what you're doing guys, grab a coffee and gather round. Something you should hear.'

So it was that the first to know of the rush toward the campaign launch are the studio team, the only ones now in the entire agency I feel any kind of affinity with.

'Listen up guys, the revolution starts here, we're going to change how communication happens, we're going to make history. I need your help.'

Vesey called back, just as I'd finished the session. He was in Washington DC half a world away. He apologised for missing my call, caught in a pre-breakfast work-out in a hotel gym.

'Budget?'

'Still working it out, but it's an open book. They've approved a completely new approach so it's not as if they can cite any precedent; nobody in the world knows how much this will cost. I've got the studio looking at what upgrades they might need because it's vital they feel completely tooled-up to meet the challenge...'

More discreet smiles all around me. I'm playing to an audience Peter doesn't know we have.

'Whatever...' he muses. 'Get Hugh to run any costs by me first.'

'Of course. You won't believe how tight this is going to be. When are you back? We'll need your input on strategy.'

Dazzling him with the far-fetched and fictional notion that not only is his contribution sought, it might actually be useful.

'Give me two days.' He lunges for the bait. 'I'll move things round.'

'More Washington stuff? What's going on over there anyway?'

'New York associates of the people I've been seeing, complicated relationships. Takes time but I'm almost there.'

'Good,' I declared, wondering where the fuck 'there' was meant to be. I knew better than to ask and trigger another cascade of coded bullshit about international assignations.

'Two days,' he repeats solemnly. 'You do what you need to get started.

I'll need to see your plan when I arrive. I'll want a status meeting with CIO and the Minister. You should also fix up a face-to-face with the Sea of Tranquillity outfit.'

And there was me doing so well, basking in the silent applause of my workmates all around. And then, the tsunami from the other side of the Atlantic. Struggling to come up for air, kicking my feet off the desk, staggering to my feet. Summon the Minister to meet my idiot boss, is that how he thinks this works? Why don't I pull in the Prime Minister and Pope whilst I'm at it? He wants Tranquillity fingerprints all over our ticket to fame.

'Peter. I don't think you understand, maybe I should explain?'

'Just set it all up, Cal,' he decrees, cutting me short.

'*Set it up. Tranquillity*? I thought these assholes wanted nothing to do with me.'

I don't know how loud my voice gets but there's a silence at the end of the line matched by the one in the room. Buttons being pressed. Explosions in my head.

'Cal,' says a voice from across the world, sighing with faux patience that's about to faux expire. 'I mean for you to organise, through my PA, the meetings.'

Of course. I'll carve it up. Me and her, unstoppable, what a support team we make. I tried to sound calm.

'Okay Peter, understood. But whilst we're on the subject, can I ask how things are progressing on the litigation front with my friends? Any closer to bringing their case forward or are we in permanent suspense due to lack of fucking evidence?'

More silence, heavy silence, all around like I've just gone underwater.

'Cal. You need to drop this. Concentrate on the campaign. Let it go.'

'Me? I'm not the one making a complaint. Why don't *they* let this go, or is the innuendo too fucking appealing? Because that's all they've got, so they've got to keep pushing it or lose face. That's what it's all about, sound right?'

'Cal. Calm down. We are concerned about you. They are concerned about you.'

'Obviously. Assholes.'

'Cal,' says the voice of exasperation, mixing in his best well-you-asked-for-it tone. 'They have a piece of digital footage of you acting in a bizarre manner. '

My head suddenly re-surfaces. Fear and loathing.

'Footage? From where? Impossible.'

'Taken at their place, I believe, when you went round. Accidentally recorded on their web-cam that was just being set up.'

'Showing what?'

Exasperation.

'I don't know, Cal. They sent me the clip on email attachment but I haven't been able to open it. Not from here.'

They are concerned, about me, my state, presumably. So they send an incriminating clip to my boss. Too kind.

'Peter, you can't open it because there's nothing there. Everyone wants them in on the campaign, even the fucking Minister, yet they go out of their way to show they can't be trusted. This stinks.'

'Okay, Cal. You sound tired. I told you to drop it, for your own sake. I didn't appreciate the Minister's take on this, you should have told me. Set up the meetings. I'm not going to let this chance be squandered, understood?'

So the supposedly good news briefing from underling to global supremo about confirmation of the biggest, most ambitious, influential and lucrative campaign in any agency's history ends with the engineer of the whole fucking thing being admonished, spooked and humiliated. Nice work.

I cut the phone and scanned around. What was it like for you guys? Nobody would return my glance. Not the only one freaked. *Understand me, someone, it's not how it seems*, something is not right. Believe me, someone. I thought of Caroline and how much I missed her. A thought that made my eyes well up, underwater again. *Get out, out now*, away from this building, from London, and never go back. A fork in the road; go now, quick, a path back to sanity, or stay and see it out and all its dark consequences.

'Cal, are you okay, want to leave this for later?'

Kenny Chance is eyeing me with something approximating to concern. I realise he had been taking me through the intricacies of the digital age. Class dismissed?

'Kenny, hustle up a few of the IT crowd. Peter says there's an email attachment he wants me to access and look at. He needs to know what's on it. Can you organise a look at his inbox? I'll get his passwords from his PA downstairs.'

He looks back at me and knows I'm lying. A fork in the road for him too.

Leave it with me, I can't promise anything until I see what kind of file it is. Which email, from who, when? Questions, Kenny. I'll get your answers, you get me mine. Now I'm going to get the rest underway. There's no going back.

A blank sheet of paper in front of me. A runner dispatched to accounts to bring back the running job total of all agency expenses incurred since we last sent a catch-all invoice to the merry men of CIO. Some new headings on the sheet of paper; Digital Sequencing and Response, Dialogue Sequence and Derivation, Interface Network Set-up... The name of the game is to be creative yet plausible at this stage, the more headings the better. Numbers everywhere, scrawled down, then rounded up, then doubled. Instant judgements made on how far to 'push it'; ours to charge whatever we choose, but at what stage does it stray into the criminal, to fraudulent? Not if the headings are clever enough, keep them coming.

On cue, a presence materialises to my side. Hugh McHover, live, in person, dispatched from the basement via an instruction relayed around the world by satellite.

'Cal, everything okay?... Peter says he wants your new forecast before his next set of meetings in America. Anything I can do?' For this you can read that Hugh's been given a rocket to extract the data from me forthwith, on pain of death.

'Here,' I say, handing over my work. 'First batch estimates. Get them formatted. Get the cover note typed, you'll see that we're telling CIO that unless we hear otherwise fairly urgently we will have to assume the estimates are accepted in principle, and open to us to invoice close of play today given the urgency of the campaign launch. Unless you hear otherwise from me or them by five, go ahead and invoice to these numbers, get the money in. As for profit forecast, assume a margin on that of eighty percent and we won't be disappointed. Tell the client, and Peter, we'll reconcile the whole lot later.'

Hugh appears dazzled by my assertiveness and willingness to give him what he wants, staring at the note in awe. Either that or he's struggling to read my handwriting.

'Peter will want to approve it before we invoice.'

Of course he would. 'These are advance invoices based on estimates. Tell him we reserve the right to reconcile the estimates up or down dependent on actual cost later. He can fuck the figures all he wants afterwards. Meantime, get on with it.'

I say this in such a way as to give him no option other than to do just that, and it seems as if he is happy to do so, heels almost snapping together in salute and acceptance of orders.

Kenny Chance waits until he is well clear before silently pushing a memory stick towards me across the worktop.

'It's called File One, the only moving image clip on the stick.'

'Have you looked at it?'

'Only to see it plays. The first few seconds. You at a desk.'

'What was the problem with formats?'

'Encoded, encrypted. Easy to unravel, don't know why they bothered.'

'So why did they? Was it a token effort at secrecy, pretend secrecy?'

Kenny shrugs.

'Easy enough to sort. Anything else?'

I thank him and get up to leave, a pat on his shoulder by way of gratitude.

New priority. Move out of the studio, avoid the lift, taking the back stairs down to the intermediate levels of the building. Wondering which office to use to view the mystery evidence, thinking of anywhere secure. A room on the ground floor. Head there fast, launch down the stairs.

Spiralling down, spinning towards an empty room, landing in a heap. Cursing at the time the inert computer takes to drag itself to life, punching in password and username to get it to play my tunes. Minutes pass by before a play icon is offered on the screen. I stab the cursor to cue it up, checking there's no sound at the door. The clip begins, untitled, mysterious, poor picture quality, maybe something to do with the decoding of the file, or something to do with the lighting of the original piece. Grainy muffled sound. A man at a desk, a woman talking to him. I can recognise the messy layout of Nirvana House. The woman, recognisable by outfit and hairstyle, is of course Angela Filmstar. What is of note here is how tactile she is with the guy at the desk, leaning on his shoulders to explain the computer programme, pats on the back as she exits the scene. He's awkward with this, fidgety. The guy is left alone, peering at the computer screen. He is in a white shirt and jeans, my clothes, my posture. I'm suspicious enough of anything to do with these people not to accept at first inspection that it is actually me; indeed everything on show could have been part of a set up to *imply* rather than *prove* – no face shot of the subject, no introduction to show who it is. On the computer before me I can hear the vague rumblings of the soundtrack in the montage I had watched in this same setting.

I watch the figure on screen show no reaction. Instead he surveys the office, glances to his watch, rubs his chin whilst keeping a half-hearted eye on the action before him. Gradually though, he seems more engaged, tuned in to the screen, to the exclusion of anything around him. He begins to slump forward, head in hands as if drugged, hypnotised by what's playing before him. Then the sound turns eerie; a grumbling wailing sound that instinct tells me is coming from the man not the machine he's watching. He stands, jerks to unsteady feet, begins to walk away, staggered steps, backward, before being drawn forward, downward again. His moaning is louder, and now there's a form to it. It's hard to make out his words, once more I try to increase the volume output of the computer and strain to discern anything other than the hiss coming out of the speakers. *Dad... Dad? Dad!* are his words.

Shit. Uncomfortable viewing. This is like watching a child being abused for viewing pleasure, this is someone else's distress as entertainment. Fuck them. But it could be anyone, any victim. I search for the stop mechanism, I've seen enough and the darkness of it is pulling me in.

And then, captured on camera, the return of Angela Manipulator arriving with two mugs of hot drink. Quickly put down as the man at the screen, the whimpering, sobbing man at the screen, turns to her and the camera finally finds its focus. He turns and falls into her comforting arms. And the man is me.

CAMPAIGN LAUNCH MINUS 22 DAYS

Portcullis House, Westminster, London

Bernie pulled himself to his feet as Greig came into view. The two locked eyes as was the new habit, the junior silently apologetic for his very presence at such a late hour, the latter performing an instant read of his colleague's countenance. Good news, bad news, it could only be the latter, why else the ambush?

'Bernie. You're stalking me. You know I could have you arrested.'

'I know… I'm insatiable,' murmured Bernie, in an only partial attempt to meet Greig's dry humour. Bad news. Very bad news.

'Okay. You have something to tell me, can't wait until tomorrow? We need a room or can we do it in the car?'

'No,' said Bernie quickly; instinctively, realised Greig. The briefings in the back of the Ministerial car had been the norm for a month or so, all based on an offer of a lift home. Problem was, as Greig now saw, these ten-minute briefings would turn into full blown hour-long sessions as he prompted his young colleague for reassurance, background, gossip or pushback as was his mood. All of it one way; a dependency, in the absence of any other source of comfort.

He was burning him out and he knew it would have to stop, but how? Especially when, as tonight, he was playing two roles; the messenger, there to be shot for bearing bad news, and part of the team falling victim to the very same news. Young Bernie. How much longer would they be able to call him that given the way events were ageing him, ageing them all?

Greig waited for an alternative offer. If not in the car then where?

'My office?' he prompted. 'We could be there in ten.'

Bernie shook his head, exhausted. 'Okay,' said Greig. 'Canteen, downstairs should be deserted. It's ten o'clock for god's sake.'

Minutes later he found himself dragging two chairs free from a corner table in the almost empty canteen, two other groups on the near horizon having similarly wearied end of play debriefs. Neither, he thought, likely to be as ominous or heavy as his was almost certain to be. A strange kind of jealousy began to take hold as his eye lingered on the other disparate parties. *Swap your problems for mine, right now.*

'What have you got, Bernie?' He settled down into his chair. 'Give me it straight.'

'I had a visit from Jason Watson. You know him better than me, I guess.'

Greig nodded for him to continue.

'He thought it important for us – your guys, he put it – to know that things are not particularly good. That there are bad vibes out.'

Perhaps not urgent news after all, more a statement of the obvious.

'All done in a friendly manner,' shrugged Bernie. 'Like he's doing us a favour by passing it on. All the same, the inference was that time is running out, that if we've got something big up our sleeve, then we've got to pull it out fast.'

'And you think this comes all the way down from the Prime Minister?'

'There's something else, Greig.' Bernie lowered his voice, broke his eye contact.

'What?'

'The reason we've got to come out with something, and fast.' Bernie glanced up. 'You ready for this? You're not going to like it.'

'Go on.'

'According to whoever told Jason Watson, and he said that the Prime Minister had intervened to stop it, for now…'

'What?'

'…There's something about to blow up in the media about you and Natasha… She's talked to someone who's talked to someone and they are going to go big on it. Her take. Inside story on…' Bernie halted again, clearly struggling, '… the whole thing.'

'I see,' said Greig, reaching out to pat him on the arm and pulling back. 'And the Prime Minister has stopped this?'

'He's bought time. Promised exclusives elsewhere to whatever editor, channel, newspaper. But delayed rather than stopped it, so I understand.'

'Thanks Bernie, I appreciate you telling me…'

What would Natasha have said? It was already public that Greig had separated from his wife, was living alone.

'What are we going to do, Bernie?' He smiled, the impossibility of it all giving little other option. Bernie clenched his teeth to mimic the gesture. Another shrug.

'How long until the advertising campaign gets going?'

'You tell me. Weeks? Have we got that? Or should we just go before then?'

'*Go?*'

'Resign. It's a disaster, isn't it?'

Greig saw Bernie's head nodding, as he stood up, pulling himself to his feet like a drunk man.

'Yeah,' he mumbled, 'why not?'

'What do you mean?' Greig threw a hand out to grab him by the shoulder. *Don't leave me.* A hand that was instantly brushed off.

'Who the fuck are you, Greig Hynd, will you tell me that?'

Bernie's voice was loud enough to draw attention from the security guards at the far side of the empty dining area. Greig cringed as he waved them down.

'Who *am I?* What do you mean, Bernie?' He tried to keep his own voice calm and reasonable. Friendly even. The reality though, was that he felt like shouting too, like screaming at everyone and everything. But not at Bernie.

'*I mean...*' came the reply, volume only slightly down but with an added intensity to compensate, 'I mean what do you *stand* for, what do you still stand for, what did I see in you, why did I work for you, why did we do it for it to end up like *this*, I mean...' he continued, staring at Greig, voice almost a gravelly snarl. 'Are you, were you always just empty, a fraud, a fucking great sham we all fell for?'

Something I fell for. Greig rubbed his eyes whilst he considered the accusation. Maybe it had all been a delusion, bound to run head-first into reality at some point.

'Thanks for that.'

'I'm sorry, Greig.'

'*Minister,*' cut in Greig.

Bernie looked to him, obviously wondering if he was serious, Greig deciding to give him no clues. He had meant it as a joke, but now was not sure either. *Thanks for that.* Good to have your chain pulled from time to time, was that the instruction from Jason Watson, to go in hard, wake him up? Or was the outburst all genuine, from the heart. From the man who had once saved his life.

'Minister,' he repeated, solemnly. 'As in Minister caught with pants down. As in *only ever* Minister caught with pants down.'

A flicker of a smile from the younger man. 'I know, but you Greig, of all people, given what we were trying to achieve…'

'Believe me. I'm sorry. I'm not proud of it. Too damn stupid for words, and beyond words to express what it's cost me… I'm sorry.'

'So, are you going to quit?' A rub of the eyes once more. Deep breath.

'No. This has to be worth one shot. One last shot. And I have to make as big a bang with that shot as I possibly can, not because of the Party or because we're running out of time… but because everyone's unhappy. That's what I get now. All this running around, meetings, deadlines, agendas, politics… ever see anyone happy? It's going to take an explosion to change that. A nuclear explosion. I don't know if they all realise it but that's what they'll get.'

'You trust these guys, the CIO people, Harlequin Agency… to deliver that?'

'They can be led somewhere. They just want someone else to shoulder the risk. As much part of the problem as the solution, but we can crank them up, try not to give them too much time to think… What do you think?'

'Do you really want to know?'

Greig nodded. 'Of course.'

'I don't know them, don't trust them, don't even like them. Don't know what they believe in, if anything, what they are after. And it depresses me that our future ends up in the hands of people with such high opinions of themselves but who are clearly making it up as they go along…'

'More frauds… phonies?'

A tired smile. 'Exactly. And we don't have much credibility left, Greig. One last shot, you're dead right.'

Greig leaned forward, stretching out both arms to grip Bernie's shoulders, pulling him close, almost touching forehead to forehead.

'Then let's make it count,' he said, softly. 'Make it count.' Mantra-like. 'Let's fix a launch, but through our people. Surely we've got some credibility left there? Another conference, something big, through the alliance. That's who I am, so let's go back to that for a little while. Can you get that one rolling, a one-off extraordinary meeting to celebrate the campaign. Three weeks from now, they'll give us that, they'll have to. And the agency will just have to deliver what it can within that.'

Bernie stood straight, breaking off.

'Okay. Minister.'

C DAY MINUS 19 DAYS

Harlequin Advertising Sub-Division Management Meeting,

Agency Boardroom

All eyes are on me. I hold up my agenda. Item one, Research. Item one, *what the fuck did they do to me, who was that crying man?* It had been a rough night, watching the clip, over and over. I look up to the faces around the table. *Help me.*

'Research. Harry. Campaign runs as previously planned. Our campaign that is. We're obliged to run a support campaign in parallel though...' All eyes on me, *help me.* 'Sea of Tranquillity, and frankly, I'm trying to fight that and if we run out of time, too bad. You should be aware though that there might be some supplementary elements or scenario testing for their part of the action.'

I could have been speaking in another language given the blank looks round the table. Still, no option other than to plough onwards.

'For our part, the major new element is the brief for follow-up dialogue with these respondents who take up the email or blog channels after seeing the ads – that means crunching all the potential avenues those conversations might follow, by each audience segment, by each ad. Another layer on the matrix. We need to get a lot of focus groups organised, and quickly.'

'*More groups?*' asks Harry, showing he's grasped at least the barest essentials. 'How many groups?'

'I was hoping you'd work it out, as Planning Director.'

'I'll need to speak to CIO. See what they have in mind.'

'It's for *us* to call, Harry. That's what they *pay* us for.'

'I can't do it.'

I looked to him. *The plan.*

'We'll take this outside the meeting, Harry. You can go, I'll hook up when we're done on the other points. For the rest of you, be aware that our planning resource will be stretched tight for the next couple of weeks. Anything anyone can do to help... Thanks meantime, Harry.'

I watch him not knowing whether to exit, as instructed. He swithers in his seat.

'*Go.* You might as well check availability for groups. We need to know, urgently.'

I wave him out of the room as Nick seeks clarification.

'When is it all due?'

'Three and a half weeks. Launch at a big event they've got planned. A mass rally of the faithful, Greig Hynd acolytes ready to spread the word. We go live then for two months.'

'Three weeks? I thought it was up to us to advise the earliest launch date.' Nick's voice is full of anguished outrage but his hands stay clear of his hair.

'You were right as of yesterday. As of this morning, my seven-forty am call, we're on in three and a half weeks with whatever we've got by then.'

'But this is *out* of control,' counters Nick. 'Three weeks? How can they expect quality in that timeframe?'

'This is our chance, our opportunity. If we tell them we're not capable, they'll share out the load with other roster agencies.'

'Maybe they should. I don't know how the digital boys can cope. Maybe we should share it around, let someone else suffer.'

At which point Mary turns to Nick. 'Digital are actually quite up for it. They're checking on additional specialist freelance but are confident they can cope with most of it in-house.'

Support. Imagine that. Thank you, Mary.

'You've been talking to the studio without going through me? Without the courtesy of bringing me in first?' A flurry of hands does horrible things to Nick's mane before it shakes regally back in shape. 'I can't work like this. I'm going to call Peter.'

'Nick, make whatever calls you have to. We'll take this out of the meeting meantime.'

'Not a brief, not an explanation. Not even the grace to tell me what's going on. Out of control,' states Nick, icily, looking for takers.

'I said we'll take it out of the meeting.' For the first time, my voice is raised. *What did they do to me?* A moment's silence follows.

'Sea of Tranquillity?'

'What about it, Nick?

'Care to explain, who, what, why, or anything?'

'I have no intention of going into the background history, the whole story, nor of defending or justifying what they do. We've been asked to work with them and Peter's keen we fulfil that. *How*, I haven't figured out yet. We'll just have to…'

'Take it out of the meeting?'

'Good call, Nick. Why not?'

'My god,' he mutters, loud enough for broadcast. 'What's the point?'

'What's that, Nick?'

'I said, what's the point, what do we get for all this?'

'We get paid for it. It's our job. Why we are here.'

'How much.'

I shift in my seat. 'Too early to tell.'

The shark senses blood. 'Really. Do you agree, Hugh?'

It's the bean counter's turn to swivel awkwardly. Drawn to the tentative offer of some support, repelled by the need to share the financials. 'Well yes and no,' he replies, helpfully. 'I've formatted the estimates Cal gave me yesterday, but I'm not sure we should be forwarding them to the client.'

'Why not, can I see?' To my dismay Hugh slides his paper over the desk.

'I wonder if they are excessive.' He watches Nick read through figures, absorbing the noughts. Noughts and commas.

'Cal, you can't be serious.'

From the man who demanded why.

'I don't think any of you have ever got that with scale and ambition successfully executed, comes reward. Simple as that. And this is new ground we're breaking, there's risk and reward in that too. The money is only part of it.'

Nick, Mary and Harry had gathered round, straining to read the same information. Incredulous all, nobody listening. *Out of control.*

I leant across the table, snatching the paper back without apology.

'Maybe you're right, Hugh. Maybe there's a typing mistake or two in the figures. I'll speak to you about it later.'

'How much of that do we get to see when this is all over and done?'

'You mean we as in you guys rather than the agency?'

'As in *pay* and *bonus*. Shared reward for all the pain.'

I nod and make to speak. *Shared pain.* 'Good question. Take it up with Peter.'

I stood and walked wearily to the door, heading for some solitude.

What did they do to me? I replay the status meeting. Not quite the victory parade that would have been the gig in any other agency. *The plan.* I think about the need for a plan and wonder why not? Make up for lost time.

Up and back to the boardroom, entering to find they are all still in there. Hot news this. The post-meeting wash-up lasting longer than the meeting itself.

'Harry, we need to talk.'

'Sure, we said we would. I think we should.' Harry looks to the others as he says this like it's code for something, an agreed policy.

'You guys okay with this?' I ask, with all the nonchalance I can muster. They take the hint and begin to shuffle herd-like to the door.

'Can I see you when you're finished?' asks Nick, gravely, resolutely. You're-in-for-it, he says in so many non-words. *Sure. I'll give you a call. You're next.*

The door closes on the last of them. Harry turns, he can see I'm angry and he's awesomely scared now that it's just me and him.

'When *is* Peter back, Cal?'

'Don't know. Why?'

'There's a lot of confusion about. That's all.'

'You confused?'

'Well yes… I mean, no. I suppose I get affected the same as everyone else.'

'How can I clarify things for you, Harry?'

'In terms of what?'

'In terms of stopping your confusion. I could explain, again, what we need to get done by when, what we need from the groups, what we are trying to achieve, is that the issue?'

Harry steadies himself. 'It can't be done, Cal. It's not possible.'

'Too much? Too soon? Too loose?… Help me here Harry, why can't it be done?'

'I don't know… All of it. It's impossible.'

'So you are sure it *can't* be done, but, as you say, you don't know *why*. And all you want me to say is I agree and I'll call everything off and then there will be no confusion, is that it?'

Harry draws his face tight, one great nervous twitch. Incapable of thinking about anything other than getting out of here.

'Harry.' I soften my voice to make one last effort. 'We are going to get these groups organised, delivered and processed in the time we've got, whatever it takes, whatever it costs. We need to start right away. Will you do this?'

'It will take three weeks just to recruit the groups.'

'Then we will hijack someone else's groups. Are you going to try?'

'It's too rushed Cal, doesn't feel right...'

'Harry!' I shout. 'I don't know whether you get this, but here it is. It will be done, with you, or without you. I am giving you a clear instruction, will you do it?'

'Doesn't feel right Cal, I can't...'

'Then *I'll* have to do it.'

'When's Peter back?'

I let his question hang. Leave it out there, hovering above us before it vanishes, evaporating into the stale air. Enough.

'It's over Harry, We're at the end of the line.'

'Over?' He's slightly brighter.

'Over. You're fired. Go.'

He smiles, disbelief bringing an empty joy that lasts a microsecond. 'You cannot be serious. You don't have the authority...'

'Over,' I say, standing up. 'I'll get a letter drawn up, out tonight. You should go now, think up a back story, say you've resigned, whatever... Thank you for your contribution to Harlequin, we can work out the severance...'

The platitudes tumbled out, I found myself on the verge of saying sorry, it had to end, or sorry it's like this. But I wasn't sorry, and he wasn't listening. *Over.* I was already thinking about the work I now had to do, looking forward. I thought of offering my hand, but he beat me to the door, moving with uncharacteristic conviction. Not even saying goodbye.

Out with one, in with another. Enter Nick, the mighty Nick Craig, sensing his moment, arriving to arrest the evil, to bring order back to the land of Harlequin.

'What have you said to Harry?' No problem with eye contact this time. Nick has been charging himself for this: rehearsing it outside, anxious for me to feel the intensity of this, his signature moment.

'I told him,' I say quietly, gesturing for him to take a seat rather than pace around, '...told him that... that's it. I am letting him go.'

'Are you telling me you've *fired* him?'

'I told him if he wouldn't do his job then he would have to go, so, yes, fired.'

'Cal, he had serious concerns…'

'That he couldn't explain. I've been through this Nick, done it. Got the T-shirt. How many times have you told me he's rubbish, that he should be cleared out? I do it and suddenly it's an issue. Are we done? I've work to do.'

'I don't like it.'

'What did you want me for?' My hand slaps the wood in front of me.

'You spoke to the studio,' he starts, quietly, ominously, as if speaking of something so heinous it can only be whispered. 'Briefed them without telling me, without telling me before, during or even after. Leaving me out. Removing me.'

'Nick.' Hand up, guilty. 'I get the point. Your invitation must have got lost in the post. I apologise. There's a lot on, got carried away. I was there, the guys were there… Zap. Next thing I knew, I was talking to them.'

'And what the fuck are you doing up there Cal? You know you are making yourself a laughing stock with this one-of-the-boys lark. Feeling the pressure are we? Needing some brotherly love?…'

A creative talent, Nick, for sure. Hit the nail on the head, what do you want me to say? If he had paused in any way I might have gone for it, opened up.

'You can forget about it,' he raged, impetuously. 'You're a distraction to the team. Clear off somewhere else where you are welcome. Not in my department, not in *my* studio.'

What's the strategy here, I wondered. Go in heavy, offend me, provoke me into something that can be used in evidence later? Or is he just being reckless, stupid, determined to play out these big scenes with a big voice, for big stakes.

'I'll think about my office location later. I'm sorry if I am a distraction to the boys. I'll speak with Kenny. All the same, there's work to be done, and fast. You need to hook up with the digital guys on where they are at. I'll get weaving on the research timetable and when we can expect outputs, obviously I'll give you as much time as possible to work around the revised briefs that come from that.'

A shake of head and hair. Vigorous shake. A this-can't-be-true shake, hands over ears.

'Cal... Cal... No. *Forget* that. None of this is going to happen. I refuse to do any of it until this whole mess is sorted out. I'll wait for Peter.'

At which point I smile, without knowing why, this being hardly great news. I'm starring in *Déjà Vu* – the movie, all over again.

'Are you refusing to work?'

'Re-briefs to briefs that never existed to start with, impossible deadlines, lack of budget, objectives... *Harry*... want me to continue?' he asks.

'Yes. Please do. What is stopping you from working? I'm warning you, we don't have time for this. If you won't do it someone else will have to, and that cannot be good for you Nick, think about it...'

'Not good, yeah? You going to fire me too, is that the threat?'

'If you are refusing to work, to input as Creative Director to our biggest ever creative campaign then you put yourself in danger. Understand?'

'Are you threatening me?'

An uber-rhetorical. The kind of thing you hear yourself saying when you are, indeed, thinking of the movie. For are-you-threatening-me read how-dare-you-threaten-me, or I'm-beyond-your-threatening-me.

'Are you refusing to work to explicit instructions on our urgent campaign for our most important client?'

'Are you threatening me?' he repeats in B-movie growl, giving his question higher billing than mine.

'I'm not threatening, I'm asking. Are you going to work with me on this?'

He fixes me in the eye. This is way beyond the normal posturing. I haven't seen this look many times before. He genuinely hates me. The real thing.

'I'm not working with you on anything right now. Go fuck yourself.'

I wonder if he knows how much this will cost him. I feel almost sad for him.

'Nick, are you resigning?' Things are getting clearer now. I relax into the endgame. No pleasure here, no nervousness either.

'I'm waiting for Peter, I'll hear what he has to say.'

Already mapping it out in my head. How to get through everything within the four weeks, without a Creative Director. Without his input, for sure, without the friction, or aggravation that goes with it. Instant calculation; I'm ahead.

'Doesn't work like that. I'm sorry it has to end this way. I'll get a letter to you...'

'Hey… wait a minute…' he spits, like we're off script here. '…You *cannot, possibly* be serious… I want a meeting with the Management Board, a full and frank discussion about where all of this mess is heading before you…'

I tune out and begin planning, thinking through the sequences. Research on dialogues. Amends to existing scenarios as a result of new inputs. Maybe some new scenarios scripted and shot. Assume I have one creative team per scenario all the way through. I'll need eighteen teams of copywriters and art directors. It will have to be freelance. Mary from Traffic will have contact numbers. Set up now. I stand up. We don't have time.

'Fired, Nick. It's over.'

That look again, together with a stillness. Not how it was to be played, not at all, waiting for stage direction, waiting for a line to bring it back on track, the crowds, galleries and committee tribunals that he wanted. Safer ground.

'I'll get a lawyer,' he mutters, can't-quite-believe-this-is-really-happening style.

'Do what you have to Nick, and I'll do what I have to.' I'm walking out as I say this. There's no time to wait. The *real* thing, from Nick. Shit.

CAMPAIGN LAUNCH MINUS 18 DAYS

Queensgate Serviced Apartments, Kensington, London

Greig cleared a space amongst the files on the dining table for the new pile, the polythene bag hitting down with a dull thump. He'd bought every title, and all its supplements, magazines, DVDs and free add-ons for just the one story, his first task would be to fillet down the stash to just that; the relevant pages.

He had been the first customer of the day at the newsagent's store. Self-conscious, anxious, but alone in the shop. That had been a relief. If the vendor recognised him he didn't let it show. Maybe six o'clock on a Sunday morning was too early for anyone's brain to be in full functioning mode, except for those who hadn't slept, who had been counting down the minutes, surfing online for the first hits of the story he was now confronting in print. A collection of titles on the counter. A metre deep. His face on the cover of some of them. His ministerial face, not the lined, unshaven one that offered the money for them. Bizarre, he thought. Not making the connection, or too polite to mention. *That's me, yes, me they are writing about.* Today's infamous man.

A mouthful of the hot, black, strong stuff to fortify him for the trials ahead. Then into it, ruthlessly. News sections to one side, everything else jettisoned into the sack, barely stopping to flinch at the headlines as he did so; *Minister of Very Well-being!, New Government Sex Scandal, Calls for Minister to Go Over Affair, My Saintly Lover by Minister's Aide.* Another drink, another pause. *Minister's Shame.* My shame, he thought. So much for the containment strategy. So much for keeping Natasha happy. They had never thought of the possibility that she might be too damn happy and that this would be the problem. Three days ago, the word had reached him that it was all brewing and then as each day passed, a new intensity to it all. First the advice to say nothing, keep a low profile. Then the holding statement diligently prepared by the government's media team, a statement to say he would be making no statement. Then a revised statement, speaking of his regret and sorrow. *I regret the distress these events may have caused to loved ones and colleagues and do not seek to defend the inappropriate nature of aspects of the relationship.* Written by strangers, by committee or generated onscreen by computer. Microsoft Public Remorse version 3.1. Now the final stage, other ministers being drafted in to speak on his behalf, to articulate the same remorse and talk up the achievements of the government. Defended by more strangers, his role to keep out of it, to ignore it. How it works. They had told him. His case would be handled personally by the new head of Government Media Relations. Scanning the words dancing around him he realised they had no better idea of how to handle it than he did; careers built on the notion of media *relations* as if there was some kind of strategy and control in place. Media *reaction* more likely. Head of Media Delusion.

His eye stopped on a tabloid inside page; a picture of Natasha, caught well, smiling and vivacious, taken at some awards ceremony, low-cut and shimmering. A picture of his wife and son; a blurred shot, looking suspiciously at the camera pointed at them, ushering the boy through the gate he recognised as the specialist clinic for his once-a-week assessment. *Wronged woman* was the visual inference. *Anxious* woman realised Greig, woman wondering what the hell was going on, why her privacy was being so publicly invaded. *Innocent* woman.

The despair he felt reading through the various accounts, and their various versions of the details, and the opinion pieces on the details, and the opinion on the opinion pieces which revisited the shocking detail with such relish, was mixed with a professional curiosity that the varying accounts could draw such conclusive diagnoses of him, his ambitions, abilities, and shoe size from the barest of facts. And all of it contradictory. From what? A woman he had made love to a handful of times had called a friend of hers, presumably when drunk and lonely, or high and joyful, and spoken of her love for a man in a senior job with whom she had a clandestine, and therefore difficult, unfulfilled relationship. She had described her dream of making that relationship, and by extension, him, fulfil all of its/his potential; this being an exciting prospect because a) he was a wonderful guy, and b) he had a big job to do, which was to change society's relationship with happiness. And therein, he saw, only too graphically, right on the pages in front of him, the irony. The pages that labelled him everything on a scale from manipulative seducer to hapless romantic victim, from shrewd political operative to a naïve amateur out of his depth, dead man walking to the great last hope of the Party. He was everything from point to point and every point in between, wrong and out of place in every last one of them. And poor Natasha. His mind lingered on her photograph once more, fixing on her face, for once without the usual guilt. No, this time a different guilt entirely. Poor Natasha, he realised, she didn't stand a chance.

C DAY MINUS 17 DAYS

Milestone Hotel, Kensington, London

I get a call on the Sunday, nominally a day off, but a day I'm in at Harlequin all the same. In early, from seven in the morning to get on top of everything. The call comes in around eight thirty. Where are you? he asks. No *good morning, how's tricks, are you okay?* None of it. Where are you, specifically; so that when I say the Agency it's not enough, I have to give a room reference for it to be worthwhile information. Are you alone, anyone with you? *Well, yes; who the fuck else would you expect to be here keeping me company?* The voice relaxes slightly. I think we'd better meet, he says, I'm back in London. Not at the agency, not a good move right now. And then I get the instructions as to where I find him and when.

Vesey was installed in a smart coffee lobby of some five-star apart-hotel-suite in Kensington. Sitting waiting, peering into his laptop screen at the corner table, clad in duty-free Ralph Lauren polo shirt and slacks. Didn't seem pleased to see me, despite the speed of response to summons.

'So,' he said, addressing the screen, its graphs and figures proving impossibly compelling, easily more deserving of his executive attention than the unshaven fidgeting presence in jeans and white linen slumped opposite. 'Want to tell me what the fuck's been going on?' Swear words from Peter, a man who never swears.

'What do you do to get a coffee round here?' I look around. No sign of service other than a concierge dressed like a military dictator of some fantasy Latin American state, busy pointing at suitcases and taxi doors waiting outside.

'Is there a bar or is it all done telepathically?'

'What's that?' he replies, still locked to the computer.

'Why are we here, Peter?'

'I have a meeting, less than an hour. Then a flight to catch. Then another meeting and back here. You'd rather be someplace else?'

'Probably.'

'Tough. Want a drink? They'll find you. Meantime, talk. And, thanks for warning me about Nick and Harry.'

This is sarcasm, of course.

'They been in touch?'

He folds down the screen and offers a sarcastic eyebrow over the top of it.

'What did they say?' Correcting myself. 'What did *you* say?'

'Nothing. Why do you think we're meeting here?'

Precisely. So that you can keep your options open, hide from them.

'Actually,' I say, settling into my chair, 'I quite like this place, be even nicer if you could get a pot of coffee.'

Peter waves imperiously to the concierge who gives back a quasi-fascist salute. Within seconds a waiter is bearing down on us, taking the order before he even reaches the table. Peter returns his gaze to me. *Speak*, it says, *explain*.

'A Minister in free-fall looking to our campaign to achieve a career-saving miracle. A deadline of three weeks, major launch and some kind of mass rally to re-ignite the cause. Nigel Richards wondering aloud if he should spread the workload to other roster agencies. Me trying to push through as many quotes and estimates as possible before some kind of guillotine comes down to halt everything. Reassuring everyone left right and centre that we can deliver all this, break new ground, and change the entire country's psyche. Stopping Harry and Nick from saying the opposite.'

'You fired them.'

'I had no choice. They weren't just being difficult. They weren't just being slow. They were looking to block the entire thing. You want them back?'

'Get the campaigns sorted.'

'With them?'

'Get the campaigns sorted, delivered, on time. Whatever that takes. I'll need to check if you've left the agency exposed by how you got rid of them, procedures and the rest, but for now I just want you to do the business. Understood?'

'It's what I was doing this morning before I was so rudely interrupted.'

A pause. Laptop powered down, folded and placed in his case. He stops and stares at me, his expression neutral. He could be my doctor. My teacher. A mildly disappointed godfather.

'How are you, Cal? You look like shit.'

'How do you expect me to look? I'm working every waking hour, have you any idea of the scale of this, the things I have to carry in my head? The nonsense going on at the Agency. Do you even want to know?'

As is the nature of these things, I didn't realise I was angry until I heard myself screaming. It must take an effort to keep his face frozen like that, with everyone turning round to watch, but he manages.

'I know it's tough. I know it's heavy. At the same time it kind of goes with the territory you were so eager to have. Stick with it for a week or two and it will all resolve, one way or another. Too late to stop now. No turning back, understood?'

His idea of a pep-talk. As useful as an accordion for the deaf. *You look shit but have to keep going. It might all turn out fine.* I'm angry. Angry, angry, angry.

'Who is still being awkward?'

'Hugh's refusing to issue the invoices. He's been moaning to everyone about excessive costs and poor detail breakdown, cash flow… you name it. I always thought the answer to cash flow was to get the money in but seemingly not.'

Abrupt change of expression from Peter. Now it's him that's shouting. A nice reversal of roles, except to the watching world it's as if he's about to punch me.

'One last chance!' he threatens. 'Give him one last chance Monday morning. Tell him it's my absolute order. If he refuses, he goes.'

I'd fired the wrong people, or maybe we were all just getting a taste for it.

'Peter,' I reply, assuming his previous guise of the rational against the raving. 'We have a schedule with CIO that states all our invoices have to be signed off by the Finance Director. That's why I'm stuck.'

He pulls uncomfortably close. So close I can smell his breakfast croissant.

'Absolutely. You sack him and do it yourself in the absence of a Finance Director, you become de facto Financial Chief. Then you call CIO and ask them to send a letter of guarantee for the payment, in total. We can't be financially exposed over this, they have to understand.'

Them and me both. Letter of guarantee? New one on me, in a world where there is no safer, more guaranteed debtor than government.

'You're not worried about whatever signal they might take from it?'

'…Just get the fucking letter out!'

The crowd in the foyer halt in mid-stride. Voices suddenly hush. The concierge arrives. *Everything alright?* Peter flicks an arm in his direction to send him back, the gesture ignored. *Then kindly keep your voice down sir, otherwise we will have to ask you to leave.* Peter has someone new to stare at now, flushed scarlet with suppressed rage. *Get me the letter, get me the money.*

'I'll call you,' he mutters through clenched teeth. 'Later.' Fingers stab at the buttons on his coat, ready to tear them off for their impudent refusal to be threaded.

'Peter?' I ask, almost reluctantly. 'We haven't mentioned the add-on campaign.'

Buttons under control, calming slightly. 'What?'

'Sea of Tranquillity. I've no idea what's going on, but we are meant to develop two campaigns in parallel, make them seamless. What do you suggest?'

His eye fixes me, brain whirring in the background, processing all the disparate parts of the equation; the need to land his money, the lingering charges against me by these lunatics, his need to make his flight.

'I spoke to them a few days ago. They didn't call you?'

'They're not allowed to. Banned themselves, don't you remember? Incidentally, what about that file they were going to send you?'

He's still locked in the same position, brain now multi-tasking across a whole range of equations. I wonder whether he can tell I hacked into his files.

'Not the lady. The man… Pat something… Anyway, *he* was going to call you.' Hand to forehead, memory search ongoing. Eyes closed, he begins the recall.

'Listen. It's simple. We agreed to send them the files and tapes of the whole *Together As One* Campaign. That's all they need. They'll update the strap-line to the new campaign, or their part of the campaign and edit their images and stuff into that. They'll turn it around and return to us.'

As simple as that Peter. We surrender all control and responsibility of half the campaign to a bunch we know nothing about and whose every move is as offensive as it is bizarre.

'Peter, this isn't thought through… what if…'

My hands are rampaging through my hair Nick-style as I reach out for his better judgement. He ups the volume again to halt both actions.

'Just,' he stammers, violently, '…fucking do it!'

All eyes on us again, perhaps we will be asked to leave.

'…And get the money in, understood?'

His last words are a whisper by comparison, but obviously the most important part to him. I lean back into my chair.

Two pats of his case and a parting nod, then he's off, watched by a bemused yet enthralled audience. I wonder what it is they think they have seen, a feud, some kind of business fall-out? Whatever it is it won't be the celebration of the imminent delivery of the largest communication campaign in national history, no. Between us, to be fair, we disguised that well enough. Fooled even ourselves.

I make the trip back across London to the agency, surrounded by weekend crowds; on the pavement, the tube carriages and escalators. Fighting an indescribable urge to pick on a victim at random, unburden myself on him or her. *Listen you, stranger, do you get it, I was all about togetherness, and look what it's done for us; and now I can't control it, my reputation and career ruined by idiots.Why am I going back there? Stop me.*

Let myself back into Harlequin. Nobody on reception, obviously. Few signs of life. Telephone ringing out all the same.

'Yeah?'

'Cal, it's Mary. I'm in the production office. I need to speak to you.'

Fantastic. Here comes another reassurance session, countering her *can't-do-its* with my *try-your-bests* or, more likely, *leave-it-to-mes*.

'You've got a visitor. Someone in the boardroom waiting for you.'

'Mary, it's Sunday.'

'Thank you, I was aware of that. A day off that we're all working for *your* campaign. Anyway she barged in half an hour ago, insisted on seeing you.'

'Who?'

'I don't know.'

But it's fucking Sunday. 'Why didn't you just throw her out?'

'Cal, what do you want me to do, wrestle with her?'

'Okay, okay… Leave it to me. Anyone else in if things get sticky?'

'Studio. Some creatives. Couple of guys in finance. But it's me you'll need if you do actually throw her out.'

'Yeah?'

'Can't have our MD manhandling a woman. Even if she is a nut-job.'

Fair point. Better another woman manhandled her in front of me.

'What was her point anyway?'

'Says there's stuff in the papers about a campaign for the Ministry of Well-being.'

Never ending. My stomach churns. 'Okay. Stand by, Roger and out.'

Phone down. I throw the boardroom door open, march in. Inside a nondescript middle-aged woman is sitting in Peter's seat. She springs to her feet when I waltz in.

'I'm Calum Begg, Managing Director. I understand you have invited yourself into our Agency. I must ask you to leave. If there is something you wish to discuss please have the courtesy to request an appointment.'

I wave toward the door in an expectant manner, pulling the chair next to her away to make space. She sits down. Passive assertive.

'You are about to begin a campaign to promote positive mental health, aren't you? Who are you doing it with, what's the content?'

Demanding answers, like she's entitled to them. 'Would you get out of here?'

'Greig Hynd has strange friends and strange motives. I have to know what's going on.'

She continues on questioning all aspects of the campaign. In full flow, like she is addressing a committee especially convened to furnish her with all the info she desires. As if that is my very reason for being. I haven't even asked her her name.

'You heard, out!'

'Not until I get answers.'

Another step closer. Her presence in this room, in my agency, my life, is so irritating I hover on the verge of lifting her up. She senses this, goes rigid in the chair.

'Are you using Sea of Tranquillity, are they involved? They are, aren't they?'

Any other day she would have been bounced at reception, bundled out by the facilities staff, used to dealing with anti-globalisation, vivisection, e-number additive people convinced that ad agencies like ours are at the front line of a war on decent values. But she chose Sunday. How lucky. And she sees something change in me at the merest mention of my friends.

'Yes.' She slows. 'You *are* working with them. And you'll know their methods, their techniques. Here,' she says, reaching into her oversized shoulder bag. 'Here.' Slapping down a polythene file on the table. 'Our dossier on Sea of Tranquillity, they colluded with Greig Hynd to infiltrate a conference for the Campaign for Positive Mental Health. His launch-pad to success. Used nasty tricks, subliminal sounds and disturbing imagery. Here,' she pulls out a page, 'a list of all the people damaged by exposure to their psychological barrage. All here, documented. Dangerous, must be stopped.'

My turn to take a seat, I scan the papers she pushes over to me.

'Who are you?'

'Catherine Hodge. I used to work with Greig Hynd. I resigned because of this, it was bad enough then, before they planned this monstrosity.'

I look again at the papers. Part of me feels relief at seeing what's in front of me. The list of symptoms and victims; they should have my name in there. My enemy's enemy. But it's complicated.

'Okay. I've got your file. I'll pass it on to the campaign team.'

'And then what?'

'They can decide where to go with it and who they want to talk to about it.'

'They? You're in charge. And you know these people, don't you? I can see it in your face.'

'Actually, Harlequin is run by our Board. Take it up with them. Now I'm going to ask you to leave again. This conversation is over.'

'But you know they are going to harm people,' she says. 'Don't you? You know people affected like this, you must do, if they've been exposed to these materials… Stop this. In the name of humanity, stop it.'

Name of humanity. 'I've heard you out, now you must leave.'

She unfolds her coat, puts it on with a pointedly slow diligence. 'Of course, you would be part of it yourself, wouldn't you?… You're all in it together, aren't you?'

The telephone on the wall. 'Security? Call the police. Intruder in the building.' I turn back to her, finally the message getting through.

In it together. Her parting shot, aimed at the air as Mary arrives to check out the situation. Only in the loosest sense of *together*. Mary double-locks the safety catch on the front door once our visitor is safely out. No escape for us now.

'Cal,' she says, turning back into reception, '…we need to talk. The timing plans. I don't see how we can do it on schedule.'

'It's okay. Leave it to me,' I hear myself saying, 'I'll fix it later.' Once I find my focus. If I can. Nobody left, all down to me, and even I'm divided.

CAMPAIGN LAUNCH MINUS 13 DAYS

Ministry of Well-being, New Kings Beam House, Blackfriars, London

Greig looked up from his papers to find his appointment secretary standing over him. He was startled but too tired to show it. No knock on the door, at least not one that he had heard.

'The car will leave for the House in twenty minutes.'

Greig nodded silently. The car will leave. An admirably neutral way of putting it, as if the car would leave with or without him.

'Nigel Richards is here for his update session now.'

Greig pulled still, puzzled.

'You agreed to giving him a slot when we discussed it this morning... unless you want him to accompany you in the car to the House...?'

'No. No. Send him in.' Greig gave up the attempt to dredge his memory for any recollection of the agreement, keener to guard the relative luxury of a chauffeured drive to Parliament in privacy. Keener to get it over with, whatever it was.

Nigel Richards materialised almost immediately, guided to a chair in the meeting area of the room by the secretary, taking a seat and waiting.

'Thanks,' said Greig. 'Ten minutes, yes?'

He moved across. 'So?'

'Interesting reading this weekend. I take it you saw it?'

'I did. And you came over to ask me this?'

Whatever trace of charm might have been hiding in Nigel Richards' default setting clouded over. 'I came to check you were still functioning, still focused on getting out of the mess, to see if I could help.'

'What kind of help would you propose? The same kind your media people gave?'

'They tried their best. If you're not satisfied I could try to switch the team around. Interested?'

He waved the suggestion away. A glance to his watch, signalling impatience.

'The campaign plan,' said Nigel Richards, clearing his throat as if trying to start again. 'You're happy with that, confident in what you're doing?'

'You tell me. It's your territory, after all. Shouldn't I be?'

'I had a call from Cal Begg at Harlequin this morning. They had a visit at the weekend from one of your ex-colleagues. I see she was in some of the newspapers on Sunday too. Saying that there's some sinister motive in the campaign. Seems to have a bit of a grievance and not shy in sharing it. Anything we need to do?'

'What?… Catherine Hodge?… If it helps, I didn't have an affair with her. Why is she so damn upset? You'll have to ask her. I'll let others decide if they think there's any substance to it. I don't think she does herself, or her credibility, any favours with wild allegations. There's no need for us to add anything.'

'Still, she managed to worry the agency enough for them to call… There are some astronomical bills on the way too, are you happy with that?'

'Are the two related? What's the issue here?' Greig snapped, sensing safer grounds to argue over. 'Do we have the money, can we justify it? I believe we can, through savings over time, through savings on treatment and the expense of keeping going as we do. Does the Prime Minister still support it all? That's the only issue, isn't it? And I'm sure you'd find a way of telling me if he didn't.'

Another glance to his watch, then a glance to the door, both for show. Confidence returning. Back to his grandstanding best, uninterrupted by his visitor. 'Yes, he'd find a way again. Through you, or through Bernie via Jason Watson. Through Natasha Skacel, or maybe through the very same newspapers we were talking about. Tell him I'll keep reading them and looking for clues.'

He stood up, reaching out for his jacket.

'I'm sorry if you think we…' began the other, before an abrupt hand went up to stop him.

'I think we're finished here, yes? Send me an update on the campaign, and when I can expect to see the final materials for approval, and meantime there's a car waiting.'

Nigel Richards progressed to the door, leaving with an undertaker's solemn grace.

C DAY MINUS 13 DAYS

Harlequin International Communications Holdings, Harlequin House,

Warren Street, London

Another day, another room. Meetings like the one I am about to have need to take place in relative secrecy. So it is pragmatism rather than malice that has me taking over the newly-vacated space of our recently exited Creative Director, Mr Nick Craig. A beautifully-fashioned space, as one would expect.

Hugh McDetermined comes in without knocking, entering in a spirit of experimentation, as if he has never seen this glass box, or this floor before. Alien surroundings that set him on guard. I could swear he knows what is coming.

'You were after me? Tried to find you. This the new base?'

'I had a session with Peter. Long session. Tough session, about the campaign and bringing him up to date with everything.'

A slippery smile from Hugh, playing out of character. Maybe he's prepared too. I wonder. 'That *would* be a tough session.' He lifts his hands, shrugging to the world. I had scrawled some bullet points on my case pad about how this should play. I look down to them for guidance, struggling to decipher my own writing and codes. 'He's unhappy about our income flow. Wants to get the advance invoices out immediately. As in right now, *maintenant*, pronto pronto…'

'I'll bet he does.'

Unexpected again. Blanked again. 'Hugh,' I say, reading hesitantly. 'I have explicit instructions to get these out, now, and I have to warn you…'

He cuts in, sharply. 'Or what, I'm gone too? Try it Cal, go on. Do it.'

'Hugh, it doesn't have to be like this, this is not my…'

'Yes it is. Don't insult my intelligence. Go on. Fire me. I'm not going to sign off your ludicrous bills, so you'll have to.'

I read my notes. We're at the end, reached by an alternative route. 'I'll get a letter…'

'Yeah yeah…' He's up out of his seat. 'Same letter you sent the others. Same template, just change the names. You've turned this place into a madhouse, Cal. Feeling proud?… I'll be gone by lunchtime. Get me my letter and I'll pass it to my lawyers. We'll take it from there.'

I let him huff his way out of the office. It's done. I need to get the estimates and invoices out, it's down there written on the list. Hugh's progress through the floor is slow. He stops to shake hands one by one with the people out there and I wonder what he's saying. A nauseating dizziness of doubt begins to seep into me, something I have to somehow reverse out of before it's glued permanently inside. I stand up. Slap myself hard on the cheek. Shock therapy. Lift the phone.

'Mary? Get up here now. We're going to tour the creative floor. I want to know these guys are on the case. And get the package at reception couriered round to Nigel Richards, immediately, registered delivery.'

I step out of the glass cage. Hugh is still finishing the rounds. A glance over to me, a final shake of his head and he's gone. All eyes on me.

'Who's putting the package together for Sea of Tranquillity? I want to review it.'

Silence, as if I'm speaking my own private language. A silence that speaks of insolence and incomprehension, and all points in between. I'm about to repeat myself, to push it all up a gear, when Mary arrives.

'Cal,' she whispers. 'Take it easy. It's David and Ian that are doing it, they're downstairs. I'll get them in the office, let's go.'

I'm guided back inside as the room stirs back to life. The session with the guys is fruitful. Slow to start but soon, by necessity, we are with the detail; what campaign off-cuts are we happy to supply – low enough down our own preference order to give them away to the subsidiary campaign, yet still retaining enough cut-through and quality to bear our name as producers. Which ones leave enough space for our creative allies to fill with whatever magic they deem missing, or alternatively, what can we give that leaves only token space to minimise the damage they might do to our origination? Choices. Not particularly easy choices. For all that, it's an undoubted relief to be working again. It's as if the craziness disappears, normality restored. It is, however, a temporary state.

A call from accounts as we are winding up. A problem with the requisitions Kenny Chance has raised for new equipment – software and hardware for the digital studio. Requisitions I, as Managing Director, had signed off. Requisitions I, as acting Finance Director, am now being invited to block. Why? There is no cash in our current account, any cheque we raise is likely to bounce. *Hold it there*, I say, finding this hard to believe given what I alone have billed in the development stages of *Together As One* et al, *I'm on my way down. Where is the fucking money?* I demand, Peteresque to a fault, meaning, likewise, where is *my* fucking money? I'm shown the balance statements by the sullen and ashen junior accounts staff. This clarifies only the size of the hole, not the cause of it. Twelve of them in that room; credit controllers, management accountants, work-in-progress checkers. All of them hushed, withholding information. So it seems. Is this about Hugh, some sort of joke, revenge?

'Draw me up a simple sheet covering the last six months; what we had in the bank to start with, what we billed during that time, all outgoings in the form of the costs of running the agency, what we should have in the bank, what we do have.'

Working backwards, the last bit is easiest for them to find; a great big zero. We have nothing. Absolutely nothing, nothing to pay wages, rent, even day to day expenses like the tube fares to take me across London to Peter Vesey summits. No wonder he was hiding.

'Can. Anyone. Get. Me. Some. Fucking. Answers!'

I don't know these guys, only on passing-in-a-corridor terms – less inhibited about shouting in front of them. Just as well. The accounts office stalls to a halt. Phones ring unanswered as they, paradoxically, look to me for clues to it all.

'Find Hugh if he's still in the building, before I call in the police.'

Fast forward more pointless and redundant studies of various financial spreadsheets and status documents. Fast forward the gamut of frustration, anger, incomprehension and despair. Fast forward the sighting, off-site or on of the man with some of the answers.

Enter Hugh McSwagger. Live before me, Harlequin boardroom, late afternoon.

'Problem, Cal?'

'What's going on? How the fuck could we be going to the wall?'

He may have been drinking. Maybe feeling that school's out. Maybe feeling the power in all of this has shifted sides of the table.

'You're in charge, Cal. So they tell me. Thought you were meant to have the smarts?'

'Hugh. I'm sorry everything…' The thought entering my head pulls me up short. What's the point? I haven't asked him back to make an apology. And he is smart enough not to expect it. So why has he come back, simply to ridicule?

'There's still over two hundred people employed here, including your team. Right now, we're all facing oblivion. I don't know why or how to avoid it. Can you tell me, if only to help your guys?'

'Cal,' he says, pushing back from the table, 'you're it. These are your changes. I really don't get why you're asking me. What is it you think I have?'

He plays this whole *who-me?* schmuck par excellence. A man on form. Shot through with this *reap-what-you-sow* riff from the session before.

'Where did all our money go, can we get it back? Will you tell me, or do you want to fuck off so that I can find out someplace else?'

A pause whilst he considers the options, speaking to the lawyers lurking in his brain. Sorry smile.

'It went,' broadening smile, '…on the acquisitions,' widening smile, 'where else do you think it went?' Carnivore smile. 'Surely you get that?'

A code I can't instantly decipher. A haze of inadequacy begins to envelop me.

'Just tell me.'

'Peter's purchases. *Harlequin International.* His entire trip for the last six months, buying up agencies, or controlling shares in agencies, or controlling stakes in agency mergers. Endless. The thirst for cash, for income, for income without cost. The inter-company loans, the relentless corporate re-structure. For god's sake, Cal, the need for a *plan*, to *pay* for all of this!'

Granite turns to sand beneath my feet. Quicksand. I've not just missed an episode, I've managed to pass on the whole fucking series.

'*International?*'

'You have this campaign that every government on earth will want to duplicate once it runs, according to Peter, and he's setting up to do it. He wants to be rich. Not *advertising* rich but *Bill Gates* rich. And you're the greedy bastard that wants to join him, and you have the nerve to ask me where the damn money has all gone.'

I'm playing back, frantically, every encounter I've had. Trying to make sense of it. Someone is lying. *Everyone* is lying.

'The *Board*. He always said he was doing it for the Board, the new investors.'

'You know,' chides Hugh McRighteous, 'you *must* know… that there *is* no Board, or rather *he* is the Board. He bought out Harlequin over a year ago. Another drain on income, and you're part of it.'

'Not true, I swear it.'

A not guilty plea thrown straight back, derisively. 'Then why else are you doing all his dirty work?'

To see yourself as others see you. Not so much a gift, as the immortal bard would portray it, more a knee to the groin. One you run into. Unstoppable.

'Hugh, is this just your theory or can you prove it?'

'You asshole… Just look up the Companies Register. Look up the American, French, German, Spanish market indexes. See who has been buying and selling. Ask our own bank, for god's sake; who does Harlequin own? What do the Harlequin shell companies own? Who's paying for it all?'

To my horror, I feel my eyes begin to glass up. I'd been picking up the tab all along, in every currency going.

CAMPAIGN LAUNCH MINUS 10 DAYS

Harlequin International Communications Holdings, Harlequin House,

Warren Street, London

The receptionist smiled. Pretty girl, pretty smile, shy, but still almost flirtatious. Identikit blonde mid to late twenties. Almost polished enough to be a model, or an extra in one of the very ads her employers mass produced twenty-four seven, judging by the array of shots and screen captures of their greatest hits going on behind her. She smiled again, this time with a hint of nervousness mixed in with apology. *I know, it's just that no one seems to know where he is.* Greig tried to transmit some reassurance that it was okay, he was early, it didn't matter.

He would have to stop studying her now, he realised, otherwise she would begin to suspect he was hitting on her, intent on making her another conquest, to join the one she had no doubt read about. The scandalous Minister. He turned as she pumped the buttons furiously on the switchboard to fire out another call. *Signed in at six. That's am. I know. Never mind then.*

An arrival at the main door. Nigel Richards striding in. 'Mr Richards. Good morning.'

'Morning, Minister. Where are we?'

Greig shook the other man's hand. 'Nobody knows. Anarchy reigns. Shouldn't show up ahead of schedule.'

Nigel Richards pointed his nose towards the boardroom door. 'I think you'll find we're in here, let's go park ourselves rather than loiter in reception.' He waved a gentleman's arm at the receptionist to indicate the intention. She offered no reaction, too engrossed in the ongoing manhunt by telephone.

Inside the boardroom he saw that it had already been set up for a meeting; holding slide on the screen reading 'Well-being Campaign Status Meeting' confirming they had found the right location. A tray of cups and pots lay on the large table. Nigel Richards touched the side of one of them; hot, today's brew. *Tea, coffee?* he offered. Greig took the latter as the door opened behind him.

'Guys, help yourselves, don't wait on me.'

'I won't, Cal,' replied Nigel Richards, continuing to pour. 'Especially since we're paying for it, handsomely… Can I offer you any of this lavish feast?'

'Why not, and some for Mary here, Mary let me introduce…'

'Greig Hynd,' said Greig, offering his hand. Another set of female eyes on him, another instant judgement, what had she read, what had she believed? Another hand was offered, breaking the thought.

'Minister…'

'Cal. How are you, they found you then?'

A blank stare back. Maybe he had missed all the drama. Maybe other things on his mind. Less than two weeks since they had last met, but the agency man seemed to have aged two years. Drawn and haunted. Same clothes, always the same clothes.

'I think we should perhaps get started, there must be a lot to get through.'

He watched as Cal leafed through the pile of papers in front of him. *Agenda?* he mouthed to the woman he'd brought in with him. *Never mind, you loaded the presentation?* She reached for the mouse to click the PowerPoint slide, only to find it snatched from her hand in the process. *Agenda. There. See?* Greig watched her take a deep breath, eyes closed. Things were wound tight at the agency.

'Today's agenda. Where we are at in terms of finalised creative and executions, feedback on the research carried out so far, updates on the research still to come, how these will impact on the final versions of creative, how we expect them to look, how we expect them to work once we launch. Any questions?'

He had spoken so fast, and with such edge-of-the-seat intensity it seemed almost impertinent to answer. Nigel Richards however remained undaunted.

'That's *all* campaigns, Cal?'

'Meaning?'

'Sea of Tranquillity… the parallel campaign, you'll update us on that too?'

Something clouding over inside, thought Greig, watching Cal. Someone else carrying an extra weight.

'I will *try*,' he said, with evident distaste. 'Although maybe you will know more than me. I haven't spoken to them for a while for various reasons.'

'Is there a problem with them, Cal?' Greig interjected, curious. Now he was subjected to the same treatment. A dead stare.

'Not exactly. Fucking impossible to work with is more like it.'

Greig watched as Cal closed his eyes. Crossing the line, vaulting it. Had he actually sworn at him?

'Cal,' said Nigel Richards, sternly. 'That's not appropriate and I must ask that you apologise.'

The eyes slowly opened. Red eyes. Tired. Greig thought for a moment there might even be tears in them.

'I know, I know, I'm sorry. Truly sorry, Greig… Sorry, Minister. I mean no offence… honestly.'

'Apology accepted.' Greig leaned forward. 'Do you need a break, Cal, some time out to gather your…' To compose yourself, he thought, drawing short of actually saying it.

'It's okay… We've got to get through this. Time is short.' He took a sip from his cup, wincing as if tasting ear wax. 'I blame the coffee. Lousy. One day, it will be sorted. One day, I promise, a decent cup.'

Nigel Richards smiled politely. 'The agenda then, where to start?'

Cal started to explain the campaign development process, shuffling then spreading out various papers round the table as he did so, spreadsheets and project plans. Coloured columns indicating work completed, other colours meaning completed but not researched. Endless categories, endless papers that Greig found impenetrable. All around the table, faces frozen in concentration.

'So, you *are* on top of it all Cal, on schedule?' Nigel Richards asked aloud, though addressing another chart of hieroglyphs as he did so.

'As I said, these are today's updates, where we are on each ad. Updated every six hours. Forty-two items. With Sea of Tranquillity on top, another twelve.'

Greig realised with a start that they were talking about a huge range of communications – that his previous assumption of a smaller number with differing versions was completely false. Rightly or wrongly, the whole thing was being taken in an entirely different direction. He looked again at the schedules, his alarm rising.

'Can I…' he placed the sheets down carefully, 'just see some adverts, Cal? This is all a bit abstract for me.'

'Not *adverts* exactly. The papers show a range of treatments across different media, a range of dialogues we expect to trigger and fulfil as a result of the planned exposure. If it was only *adverts*, life would be a whole lot simpler, believe me.'

Greig wondered how to react. Although this time Cal had not sworn or used any language that could be construed as abusive, the patronising, wearied air to the reply was palpable.

'Cal. Can you give me a minute, can you come with me a second? I need some air. Something about this room, or maybe the coffee, as you say. Anyway, can you? Come on. Excuse me everyone. Won't be long.'

Greig stood and moved to the door, ushering Cal along. The other moved with an awkward chair-dragging lack of grace. They passed the girl on the desk, busy pretending not to notice. Out to the doorstep. A pleasant day, dry. Greig saw the brass doorplate's half-hearted shine. In need of attention. He put his arm around Cal.

'Clean air, or as clean as we can get in the city. What is it with that room?'

The younger man was silent.

'I'm trying to get my head around the campaign, Cal. I want to understand. Need to understand. I've got a lot riding on it, frankly, *everything* riding on it. I'm not saying that to add pressure, but to tell you I'm on your side. I *want* this whole thing to succeed and I'm *not* in any way hostile. So I simply *refuse* to be talked to the way you are. I'm not talking about respect or protocol but just as a human being. Someone on the same side. Do you understand, Cal?'

His professional voice. Dr Greig voice. Enjoying his own improvisation.

'I do, Minister. I'm sorry. I apologise.'

'Greig.'

He took his arm from Cal and turned his face to the activities of the street.

'How long have you worked here, Cal?'

'Five years or so.'

'Good place?'

'Has been. Not so sure now.'

'Pressure, stress. Something else?'

Cal turned, frowning.

'All of that. Shall we go back inside? They'll be wondering what the fuck...'

Another grimace and mouthed apology. Greig's arm reached out once more.

'No. Let's stay here. I need to understand what's planned. Simple layman's terms. You're good at that, Cal. It's your strength.'

'It's complicated... I...'

'Doorstep pitch. Come on.'

Eyes closed. Inhaling and expiring in numbered, calm-down sequence.

'We have a range of ads that promote togetherness, community, harmony in a variety of guises since for different people *togetherness* means different things... for old timers it might mean cosying up, for the young it means hanging out... Anyway, different variations showing what a wonderful world it could be, reaching their target segment by the channels that are most likely to reach them... TV, internet, social websites... The ads are tested to perfection, tap into a need, a craving we identified years ago. To that we've added a personality, *you*, Minister, as the face of government, wanting the same thing. Not even promising to make it happen, that's the *new* thing, the *clever* thing, but being just like them, just as vulnerable.'

'Okay, and how do you add in me?'

A shake of the head. 'We'll show you. There's an issue with over-exposure. Kind of dulls your reaction to them. We've so many variations that if we played one after the other we'd be in there all morning, and you'd be a zombie. Hence the grids explaining what's in them. I didn't know how else to make it clear. Didn't want to scare you. Didn't mean to swear either. Just happens. All the fucking time.'

'How do you put me in the ads, Cal?'

'Shoe-horned in. Copied from the Sea of Tranquillity people. Just cut away to a shot. All to do with the emotional landscapes of the piece rather than narrative flows. It can look clumsy and any creative guys hate it. Works though, spectacularly.'

'How do you know?'

'We ask at research. Not outright, but we ask a range of approval statements and measure strength of agreement. So we feed in a statement like *Government cares about everyone's well-being,* we get an okay score. We say *Government is actively protecting my well-being,* we get a slightly lower score, adequate, okay. All the way to *my mental health is important to Government.* The real fireworks happen with the emotional scores, that's the really clever bit.'

'*Emotional scores?*'

'For emotional we'll show a picture of you or the Prime Minister and ask something like, *I'd be proud to have him as a friend.* Or, *he cares about those less well-off than him.* You gave me the idea when you said you would take it all on, remember? Thought you were offering to be Jesus. So I set up the questions to see if you *could* be Jesus, everything other than *this guy walks on water,* anyway we get the answers then tweak the ads to push the scores higher. And it's a sensation. You'll be a superstar. We're still altering the executions based on research feedback. We'll do that to the wire, right up to launch.'

'Anything else to be done?'

'The dialogues… I'm not happy with them. I'll find some way of doing it. I'll have to. And those Sea of Tranquillity fuckheads, I haven't seen their stuff and it worries me. You really need to check what they're up to.'

A hand up, gently assertive. 'They'll be fine.'

A flash of something in the other's eyes, not what he wanted to hear. Breathing deeply again, an effort for him to keep control.

'We've got ten days to launch.' He sighed. 'Come on, there's a schedule inside.'

'Okay Cal. We'll go back. Show me some ads. A safe amount.' Greig gave a smile. 'I've got to ask you to go through your résumé one more time, if you would, for Nigel. And if you could miss out the stuff about Jesus that would be great.'

'Where's your other helpers today?'

'Setting up the launch. You'll have been briefed about the new convention?' A nod back. 'Maybe you could give some thought to that?'

He felt a surge of guilt as he watched Cal's blinking brow-rubbing acceptance of the additional brief.

'Come on, Cal,' he said, guiding him back through the door inside. 'One more time, then we'll leave you in peace to get on with it.'

Silence in the boardroom. An icy glance from Nigel Richards.

'We're okay here. All under control, Cal? From the top if you please, simple layman's terms again, we're all on the same side, aren't we?'

C DAY MINUS 6 DAYS

Harlequin International Communications Holdings, Harlequin House,

Warren Street, London

Maybe Nigel Richards had his own troubles to smooth over back at his place. Maybe he thought it best to let the dust settle, metaphysically speaking. Maybe vengeance is something he only savours when served cold. Whatever. He let me stew overnight before putting his call in.

'Cal,' he starts reasonably. 'If you ever,' he slowed, '…ever,' gear-change up, 'do that to me again, or go near any kind of display even approaching yesterday's… I will personally remove your balls from the CIO roster. Understood?'

Understood, in that it is a hollow threat. It is hard to think of any behaviour that would trigger such a move, given the state of play. Swearing at a Minister, over-charging, creative going to broadcast without client approval, all becoming de rigueur and there is nothing he can do about it except posture, make these calls, so that he can say he made the call.

'I'm sorry,' I say. So that I can say I said it.

'Well, we got there in the end, didn't we?' he says, brightening. 'Bit of a chaotic start but I thought you did well after that. You have a gift for getting it over when you talk it through. Only issue for us is that none of that comes across in the documents, and we need written plans and results for the file. When can we get them?'

Fuck knows. There's as much work in scripting these for posterity as there is in developing them to start with. Make your choice, Mr Richards. The campaign or the story of the campaign. Can't have both.

'Maybe,' I reason, thinking aloud, thinking fast, 'we could just take a film of me, talking it through – otherwise I've no time to do this.'

'Cal, I appreciate that. But at the same time we are processing through millions on a campaign that has no formal approval or documentation. I want you to write up everything you went through yesterday. That's a formal request.'

Another request. Add it to the pile. 'I'll respond as best I can. There is something I've got to raise with you before I do that. Some good news.'

'Yes?'

I put both feet up on Nick Craig's old desk. I look out to the room of creative talent beavering away. *Listen in guys, listen to the master.*

'You'll remember we wanted to put a face to the campaign. You'll remember the need to personalise. Hence the need to use Sea of Tranquillity to achieve that. You'll also recall how difficult that has been and how we are in danger of running late with their part of the delivery?'

Prompted, Nigel recalls, albeit suspiciously. 'Yes…' he hisses.

'You'll remember from yesterday that we had managed to do that with our wholly-owned part of the campaign, the approval ratings we showed? Well, there's new figures in today, on the latest executions with the imagery of the Minister, copying, in fact the Sea of Tranquillity style. And the news is…'

I wait for him to bite.

'Yes?'

'The news is our scores are falling off the scale. *Someone I would love to have close to me, someone I'd be proud to call a friend.* Scarily high. So high I'm getting complaints from the research people. Respondents wanting to go off and consummate their new-found love. And that's just the men.'

'So?'

'So we can drop the other half of the campaign. Job is already done, elsewhere. No need for it. Redundant. Simplified.'

There's a quiet at the other end, Nigel breathing silently, working through the angles. It's a slam-dunk case. How could he possibly see it any other way?

'That's your recommendation?'

I sit up eagerly. *Watch me boys. Watch the master.*

'Absolutely. It's over-kill, potentially confusing, wasteful.'

'I get it,' he cuts in. *Over-kill.* 'Leave it with me. Send me all the latest results.'

'But Nigel, if we are going to abandon it they will need to be told…'

'Leave it with me.' He shoots, again. 'And let me see those scores.' Slam-dunk.

I make my goodbyes and close the call. One major irritant and source of stress manoeuvred out, or soon to be. A victory, albeit yet to be confirmed. For the first time in months I'm moving in the right direction. I smile to myself, uninhibited, even in Nick's glass box. *Look, people, we are winning again.* My smile fades as I realise no one is looking. There's no one to share this triumph with anymore. How I miss Caroline. Correction. There is someone who would be keen to share the new detail, and he's outside this room. Peter Vesey is all smiles and pats-on-the-back to the sycophants willing to bathe in the glow of his love. Unannounced, as ever, re-establishing his domain. This time though, I feel more than ready for him.

'Well, *you* get around,' he says on entering, in a what he probably imagines as subtle referral to my latest choice of office.

'Could say the same about you,' I counter. 'Where was it this time; New York, Paris, Ulan Bator? What's next, the Board want you to cut a deal with the lost tribes of the Amazon, or an Eskimo collective on the Pole?'

Going in hard. Too hard. He stares at me. He knows that I now know. No Board, no hiding anymore.

'Listen,' I add, quickly, in a *making-amends-we-can-still-be-friends* kind of way. 'You might like to know. Letter of guarantee CIO won't do, but they have paid fifty percent already of sent invoice, the rest due by end of this week.'

He pretends to take this in his stride. Like it's non-news. Really? His heart will be pumping at the thought of that cash flowing in, keeping the dream of the Global Vesey empire viable. I squeeze in another of Cal's greatest hits. 'The short term creative and research bottlenecks have been fixed too. We're using a handling house to arrange the admin of the freelancers, just as well, there's hundreds of them, look...' I offer up the latest matrix. He shows less appetite than Greig Hynd to engage with the minutiae. As could have been predicted.

'What's that costing us?'

'Set fee, plus agreed mark-up on the freelancer rates. CIO have approved it. And we mark-up their mark-up. Everybody wins...'

This is enough to shake him off the scent. Besides, he has other issues weighing heavily. Heavy as fuck.

'We need to talk. You'd better come downstairs.'

For *we* need to talk read *I* need to talk. To talk *at* you.

'Actually, I'm a bit busy right now. Calls to make, last minute things, adjustments. Got the show to put together for the Minister's launch on Thursday.'

'Cal, come down. Now.' His master's voice. What the fuck?

'I'm sorry Peter, but no. This thing's going like a train, this is the final stretch…'

I'm not to be moved and he begins to get it. *Fuck you. Liar.* His eyes narrow. He brings over a canvas chair, plants himself in it.

'Angela at Sea of Tranquillity.' He says this like it's some kind of sentence, with purpose, structure, and self-evident truth.

'Haven't seen their stuff yet.' I shake my head. 'I've played fair, sent them a range of semi-finalised treatments over a week ago. Not a thing back. Haven't hassled or harassed either. All in their court. So?'

He turns and makes a show of checking the door is closed. Looks back to me.

'That's *not* where I'm coming from,' he says, in a clipped I'm-about-to-lose-patience way.

'I've just been over there and been through it and they're worried. Extremely.'

'Good. Does that mean they'll get a move on?'

'About *you*, Cal. Worried about you.'

'Really? How surprising. Another complaint?'

'Will you let me finish?… They showed me the *film*, Cal. All the footage. They think you're having a breakdown…'

Breakdown?

'Based on… what exactly? What are they trying to achieve with this?…'

'…Or about to have a breakdown. They are trained psychologists, Cal. I have to… Have to at least listen.'

'And what else are they saying that you're listening to?'

'That you shouldn't be running a campaign this size, with these pressures. It isn't going to do you, or anyone, any good.'

Another look outside, no signs of interest from the other side of the glass. Sea of Duplicity. They want me out. A pre-emptive strike. 'I can assure you, I have never felt better. *I* am on top of this. We are *six days* from launch. Continuity is everything. Besides, I think you'll find it's them who no longer have a place in our campaign.'

A good comeback, upping the stakes, playing my hand strategically. *Too late friends, it's a done deal. Watch and learn.*

'What? *What* do you mean?' The venom has come back into Dr Pete's tone.

'There's no need for their particular input anymore. It's covered. By us. We've taken the elements we need and incorporated them. We have the personality, the emotional zone, covered. We can drop their half. I've told CIO already.'

'*What*?' screams Peter, jumping up. 'What have you done?' From concerned to raging mad. 'And don't you think there's something highly suspect in that?'

Of course there is. Everything about it is suspect, it's the Harlequin way. What's the specific that has him so irate? 'I'm sorry Peter, I don't know...'

'We've *billed* for it... estimated, quoted and *billed* for this work. What are we going to do now, write that off?'

The money, you asshole, the fucking *money*. He's panicked that I've just knocked a couple of zeros off his income projection.

'We can adjust our fee for the additional work we have done to our bits.'

A slam of the hand on the table stops me. Oh yes we have an audience now, he's made sure of that, faces turning towards the office and the who within it. And for once it's not *my* meltdown they are witnessing.

'But it wouldn't be the same, we won't make the same. *Look*, we have forecasts, projections based on that income, detail we've shared with our bank and fund managers. You... cannot fucking... mess about with it, Cal, don't you understand?'

How dare I interrupt the smooth flow of international commerce? *Make the money and give it all to me, you moron.*

'I was simply trying to safeguard the campaign, without which everything else counts for shit. I want these guys out. They have no place in it anymore.'

'When was this decided?'

'A few days ago.'

'I'll call Nigel Richards. Explain there's been a mix up. A change of opinion.'

'That will make no sense to him. I've sent him results, justifications... the works. He'll know the only motivation is money. You can't...' This time it's my voice going through the changes, evening out at plain hostility.

'Don't,' he points, 'shout at *me*, Cal. I know it's your habit, part of what you're going through, but I will not tolerate it. And don't,' he says, changing hands for an assault by a different angle, '…tell *me* what *I* am and am not allowed to do.'

I can only wonder what they make of the spectacle outside. The shapes being thrown, the clenched fists. Harlequin's international man-of-mystery jets in and unleashes a one man comedy wave. Only not in any way funny.

'Yeah.' I look to him, voice sour. 'I'll leave that to the fucking Board. Yeah?'

I know, you know. I know.

The same expression comes straight back at me, only less friendly. 'Get out of my sight Cal, I've got to call Nigel Richards.'

You and me both, I realise, checking my Blackberry is tucked in my pocket.

The jacket is thrown over my shoulder, I step outside, and start the search for another new office. Multitask. Walk and dial as I go. Hands shaking.

Nigel's phone rings out, then switches me to his voicemail. A polite tone invites me to leave a message. *Call me, for fuck's sake.* My feet are clattering down the steps and I'm breathless as I hang up. Try again in five minutes. Calm down.

Where to go? My old office. Can't face it. Graveyard. Think. A fugitive in my own fucking agency. Call Nigel again. Steady breathing. *Nigel, can you call straight back, it's urgent. Do it before you call anyone else. Anyone.* I hang up. Fuck, that must sound even worse than the last one, calm down. Why does this matter so much? Because something is going down, I can feel it. Angela Manipulant is one step ahead again, they are in my agency, in my campaign, in my head. They think they can remove me and have free rein. But to do what? Has to be bad. Very bad. I just know they want to ruin my campaign, and they've locked onto Pete Vesey's greed. Is that it, am I seeing it straight?

I sit down on a step. Somewhere between the second and third floors. I get a number for RSGG on a search. *I'd like to speak to Caroline O'Hearn please.* Need to speak to her. *It's Calum Begg. She's out? When is she back? Urgent? Yes, to call me, on my personal number, the number I'm giving you now, not through the agency.* It's important, the numbers. *You'll tell her that? Okay.* I hang up. No one around. Nowhere to go. Calm, Cal. What will they think of you with calls like that? Sing to myself, switch off, take a sad song and make it better. Hey Cal. My phone rings. Agency Blackberry. I almost drop it in surprise. Nigel Richards, thank fuck.

'Cal?'

'Yes… Nigel, listen, Sea…'

'Cal? Sorry… it's a bad line, lots of echo, where are you?'

'At the agency… between rooms. Nigel, I needed to talk…'

'Cal? Sorry. I've got an urgent instruction for you, something you're going to hate me for, but I need you to turn it around. I know time is critical but this comes from the top, the very top.'

'Yeah?'

'We need you to replace the imagery of the Minister in all the executions. To take it out. Do you understand?'

'*Replace*? With what?'

'The Prime Minister. You put him centre stage. Him only. That's how it's going to be. Make it happen, whatever the cost.'

He must think I'm as bad as Pete Vesey. He's missing the point.

'What about Sea of Tranquillity?'

'They will get the same instruction.'

'That's not what I mean… we are going to drop them, we agreed…'

'My instructions are that the campaign is to go ahead as presented and as currently developed. Except with the Prime Minister instead of the Minister. I've got a message from Peter, does he feel the same?'

Not exactly. 'Nigel, I've got bad vibes about all this. Dreadfully bad vibes. We both need to stop and think about all of this.'

'Of course,' he says. A chippy, British and efficient *of course*. He hasn't any idea. Or maybe he's part of the whole thing. In it together with them. Fuck, that's it. Hit reverse, fast.

'…Okay… I'd better make a start with your changes. You'd better send me whatever image files you've got of the Prime Minister.'

'Already on its way. A courier dispatched a while ago. Probably already with you Cal. Best of luck. Give my regards to Peter.'

I hang up. Scour through the list of stored names on my phone. Someone to talk to. Hit the button. Dialling.

'Harry?'

'Cal?'

I can hear the surprise in his voice, thrown. Children squealing in the background. He's in a park, playground. Surrounded by people.

'Harry, sorry to interrupt… Harry, listen to me… Remember when we talked about the campaign, and you used to say we had to be cautious… you even said that it was a set-up, do you remember?'

'A *set-up*...' he echoes, dreamy, ever more distant, like his medication is kicking in. Like he's squeezed his morphine drip button.

'...Harry? What did you mean? What kind of set-up?'

A delay at the other end, message lost in fog, punctuated by the soundtrack of children playing. 'Cal?' he says, eventually. 'Cal, I, I don't want to think about it any more... It was your thing anyway... Cal?... Cal, goodbye, you're on your own.'

I stare at my inert phone. How right you are, Harry. I sink further into the stairs. I can hear footsteps ringing out from somewhere above. I pull myself to my feet.

Heading up, with as much purpose as I can muster, I pass the owners of the clapping steps, finance guys, notebooks and files to hand. Deep breath, ooze confidence. A perception thing. *Okay guys, what gives?* We're busy doing the analysis Peter requested, don't you know? He has been interrogating our finances. Cash balances by the second. Are you joining us for the meeting? Not exactly. Not invited. *I need a plan.* Where shall we tell him he can find you if he needs you? *That's okay guys, I'll get him later, for sure we'll catch up.*

Moving quicker, two steps at a time, back toward the digital studio, hoping Kenny Chance is around. Every minute will count. I burst in, launching myself at him. He looks up from his screen, tired eyes addressing me. *What now?*

'Kenny, can you call Mary. Change of brief. Urgent. Ultra urgent.'

He winces and lifts the phone.

'Not my doing, Kenny, not my idea of fun.'

The phone goes down. 'On her way. What's the change?'

'PM in, Minister out. Every ad, every execution, they've sent images of our Prime Minister at work and play, it's up to us to choose. I dare say we can throw in any pictures we think more appropriate. They just want him to be a star.'

Kenny's gaze back at me is loaded with exhaustion rather than understanding, I'm talking to myself, thinking back to my conversations with Nigel Richards. Research scores off the scale, the Minister as superstar, *a man I'd be proud to call my brother.* It was me, *I'd* sold it. Holy fucking mackerel, how I'd sold it.

'How are we going to do this, Kenny? How can we divide up the changes required? Show me how we access the files and substitute the fast-grab stuff.'

'I'll show you… But I don't know how we can do this in time to get broadcast clearance through the authority…'

'Don't worry about that, we'll switch copy on line, get retrospective clearance, how it is going to work?'

'Never heard of that. Is it legal?'

'*How will it work?* Show me now and give me a file with the passwords and entry codes. I'll do some of the edits myself, it's all-hands-on-deck.'

Someone else approaching, soft footsteps. Another chair pulled up to join us.

'What have we got now?' she asks.

'A new directive. A new star. Swap every capture of the Minister with the happy smiling face of our Prime Minister.'

'Says who?'

'The main suspect would have to be the Prime Minister.'

Mary smiles. Face at once sour and sweet. 'Greig Hynd knows this?… How are we meant to do it all in time?'

'Us and Sea of Tranquillity. Same deal. We'll have to find a way, speed up the edits. I don't know. Automate it.'

'They didn't like the treatments then?'

My turn to copy Mary's take on pained pleasure. 'Oh no. They liked it. Only too fucking much, that's the problem.'

Again, I'm talking to myself. A one-man monologue of profound. Mary's already taking another call. She waves at me, gets my attention. Mouths *Peter*. I shake my head. *Not up here,* she says, *I'll tell him if I see him.* A fugitive in my own agency. *Kenny, show me how to do it, how to access it, this is important.*

And then of course the inevitable summons. *Come, now.* His PA conquering her vertigo to make it all the way up to the creative floor, tracking me down. Paranoid? Yes. What's going on, what's the plan, who's in this thing, are they all in it together. *Togetherised.* Oh my god, calm down. Think straight.

In the end, not paranoid enough. The very last summons. I am drawn into Peter's lair.

'Got you at last then.'

Peter says this without any overtone of friendly triumph. The inflection is all about the weary effort involved, wasted effort. Prison camp commandant.

'What's going on, Cal?'

It's hard not to be impressed by the panoramic breadth of the question.

Choose your place where to start. Any place. What's going on? You fucking tell me.

I'll try the obvious answer.

'We are working round the clock to break the biggest ever government campaign in history. The most far-reaching, influential and important one in this agency's history. That's what's going on.'

History will show that this is an accurate summation, or would have been accurate if events hadn't quite overtaken it the way they did, but it's not what he was looking for. This is a trial, a closed-court show trial.

'No. I mean, what's going on?... The campaign is a mess. No one bar you seems to have a clue what's happening. Now I hear about another change. *Huge* change, complete rework. And when were you planning to tell me?'

'To what point, Peter?'

'So that I can help!'

'Help? In what way?... Writing briefs, editing?... What were you going to add that wasn't being handled?... How would taking time to bring you up to speed when you've been fucking *miles* away do anything other than slow the rest down?'

My courageous heresy does make him pause, if only momentarily.

'I would have got involved with the client, influenced them to not make the changes...'

This makes me laugh out loud. He was going to call the Prime Minister, tell him not to be the star, to resist the limelight and all the immortality it will bestow. *Pull yourself together, Cal.* If he's miles away it can only be your fault. 'With all due respect, I don't think they would have bought that. It's pretty far gone for that kind of intervention. Anyway, that was my call.'

'Well,' he says, quietly, still confident he can salvage a winning point. 'I guess we will never know, will we? Since you didn't give me the option.'

Rekindling the fire. 'Well then,' I mimic, pointing to the phone. 'Do it.'

Words fade out. A knock on the door, PA re-entering. No. Waved away.

'It's a shambles Cal, a complete shambles. You haven't carried your team with you. You disappear, reappear, no one knows where you are... We have a Minister left hanging around reception before Nigel Richards rescues him, and that's before you start swearing and have to be taken out for a talking to...'

He waits to see if I'll challenge this, to see if his intelligence is accurate. I'm more concerned with where it might be leading. With good reason.

'Too much change, too fast. You've lost the team, and there's too much disruption, and you, I'm afraid, are the cause of that disruption. So I've got to act.'

I can tell by the way his eyes switch off that this is all pre-rehearsed in his mind, coming out, as it does, as if he's reciting a fucking shopping list.

'I think you need time out. A break. I think you need to play your strengths rather than get stretched across areas that you're not suited to. I'm going to restructure.'

He waits to see if I'll challenge his right to do this.

'I'm making you head of Harlequin Solutions,' he offers, generously, '... the planning and strategy side of the business. It will be stand-alone, so that it charges the other delivery sides of the business for its involvement...'

It's typical of how his mind is wired that he works backwards from the money. I'm already pining for the simplicity of virtually autonomous sub-divisions.

'You've lost me.'

A face turns on me that spies an idiot. *Can't you follow?* 'The advertising, public relations and digital divisions.'

'They are the bits that face the clients.'

Another ace. Why ask the obvious? 'Yes!'

'So what involvement does Harlequin Solutions have with clients?'

Leaning forward, *tiresome specifics*, can't you see the genius of the plan? 'It will face the clients when invited to by the other parts of the business.'

'When it's *contracted* to?'

'*Yes!*'

I was being sarcastic but to my dismay I have elicited a genuinely enthusiastic response. *Keep up!*

'So all we have to do is wait for Harlequin Solutions to win some contracts from Harlequin Advertising and we're off and running?'

Enthusiasm waning. '*Engage* with other divisions. Scope and then win the business. Playing to your strengths, concentrating on what you used to excel at.'

I note the past tense.

'So, who else is with me in Harlequin Solutions?'

A shrug. 'You'll be able to build a team, based on the workload you build up.'

'So, just me then, right? When you say *Harlequin Solutions* will have to engage, you actually mean *I* will have to engage, win contracts, scope, scrape, scramble.'

'Cal,' he cuts in. 'It's *your* platform. *You* build it. *Your* opportunity.'

At last, a return to the big 'O' word. My *opportunity*, why am I so blind not to see it?

'And when does all this take effect?'

'Immediately.'

'Haven't you forgotten something, like the campaign about to break? Do you want me to scope and win a new solutions contract before we do our stuff on that? Want me to go round with a fucking flow chart that shows how the new model will provide even more magical Harlequin moments at a fraction...'

I hit my stride into a long rant that gained in volume at the cost of purpose or logic. I could hear myself shouting, but couldn't necessarily follow what it was I was asking or stating. All I knew was that I was upset. There's just one thing the new structure lacks, Pete baby. *Everything*. He waited and waited. His PA re-emerged. This time he let her stay and watch until I began to go under.

'I will send you a new contract. I suggest you sign it.'

'Why the fuck should I sign anything?'

'Because if you have another little episode like that I'll seriously consider whether to offer you anything at all and suspend you instead.'

'I'll not sign anything.'

'Read it, re-consider. There'll be a sizeable pay-rise in there.'

'I'd better get back to work.' I make to leave.

'The re-structure has immediate effect, Cal.'

'Meaning?'

'I want you to go home and wait for the offer.'

My turn to smile. The incredulity of it all. I'm history.

'You can't do that... Are you firing me?'

'Quite the contrary. Making you a better offer, one that plays to your strengths. After receiving client complaints, staff unrest, rapid staff turnover, and erratic behaviour, we still offer you a better contract. Think about it.'

Which is his way of saying don't think about it: checkmate. Do not pass go, do not call your lawyers, it's all been worked out and you lose in every scenario. You lose. I'm staring at him, blinking. Screaming again but only in my head. *The plan, my plan.* Say something clever Cal. Not paranoid enough. That's the problem.

'You go home. You *do not* contact the client without my permission and without me present. Any contact they attempt with you, you divert to me.'

'Working from home?'

A sweep of the hand, as if a wasp is buzzing irritatingly close. 'I'll get IT to check your connection, get you networked. Whatever... I have to act and I want you... to take a break. Immediately, understood?'

Well yes and no. You want me out, but quite why I do not, as yet, get. Out but I'm hanging in. Just. I stand up.

'A few things to clear first. I'll consider the offer when I get it.' I make for the door. Hanging in. Only just.

C DAY MINUS 4 DAYS

Cal's Cell, Highgate

The intercom buzzer. Lying in bed neither asleep or awake, sometime in what seemed early morning. I realise with a jolt that the flat's intercom buzzer is about to overload with urgency, shake itself off the wall as a result of the abuse it's getting from someone at ground level outside. An angry wasp trapped inside the box. More buzzing, impatient rhythm. A fucking swarm.

Stagger through to the hall. Who is it? Delivery, says a terse voice from the other side. Signed delivery. As if I should have somehow known. As if my ignorance of this scheme was creating a life or death delay in its own right. My hand flicks the switch and the intruder is in the building, vaulting steps on his way up. Seconds later my door itself is shuddering, pounded from the other side. Let me in!

I look for clothes, glancing at the time as my jeans roll on; bordering eight thirty. When did I last sleep that long? Am I dreaming, am I really here, why am I not at the agency? My mouth is dry. Craving coffee. Strong coffee. Door opens, and Jesus Christ he's standing there like he's my assassin. Black leather version. Helmet still on, ultra heavy breathing behind it, like Darth fucking Vader. I can feel my heart trying to break free of the bearings in my ribcage, about to jump out of my throat. I'm dying and he's thrusting a wad of papers at me. Have to sign. I comply. Acknowledge receipt. He's still not happy. Have to sign. *The Contract.*

Contract? His hands are free of the gloves, curiously fleshy, vulnerably human under the shield, flicking through the pages. More lines where I should sign. Trying to read. What's this? *New terms and conditions. Amendment to role and responsibilities.* And more. Let me study it, can't do this like this. The helmet shakes its head, menacingly. *Must sign now.*

Immediately. He's not up for negotiation. Then again he's the delivery man. I must be dreaming. I read again. *Head of Harlequin Consulting*. Salary tripled, Jesus Christ. He thinks he can buy me as cheaply as that. Sign! He wants a signature, I think it deserves an autograph, reluctantly taking the pen, *Ringo Starr*, I scrawl with a flourish. Helmet man is happy to take it, pack it away and exchange it for my copy. On his way for now, I wonder if they'll send him back when they decipher the code. Maybe they won't. Phoney signature for a phoney contract. Everybody wins.

I sink back on the bed, go through my copy. Interesting read. A contract that condemns me to house arrest. Never to leave my flat in working hours, log on, clock on and wait for the call 9am to 6pm every day. Further hours as notified as and when they are needed. Their need. They need to know where I am. A sitting duck. Time to get moving. I jump to the wardrobe, pull out a white shirt hanging ready, jeans to go. The working outfit of choice. Why fuck with the formula?

CAMPAIGN LAUNCH MINUS 3 DAYS

Ministerial Car, London Centre

The car pulled up in its lurching, impotent way again. *Here?* Greig looked out through the pouring rain, bodies rushing past each other through it, heads down, faces pulled tight in concentration, as if by bracing themselves against the wet they could avoid its excesses. *Wootonomy Café*, read the name printed over the door. Was this it?

'He said the internet café off Tottenham Court. *Wooty's*, something like that... I'm sorry, I didn't press him... thought I was doing well to get any sort of commitment at all from him, to be honest.'

Greig looked at Bernie, weighing up his desire to probe for more detail, and his need to unleash the frustration welling up inside. Nothing ever straightforward. Nobody ever in possession of the full picture, or revealing their position on it. Detective work, always searching for the damned lines of enquiry.

'So, do you think he was genuine about meeting up, or was he just throwing something to make us chase our own shadow?'

Bernie's guilty yet unbowed schoolboy look.

'I just don't know... I'm sorry I just don't know... I did what was asked...'

Tetchy, and unapologetic despite the language to the contrary. All of Greig's seething exasperation shot straight back at him. Outside, a traffic warden staggered through the downpour to gesture to the driver. *Move on.*

'Okay. I'll check it out. And... I'm sorry too, Bernie... Keeps getting better, doesn't it?'

An anaemic glance back. He leaned forward and tapped the glass. A light came on. Communication open.

'We'll call it quits here, yes? You take Bernie back to the Department.

I'll make my own way to the House for evening session, pointless wasting any more time, thanks for your patience.'

A sideways nod to Bernie as he leant deeply forward for the umbrella rolling on the floor. 'You keep your ears open…'

He didn't wait for the reaction; happy in some way to be out of the steamed up interior, out in the raw exterior. He stood still under the cover of his umbrella, enjoying the rhythm of rain on the canopy above.

Real life, cyber style, greeting him as he walked through the doorway. Modern café society. Everything arranged around clustered computer stations, like battery hens hooked into a constant feed.

He queued at the counter, service quick, depersonalised, then sank into a chair with his cardboard cup of foam.

'Want to know why you've been pulled from your own campaign?'

Greig put his cup down hurriedly and thought about offering his hand. But the mood seemed to argue against it.

'Cal. Are you going to sit down? I mean do you want to go someplace else?'

'Do *you* want to go somewhere else? Not good enough sir?'

'Not what I meant.' He stopped to show he wasn't into the confrontation that seemed inherent, even desired by the other. 'Cal, you okay? We've been getting all kinds of signs… I didn't mean anything about this place… If you're happy, although you don't seem happy, let's stay, let's talk.'

'Don't bullshit me. You want to know why you're out, if I know why. If I did it… So you do this I'm-your-friend stuff to get under the skin to find out. Yeah?… Only I don't want you under my skin. I don't want anyone under my skin but me. Just be straight. All I want is for one fucking person in this world to be straight with me.'

It was the same thing as in the newspapers, thought Greig. At one time, not even so long ago, the accusation would have been enough to prompt a flurry of angsty introspective examination of motive and method. But now, curiously, he was immune. Someone thought the worst of him. So what? Someone was of a mind to misconstrue every action that had his thumbprint on it. So what? Can it hurt? It can be uncomfortable, but the more you died inside, the less you hurt.

'Cal, I don't recognise anything in what you say as being close to where I'm coming from. I'm sorry if you picked it up differently. I thought it would be good if we could talk. Like two human beings. Two men under pressure. That's all.'

'So *I'm* the problem then? I'm getting this all wrong? Mr fucking Paranoid fucks it up again, even though they all want to screw him?'

Greig raised his head to judge whether anyone else was tuned in. Cal's voice had been loud, noisy and charged, yet in this environment of headphones, web-cams and buzzing commerce, it could pass unnoticed.

'Cal...' he soothed, soft and slow. 'Are you going to sit down? I'm not going to continue any conversation in this manner. We can talk normally, or not at all. It's up to you.'

Hardly meant, or pitched, as a knife-edge decision, yet one that showed every sign of being treated as such. Cal looked dreadful. Drawn, agitated, restless. Feelings of persecution, sustained threat and sense of alarm not far behind. A classic case of someone crossing the line. The man before him, in the process of leaving behind those *under pressure*, the vulnerable part of the graph, now about to land in the *under treatment* section. Pushed, or always likely to fall?

'What are you looking for, Cal?... Is there something wrong?'

The question served to prompt a change, or at least to coincide with one. A chair pulled up solemnly alongside; a resigned stare.

'Well... You're the shrink, you tell me, maybe that's what you came for.'

'You think I want to spy on you, Cal, examine you?'

A sudden, sour laugh. 'Very good. Oh yes, very good, doctor, give a question to a question. All the answers coming from one side. You're as subtle as Pete Vesey.'

Greig watched as Cal stopped and scanned his eyes round the room, not as if he was wary of being watched or trapped, thought Greig, more to do with a quick weighing up of options. He returned his attention to the cardboard cup, on the dividing line between them.

'Listen, I'm not playing this game... You're the one who wanted this meeting, what is it you want to know? Just give me it straight. I'll see if I can answer and if I *want* to answer. Maybe that's how we can get somewhere here, yeah?'

Greig found himself looking for guidance in the same coffee container as Cal. An unlikely source of inspiration, yet one he was drawn to. Losing his touch. There was a time when he could connect. He had built a career upon it, this gift for cutting to the heart of the matter, finding common ground, engaging. And then, just when his whole mission depended on it, it had vanished.

'I just want to know, Cal... And *I am* giving you this straight.' He paused, when had he ever heard himself before having to reassure anyone he was honest? '...Changes to the campaign, so I'm told through... last minute changes to content, ads that I'm not going to see... And I ask for the reasons, the context, expecting to hear from you and I'm told you're not available... transfer of duties, new responsibilities, none of it making sense. So I wanted to hear from you, one-to-one.'

'Like, why have *you* been dropped from the campaign?'

Every time, a brick wall. It was everywhere, every conversation, every action, turned inside-out and upside-down, re-interpreted to demonstrate that his true purpose was as devious as his method. One day he had woken up in a world where no one believed him. He had learned not to let it cut him the way it did at the start, but he was still left with that wall, hitting it over and over. Perhaps it would one day end. Maybe the universe would mysteriously somehow re-align its axis. Straight answers to straight questions. *I'm giving this to you straight.*

'I asked for this meeting... You are right. But I'm losing patience. Maybe because of your implication that it's all about *me*, or that I already know the answers and I'm trying to find out how much you know. Maybe there *is* a conspiracy, Cal... All I can say is if there is one I'm not in it. Maybe they don't like me either.'

Back to the cup. Contemplation. An audience of one who may or may not have been inclined to listen. Two if he included himself. *Think what you like, Mr Cal from Harlequin whatever, but I know what I'm about.*

'Thanks for that.' Cal coughed, unmoved. '...Okay then... Let me share some of my experience, my *take*, if you will.' A slight lean forward. 'There I am. I'm working on a big government campaign. All the king's horses and all the king's men love it. Love me. So the campaign gets bigger. And I get a *brand new* Minister to sign off the whole thing. And now I'm hot, dead hot, everyone wants me as their new best friend. What I say goes.'

A glowering flash from the other side of the stale coffee. *Get this?*

'...And then a side show from a bunch of nobody freaks becomes a campaign in its own right, then a part of the *same* government campaign, then all of a sudden it's the main event. So I challenge this, go to see them, basically to pretty much drop them back into the obscurity they deserve. And they set me up, psych me out with exactly the same shit that should have them dropped from any campaign, public, government or otherwise, yet it's *me* that's the fall guy. They go from saying I shouldn't work on *their* campaign to I shouldn't work on *any* campaign full stop, and the only person I can think of who finds this more convenient than my idiot boss with his delusions is you, Dr Hynd, who insisted they be part of the whole fiasco to start with. *You* who so fucking indignantly is *not* part of any conspiracy. So forgive me for not buying into the legend but I'm too sore for that.'

Greig's immediate inclination was to walk, to write this off as a bad use of time. Listening to the rambling diatribe he had clicked back into the mode of his former life, diagnosing by learned instinct. Here though, was a persecution complex like no other he had encountered. For one, it was unusually logical, focused in fact. More importantly, somehow it had himself at the centre of the web. And yet elements rang true. Everybody thought he was lying, and he himself seemed to have given some measure of substance to it. However unwittingly.

'Nice to know where you're coming from… Can I ask, then, the obvious question; if I'm the creator of all this, then why am I dropped from my own campaign?'

Bloodshot eyes, unblinking, meeting his gaze. Angry eyes. 'You know, you must have known, the way you pushed it, that this campaign would make a… a what?… Hero? Demi-god? Idol of its star? Meant to be you, because you know what you'd do with that power. You're safe with it, responsible. Like Superman, you'd only use it for good. And guess what, the Prime Minister thinks he's got better uses for it… Not part of the conspiracy? You've been sidelined, my friend. Join the club.'

Greig returned the lingering eye contact thrown his way at this conclusion. The bastard. His flailing punches suddenly landing, painfully.

'The PM's office has told you this, confirmed it?'

Cal stood up, reaching to his jacket on the back of the chair. 'Be serious. Decide which fucking hat you're wearing. Government propagandist, psychiatrist or whatever. Just stick to the same one. You know where I'm coming from, you recognise what I'm talking about, don't you?'

Greig made no effort to stop him leaving, trying instead to gather a line of concentration in amongst the cacophonies triggered in his head. He needed time to replay it all, compare with his version of the truth. *Which hat to wear.*

'So you're no longer part of the campaign then, Cal? I'm sorry to hear it. Thank you, honestly, for your contribution. I enjoyed working with you. Short though it was… And of course, if there's anything I can do for you, please…'

Face suddenly near. 'I'll tell you what you can do for me if you're *not* part of it, the conspiracy… Get me in front of the Prime Minister. Let *me* ask him where he's coming from, yeah? Best behaviour, promise. And, let me tell you, a heads-up word to the wise… I'm *still* part of the campaign, you'd better believe it. In fact, get me my audience or you'll all regret it.'

'I don't see why not, Cal, let me see what can be done. I think you deserve it.'

In fact, he realised with a faint glow of pleasure, they deserved each other.

C DAY MINUS 3 DAYS

Oxford Street/Warren Street, London

Dr Hynd's performance left me cold and clammy. His brand of sincerity has spoiled one of my new hangouts, something else to resent him for. I'm networked up at home and have all the access codes one could dream of, but am wise/paranoid enough to carry out my work from a series of moving locations, internet cafés and the like, where no one can monitor my activities from switch on to log-off to sleep, whatever that is. Anyway, I had to be rid of the man and stormed off into the side streets, looking to lose myself in the arteries of the city. London, not a place for bumping into friends, or lovers, until today. Angry, angry.

'Cal... Cal?... *Cal?*'

The voice stops me walking. Invades a clouded consciousness. Caroline and partner; her beautiful, radiant, serene. Him relaxed, catalogue handsome, spray-on charm applied instantly. Two approaching smiles.

'Cal.' She steps forward. A kiss. As in a *greeting* kiss. Pointless. 'You keep calling me? Sorry I couldn't get back... I've been worried... How the hell are you?'

Thinking of a reply. Where to start, Caroline. I called you once, bitch. Maybe twice. Hardly the act of the borderline stalker you're mapping out here.

'Oh,' she breaks off, apologetically, 'sorry, this is Simon. One of the guys from the media buying agency at CCDP. One of the *good* guys...' She laughs. He laughs back and I notice they are holding hands. *One of the good guys at the media buying agency.* What you'd call an oxymoronic intro in adland. On a par with *a friend I made in prison.* He shines and offers me his hand, still warm from her touch.

'Pleased to meet you Cal, a famous man.'

Another shared giggle on a wavelength unavailable to me. Bodies buzzing by, all around. We shuffle to let everyone through. It's only us in the slow motion bubble, everything else is on fast-forward all around, everything blurred.

'So how are you?... I called the agency but they said you were off-site... Then I got a call back from Mary and she told me about the breakdown... Everyone's worried for you...'

Fast-forward, then freeze-frame. '*Breakdown?*' Pull-in on extreme close-up. 'Did you just say *breakdown?*'

She gropes blindly for reverse gear. 'Well... I mean... Mary said there were things going on...'

'You said *breakdown...* who is spreading this shit?'

'Cal, calm down, will you? You're shouting at me... There's no need, nothing to be ashamed... You'll bounce back...'

Refusing to get to the point. Time is of the essence, Caroline, can't you get that either?

'*What... fucking... breakdown?*'

I don't realise I have grabbed her until I find myself in a struggle with her new fuck-partner. Not the best tactical ploy on my part, allowing him the role of dashing knight opposed to my dastardly villain. Bad move. People watching. Caroline's tears. No answers. He puts a shoulder between me and her. For a moment I consider taking him on for it. It's like he's steeling himself, ready to attack in some Clark Kent hold-my-glasses way.

Not to be though. Lost this battle, but the war is still on. Need to think, regroup. Sorry Caroline, honestly. Make it up later, make you understand. Pulled downstream by the flow of the people around. Carried by the current further and further away. Caroline and friend diminish in size, her heaving shoulders more and more remote. I'm spiralling off in the next torrent, just letting myself go into the tsunami tide. Head above water until the next land mass comes into view, jutting out of the turbulence. There it is ahead, drawing me in through the whirlpool of rage. Centre of the storm, heart of the beast. Harlequin Agency.

Breathing deeply, hiding the effort of this behind my hand, entering the building as if yawning with the tedium of it all. A smile for reception. *Peter in? I'll make my own way, creative floor?* A wild look comes shooting back, hand instantly to telephone; he's here, yes, now arrived, on his way up, alert, maximum alert.

'Cal,' Peter says, lifting his attention from the papers before him. 'How are you?... You know you are not meant to be here and I'll have to ask you to leave?'

I sit down, pulling a chair close. Director's chair, wood and grey leather. More of a room adornment than practical furniture, surprisingly comfortable all the same.

'How goes the finalisation? Are we on schedule?'

I nod to the spreadsheeted timing plans I can see he's been studying. I know them well enough to recognise them upside down. My work.

'Things are bad enough for you, Cal. Leave now, before you make it worse.'

'I'm not here to make anything worse, just to clear something up... Are you, as my employer, pushing some kind of angle to the world out there that I am having a breakdown and that you've removed me from the agency as a result?'

A frown creases into being across a magisterial forehead.

'*Cal*... We've just about got a handle on this but we're about to go live. I'd be failing in my duty to get distracted by hypotheticals... Anyway, I've tried to tell you you're in trouble, don't dig deeper.'

'Could you, with all due respect, just take me through the trouble I'm in and how being here, asking a simple question, a yes-or-no and hardly *hypothetical* question gets me into *worse* trouble?'

I make every effort to let this out slowly and reasonably, to stay seated, cut out the gestures that would be noticed in silhouette outside. The only raised voice is his. I am, tenaciously, miraculously, keeping it all together. Just.

'...Well for goodness' sake... where do you want me to start?' he blusters. 'You're under investigation from a serious client complaint, we've got our own internal enquiry into the procedure you followed or didn't follow when sacking three senior members of staff *and*,' he emphasises, like he's just found the solid ground his feet were kicking for, '*and*, you're in breach of the new contract.'

His sudden glee at the last is a thing of mystery to me. *The fuck?*

'You'll need to explain, maybe I missed something.'

A glance outside, tight mouth. *No time to lose but I'll grace you this anyway.*

'You're off premises here until new premises are found. *Contracted,* Cal. You're breaching the new contract by being here. That's serious, I'm afraid.'

Serious and surreal. What contract? I've signed it but only under a phoney name. I am just about to say the same when something stops me. If I object he'll say it's a disciplinary matter, requiring a hearing and send me home to wait for it. The only place the contract exists right now is in his head, but that's enough for him to hammer this home with zeal. I'm in breach, he's decided, it's official. Check.

'I've signed it but I've been suffering severe stress, and I'm not sure I can trust my judgement. Not sure if I even signed as myself. I'd like someone to assess the contract, my signature, and my state of health before we conclude. I'd like to see a plan from you, my employer, as to how you will handle my situation and arrange a suitable work plan that is sympathetic to my condition, a condition you have remarked upon on many occasions but have shown no sign of accommodating.'

Checkmate. The just-fucking-do-it man tasked with a plan, formally. As good as it gets. He scrambles for a way out. Swallows hard, this isn't *helpful*.

'Cal, if you're going to get hysterical and lash out then I have to ask you to leave for the safety of those in the agency.'

I twitch in my seat, rocked by the nastiness of this. He'll start beating himself up and scream for the cops next. Breathe deep. 'I wouldn't worry about that, I'm perfectly calm. Just want an answer. Are you spreading a lie that I've had a breakdown?'

Staring at me with a look borrowed from the man we both stole the room from. He does hate me. 'You can't threaten me,' he shouts, fingers suddenly flailing in operatic gestures. 'Get out!'

I sit on my hands, keep quiet. We're being watched, he's making sure of it. Reacting to things that haven't been done. The phone is lifted.

'Nancy. Get the guys on security duty. Ask them to come and remove Cal… for his sake and ours. Threatening behaviour…' Phone down. Staring again. Total war.

'You didn't ask for the agency straightjacket then Peter? Fabricated enough as it is? Think I don't know where you're going with all this, think I didn't plan for it?'

No time for this, as ever. Up on his feet, short march to the door, opening it in what he deems an inviting manner. 'Now, Cal. Go. Better that way, believe me.'

'That's the problem, right there. I don't believe you, not a fucking word…'

And there, despite my very best intentions, words suddenly getting louder, shouting, open door, every head in the room tuned in. His voice softer. 'I cannot have you threatening the agency or its people Cal, I have to ask you to leave.' Real authentic, cappuccino gravitas.

Can't stop myself shouting, hearing myself scream.

'You cheap bastard, lousy cheap phoney bastard!'

At which point the acid PA arrives, stage left, hand to chest in horror.

'Well?' I demand. 'You going to hit me with the departmental taser gun? What is it with you people, can't you see what's going on? Sneaky Pete becomes the next fucking media mogul at your expense. Ask him about his travels, his purchases, his friends at Sea of Tranquillity and how it all adds up…'

It makes sense to me, sort of, as it cascades out, sparkling and flashing with rage. Almost makes sense, the pieces in my brain snapping together jigsaw style, whilst clashing together meteor style in the same instant. No one's contradicting me anyway. No one in the crowd that's gathered, vultures all. Pete happy to give me the floor. Only too happy. Drawing breath I spot Mary, propped up amongst the mass, head down.

I have to stop. *You've lost it Cal.* The impossibility of explaining suddenly drops on me, heavy, suffocating.

Breathe deeply. Stride to the door slowly, pausing to inspect the guard holding it ajar. Keeping my voice low and slow, playing to an audience of one.

'You horrible phoney bastard. Hope you know what you've done. Hope you're proud of it.'

No reply, none sought. A lonely walk to the stairwell. Lonely in the quiet, but maybe it's better that way. I got what I came for anyway. Nothing.

C DAY MINUS 2 DAYS

Media Suite 1, Central Office of Information Exchange, London

Nobody asked the simple question; why? Why would anyone collapse like that? The Prime Minister stands over him, shows appropriate concern and makes the right noises. So too our victim. He's over-tired, over-caffeined and apparently over-it-all, happy to get back up on wobbly legs. Only the start for you, my friend. But we are all so happy to accept the opposite because the truth is a lot less comfortable. No, the truth lies in the ads you just saw, and yes, what a show.

The darkness in the room. The files on the stick primed to play in sequence; first the YouTube float, two minutes thirty of audio visual straight to screen that forms the basis of sixty-and thirty-second cut-downs for HD television, themselves shown in the same narrative sequence of the longer combined YouTube viral email. Then onto a random selection of the outdoor ads, which would act as prompts/reminders for the core masterwork already shown.

On the screen: a young mother pushing a pram uphill on an uninviting night; an old man lost and bewildered in a shopping centre; another, older mother, watching her daughter playing with dolls, the dolls asking each other through the voice of the girl holding them what it's like to feel safe, wanted; then a sudden cut to the harsh lights of a hospital emergency ward, a doctor explaining flatly to a distraught patient that there's nothing he can do. The scenes somehow play concurrently – actually through a flickering series of cuts that seem to transport the viewer from one place to another, on a superficially random time shift that only makes sense in that the emotional trigger that cuts the story from one thread to another does make some kind of intuitive sense. The colours, tone and despair of each section's hero hint we're about to move again, each after only the shortest of interludes. One hundred and three focus groups taken to fine-tune and pinpoint each moment of change.

And all the while the soundscape too is taking shape – threatening bass grumblings begin to find a pulse, then a loop, and then female voices like a celestial choir find a form for their words: '*Whatever doubt, whatever worry, whatever never, whenever you feel right under the weather, remember this remember all, you know it's fine, we're in this together.*'

These are the unlikely tones of one-hit-wonders Hexagon; a six-girl multi-ethnic all-colours-of-the-fucking-rainbow coalition singing their dedication to each other, right up here in the mix and lending a brutal efficiency to our plea for our nation's mental well-being. Or the Ministry of Happiness' plea, to be exact. The melody seems to drive a more coherent narrative once the listener forgives the clunkiness of the under the weather/ in it together couplet. The images change as we reach the bottom of the curve of despair for our stars, now being replaced by generic shots: the isolation of heads in hands; figures walking away from each other; a newborn child's feeble cries. Then, finally, we are slowing right down in visual pace, to a lingering study of one man, his isolation, his moment of dislocation. It's the man in this room, of course, the Prime Minister, shot at the Party's Special Convention, back to resurrect the party after its fall from grace, back to resurrect the country after its dissolution and economic collapse, back to resurrect us all, and shown here overwhelmed by the call.

The voiceover gently pushes the feisty Hexagons aside. The voice itself is calm, measured, distant, not the Prime Minister's, as if someone is passing judgement from afar with a sort of forward hindsight.

'*The challenges we face can leave any of us feeling small. And while everyone's challenge is different, the choices we face are all the same.*'

Then we're into it again, the splintering of images, the previous characters brought back, revisited, but this time flickering like cards in a deck being flashed before us; impossibly fast, too fast to make any kind of narrative sense, but a feeling of understanding resonates in the viewer somehow – slow the visual right down and you'll understand why. You'll see it; our man is reaching out to them, embracing them, holding them, lifting them. Shadow shots of course, taken with a stand-in with the camera from behind, inter-cut into the edit so fast it's like an explosion before the eyes. This is ripped off from the techniques of those purveyors of psychobabble known as Sea of Tranquillity. Their method furtively passed on. Their madness about to be set loose.

My nemeses have somehow bestowed an entirely different kind of enlightenment to the one they spend their lives proselytising, though it's still recognisable up there as their thing. Show people coming together and you've got something powerful. Show it fast with all kinds of colour-coding, background noise and ambient cues and you add an exponential element of force. Put it together; test it, fine-tune it so you know where it kicks hardest, and you can sell anything. Happiness. Compliance. Anything.

'The times when we are most alone can be the times when we are most united,' soothes the voice of reason as the sun, literally, rises on our screen and this time we take our final, leisurely tour of our heroes, alone once more, but resolute, somehow contented.

'Never be afraid to reach for help when you most need it. Only we can make it in this life, we together.'

The outdoor work follows next on the screen, there's no sign of movement from today's test audience and I don't know whether they realise we've switched mediums or are lapping this up as one seamless trip. Scenes from the London Underground, the hustle and bustle, the bombardment of the senses, then a fix of silence and a sudden, startling, lucidity – a poster on the wall, black copy on a white background in quotation marks, classically old-fashioned typeface, like a lift from the Holy Book.

'You can be a beacon in your moment of greatest need.'

The screen goes dark and the room becomes one huge total immersion tank for the radio campaign. A female voice this time, late thirties, professional, caring – like the doctor you want to take home with you to be your prop, to get you through life – except that she's telling you that you can do this for her:

'Can I count on you when I need you; are you my beacon of light?'

And that's it, over and over in a series of vocal variations. Old, young. None sounding desperate, all sounding credible. I know this because it's been my life's work to select and test and tune these voices so as to know the effect they are having on this room right now and will have on the world outside it. C Day minus two. Do they know what they will have on their hands? A Well-being Nation. Officially. Now blog entries are up on display, phoney of course, as they all are. These ones written by Harlequin copywriters for display purposes, ahead of the automated ones which will flood cyberspace post-launch. *'Did you see that? That was me up there! I really connected, I know what they mean, they care!'*

And then, because I've programmed it so one campaign lifts as the other finishes, the memory stick fast-forwards us to the yet more fearsome, more experimental territory of the Sea of Tranquillity launch, now playing, for reasons unknown, at ear-splitting volume out of the auditorium's sound system.

The Tranquillity chant is upon us; circular, soaring, but with no obvious start or end point. Designed to be hypnotic, a mantra for those who find mantras hypnotic. Those not like me. We're in the same colour-coding onscreen, with the intense blue wash hotting up into warm lavender, for those who can find lavender warm. Into hand-holding, anonymous hands without any kind of narrative back story, hands that greet, clap and pat, a connection of hands. We're into obvious territory here, it seems, and I look away from the screen, because unlike the others, I know what's coming next and I'm meant to have a conversation at the end of it.

I've tried it, and I know the sequence length. Three and a half seconds. I know it seems longer. Far longer. I know it does something, something we and our client stumbled upon, and got through a hundred and more research agencies trying to bottom out. Without any noticeable success, to be honest, but some spellbinding post-rationalisation about rational vs emotional liability, emotional equity, emotional self-worth. If the first ads break all the rules and leave the viewer with a yearning nostalgia for something he never had, yet make him feel good about himself in the process, the second lot push the same buttons harder on the Richter scale, dissembling what's just been created. And it all happens in just three seconds. Three seconds of every hand in the world – again through the same flickering, subconscious fast cut from continent to continent – hands shown again, disembodied, drowning not waving this time, literally going under the waves, swallowed by an earthquake, flailing under fire. Three seconds of extreme disorientation, showing nothing but saying everything, at the end of which, so the tests confirm, you can sell anything. And here we sell the Prime Minister as almighty salvation and watch everything fall apart afterwards.

A man on the floor. The exiting PM. An impostor adman.

No questions at all. And no answers.

CAMPAIGN LAUNCH MINUS 1 HOUR

National Exhibition Centre

Greig read through the notes another time, determined to reach the end. He had already tried more times than was worth counting, sometimes interrupted, sometimes simply losing the will to go on.

'You seen this stuff?'

Greig glanced at the thick sheaf of newspapers Bernie had in his lap.

'Give me a clue.'

'What's the point… Have a look yourself.'

'Not if I can avoid it, anything I should be aware of in the speech?'

'You tell me.'

'No, Bernie, *you* tell me. What's the gripe?'

Another prolonged pause as the younger man studied the damming evidence, almost as if for the first time, thought Greig. Or if wondering how to position this to best effect, whatever that was; spite, compassion, despair, whatever.

'Cabinet reshuffle, new energy in, dead wood out. Anything older than five months is passé.'

Despair, realised Greig. Other elements added to the mix but that was the principal ingredient. It wasn't just *his* career that was evaporating.

'So who gets my job, any speculation?'

'No,' said Bernie, looking up for once. 'No speculation. It's a done deal. All the papers unanimous… Stephen Aytoun, junior minister at Enterprise and Logistics. Ambitious target-setter, pragmatic, output driven, not a dreamy philosopher… Already fitted for the suit… Met him?'

'No…' sighed Greig, reluctantly absorbing it all, '…or if I did I can't remember…' Was it true? Didn't matter, they wanted him to believe it could be. Wanted the whole world to know just how tough, decisive, pragmatic they were. And this was the preferred channel, nothing as difficult or time-consuming, or honest, as a face-to-face meeting. A Prime Minister who had to be kept above all that. All-seeing, all-knowing, spreading his wisdom through the laughing hyenas of the press pack. 'I know the type though, met that a thousand times... Bernie?'

A meeting of eyes in the windowless room. 'I'm sorry.'

'You really think it's gone then?'

'If it's any consolation... I wouldn't rate the new guy's chances that high either.'

Greig studied the other's face, certain he could spot tears forming in the quiet that descended between them. He almost envied the engagement with whatever emotional core triggered them, now feeling beyond all that. The fast-track Minister, now the fast-track ex-Minister with a trail of devastation behind him.

'What about this speech then, the campaign?'

Not so much a genuine inquiry, more a concerted effort for Bernie to drag himself away from the maudlin quagmire.

'Yeah. Once more with emotion. How is our launch anyway?'

'Launch? This is it.'

'The ads. The posters. The internet stuff?'

'I believe...' replied Bernie, lifting his glasses to his eyes, dry, blinking back into default status commander mode, '...everything starts from this afternoon, after the speech. Materials out already have had very positive reviews, already thousands of hits to the website, already clogged with comments, both good and nuts.'

'*Nuts?*'

Bernie threw his hands in the air. 'Apologies... eccentric, unconventional... left field, what do you want me to say?'

'What's going on?'

Bernie's hand-waving seemed suddenly to extend to his arms, a windmill of prevarication. 'You know... people who've caught the leaked internet stuff... Catherine territory, we're sending out subversion on secret frequencies, screwing up the magnets in their brains...'

'*Catherine* territory?'

'You know... her thing, the brain-washing thing.'

'Accusing us of that before we've even *launched?*'

'Maybe her doing, maybe she had them all primed.'

Maybe, maybe, maybe. Greig looked at the script in his hands.

Soon to be someone else's problem. Maybe his job, his only achievement, was always meant to be simply making the link, opening up one whole new dimension in politics and public life. One common aspiration. *Togetherised* society, not such a bad legacy.

'We do the speech and then what? What's the schedule?'

'We…' Bernie leafed through the notes at his side, '…rather you, host the reception here with sector leaders, then photo-call, then a catch up with the Positive Mental Health lobby groups, then the House and a ten o'clock vote.'

'Is it an important vote?'

'I don't know.'

'Then it's not important. They can do without me. Cancel the reception here too. Tell them I've been summoned to a vote at the House. True, yes?… Got to get out of here, get away from it all. Understand?'

The understand bit wasn't a test of compliance with the instruction, he realised. It was more to do with the shared sense of disappointment. Failed initiatives, each bringing a modicum of success blighted by the new baggage they created.

'It's up to you, Greig. It's not me answering to the Party machinery or the new Alliance for Positive Mental Health… Might take it badly but…'

He checked the time; three thirty, due on stage in less than ten minutes, the words in the script still making no sense whatsoever. At one time it wouldn't have mattered, they would have been at best a base from which he would have improvised an address. Maybe he still had that in him. Ten minutes to go.

'Screens are everywhere, right?'

A nod back; half-hearted, uncommitted. Enough.

'Let's get out of here anyway. Let's do it now, okay?'

'We're meant to wait for our cue. Lunchtime news, post-speech interviews…'

'They'll already be trailed… Together with the PM's view of my performance. They'll all know more about this speech than I do, damn it, no… Let's go, make something happen, not wait for it.'

Standing up, then to the door out into the corridor and the main foyer, all the while assuming that he was being followed, though never turning round to check, fear of reality colliding with the role of confident, decisive Minister he'd chosen to play. Thankfully he knew the route, remembered the venue, the same room, he realised, where they had celebrated the post-gig triumph, the fall-out with Catherine. A room associated with everything to do with afterwards, the aftermath, why had they holed him up in there? Why not have him outside, mingling, mixing with the crowd, *his people*. Or what had been his people. Moving quietly amongst them, confidence fading, no one returning his glance, no cries of recognition, nor encouragement. Curious stares darting away when caught, caught watching the car crash of a career in its final moments. Derek Rove up ahead, a cluster of suits attending.

'Derek... Anything I should know before show-time?'

Pained smile, strangled at birth, the Party man instantly pulling him to one side, cradling him into quiet with an arm around the shoulder. Sound protection rather than affection. Quarantine rather than intimacy.

'You'll do great, Greig, you know the script? PM's very big on everyone sticking to the script.'

'Indeed. And the stuff on today's newspapers, part of the same script?'

Pulled closer. A shout to his ear. Painfully loud. 'You'll do just great. You know what's at stake.'

Bernie arrived, having been ambushed in the crowd. Shouting too, above the din. 'Jason Watson needs to see you straight after. Interrogating me about a meeting you set up for the PM a few days ago with the ad agency, didn't know anything about it. Insists on catching you the moment you're done...'

So Cal had got his meeting, what had he been told, what had he gleaned?

Greig walked onwards without giving any response and staggered up the steps, grateful for the darkness in the room off-stage. Music echoed thunderously throughout the chambers, bass lines growling like earthquakes far below. A familiar route, closer to the stage, this time shining brightly with only the projected logos and campaign headlines. The music becoming recognisable, higher register sounds adding melody and voices, the Hexagon girls harmonising their appropriated hit. 'We're all in this together,' they chorused as he waited, his very last cue. He felt the breath being squeezed out of him. Empty beyond anything he had ever felt. And still the chorus echoed all around him. All in this together. If only.

C DAY MINUS 1 HOUR

iCafé, Central London

Carlos puts an ambitiously frothed coffee on my desk, for a moment it looks likely to spill but doesn't. He smiles apologetically but excitedly, he's made a new friend, after all. *Thank you, Carlos*. Spotted me hanging round here for hours on end and made my acquaintance, suspecting some kind of cyber soulmate. Nice guy. Tells me he's Portuguese, though probably North African, that's my guess. I spun him a line about being a post-grad student. He's a student too, showed me notes, commiserated over assignments. Seems comforted by my presence here, even though the conversation dried up a good hour ago. Same thing for me with him; I take reassurance from him and all the others simply being here, all of us nested in our virtual community, shoulder to shoulder at the workstations, togetherness of sorts, tapping away with the world on our screens.

I take a drink, turn to thank him again. He's not looking. Reach into my rucksack and pull out the list on headed agency paper of the log-ins and passwords of the Harlequin payroll; my insurance policy, requested a week before the roof fell in. I wonder when they'll catch up with the fact I have it.

A few hours since I last logged in, the intervening time evaporating in a series of searches through news sites for detail on the breaking campaign. The love-rat Minister of Well-being, his conference today, the imminent Cabinet reshuffles, and the PM's new campaign for togetherness and positive mental health across our nation. And Sea of Tranquillity, endless searches on my unlikely nemeses, their players, their words and phrases. Angela Ambush and Pat Bromide. Every spelling and variation, everything tried, like I tried yesterday, the day before. For a supposed technology-savvy new-age bunch hot for communication, they leave a spookily empty vapour trail on the net. No, the only site thrown up is a self-help action group Together-As-One-Victim's-Voice as set up by a familiar face. Catherine confronts the world from my screen. Not easy for her, that vulnerable-but-resolute-and-engaging trick. Catherine, for fuck's sake, you'll give us all a bad name.

Trying to remember who I was last time, I toy with the notion of going in as the great Pete Vesey himself, but no; Kenny Chance will do nicely. Log in as one of Harlequin's best.

I put my headphones on, shut out the world, relax whilst I revisit the scenes of the crime. Four hours worth of Beatles' songs from 'Love Me Do' to 'Her Majesty' and all points in between, on random play. Aural tranquilliser. Telling me when to switch cafés as the song cycle ends and I recognise we're full circle again.

I'm scrolling through the catalogue of executions lined up and ready to despatch to all outlets, all expertly indexed, the now vindicated outputs of the derided matrix system. My ads, all of them, unchanged. My system. More than forty separate Harlequin adverts, eleven separate Sea of Tranquillity run-throughs, I can tell by the clock numbers that these have not changed either, won't now. These people who supposedly wanted nothing to do with me end up with my approximations of their work, completed out of exasperation and despair at them never completing their input on time. Tranquillity as imagined by the freak they created and reviled. Close my eyes to calm down, Paul is singing 'Good Day Sunshine' as I detach from the fractured eclipse/Prime Minister-attendant montage of the masterwork. I push the escape button. Why are we trying to hypnotise an entire nation? Prime Minister, I need to know. Why wouldn't you tell me? Drop down into the dialogue section, introductory copy, a range of answers to likely initial requests from those sensitised by the ads and looking for more. People who will visit the website looking for real togetherness and getting an airbrushed answer, scripted by yours truly. Hundreds of thousands of our audience, maybe millions, entering into a conversation with government about how they *felt*, how they would *like* to feel. In reality, talking to me, driven crazy by the effort it took to second-guess them all, to predict their whims and whinges. Nineteen thousand words of dialogue already prepared, emptied out of my fried brain, just waiting for their need. I'm ready to cry. Pride at the achievement, pain at the personal cost, anger at the lack of recognition. Stolen from me, because it seems to suit everyone that way. I'm tired, grateful for the coffee and its caffeine kick, I rub my eyes, log out.

Open eyes. Breathe. A look around my friends at their machines, watch out guys. I know what's heading your way. Calm, Cal.

Another search, can't stop myself trying. I type the words *Angela, manipulative* and *bitch* and press enter. A list of relevant headlines fills the screen, most of them porn related. I type *phoney, charlatan* and *transcendental* and peruse the list this generates.

We've lost the sex-sites, though we've simply swapped these for meditation course banners, online chat-room invitations and cult survival forums. Paul starts singing 'Hey Jude', as if in sympathy for the pointless quest. Type *awful, New Age, bastards, take a sad song*. Begin to smile at the results. Therapy in just getting it up on screen, getting it out. *Make it better.* Last words, for fun, lightly entered, *international, psychological, terrorists.* The list comes up, short list. I hit return on the first line it offers, intrigued. Maria Ivanovic, jailed three years in Zagreb, deception, fraud and menace. *Better, better, better* screams Paul as Angela Pseudonym's sullen, scary face lights up the screen. Reading quickly, suddenly, reading faster than the speed of the light it takes to reach my eyes so that I'm almost downloading instantaneously: Maria Esnaur, AKA Angelica Ivanovic, Doctor in Psychology, Sofia University. Deported Croatia, deported Singapore. Arrested and detained Jakarta, subversive behaviour. Hit enter again, new entry. Dr Sean O'Neil, Renegade Psychologist, University of Brisbane. Sacked, conduct unbecoming. University of Kuala Lumpur. Resigned. Deported Singapore. Staring eyes and shaven head in picture. The man I met a caricature in beard, glasses and wig. Angela's bubble perm, a wig. An obvious fucking wig. Here she is again in another pose; icy, formidable, sexy. New age Baader–Meinhof. The tagline refers to their *State of Mind Revolution In Progress.* Hit enter. Anarchist e-collective, anti-government, anti-censorship, subliminal programming to undermine authority. Banned everywhere, banned from recruiting, fund-raising, experimenting, from internet access. Suspected support for radical insurgents across the Middle East. *Wanted.*

I'm standing up, jerking to my feet so fast the headphones fall off, coffee knocked over. I may have made some sound because everyone is looking over, maybe I started something. Puzzled smile from Carlos. *You okay?* I don't know… His expression lingers and he reaches out to touch my arm. To reassure, or to hold. So many questions all of a sudden starting with him. *Who are you, how did you find me?* I snatch my arm away, snatch my rucksack, throw the iPod into it, run for the door. They're taking us down, taking everyone down. Infiltrated my campaign. Stole it, from the very start.

The street outside. I'm running. Running fast, faster than I ever knew I could.

CAMPAIGN LAUNCH, ZERO HOUR

National Exhibition Centre

Screens everywhere, Greig reminded himself, moving hesitantly forwards. Try as he might, he had no recollection of how his address was actually meant to start. *Welcome to the launch.* Or *Today I'm delighted to be able to share with you all.* Or, *Today we launch?* He was sure all three had been on the scripts he had tried so hard to memorise. Maybe the latter, had to be. Today wasn't about the people in the hall, the remnants of his once great movement, no matter what their invites might have stated. Today was about the television cameras there to capture it for the news bulletins. The struggling Minister, reaching out for lost credibility, or the exiting Minister, as some were doubtless already briefed.

How do I look? he had asked Bernie at the last. *Beautiful, boss. Never better. Do your thing, it's what you're born for* had come the reply, doubtless meant as a compliment, but if he lingered on it, anything but. A mouthpiece. Empty suit. Spokesman. The hall around had been filling, now almost done. A call to order over the speakers. Lights up. Standing waiting at the front of the stage, frightened to look up. Familiar faces in the front rows, Nigel Richards and his men, Natasha, Bernie, Jason Watson and his Party henchmen. *I don't want to do this.*

He took his seat on the stage as the introduction began, a middle-aged man talking about the challenge of healthcare provision in today's fractured society, the extinction of community care and the need to replace it with a new model, reflective of new community. *New community,* the words stuck in his mind, vacuous, empty. Spokesman words.

'Dr Greig Hynd, ladies and gentlemen!'

His cue. He rose to his feet, corners of his mouth pointing downwards of their own accord, mouth dry. Screens, the screens. The perspex pillar came into view, words projected on it sideways, visible only from his side of them. Instinctively he latched onto it, then spotted another to his left, then another to his right. Positioned so that he could address the audience from any angle and not lose his prompts, so that he could feign the engagement with them the situation demanded, and not betray the mechanics of sticking to script.

He began to read aloud, announcing the words as they appeared, and then started scrolling as he progressed through them. 'Ladies and gentlemen. Guests, fellow stakeholders in our nation's well-being...'

Fellow stakeholders? Was that how they expected the audience to recognise themselves, something they seriously thought they would respond to? Surely he should have spotted that, scored a red pen instantly through it, edited it out. Too late now, he'd said it. No choice but to continue. 'This government has long recognised the need to mend the fractures in our communal spirit, and indeed the benefits not only to society, if we can begin that healing process...' He wondered if his face betrayed the horror he was feeling as he heard the words echo around him. Words coming out in his voice. *Communal spirit, healing process.*

He turned to the other screen, looking once more into its display, following the autocue, there to help him fake the spontaneity that had once come so naturally. He found himself grateful for the presence of the glass podiums, there as barriers, shields between him and the crowd, keeping them all at bay.

'...Which is why government departments, like mine, working closely with the Prime Minister's office...' It was like reading aloud his own confession at some state show-trial. Words so manifestly not his, he wondered if anyone out there would know. 'This government... our Prime Minister... our society... the Prime Minister's ambition...' He was now almost speaking in code, emphasising every claim of ownership, as written in the script. Written so that when the news-desks edited it down for soundbite viewing they would be sure to capture mention of the key player, whether they wanted it or not. Still sounding all the more absurd in this hall, in this moment. Sounding like his own denunciation. '...And we would therefore invite you all, as the most important stakeholders in our bold new initiative, to preview some of the messages and images we will be giving out to that fractured society as the first part of that process. Thank you.'

He sat down, cautiously drawing out a handkerchief to wipe a sodden brow, then hiding his stinging eyes behind it as the ads began to play on the giant screens descending in each corner of the arena. The theme tune ear-splittingly loud, together with the sweep of colours on display, from swirling greys to blinding light, a blanket of camouflage for him to hide behind. He began to get up. *Get me out of here.* An outstretched hand stopped him. 'Q and A!' whispered his host, pointing back at his seat. He took it once more and reached for the handkerchief. Hiding his brow underneath. Lights up. Facing the audience again, too soon. Pretending to look out expectantly but really focusing in on the screen prompts. Questions chaired by the speaker who had introduced him. Plants, obviously, his answers right there on autocue. Then a shout challenging the delicate choreography.

'*I've* got a question. Why are you avoiding me?'

A voice from the back of the hall. A woman's voice.

'I think we may have time for one more...'

The chairman waited for the last of his written queries, but the insistent demand of the protestor became harder to ignore.

'Please, Mr Chairman, you have to let me speak!'

'Question here,' he said, embarrassed, pointing to the pre-arranged query.

'Can we have order please?'

Greig looked through the perspex to the source of the disturbance. Security had stepped in to remove the woman responsible, but her voice cut through. Cut right through everything.

'Greig! Greig, why are you doing this? This propaganda, this *ruinous* propaganda that will cause more damage to the vulnerable instead of healing anything... *You know* it will... why, Greig, why?'

The sweat on his forehead again, almost dripping. The woman at the back of the hall, being manhandled out. Her hysteria.

He began to speak, for once not reading from his cue, though forgetting his radio mic was still on. Speaking to himself but sharing it with the watching hall, and the cameras trained on him.

'I don't know, Catherine... I really don't know any more.'

C DAY PLUS 1 DAY

On the move, London

Sabotage. One man versus the world. The nervy train-wreck Cal, the poor bastard scurrying along the streets of the city, forever looking over his shoulder, too agitated to sleep, then thirty-six hours flitting from workstation to workstation, choosing a random, unlikely orbit through the all-night cyber-cafés, on the run. Outcast.

There was no plan of how to do it, everything fell into place kind of organically. Logging in, the music in my earphones, the iconography of the campaign as was, and the imagery in my head becoming one and the same. Two-hour segments. Logging in as the entire agency across those thirty-six hours. Internet security had been part of Harlequin IT department's responsibilities, which was part of accounts and services, which was on Hugh McDeparted's remit. Nonexistent security, he should have been made to resign over it, if I hadn't already sacked him. A three-day run of it before the stable door, as it were, was bolted. Three days to save the world.

Cut and paste, over and over. Get up, walk the streets, find a new café, install myself at the workstation, choose an identity, username, password, check the ads awaiting dispatch, dip into the dialogue sections. Then the new bit. Free-fab-four dot com, whatever. Go into the ad, delete the frame with the Prime Minister, replace him with John Lennon, sometimes even Ringo. A thoughtful George, an empathetic Paul. Sometimes all of them, if the image strikes me as having the cut-through. Over and over, sometimes taking an hour to amend a single execution. Then switching to the dialogue and pasting in a verse or chorus of the boys' gnomic wisdom. *Imagine No Possessions, Let it Be, All You Need is Love.*

Above all, doing this relentlessly, whilst I could, before the shutters slam

263

down and the stars of the new direction of the campaign are noted. And *that* was the genius part, exchanging one subliminal, manipulative image for another, albeit hopefully a more benign one, taking the whole thing somewhere less sinister. No way for the owners to call foul, at least publicly, without revealing the true purpose of the images that were in there to start with. There are worse things in life to believe in than this. *This* campaign, as my father himself would have said, is a *Beatles* campaign.

CAMPAIGN LAUNCH PLUS 4 DAYS

Ministry of Well-being, New Kings Beam House, Blackfriars, London

There was work to do, of course, briefings, appointments to prepare for, letters waiting for his signature. All of it left untouched, all of it, he decided with logic inescapable once he had let it enter his thoughts, to be left for his successor to deal with. He himself would be better occupied simply enjoying the room, reflecting back on a career so well intentioned. And so short. Allowing himself to take in the detail of his office so that one day he might remind himself, and prove to himself, that it had all actually happened. Here it all was, one final time; leather chair, walnut desk, glass-topped coffee table in the meeting area. Never used, never would be, he mused, stroking the arms of the chair. He had come in to clear his desk but found he had nothing of note worth lifting. Nothing personal, not even a shot of his family. His children. His wife. Maybe it had all been doomed from the very start. Unbalanced. Someone entered through the door unannounced. Marching in.

'Brought you this. Campaign update. You'll need it.'

Greig had no interest in the plastic file the other tried to hand to him, leaving it to be put on the desk. 'Save it for the new guy.'

'You'll need it for your meeting with the Prime Minister, he'll want a briefing.'

'Why don't you just tell him, cut out the middle-man. Spare me the humiliation.'

'Humiliation?'

He leaned forward to challenge Nigel Richards' puzzled demeanour at closer range. 'He's summoned me there to fire me. You know that, don't you? Someone else has already taken all this on, reshuffled in, whilst I get shuffled out… Called to Downing Street so as to send a message to all of the world. And here's me thinking public executions were a thing of the past.'

'You need to read the brief, if you don't, it won't reflect well on the department.'

Greig wondered which department was being referred to, his own or CIO? Whatever, somewhere, someone wouldn't be happy with him. Yet more people he had let down.

He looked to the file. 'Where are we at anyway?'

Nigel Richards flicked through it almost like a man leafing through a catalogue. A detachment you could almost admire. It was how civil servants like him would outlast every minister they served. Already loyal to the next one. Had he ever believed in any of this? Had it been a set-up from the start?

'Record numbers of responses to the campaign website. Record levels of awareness, engagement. So, on one level at least, a success... The campaign itself was pulled late last night, immediately withdrawn from radio, television and internet broadcast, the posters and other ambient will take a few days more... And there will be copies of the treatments doubtless passing through unofficial channels for some time to come. Not for mass viewing though, that's all over.'

'And the damage?'

'Still being assessed. We have reports of psychological trauma, fits, flashbacks, hysteria... Doctors' surgeries inundated, hospitals the same. You'll know better than I how hard it is to actually substantiate... *authenticate*, rather, the source. Such behaviours could simply be numbers of already vulnerable people succumbing to the media bandwagon...'

'But there are patterns to it?'

'Oh yes, for sure... The whole Beatles thing, people thinking they *are* The Beatles, The Beatles *talking* to them and sending signals or just having a new *dependency* on Beatles' music. That could be all down to the rather bizarre turn the campaign has taken and then again, if you will, it could be a reflection of the media picking it up. I'm told the television channels are saturated with old clips, songs. That has to be part, not all down to one campaign.'

And that's what I tell the Prime Minister. 'What about the serious cases?'

'In the brief. A number of people being detained for their own safety. Slight increase in those numbers from the average we would expect to see. It's not really about the caseload, it's the fact they cite the campaign as cause. Interesting.'

Interesting for who? Greig stared at the clock. Almost time to leave. His last reflective moments in the role ruined by the presence of the man who insisted on briefing him. Useless information all, it was still resignation territory, even if the PM *had* loved the progress he was making beforehand.

'Anything else?'

'You probably need to familiarise yourself with what had been intended, the lines of enquiry into how and why it was altered.'

'Before or after the Prime Minister altered it?'

A pause from Nigel Richards, polished reply for once freezing dry in his mouth. Eyes looking to Greig as the questions were processed in rapid time. *What are you inferring, what do you suspect, how much do you really know?* Greig returned his gaze, unblinking, determined not to signal any clue, leaving him lost for words, literally. A knock on the door. Time to go, assumed Greig, standing up to acknowledge his secretary, but behind it was another man, Derek Rove, looking flushed.

'Thought I'd escaped you as well,' said Greig, flatly. 'Come to measure up for the next inhabitant?'

'Has he read the brief?'

Greig and his comment were bypassed as the Party and Government man checked the status.

'We've talked through it. He'll take it in the car I suppose.'

'He needs to be on top of this. I'll go with him.'

'Excuse me,' interrupted Greig. 'I'd rather you didn't, I'd rather just do this and get it over with, on my own.'

He turned and moved to the door but found he was being followed.

'It's not your choice, Greig. There are things you will need to know.'

Greig walked onwards regardless, but could hear the clicking heels of his pursuers as he made his way down to the ground floor and out. Reaching the reception area he saw the media scrum outside, the photographers and reporters waiting in noisy ambush. *Public execution.* He turned to say goodbye to the staff on duty at the desk, but the commotion outside was distracting, besides, Derek Rove pressed close to invade whatever privacy he might have required for any kind of genuine exchange. The crowd outside stirred as they caught sight of him and prepared for his arrival. It would be a test of courage just to push through them and get to the car and he began to wonder why he should have to go through with it. Couldn't he just take the call, a letter?

'What are you waiting for?' Derek Rove was so close Greig could feel his breath on his ears. People everywhere, waiting for him, expectant of him in some kind of sinister way, as though he had wronged them and was now being called to account. People everywhere, reading their newspapers full of details about him, his crimes and his vanity, wronged them all. *I can't go through with this.*

'Move, or we'll be late.'

An arm went round his shoulder, steering him and propelling him through the glass doors. Into the maelstrom. *Minister, why have you cancelled your campaign? Minister, have you offered to resign? What help for the victims of the initiative?*

Head down, eyes to the pavement, he let himself be led to the limousine, door opened, pushed along the back seat as they sought to make their exit.

'Okay?' Derek Rove obviously meant this more as a statement than a question, slapping his hands authoritatively as the car began to accelerate away.

'Let's get this straight, the where-we're-at, yeah?'

Greig closed his eyes, happy to close it all out. A nightmare. And he wasn't coping. The first time in his life he had ever felt that way. Making a career out of treating, assuming the role of protector of anyone who felt the way he did right now, unable to trust his own judgement, beyond caring, beyond despair.

'Listen to me for Christ's sake, this is important.'

A shove to his shoulder to snap him out of his reverie. *He pushed me. He thinks he has the right to do that.*

'Your campaign is serious mess. You had to pull it the minute you heard there was a possibility, even the smallest possibility, that it might be undermining the mental health of the vulnerable in our society. It is not clear whether that is or is not the case but you took decisive leadership action to arrest any potential threat. The aims of the campaign were entirely different. The ads you personally approved were in a different format. You have asked the agency involved for a full explanation. There will be further investigations. You do not rule out a full enquiry, later. In the meantime we will concentrate all efforts in helping those affected, and ensuring our health services have all the necessary support to do this. Get it?'

Eloquent, if predictable. Limitation stuff. Who was this meant for? Surely the Prime Minister would recognise it in all its vacuous glory.

'He's going to buy this?' Greig wondered aloud. 'I mean, what's the point? It's over. I'm happy to go. Blame me for everything. Stop the damn car right here and tell him I'll go. Driver.'

Greig leaned forward to engage directly with the chauffeur. Change of plan. Eyes in the rear-view mirror acknowledged his call. He found himself pulled back, literally; manhandled back into the seat, into listening mode.

Derek Rove pushed his face close, menacingly close. 'I'm all for the *mea culpa* stuff, Greig, but there's a time and place. Your campaign was infiltrated, sabotaged from the inside, not yours or the government's fault. Tragic consequences, maybe, not *our* fault… You stay with this until the end. There's too many careers at stake for you to sleepwalk into this man-of-principles shit, understand?'

Greig shook his head. He didn't. *Stop the car, I cannot trust my judgement any more.* 'Who would have sabotaged it from the inside, you mean the Department?'

'The agency, they fired the Account Director. *Conduct unbecoming.* They think he left a time-bomb behind. Offered him up straight away.'

'Who, who are you talking about?'

'Their top guy, Peter Vesey, offered to turn over everything they've got, he's just seen millions worth of government contracts fly out the window, offering to trade names for future assurances about work. Out of that it transpires that the Account Director you dealt with screwed the whole thing up on purpose.'

'I don't believe it.'

'Not everything is how it seems, Greig. This guy, Cal Begg, it's in your notes, had some kind of feud with Sea of Tranquillity, fired anyone who questioned him, he siphoned off close to a million from the budget, put research and other freelance costs through handling houses charging commission, only they didn't exist. He was his own middle-man. Another reason why his boss is pissed off… He's been sending money to a brother abroad who may or may not exist… It'll take time to unravel. All the same, you've been done, we've all been done. You wait to hear what the Prime Minister has to say. Think bigger picture. Don't be in such a hurry to fall on your sword. There might be a way out of this yet.'

He looked out of the window, the car was pulling into Whitehall, nearing Downing Street. Crowd barriers had been erected to keep public and press at bay. The car door was opened from the outside, a porter waited expectantly for him to exit. He reached out for the folder, grateful for something to hold, to occupy his hands, as he picked his way to the front door.

Inside the building, a host of men ushering him upstairs, no time to stop, reflect, take it in. He was being processed, pushed through the workings of the machine. Up another stair, then pointed to a room, the Prime Minister's private office, the wooden door opening as he arrived, almost automatically.

'Greig. Thank you for coming. Some water?'

He accepted with thanks and sat down at the table, glass and file together in front of him. Mouth dry. He sipped nervously.

'Such a busy day,' said the Prime Minister solemnly. 'Guess we should keep this to the point, for all our sakes. Yes?'

Greig signalled his agreement. *Make it fast, clean.*

'I understand we have a mess on our hands regarding the Well-being campaign. Irregularities with the ads?'

Another reach for the glass before he began to formulate his response. 'Prime Minister,' he coughed. 'The materials themselves have been withdrawn whilst we seek an explanation. I realise of course that as the Minister...'

The PM told him to halt, a palm of assertiveness ushering his silence.

'But there's some pretty serious fallout from what's already gone out, as I understand?'

Greig turned to the briefing notes, redundant in the face of a better-informed interrogator. 'There could be... probably... still trying to discern what...'

Another palm.

'As you know, Greig, I've been planning to alter the shape and responsibilities of Cabinet... I had been concerned with the alignment of responsibilities to the government's objectives, and the challenges it faces.'

To the point, reflected Greig, suddenly illogically nervous. Nodding encouragement to the PM to seal the inescapable fate.

'And then...' continued the Prime Minister, hands offered skywards in exasperation. '... *This*.'

He paused momentarily to let the impact of his words resonate.

'Pretty good example of the kind of new challenge we're facing... the hijacking of modern technology and communications to dangerous ends, putting at risk the most vulnerable in our society, putting, frankly, our national security at risk... I mean, what were these people trying to do, turn us all into zombies? It beggars belief.'

At last he indicated the path was now clear for Greig to respond.

'Prime Minister, I take full responsibility.'

'You are someone,' came the rapid interruption, 'who has championed the rights of our most vulnerable, Greig, you have done that passionately and credibly. One of the reasons why I wanted you to be part of this government. I want Well-being, as a Ministry, a cause within this government, to include *protecting* our society from any element that would seek to harm our well-being. I want you to head up a new expanded department with a mandate to monitor and regulate access to the new channels of communication that have been exploited so dangerously. I know you will be conducting your own departmental enquiry, I think it would be wise to also consider what immediate powers government now requires to prevent this happening in the future. Ready to take this on?'

'Prime Minister I... I...' *I what?* The thoughts in his head swirled, impossible to capture. He had wanted out, at any cost, but had been told this notion was selfish. He had once been committed to whatever it was the Prime Minister had described but had lost his way, lost focus, all credibility. And what was it that was being offered now, a job as government censor?

'Prime Minister, I'm not sure... I mean, my first thought is that this would seem a substantial change of remit... more to do with regulation and *control* than... I'm not sure I have the background you would need in such a...'

Halted again, rudely, sharply. 'Greig, can I be blunt?'

'By all means, why would you...'

'*Greig*,' said the PM, throwing his name at him like a slap to his cheek to bring him to his senses. 'A lot of faith and Party currency has been invested in you and to date, to be honest, there's not been an awful lot of return. I know your programme matters to you, I *know* you are capable of delivering it. It's only that the events of the past few days have shown there are *other* critical factors that *must* be addressed before we get to that, and yes it's... *control* of the messages reaching our public, control of any message that might be deliberately aimed at destroying their well-being... Greig,' he said again, this time wrapping it in a warmer blanket. 'If I let you go now, your programme goes with you. If you go now, you condemn yourself to be remembered as the Minister who was never there... with only this mess as your legacy. I am asking you to stay, to turn it around. Do the job you were meant to.'

Greig turned away from the Prime Minister, consciously seeking some way to deflect the power of the pitch being played to him. His eyes were met by those of the Cabinet Secretary, silently stern at the side of the room, sitting in quiet judgement. Contemptuous judgement.

'Again I have to say I'm not sure…'

'We don't have time. We have to be *decisive*, Greig. All of us. I need your answer now. Can I also say, I think you're missing the point.'

Greig turned back to face him. *What point?*

'If you commit to being part of the solution, you have all of us, the Cabinet, government, Party behind you in support. Turn your back on that, you'll be on your own, absolutely alone. Let us help you, Greig.'

A smile, like he meant it. Like he genuinely saw it that way. Stay and be part of the gang, be protected as part of the pack, or we will have to turn on you. Decide now. He thought of the melee waiting outside, waiting to devour him. Walk out unprotected, or into the bullet-proof car. Maybe it had been arranged that way.

He stood up, heavy on his feet, thinking only of leaving the room, getting away. 'I'd better get back to the Department. Better get started then.'

The Prime Minister didn't stir, perhaps already focused on the next meeting; the next exercise in coercion. 'Thank you, Greig, get in touch once you have made some progress. We'll need a review of immediate options, emergency measures we should think about imposing right now, get that worked out sharply.'

Greig watched the silent exchange between Prime Minister and Cabinet Secretary. They had already worked it all out. His job would be to front it. The Minister as spokesman. With all of the Party and government machinery behind him. How lucky he was to have such support, something he would never be allowed to forget. He deserved it.

CAMPAIGN LAUNCH PLUS 6 DAYS

Finchley, North London

She had finished reading the article and the full page analysis that went alongside it, authenticated by the unnamed insiders the government seemed to field when it wanted to share its thinking. Read it all, slowly. Still it made no sense. She started from the top again, there had to be something she was missing: the link from the aspirations of the campaign as she had known it, to where it was now, was nonexistent, yet presented as a logical flow. Try again.

The second effort was immediately interrupted by the actions of her son, excitedly pointing to the picture of his father on the same page. A flash of anger in her face turned soft in the same instant. *Calm down, yes it's Daddy, calm down.* She planted him in his high chair and moved to the other side of the kitchen, locating the plastic scissors in a drawer of culinary debris. *There, have it, Daddy.* The boy studied the image she had cut free from the newspaper, sated and satisfied in some way. Maybe he would keep it with the others in his bedroom or maybe this one would be discarded like the others of the more recent vintage. She wondered how or what it was that triggered the distinction, surely he couldn't be sensitive to the change in the man as witnessed in the photographic record, or was he? Maybe the journey from thrusting irresistible force to haunted hollow shell was there for anyone to see, especially those that loved him. Or perhaps it was something more mundane, backdrop, whether he was wearing a suit, smiling or not, faking it or not. She had meant one day to go through the set that he had made; somewhere in there was another clue, another piece of the jigsaw that made up her son's personality. But she was hardly impartial, and there was still too much hurt lurking at the core of the exercise.

Staring ahead, her eyes focused with automatic discipline on the day's schedule typed out in bold on the kitchen notice-board. Monday: eight-thirty, breakfast snack; body massage for the boy, wind-down time; nap. Ten fifteen, medication; ten thirty, call speech therapist; eleven-ish, arrange consultant appointment, rearrange missed session; three twenty-five, pick up Sophie from school; Dr Harrison beginning at four. Pack snack and extra clothes for Cameron. Things to do. Somewhere in there she might carve out time for herself to eat, or even read a newspaper. Such was her life now, since the split, an endless 'to do' list, with so much to do that she would panic if it wasn't written down and formalised. So much to do if she was to do the right things for her children, her son locked in a world of his own, her eight-year-old daughter struggling to cope with the trauma of her parents' separation, alternating between the bitterness of an adult and the impossible needs of her brother. The therapy might eventually moderate that. Something would have to. It paid not to look too far ahead, for any of them, such was her life.

She lifted Cameron free. He held onto his new picture, concentration still fixed, almost heavier in her arms because of it, inert and stiff. She carried him through to the lounge where his playpen was installed. He'd soon be too big for it but it would have to suffice for a month or so more until she could finalise a strategy for the next phase of his development. In the meantime he had a few favourite pastimes guarded within the same soft captivity. She set him down and turned on the television, another proven distraction, with the main channels preferred to the children's ones, something about the ambient stimulation those offered rather than the more intrusive kids' fodder that irritated him, TV as wallpaper. Another clue somewhere, another piece.

Back to the kitchen, taking a seat and sip of cold coffee, where was this going, what was going on? She had been simply too busy to follow the showbiz tale of her estranged husband's career arc, but something was telling her to tune in now, that the dynamics had all changed and she had to understand them. The panic attacks about not being able to cope had returned and somehow all this was connected. Something telling her that her family was at risk, because of something wrapped up in this, turning dark, darker than it ever had been, if that was possible.

The page was inevitably easier to read with the snapshot of him removed, although it still made no sense, except in discerning more fully the political opportunism of the Party, turning disaster, if not into faux triumph, into their own assumed heavy burden of national leadership. She thought of her husband, caught in the spotlight at the launch, challenged by the feisty Catherine, *why Greig, why*? His lost, terrified response. *I don't know*. Played back bizarrely in a manner beyond spin by the same Party machine as *I don't understand the question* but fooling no one, especially those that knew and loved him, those like her. A lost man. And that, looking back, had been the chill that rippled malevolently the first time she had the premonition that the worst was yet to visit. Her family was at risk. Even with him exiled, pulling further away, the shadow over all of them was growing. How could it be? There were few clues.

How long ago was it that she had invited him to come along to a public meeting she and Catherine had organised? Sparsely attended, and those few there as usual being those with a personal grievance against the public health system, not even necessarily those maltreated by the mental health side of it; but anyone with anything to say about perceived inequities in treatment, eager to believe the worst and put their support behind those with complaints to air. She had found of course that this wasn't necessarily a bad recruiting ground for the wider, grander yet more abstract course. Perhaps she herself had been cynical from the very start, perhaps that was where the concern always lay. But there would be nights when the connection was made, a handful or maybe even just one soul in the rows of empty seats getting the clarity of it all. Yes, this is not part of the agenda, this *is* the agenda, the trauma we inflict upon ourselves as a society to escape the day-to-day stresses of modern life is self-perpetuating, and I too have the courage to challenge it.

He had watched with wry bemusement; detached, aside from his love for her. A smiling onlooker, somewhere in the middle rows, a presence she would try to ignore as she made her presentation, cheeks flushed, voice lecturing as she vied for attention. It was his idea later to make the pitch more scientific, introduce the graphs, the visuals, vary the face and light. A psychologist, like her, junior to her in fact in those days, but with a different grasp of how it should play. All about persuasion, a compelling case that people can feel righteous about, victimised by, he said. *They* are not our enemy, so why harangue them as if they are? You try it, she had said, and they swapped places in the hall. She had watched him electrify the scant crowd, and taken pride in the fact that they had a new star, a messenger to take it all to another level. Their daughter would have been conceived in the same glow.

She had continued watching, and he had only ever got better. Although making essentially the same pitch, he had found new intensity that drew the crowds to him. Everybody's friend and, eventually, the Party's friend.

A second tremor of anxious guilt across her chest. That was it, she thought, another clue, one she had missed amidst all the bitterness. He had never seen it as selling out, joining the part of the establishment that had caused the very problems he campaigned against, no. In his naïvety and eagerness to charm, he had never tried to eliminate the source of the tumour. It had always been about alliances, engaging unlikely stakeholders. Always about making friends. After all, wasn't that why she had left him, because of the same kamikaze drive to please everyone? He had thought, of course, she was throwing him out for his betrayal, and probably still did. And the world had thought, of course, that he had left her, traded her for the updated model. The truth, she realised, with a stab of guilty regret, was that the moment he introduced the Party as a legitimate partner in their marriage whose views required consideration, if not outright obedience, it was over. *The Party thinks we should separate for a while, and I don't know what to think.* And she had realised she was on her own. *I know what to think, I'm on my own fighting for this family and you are going to be a distraction, when I will need everything I have and more for our children's sake. You don't know what to think? Then go.* Sending him away. Not as punishment but as preservation. It was meant to regulate their lives post-marriage. She had taken no pleasure from his free-fall since, sometimes wondered if she should reach out. But her hands were already full, there was no room for another dependent. *Minister Number One*, the newspaper said, *Big Brother watching you. Minister of State Censorship, Minister of Anaesthesia, keeping you all sedated. Minister of Tranquillity.* He hadn't looked like it. Perhaps only those who loved him would be able to tell.

Screaming and grunting from the other room, a quickening of her heartbeat, same as the panic attacks in the night. Running towards his playpen, another fit, a seizure taking hold. She entered the room to see her son standing, white knuckles gripping the pen walls. On the television, facing him, another image of the same Minister with a scrolling banner above it, *Breaking News*. She didn't need to read the detail underneath the headline. Premonition had already told her. For all her son seemed happy to once more recognise his father, she knew already with a conviction that could have crushed her through the wall, that despite all her efforts, for her, her daughter and innocent son, their universe had just got darker, irreversibly so.

CAMPAIGN LAUNCH PLUS 14 DAYS

Central Institute of Mental Health, Phelps House, Twickenham

The car had picked him up direct and early from his flat, it had not been explained to him why it was important that the whole visit and media conference take place around breakfast, but he assumed it was all to do with dominating the lunchtime and early evening news bulletins, or simply to minimise the crowds these appearances were beginning to draw. Come and meet the guilty man.

A crowded car, to his irritation, Derek Rove up front, co-pilot to the driver. In the back seat, Jason Watson perusing the day's speech and press pack, reading and re-reading, circling random words in red pen, greeting Greig with an empty frown as he entered and pushed Bernie along. Safety in numbers, here to keep me on message, or to stop me from running away.

'Jesus Christ,' said a voice in the front of the car.

'What? What's up?' Bernie levered himself forward to survey the upcoming scene, squatting and holding himself between the passenger and driver seat. 'Wow. Are they all there for us?'

Greig tilted his head to one side to catch it and then leaned back, eyes closed. *They're unlikely to be there for anyone else, Bernie. Come for the best show in town. The only show in town.* He could feel his heart beginning to complain about the increased demand for blood to be pumped, at high pressure, through his every vein and artery. He tried to blank out the vision but it was too late, implanted in an instant, hot-wired into his consciousness like a flashed scene from one of his ads; the hostile crowd, predisposed to anger, now given extra licence by the abrupt change in government strategy, you have all been wronged, abused by alien agents, come and vent your feelings in a festival of rage.

'Foot down, drive on, drive around the block, we're not getting out into that. I'll make a few calls and find out what the fuck's going on.'

The speed of the car picked up as the driver responded to Derek Rove's command. Greig kept his eyes closed, the phone calls kicking off around him; Derek Rove's staccato interrogation of his men on the ground, Bernie's more polite requests back to Departmental HQ to those with access to the news channels – *we need feedback, how is this being set up,* Jason Watson's ongoing commentary to Party HQ of the events and next stage of play. *We're still in orbit, trying to get intelligence of what's facing us, we'll let you know when we're going in, if we go in. Okay, agreed.*

'Press conference delayed half an hour until we know what this is about. The word will go out to the media that we've had to postpone.'

Half an hour. He thinks this can get fixed in half an hour. He placed a hand to his chest, pushing his heart back into its cage. Bernie terminated his call.

'It's a demonstration. They're all saying they've been brainwashed.'

'If only,' barked the man at the front, phone still pressed to his ear. 'Then they'd all be nice compliant zombies... How can they be brainwashed and aware they've been brainwashed?'

'Because they think we've tried to brainwash them and failed, but damaged them in the process.'

Derek Rove put down his phone for a moment, and turned in his seat. 'Shut up, you prick.' He turned round again and lifted the mobile to continue.

Greig felt Bernie's form sag into his seat. A kid, relaying his information as best he could. Walking into punches. *Stop the car, let me out, I'm better with that crowd that hates me than you in here crushing me.*

'We're to go back round again, the police have been primed; should be there to let us through. We're not to let the half-hour deadline slip, can't be later than that or it detracts from the story. The presentation is a media-only event, no public. We've only got to get through them on the street and lobby inside and we're okay. Okay?'

Jason Watson talked loudly, decisively, as if he were taking command of the situation. The reality though, realised Greig, was that he was simply pitching Party orders, freshly transmitted, to the front passenger whose rottweiler mood dominated. 'Take us round to the entrance again,' he mumbled to the driver. 'Let's get this over with, we'll just have to bulldoze through.' He turned again. 'You all follow me, yeah? Heads down, stop for nothing, no comment, zilch.'

There was no challenge to this latest assertion, the car and all occupants quickly fell into a grim contemplation. Like an aircraft flying over enemy territory, thought Greig, about to jettison soldiers onto the battlefield. Stop the car.

'I think I should address them, see what concerns they have.'

Derek Rove turned again, already scowling, as if angered by the effort it took to twist round. 'You're joking. That's the last fucking thing you do… We get in, deliver the lines, get out. We don't stop to talk to anyone; clear?'

Greig found it easy to ignore him as the car drew up at the kerbside. He closed his eyes, then clicked the door open and launched himself out.

Outside, the drizzling rain, hundreds of people on the steps of the Institute. The gathering took a few moments to realise his presence amongst them, led eventually by the press pack rushing to capture his arrival on what seemed like a hundred cameras. They began firing questions, a barrage arriving all at once, a thousand explosions in his head, attention pulled in every direction, endless shouts demanding answers. 'Minister!' 'Dr Hynd!' 'Greig!' Every variation of his name and title, sharing nothing but the same indignant urgency.

It was impossible to focus on what anyone was asking, let alone begin to address them. Impossible too not to smile, a smile of shock and wonder, the flashing lights, angry faces, a wall of it. They *hated* him.

Movement and jostling in the crowd, some elements pushing through to get to him. To his side, the burly presence of Derek Rove materialised then pitched forward, looking to clear a path to the building. Greig looked up. The Institute, an ancient building, a hundred and fifty years old. August, faux Greek classical with its pillars and columns, he had been here before, so many times; as a student, as a guest lecturer, positive memories. Now back, summoned as traitor, here to answer for his crimes and misjudgements.

A hand in his back pushing him forward, he turned to see an anxious Jason Watson urging him on. His feet tripped on the first steps to the howls of the crowd, in an instant he realised this would be one of the primary images for tonight's news broadcasts. Pushed up and on again, relentless pressure. He stopped to look for Bernie, anxious himself that they leave no one behind, then realising, as Bernie had said, that he was the heat, and proximity to him was not going to be pleasant. Still the questions ringing out, mixed with cries of 'shame'. He was reaching the top of the steps.

A short stone plateau and then the grand entrance doors. He noticed that he was losing ground to the team again, almost as if the other two were being sucked forward.

Another cry, this time from a voice that resonated. *Dr Hynd! Please, Dr Hynd, I want to speak to Dr Greig!* This was a voice of distress. He scanned the faces to catch its source. And there she was, the old acquaintance, if anything looking more together than she had the last time, less frail. He moved on his tangent toward her, what a journey it had been since they first met, the very day he had gone to make his play to the Party, the very day Nigel Richards had first outlined the impossible future. Why hadn't he let her stop him then? He realised he didn't know her name, but still addressed her as if he did, struggling for words, resorting to doctor and patient words as he had last time. *You are everything you say you are not.* Maybe she had been right. Maybe they were all right, the only one who had it wrong was himself. He *was* everything they thought he was, it was his lonely delusion that stopped him from seeing it.

'Hello... Are you okay?... What can I do for you?'

A look of utter terror in her eyes. Facing the Antichrist. Hand to her bag, drawing out something small, metal, a box, no, a toy gun. She pointed it at him, aim unsteady, shaky hand and jostling crowd making it veer from one angle to another. A slight quieting of everything around him. She needs help, he thought, focusing on her hand. The flash at the end of the barrel, a surprise. A sudden, thumping, push to the chest. His shoulders falling backwards, a view of the classical stone columns meeting the Latin inscriptions on top of the roof. He had been here before. Happy memories. Feeling light, drawn to the light and the lure of the memories.

CAMPAIGN LAUNCH PLUS 30 DAYS

St Augustine's Church, Highbury, London

She hadn't wanted any of it, the solemn ceremony, the state funeral, the full regal majesty of the Prime Minister in black. Mourner-in-Chief. He had made his way slowly toward her, grim nods of acknowledgement to those gathered on the steps, then given her a special kind of look, a man with a face for every occasion, she had thought, and here today a new one; partly compassion, perhaps genuine, partly his own grief, probably not, and part icy warning, play this part, do your duty, live the role. Wholly genuine. Because she had not wanted this, and had made that clear to his emissaries from the start. Not to be though, it was only going to be this way, and she would have to comply with it or face the consequences. That's what the look said, she realised. *Don't ruin my show.*

What she had wanted? Family only, close friends. A small service in a smaller church. A chance to bring her children, to let them say goodbye to their father. Both children. But that wouldn't work with the cameras. Any inappropriate behaviour would cut across the dignity of the occasion. *The Prime Minister's show.* Any of it she could have coped with, in the quiet, low-key ceremony she had wanted and insisted upon. They wouldn't let it run like that though and let her know that all costs would be hers to deal with. As would the media attention, the security plans and any number of other logistics if she wanted to run it alone. And then there was the messy business of insurance pay-outs and pension matters, none of which had been properly set up in his lifetime, all of which could be expedited if she would comply. *Poor Greig,* she couldn't help thinking, even in death they still owned him.

A hug outside from Catherine. A silent embrace as slow as it could be in the crush. Two women who knew each other, everything they had faced.

The Prime Minister had found her and then they made their way to the top pew inside the church. She had not taken his arm yet it still felt to her like the slow procession of a newly married couple. Escorted to her seat in the front row, a privileged seat, there to watch the spectacle unfold. Looking back at line after line of faces, not all of which she recognised. Professional faces, civil service faces, departmental. His other life. She had been assured that Natasha Skacel would not be there but still found herself scanning nervously. Feeling alone, missing her children. Someone else's show. Maybe they would have their own private version later, surely that could be arranged, once this charade was over.

'A man capable of great love, who, by his selfless example, was capable of inspiring the great love and respect of all who worked with him in service of the mission that was his life, who will certainly be missed by his colleagues in Cabinet and government, and right across the health service to which he devoted so much of his life...'

She let the Prime Minister's words wash over her, looking to him with an intent that could have been mistaken for concentration, or intense empathy to his oratory, but was instead the opposite; a desperate attempt to focus on anything that would absorb her enough to deflect her from crying. *Greig, you stupid bastard. You put yourself in the hands of these people.*

'...Missed not so much for his outstanding abilities, and his commitment to community, but that *same* love...'

The Prime Minister was warming into his delivery, and she wondered if he knew at all to whom he was referring. Perhaps it got in the way of the best delivery if you did, perhaps you could only perform like this, with the poignant pauses, the subtle hints at breaking emotion underneath the statesmanlike drone, if you were at a distance, if you were playing the part. *Love, devotion, life, commitment.* The Prime Minister's words seemed to be on some kind of loop, as if his address had been written by a committee fooling around with fridge poetry magnets, the kind beloved of her daughter, and Greig himself, in the days when they lived in some kind of domestic harmony. Before he decided that saving society's well-being took priority over his family's. Before he ever realised that if he had told every family to look after itself he would have got where he wanted by a natural route. But he was a man for the toughest challenges, and engineered his life so that they would always be that way, goading everyone into it. *See how high I can fly.* Foolhardy, right to the end. Why doesn't the Prime Minister mention that? Appropriate. Seeing how it killed him. *Killed us all.*

She was aware of the silence. The Prime Minister had finished, reaching his conclusion but to no ovation, just a climb down from the pulpit to be beside her again. An immaculate man, white shirt, black suit, black tie. All of which would have been brand new, all of which so exquisitely tailored his own creased face and wiry grey hair seemed thrown into chaotic relief by comparison. Maybe it was better to blend into your funeral clothes, let them reflect your lived, worn, exhausted inner self, she wondered.

Another voice. A minister of the church offering the divine take on death in general, as if that might be of comfort. She could have spoken herself, she realised, the one concession they were willing to offer. Yet by then it had felt that in doing so she would somehow legitimise the whole thing, be speaking to no one other than those curious to hear the voice of the Minister's wife, the wronged woman. Not as beautiful or young as Natasha. No speech today. Perhaps next time there were things to be said, once she settled on the exact lines. Something about how he had believed, they had *both* believed, in the power of a common cause. In sincerity, transparency. In wanting to be happy and the right to ask for help in being so. In the natural, noble, instinctive and yet continually abused and exploited human quality in wanting everyone to be happy. Something to be said.

Her concentration was drifting, losing her sense of where they had got to in the event. No matter, she was a passive partner, could fall in, take direction. No hurry, a car would be waiting outside. She would miss him. The children would miss him. She should have brought them along. Maybe they would have enjoyed it at some level. Her poor son, the only one who would have had licence to be himself. Loving the presence of his father, but not the man himself. No, he wasn't a bad man. Capable of kindness, insight; stupid and vain, like the rest of us. *Greig, you stupid bastard, you put me in the hands of these people.*

She swallowed hard and fixed her gaze rigidly on the stained-glass window, forcing herself to take in every last detail. Her head beginning to ache with the effort required. Determined not to cry.

CAMPAIGN LAUNCH PLUS 31 DAYS

Sheeba Coffee Shop, Warmoesstraat, Centrum, Amsterdam

The espressos were laid down before them a little more carefully than might have been normal, especially, she thought, given the vibe of the place. Asking if everything was okay, eye-contact lingering again longer than would have been necessary. Did he know he was being eyed up? Probably, though he showed no sign of noticing. Probably took it for granted, because there was absolutely nothing modest about Sean. The alpha male in residence. Frayed combats and high-tech sandals, a warrior surveying the scene. Out to change the world, as was his right, his self-appointed mission. Made you realise how good he was at the whole fake identity gig, playing a hapless academic like Pat Brosnan, tougher for him than most. Now relaxing, back starring as himself, arrogant, oblivious to any fault. In a city of cafés but choosing a tourist trap like this, presumably to blend in anonymously, then strutting his stuff like a peacock amongst pigeons. There to be admired, in all his glory, little time or patience for those with an air of defeat.

'What do you want, Natasha, why are you here?'

He said it as if either the question or the coffee was a source of mild distaste. It was unlikely to be the latter, a smile flashed back to the appreciative waitress saying as much.

'I need some money or I'm going to starve.'

'You had a job didn't you? Didn't that pay?'

She put down her cup. Bastard. He was serious. He honestly thought she should have stayed put, brazened it out, sang-froid.

'Sean, you *do* know there's a public enquiry underway. There's an army of them let loose, poring over everything… interviewing, interrogating, and that's just the start.'

'And doing a runner won't really draw attention to your little cameo, will it?'

'Oh fuck off. Would you really want me still there fessing up, was that part of the plan, where's Pat Brosnan then, why are you here and not there?'

She waited for an answer that didn't come, a loaded silence lingering in its place, contrasting with the bustle all around. Amsterdam in the afternoon sun, a scene playing for her with its inhabitants cycling, blading, walking. All of them moving as if free, without baggage.

'Look, Sean, I need some money. I'm due some, are you going to help?'

'I'll think of something. You having a beer?' He waved over for attention.

'Surprisingly good dope here too,' he grinned, '…though you've got to go inside for that.'

The afternoon sun. A drink had a lot to offer right now, but not with him, not like this.

'Can you commit to something for god's sake? I'm through with hanging in there. Unless you want me to take out cash from my bank account and bring the world to your party right here.'

Another smile as the beer arrives, talking to her though fixing the other's gaze.

'Oh Natasha… why not, then? I'll slip you something. But that will be it, until the next special.'

Next one.

'If there is a next one Sean, let's have a better plan.'

'*Better* plan?' he spat, unable to resist the bait. 'We had a great plan. Almost worked out perfectly.'

'Not for Greig Hynd it didn't…'

The words were out simultaneously as she thought them, formed and spoken before she could halt herself. Straight from the heart. How could she have coped with a real interrogation? Out before she could stop it. Seized on by anyone not weighed down by the same baggage. Seized on now, from across the table.

'Spare me the tears for Minister Hynd. He knew *exactly* what he was getting into from day one. Saw it, knew it, bought it all… thought it would all be worthwhile because it was all for him. Only ever had doubts when it was hijacked for someone else who wanted it more.' Sean halted, lowering his voice. '…Which of course, was part of the plan.'

'Like his murder?'

A quiet, satisfied laugh as he contemplated his glass. 'Darling Natasha. Would that I could predict and plan to that detail. You really do have me down as a criminal mastermind, don't you?'

'He didn't deserve to die, Sean.'

'...Whatever, not *my* doing. Remember, this is a guy who thought anything was justified, so long that it suited his admirable purpose.'

'He's not the only one.'

'Listen... You either believe in personal freedom, freedom of speech, freedom of thought, and believe that that's worth defending when it's under attack, which is from the Greig Hynds of the world... You believe in that or you don't, Natasha. And I remember a time when you didn't take as much persuading and were more than willing to be a foot soldier in the war... That all changed now, has it?'

A foot soldier in the war. And him the general, of course. Her eyes stung again, to her own surprise.

'Where's Andrea?'

A dismissive wave of the hand. 'Lying low. Need to speak to her?'

No thanks. So it had been only her who was expected to stay and face the music.

She stood up. 'Get me some money, Sean. I'll give you until tomorrow.'

His hand out to stop her from leaving. A change in tone.

'Listen. It was a *great* plan. I'll get you some fucking money if that's what this is all about. But remember, we did a fantastic job. We're winning, and you played your part in that and should be proud of it. One more like that and we bring down the whole system.'

She was already standing, poised to go, her feet now led her away, away from the lecture, away from the crazy universe of his table. She found herself walking into the interior of the café rather than out along the canal. Going further inside, everything suddenly dark, starved of the bright sun, neon signs buzzing silently behind the bar. It was almost empty, mid afternoon but with a deserted midnight ambiance, a few balls clicking lazily on the pool tables to her left, a haze of smoke brightly lit over them. She waited over a glass-topped counter, absently studying the display of cigarette papers and pipes caught beneath it. A heavily bearded young man sauntered into view opposite, somehow exuding an air of mellow impatience.

'What have you got?' she asked him, sizing up the notion of choosing something, or just being led into it. 'Something that will take me somewhere, what's your strongest?'

'Skunk?' he mumbled.

'Whatever... Something that works... Something easy.'

She realised she'd probably offended the etiquette of the transaction though she lacked the will to apologise. His hand reached under the counter, slapping down a pair of ready-made reefers, these swiftly joined by a small bottle of poppers. 'Draw on this, sniff this. It works.'

'Can you give me a lighter?' She passed over a note in exchange, then turned to settle in a booth she occupied alone. Sean was still out there. Time to exit her universe too, if only for a day or so, out of orbit until the pain subsided. She cleared a space amongst the empty bottles on the table top. Cigarette to mouth, hand holding the lighter shaking slightly, the man at the counter watching her. Eyes closed, inhaling deeply, a burning shock to the lungs. A queasy dizziness gripped her chest, everything slowing, reaching for the bottle, fumbling to open it. Inhaling again, this time accelerating the speed with which everything powered down. Greig Hynd's face, the faces of his children as shown on the news, all still there in the front of her mind but no longer triggering the pain. Further detached with every draw. Opening her eyes, focusing on the printed name of the reefer she had in her hand, locking onto it. Amsterdam, the rest of the world turning outside; inside on her own, stuck in this moment, reading the name, over and over. *Tranquillity Express*, said the lettering, her eye unable to move from it.

C DAY PLUS 400 DAYS

Tranquillity Guest House, Sihanoukville Beach, Cambodia

Nearly five o'clock, the guests will start coming down in the next half hour, nobody likes to be too early but for sure they'll all trickle in long before the official seven pm start. And why not? We're in paradise. The incense is burning, wind-chimes playing a mystical random scale and the ice-bucket is full of chilled Angkor beer. Quite a set-up, even if, to be fair, it gets ever more establishment. We've got better furniture, wicker sofas and the like, we put out rugs and drapes and have created quite the post-colonial ambiance here. Come a long way in a short time. Self-taught, though I've learned a lot.

People come here from very far away. Single backpacker, professional, West European, or American, anything over thirty, male or female. If I was wearing my old hat I'd create some kind of demographic tag for them; *Part-Time Mystic* perhaps or *Lonely Planet Voyager*. They all travel so far to escape and then get overwhelmed by their loneliness, the one thing they can't help but bring with them, the constant companion in every journey, no matter how far they go. Imagine a guest house for discerning people like that, who will pay a reasonable premium to stay somewhere nice, and with a new age community dimension. Clean rooms, breakfast hall, veranda and compulsory evening aperitif where they must come each evening pre-dinner and be prepared to share one secret with the proprietor and his staff. After that they are free to dine alone or ensemble and then return to take evening drinks watching the waves as some retro-rock soothes in the background. The Floyd, *Wish You Were Here*, Leonard Cohen, Moby, maybe even The Beatles, though I've got to be selective there. I've had people asking me if I'd ever seen 'that crazy campaign', people turned onto it all by the same campaign, people weeping because of the associations triggered by the same music as *those* ads. But *no, I've never seen it, did you like it?* Can't choose anything that cranks the whole thing up when the aim is to mellow out. George Harrison, there's the ticket – *All Things Must Pass.*

I'm down early, restless tonight. Wondering what I'll hear. Five guests, an unpromising lot; a Canadian, a German, a Belgian and two English schoolteachers who won't last their holiday. Mr Teacher is just that, sensible, still thinking he wears the trousers. Mrs Teacher is itching to roll, style cramped by the paired identity. Up for anything. I can tell she's into me, eager to break my back story, suspecting hidden depths, intrigued by this man of mystery. I'd love to give her the surprise she craves but won't of course. Been tempted before by better-looking girls and have held firm. Tonight will be no exception. Besides, I'd rather hear about them. Amazing what they reveal once you start listening.

Happy? Yes, I guess so, I've got a thriving business in a chilled-out, non-competitive way. We have fan-mail, devotees, people who swear they've found something here, unaware they've poured their hearts out to sweet natured Khmer girls who've barely understood a word of it but smile benignly because that's their thing. Never underestimate the power of a sunset and cold beer, and a solitary soul finally feeling comfortable around others. *Togetherness.* Yes, I'm proud. Come down early to reflect on that, and my own journey that I never share.

So, am I proud of creating the new Beatlemania that eclipsed anything that passed for success in their heyday? Yes, I can now allow myself a smile at that. There are worse things to be accused of. I just think of what would have come to pass if it had been Prime Minister mania as per the brief, or mass neurosis as per the *Sea of Tranquillity* steer, but obviously, I'm alone in that analysis, the only one close enough to it to see how it was shaping. History portrays me as having been in league with the latter lot, eager to shock the world into anarchist, anti-government utopia by demonstrating how the politicians sought to brainwash them all. The cure being revulsion at the method's worst excesses, as if that makes sense. Angela Antichrist. And now I live under my own pseudonyms. There's irony. Did they know that I would react that way, pull the plug on my own masterwork? Perhaps. More likely they saw Sneaky Pete as the better ticket to ride, tapping into his delusions of global grandeur in an instant. Me out, him in, that would have been the strategy, simple as that. And for sure, they got how the politicians would always play it, way before your floundering adman did.

After that it was catch-up.

I had it together enough to get some money out so that the lifestyle I now enjoy would be not only possible, but comfortable. Proud of that too, in a backwards look-at-strategy-from-the-ashes kind of way. Never knew I had that in me. Makes me wonder how hard I was being pushed. Done at a time when I was fulfilling the role that had been set up for me; meltdown time. I worked solid for days amending all materials before the idiots at the agency finally caught on and froze out the old passwords, shutters down. The campaign itself pulled half a day later. Sometime after that I noticed plain-clothes cops discreetly asking questions about the habits of regulars at the internet cafés I had been using, flashing ID cards to give themselves away. Log off quietly Cal, visit to the bathroom then quietly out. Just paranoid enough, thank you. One way ticket east, first class. Bought online that same afternoon.

I sometimes dream about another chance. Fantasy of course. There's no more Harlequin: going under, under the weight of its debts from the purchase of all those foreign agencies who were going to run their own *Tranquillity Now* campaigns. You have to admire Pete Vesey's boundless ambition, wanting to go from mediocre adman to richer than Midas in one step. Online, I follow his new routine, fame as a stand-up on the after-dinner-lecture-circuit, *my-time-at-the-heart-of-the-Tranquillity-scandal*. He plays it straight mostly, although sometimes for poor-me laughs, it takes him all over the world, so perhaps some satisfaction there. I can see him now, working the tables at some industry-association bash, swapping business cards in an orgy of networking, talking up deals, mergers and ventures that will never happen. Adman's Valhalla. Alas Dr Hynd, former Minister, now saint. I think about him, wonder where he was heading when it all came to such a sudden halt. In many ways being shot was his perfect career move, getting the martyrdom I always thought he craved, although martyr to what depends on to whom you listen. There's internet talk about his widow taking up the mantle again, and I wonder sometimes if she'd be interested in help. Then again there's no Nigel Richards or Derek Rove there to make the bridge, they've all been pensioned off or recycled as part of the post-campaign purge. The only one of course doing well and still with us is the Prime Minister. I try not to think about that too much, having promised myself I'd never be as angry again. Switch off the mind, relax, and float downstream.

The guests will arrive any moment, and they've bought into a different

Cal, in fact they don't even know him as that. Time to be someone else, I didn't like the old Cal that much anyway. Better to re-invent, should have known that the first time around. Nick Craig can flounce, pout and shout and make a career out of it; me? I begin to snap, crackle and pop and they send for the ambulance. Why? Because it's out of character, stupid, and no one likes anyone to act out of their character, whatever it has been decided that is. Change persona, reap the benefits. There should be a campaign for the whole nation to change persona, now there's a challenge. Interesting. The wind chimes are gently tolling and I let myself linger on the thought. Maybe I have one more campaign in me after all.